To Brenda —
Blessings

REBELS IN PARADISE
BOOK 3
RESURRECTION DAWN SERIES
In the Continuing Saga of Victoria Martin Tempest

BY M. SUE ALEXANDER

M. Sue Alexander

#88

M. Sue Alexander

This book is a work of fiction. Names and characters in the story are a product of the author's imagination. Any resemblance to actual persons, living or dead, events or locales, is coincidental. Should you purchase a copy of this book without a cover, be aware this book may be stolen property and neither the publisher nor the author has received payment for a "stripped book."

SUZANDER PUBLISHING, LLC
BOOK 3: RESURRECTION DAWN SERIES
REBELS IN PARADISE
FIRST EDITION 2005, USA
Copyright © 2005 by M. Sue Alexander

All rights reserved. No part of this book may be reproduced in any form, either by electronic or mechanical means, including information storage and retrieval systems, without obtaining written permission from the publisher, except by a reviewer who may quote brief passages in a review.

Scripture quotations are from the *Holy Bible: The NIV Study Bible*. Copyright © 1985, the Zondervan Corporation and used by permission of Zondervan Publishing House. All rights reserved.

Cover design by Ron Watson of Clarksville, Tennessee
Photo provided by M. Sue Alexander

SUZANDER PUBLISHING, LLC
PO BOX 135
VANLEER, TN 37181
www.resdawn.net

READER OPINION

"It's a ministry that you do. Keep up the good work. I love this story's Christian message—not easily found in foreign countries," says Juli Beckman, Christian missionary to Holland.

"This compelling narrative causes one to reflect on the ultimate realities concerning Christ, salvation, the end time—the evil influences and the penalties for participating," states Dr. Jim Chatham, pastor for First Baptist Church of Dickson, Tennessee.

"I love this story because I can relate to its characters. Not much of a reader, this book held my attention until the last page," says Stewart Culpepper from Dickson, TN.

"In each book the characters get more exciting. It is such a good Christian-based book full of suspense. Any reader would enjoy this exciting series," says Janice Odom of Burns, TN.

"Alexander has an imaginative gift which she reveals in flowing, natural dialogue in the strength of this tightly woven plot. I have been satisfied with new developments in each new book," proclaims Anita Story Foster of West Palm Beach, FL

"Victoria is cool," says Florida teen, Heather Ryan. "Story has exciting and surprising cliffhangers—couldn't put it down."

"Intriguing mystery kept me hanging on to the last word. Author is truly blessed," says Faye Turner of Burns, TN

"One of the best written mysteries I have ever read," proclaims Carolyn Lathrope of Westmoreland, TN. "Can't wait to read the next book in the *Resurrection Dawn* sequel."

M. Sue Alexander

AUTHOR'S DEDICATION

Praise to the Magnificent Godhead for inspiring this amazing story in a 1997 dream and perpetuating the plot through yet another book. Bless all who have read this work and offered constructive opinions. Thank you, husband, for sticking daily with me through the ins and outs of writing. I salute my editor, Nell Meriwether.

AUTHOR'S NOTES

Resurrection Dawn 2014, a novel series set in the arena of pre-Rapture, Biblical "end times," is not to be viewed as prophetic fact. A specific time frame has been selected that best fits the story plot, and only God knows when the Antichrist will rule.

Victoria Martin Tempest, the victim of an automobile crash on April 13, 1989 that crippled her memory, remains focused on solving the twenty-five-year-old crime that resulted in her attorney-husband's death. Suspecting that Dick Branson was responsible, proving it is difficult in light of his political connections, expert lying, and continual interference running.

Private Investigator Georgie Hendricks has twice gone undercover and obtained proof that Dick Branson violated the law. Posing as a Tennessee Gas Authority employee, she collected contaminated soil samples from a quagmire back of Branson's property. Later, as homeless Jaycee Moore, she snapped photos of Branson employees packing cocaine inside packaged meats, but evidence was stolen when she was kidnapped and taken out of the country.

At the conclusion of book 2, *The Christian Fugitive*, Victoria and her mother, Kimberly Ann Martin, escaped Green Gables federally assisted complex with the help of Texas Holmes. Glimpsing a chance at new love, Victoria is plagued with mixed feelings over loyalty to her deceased husband and a new life with Texas.

While the road leading to absolute truth is rocky and twisted, Victoria is determined to prevail with God's help. In Rome, she meets the alleged Antichrist and her young son, Daniel. Enjoy *Rebels in Paradise*, the next sequel in the *Resurrection Dawn* series.

M. Sue Alexander

"But mark this: There will be terrible times in the last days. People will be lovers of themselves, lovers of money, boastful, proud, abusive, disobedient to their parents, ungrateful, unholy, without love, unforgiving, slanderous, without self-control, brutal, not lovers of the good, treacherous, rash, conceited, lovers of pleasure rather than lovers of God—having a form of godliness but denying its power..." 2 Timothy 3:1-5, from The NIV Study Bible.

WEDNESDAY, MAY 14

1

Nashville, Tennessee

Jon Branson was seated in his Chevrolet when he heard a whirring noise overhead. He glanced up and saw a Bell helicopter swooping over the parking lot. *Good.* Texas Holmes had rescued Victoria Tempest and her mother, Kimberly Ann Martin, from Green Gables. Now Kimberly Ann would not be required to submit to voluntary cessation, equivalent to assisted suicide. Being a fugitive wasn't so bad, considering the alternative.

Jon knew God was on his side. Somehow he had evaded the police up to this point. However, seated in his parked car outside the assisted-living complex made him feel more like a sitting duck on an open pond. Anybody could walk up and take a shot.

Overhead, the swishing sounds of the helicopter grew softer with distance. He'd miss the troubled debutante from Fernwood, but life would go on just fine without Victoria. Anyhow, it was time for him to head back to Selmer and tend to business.

A knock at the car window diverted Jon's attention from the friendly blue skies. There were still shades of gray on earth when it came to choosing sides: good versus evil.

But in time Jesus would make all things right.

Jon let down the window glass and peered at the police officer. "Can I do something for you, Sir?" A lump formed in the back of his dry throat. Getting caught *now* was a bad idea.

"You might," came back the reply.

A friendly smile masked Jon's true feelings. In case of unexpected intervention, such as the occasion at hand, he carried his Benjamin Bolt identification credentials. Three days a week as Ben, he worked a half-day shift at a Selmer, Tennessee gas station minding the cash register. A mundane job, but a welcome change from safehouse work. He even maintained a local Selmer apartment that he shared with a Spanish beauty, Latisha Mangosa.

She was a Christian convert and full-time Selmer resident who kept up with their mail and bills. Grateful to share the rent with someone who made no sexual advances, she vouched for him when his Benjamin Bolt credentials came into question.

Latisha was the best. On dreamy days, Jon gave serious consideration to courting her, but she was already taken. She was very much in love with a young Latino named Antonio, the possessive type who looked like a movie star on the big screen and flexed his muscles like a Roman gladiator. In lieu of the competition, Jon had not tested the romantic waters.

Besides, he was entirely too busy with running Safehouse #36 to fall in love, get married, and start a family.

Jon refocused, realizing that the officer was speaking to him. "Did you say something to me?" he asked.

"Yeah. I need for you to step out of your vehicle so I can search your car for a missing fugitive," Officer Matthews stated his business. "*Now*, if you don't mind."

"Sure," Jon complied and exited the vehicle, standing a few feet away while the officer completed his inspection.

Office Matthews walked around Jon's Chevrolet, stooped over and looked under it. "Pop your trunk," he told Jon.

The officer didn't bother to say please.

"Sure." Jon used an automatic remote to open the trunk. "What's the problem?" he casually asked, thinking it was a nice day despite the hassle. Life had its virtues and unexpected twists.

"We're looking for a gal—oh, I'd say in her mid-fifties, though I'm told she looks a bit younger." Matthews' flashlight tunneled light into the dark trunk. "I see you keep two spares."

"Yeah, it's always good to be prepared." Jon wasn't talking about car trouble. "Who's the fugitive?" He tried to appear calm as the whirring noise of the helicopter diffused in the air.

"A woman from Fernwood, Tennessee." Officer Matthews made eye contact with Jon, one eyebrow noticeably set higher than the other "You might've heard of her."

"Oh?" Jon showed interest. "Who is she?"

"Victoria Martin Tempest."

"That gal pictured on TV?" Jon tried to sound impersonally interested, all the while his heart jumping.

"Yep. Some claim she's the richest widow in Hardeman County, though her money ain't doin' her no good now." Officer Matthews still trusted in the American system of justice.

"What's she done to create such a ruckus?" Jon asked.

"Seems that the fugitive is wanted for questioning in the murder of her husband." Matthews spit on the concrete.

"Interesting." Jon blinked, showing no interest in furthering the subject. "Are we finished here?" He didn't want to prolong the search, afraid that the officer would become interested in the high-tech equipment installed in his Chevrolet.

"Sad, if you ask me." The officer slammed down the trunk, walked around the side of the car, and shined a beam of light into the floorboard of the back seat.

"Why is that?" Jon made eye contact, trying not to appear nervous. *Just keep talking like nothing is wrong.*

"That a person has to go to such lengths as to take another life." The officer stored his flashlight in the holder attached to his black belt, seemingly satisfied that Jon wasn't harboring a criminal.

"Yeah, I guess," said Jon. "The jury will decide her guilt, huh?" *What happened to innocent until proven guilty?* "Are we done here?" He had to report to work in Selmer at three.

"I see you have a Selmer tag. What brings you to Nashville?" Matthews queried, not in a hurry to move on.

"A friend of mine has a mother in this facility." It was the truth. Jon had known Kimberly Ann Martin for years. "I stopped by to say hello but didn't get in. Guess I'll try again when I'm in town." He peered at Officer Matthews who didn't comment.

Jon approached his car with his keys in hand, wondering what wild tales Victoria was telling Texas about now. He'd hear all about their trip later. "Can I go now?" he asked the officer.

"That's mighty nice of you to visit the elderly, fella." Officer Matthews was stuck on Jon's last statement. "Folks today don't often think of other people's needs. Not the way it used to be when I was a kid." He removed his cap and scratched his head.

"I guess not," Jon agreed.

"You can be on your way now. Take it easy on the pedal, though. Got speed traps set up within a fifty-mile radius of Nashville. You don't won't no speeding ticket, son."

"No, Sir." Jon saluted the officer in a way of saying thanks. Slipping into the driver's seat, he rolled up the window and popped the door locks. *Close call,* he thought to himself.

Jon heard the soft purring of the fine-tuned Chevy engine and slowly pulled out of Green Gable's parking lot onto a main throughway. Breathing a sigh of relief that Victoria was once more safe, he headed north on I-65 when his cellphone beeped.

"Yeah, this is Jon"

"SS4639 reporting in," a familiar male voice responded. "All's well in heavenly places and going as planned."

"Roger," said Jon, shutting down the phone.

It was Texas checking in. His plan was to fly Victoria and her mother, Kimberly Ann, to a private Christian Protection Agency facility nestled in the foothills of the Canadian Rockies. Victoria would stay on for a while, until Kimberly Ann became acclimated to her new surroundings. Then, they would talk more about the next step involved in solving her husband's murder.

Jon agreed with Texas that Victoria needed to get a handle on how to clear her name of a murder charge. Until then, the police would not give up their search for her. Meanwhile, Texas was heading back to Dallas to tie up a few loose ends at his ranch.

As soon as Victoria felt her mother was well enough adjusted to be left along, and she had come up with Plan B—still very much up in the air—Texas would phone Jon and clue him in.

Jon had basically told Texas that it was up to him to assist Victoria from here on out since he already had far too much responsibility on his plate. With romance in bloom, the CPA media specialist readily took to the idea of protecting the fugitive.

Then, there was Jon's malicious father, whom he had not seen or spoken to since the night he'd rescued Victoria from the hospital. By now the smart business tycoon had probably figured out where his rebellious son stood when it came to doing the right thing. At some point, there would be an unavoidable showdown.

Jon loved his father deeply, but hated Dick Branson's worldly ways. One day before very long, maybe he'd schedule a time when they could speak privately. Jon let his mind wander.

They could have a casual lunch together somewhere in a public place where his daddy wouldn't make a scene. He would explain why he had helped Victoria Tempest escape from the hospital and discuss God's plan of salvation with him.

Jon had been praying that his daddy would become a Christian ever since he accepted the authenticity of the Bible and felt the power of the Holy Spirit. Then what would Richard Branson the Third have to say in his defense?

It was sure to be an interesting conversation.

2

Victoria noticed the mountainous terrain below them, nose pressed flat to the window glass. "Where are we, Texas?"

"Those are the Appalachians." He pointed below. "We're over the Carolinas, headed up the eastern seaboard into Canada and keeping a low profile. I'll check in with the local aviation towers periodically and inform them I have federal clearance to transport microchips for a California company I work for."

"Will they believe you?"

"Yes, because it's true." Texas grinned at his passenger. "I have a contract with GyroDynamics, Inc., to deliver their products to companies in the US, Canada, and Mexico."

"Busy man, you are," Victoria remarked, smiling coyly.

"When I'm not working for Gyro," Texas explained, "I'm moonlighting for the Christian Protection Agency. My credentials are legit, and it gets me into the friendly skies weekly."

It pleased Texas to see that Victoria was so open to asking questions, in his book a refreshing trait for a pretty woman.

"My, Texas," Victoria's dark eyes widened with approval, "aren't you are a bundle of surprises?" She looked down to hide her blushing cheeks, straightening her nurse's uniform.

"And there's more to come," Texas said with a lengthening smile. "How's Mama doing back there?" He cranked his head to the side to grab a peek. "You comfortable, Kimberly?"

"She's sleeping soundly." Victoria glanced over her shoulder at her mother whose eyes were shut tight.

"No, I'm not." Kimberly cracked one eye. "I can't stand heights, so I'm keeping my eyes closed. You two just keep on talkin'. I'm a listenin', and you don't have to worry about me."

"So tell your daughter some more about Daniel," Texas said to Kimberly, knowing Victoria was dying to ask about her son but was too afraid of the answers she might get. "Are you ready to hear the truth, dear?" He glanced over at his passenger.

Dear? Victoria loved the way the endearing word had slipped so easily off Texas' lips. *So understanding and compassionate.*

"Uh, I suppose," she answered, her vulnerable heart leaping with uncertainty. Was she ready to hear about a son she had birthed and forgotten? Once she knew where Daniel was, could she face him with half a memory?

Kimberly sat up and took charge of the conversation with confidence. "After Victoria's accident in 1989, and Jeffrey's death, none of us believed my daughter would survive so serious a head trauma." Her eyes were alive with memories.

Victoria searched her mind bank for a scrap of memory. To her dismay, nothing surfaced to support an opinion.

"I've never seen Mark James look so despondent," Kimberly Ann continued. "You'd have thought he was responsible for Victoria's condition," Kimberly said with a disparaging sigh.

He might have been, thought Victoria, though she was not yet ready to expound on her theory.

"Did Dick Branson visit me at the hospital?" she asked. The smooth criminal had surely put on a show that out-shined any circus act in order to divert suspicion.

"Now that I think about it, he did come a lot," Kimberly replied. "He was Mark's good friend, you know." She was delving into memories too long stunned by prescription drugs.

"Mother!" Victoria protested. "Richard Branson the Third is nobody's *good* friend! Although you can bet your boots he'd like to make the citizens of Fernwood believe he is!" She had a short fuse when it came to Dick, a temper that needed taming.

"You sound almost angry, dear." Kimberly had no idea where her daughter's fury came from. "Did this man do something to hurt you?" She truly wanted to understand.

"It would take hours to explain, Mother. May I have a rain check?" Victoria glanced over at Texas. The sordid tale was one she was not ready to share with a potential—what?

Friend? Or some one with whom she could entrust her heart?

Kimberly yawned and reached inside her purse. "Darling, do you have any aspirin? I have a slight headache." She felt tired, ready for a real nap. The morning had been surreal.

"Mother? Is there any special medication you should be taking—for your blood pressure or thyroid gland?" Victoria didn't want to discontinue any treatment vital to Kimberly Ann's health. "That last thing I want to do is hurt you in any way." She recalled Karen's admonition to leave Grammy alone, that she was happiest where routine prevailed. Had she made a mistake?

"I do get one high-blood pressure tablet each morning " Kimberly thought a second. "And they gave me something to quiet my nerves. Actually I feel much better without those blame pills!" She let out a chuckle. "Hallelujah! I don't know when I've felt so free!" Her comment brought a hearty laugh out of Texas.

Victoria smiled, certain she had made the right decision in removing Kimberly from Green Gables. Going to Canada would be a new start for both of them.

"When we reach our destination, I'll make sure Kimberly's first stop is at the CPA clinic." Texas fondly peered at Victoria, who mouthed an inaudible thank you with her lips.

"And Kimberly," Texas continued, "you'll be interested to know that the CPA care facility where you will be living is fully equipped to handle any medical need or emergency."

"Tell me more, son," said Kimberly, slouching comfortably in the back seat. "Sounds like Paradise to my aging ears."

"The exciting new complex has access to a small village with stores, hair salons, restaurants, and novelty shops. Many elderly residents choose to work in the village. No one has to sit around and twiddle their thumbs with the multitude of available activities. Or course, it's up to the individual. We practice democracy."

"Wow!" Victoria eyed Texas with deep appreciation.

"Double wow!" said Kimberly, laughing.

"The system seems to work well and the residents thrive." Texas reached over and patted Victoria's hand, hoping she felt better about Kimberly's change of environment.

"What you just said, Texas, reminds me of how the first-century Christians lived—together and sharing in everything." Victoria thought about her past, as much as she could recall. "In some ways I guess I'm still an old-fashioned girl."

Texas smiled, rolling his eyes while shaking his head.

"I already like the place a lot better than Green Gables," Kimberly Ann said. "I'm not stupid." Her voice took on a chilly seriousness. "I know my death was only a couple days away; I just chose to ignore the fact. If Victoria—and you, my handsome Texan—hadn't come to my rescue, I'd be walking in Heaven by Friday afternoon. Not that it would be so bad." She smiled.

"In God's time, Mother, not the government's." Victoria indignantly turned around in her seat, grasping her mother's hand.

Kimberly Ann had tears poised in both eyes.

"Whoever came up with the lame-brain idea of killing our most important citizens ought to be prosecuted to the fullest by the law!" Victoria was appalled by the sudden fury that had surfaced. Not understanding how society functioned, she badly needed to get her emotions under the control of the Holy Spirit.

"Except *voluntary cessation* was voted by the people as the best solution to our healthcare crises," Texas pointed out. "Unfortunately, most people believe that an early death sentence is a better solution than dying alone at home from a terrible disease." He banked the plane to the right, reaching to adjust the dials on the computerized control panel. "Sorry, ladies."

"Hold on to your stomachs!" Kimberly let out a whoop, immensely enjoying the ride.

"Look, gals!" Texas exclaimed as he pointed down with his left hand. "You can see the Great Lakes from here."

"Beautiful!" Victoria exclaimed, holding a hand over her eyes as a blade of bright sunlight momentarily obscured her vision.

"It sure is," said Texas, his eyes keenly fixed on Victoria as he banked the copter sideways. She blushed, aware that Texas was referring to her. However, his attentiveness was most flattering.

"Lovely," Kimberly commented on the scenery below.

"The rolling waves look just like whipped cream moving inshore," Victoria remarked. "I wish we had time for a dip."

As a child, she had once visited the Gulf of Mexico with her parents. Victoria faintly recalled putting her foot in the cold water. Everything after her automobile accident was a blank.

"Why the sad look?" Texas tuned into Victoria's feelings.

"I'm not sad, just concerned." She evaluated her situation. "Texas, when I remember—if I ever do recall my life during the past twenty-five years—I wonder if I'll like myself."

Texas smiled. "You hear that, Kimberly? Is there any way we are going to like your daughter less because of her past?" He reached over and patted Victoria's hand.

"Wait!" Victoria exclaimed. "My daughter, Karen—entirely too much like me—offered her unedited opinion of how she viewed the *me* before April 14. I absolutely hate the image she painted." Karen was a straight shooter, for sure.

Kimberly sighed. "Most folks I know feel no animosity toward you, honey. Karen was a little harsh, don't you think? People who loved you most empathized with your situation."

Texas glanced over at Victoria. "What about Karen's opinion worries you?" he asked. "Are you carrying guilt?"

"Of course, I am. What if remembering becomes too much to bear? I know I've broken God's commandments. What heinous acts have I committed and conveniently forgotten?"

Victoria grieved deeply in her spirit, feeling as if her heart would explode with agony. "Maybe Karen is right about me."

"Don't be so hard on yourself, Victoria," Texas warned. "We all live with regrets." There were things he hadn't told her.

Quiet as a kitten, Kimberly listened in deep thought.

"You're right, Texas. I should give myself a break." Victoria wrung her hands as fear capsized her emotional security. "It's my prayer that grace will prevail in my life." Like it or not, human storms were far more devastating than the dangerous physical ones. And how could she flee from an invisible storm?

Texas hated that he had no more comforting words to offer. Thank God, Kimberly had some motherly advice.

"Victoria? Have you considered that God may have erased your memories so you could better fulfill His purpose in the present?" Kimberly's tender heart filled her mind with a godly wisdom coming from a long, faithful life of walking with Christ.

"And don't forget about God's forgiveness," Texas reminded Victoria, thinking of the time they were alone together in the garden back of the state mental institution. "Grace is amazing."

"Yes, it is." Victoria was reminded of her position in Christ as a daughter of the King. The truth of how she really felt surfaced.

"I've made such poor choices in the past," she admitted. "What wonderful deed could I perform for God that someone else couldn't do so much better?" She felt limited in talents.

"Time will tell, dear," said Kimberly. "Time will tell."

3

Karen paced Mark's den, worried over how her mother would survive inside a jail cell should she be caught. Victoria Martin Tempest was as naive as a trusting child.

"I wish Sheriff Grimes would phone and tell us what's going on," Karen fussed. "How can it take this long to find two women in a care facility? Maybe we should drive over to Nashville and evaluate the situation ourselves." She was getting worked up.

"No, you should take a nerve pill and relax," Mark advised.

Sympathetic with Karen's concern over her mother, he was baffled by her duplicity. While she seemingly supported and loved her mother, she had seduced him into bed. How would Vicki feel about that indiscretion? It didn't make a shred of sense.

But then, Karen seldom did.

"I admit I'm a little on edge, too." Mark drew Karen into a conversation, thinking she had been far too introspective for her own emotional good. In fact, she was bordering on depression.

"What?" Karen paused mid-floor. "You think the police shot Mother and they're not calling because she's laid up in a hospital somewhere fighting for her life?" She leaped to an unsettling scenario. "Well, I won't stand for police brutality! I'm going to Nashville and find my mother! Where's my purse?"

"Now?" Mark reacted, restraining her by the arm. "We are not going to budge from this condo until Sheriff Grimes phones." He was amazed how so fragile a mind reached wrong conclusions.

"Then what?" Karen defiantly crossed her arms and began pacing the floor again. "Don't stare at me, you hear? I'm not responsible for what's happened to my mother!"

"Nobody said you were." Mark collapsed in his leather recliner, reaching for the morning paper. "I can't believe the news is so biased. They've convicted Victoria before she's had a trial."

Privately, Mark had to admit that Victoria's prospect for achieving happiness on the run was looking dismal.

"Like I said, police brutality," Karen mumbled. "Anyhow, why should I feel responsible at this late date? Did I have anything to do with the break-in at my father's office? Or create the storm that contributed to Mother's accident? Is it my fault her memories switched on April 14?" She blamed God. "What?"

Mark chuckled. "No, dear. None of the above." He left his easy chair to wrap a reassuring arm around Karen. "Let me make you a cup of hot herbal tea. Maybe it'll calm your nerves a bit."

"You really believe Sheriff Grimes will soon call?" Karen needed Mark's reassurance. "Because if he doesn't, I'm going to go crazy and you'll have two loony women on your hands!"

"He'll call, but if he doesn't, I can certainly handle it," Mark assured Karen. "I have in the past, and I will in the future."

"You don't much like talking about the past, do you?" Karen scrutinized Mark with her hazel eyes. He didn't answer, just stared. "Well? Aren't you going to answer me?"

"Uh, sure." Confused over where his loyalties lay, with Dick or Victoria, broaching the subject of the past deeply troubled Mark. His conscience told him the right thing to do was to level with Victoria's daughter and tell her what actually had happened the night her father died. But his good judgment advised him that a confession was foolish, his heart couldn't take the results.

"Explain, please," said Karen.

"Discussing the past does bother me," Mark admitted. "But for now, couldn't we just concentrate on the future and finding your mother? Meanwhile, let me fix you some hot tea."

"I don't want hot tea!" Karen despondently threw up her hands. "I want Mother back!" She picked up her jacket and headed for the door. "I'm leaving now. I'll phone you later."

"Don't be so irrational!" Mark grasped Karen's arm to stop her from going, having had enough of her testiness.

"I'm not. I'm being responsible."

"So you say," Mark replied. "Face it, sweetheart! You really don't want your mother to come home because you know I'll be waiting for her." He'd probably said way too much.

"What?" Karen's face turned beet-red then melted into a chilly complacency. "You would take Mother back?" She didn't call Mark a fool, but she thought it.

"I'm sorry," was on the tip of Mark's tongue, but he didn't say so. It was true he loved Vicki first, with all of his heart.

"Mark?" Karen calmly said, as if detached from reality. "My mother does *not* love you." She huskily laughed.

He recoiled from Karen's statement.

"Oh, yeah, Mother would care plenty that I'd given my body to a man old enough to be my father. But your *Little Vicki* won't miss *you* one bit." Cruelty threaded Karen's words.

Deep within, Karen knew Mark was correct in saying she was jealous of his affection for her mother. And though Karen's devotion to her family was solid, she wanted Mark for herself.

"Be careful of what you dish out, dear," Mark warned. "Words have a way of coming back to haunt you." His violent outbursts in the past had earned him a place in heartache history.

Silence filled the room as Karen and Mark considered the futility of arguing. Would it bring back Victoria any sooner? Or restore peace to their lives? Would it change the past, or alter the future? Now, more than ever, they needed one another.

"I'm sorry," Karen was first to apologize. "I know you love Mother. And she loves you in her own way." She swallowed her pride with courage. "This is a horrible situation for all of us."

"Given." Mark shrugged his shoulder.

"There's no way to remedy the situation short of clearing the charges against Mother," Karen said. "Can we do that for her?"

"I honestly don't know if we can." Mark watched Karen sink to the floor in a pool of tears, weighted down with emotions, shaking hard from worry over a situation beyond anyone's control. He had to find a way to help her cope with the crisis.

"It's my fault, honey," he said. "I came down on you too hard." He would take the blame. "Let's call it even, shall we?" He bent down to comfort the woman he cherished like his own flesh.

Even, thought Karen. It was better than she deserved.

"Let me help you off the floor." Mark offered a hand.

Accepting Mark's support, Karen came to her feet and loaned him penitent eyes. "I love you, Curtis Mark James. Nothing will ever change that. Not the truth about the past, or the future."

Karen somberly traipsed into the kitchen.

A few minutes later Mark heard the microwave in motion. He placed a small white pill under his tongue to control his skittering heart, chagrined that he hadn't protected Victoria from her enemies. She didn't deserve to suffer like this. Neither did Karen. What a calamity fate created the night of April 13, 1989.

And what was he to do with Karen's raging hormones?

"Shall I bring your hot tea with honey?" Mark heard Karen's lilting voice call out from the kitchen as she regained her composure. "Sure," he answered, noting that it was 11:30 a.m.

Why hadn't Sheriff Grimes called? Had something terrible happened to Victoria to cause him to withhold information?

No, Karen would be the first one notified. She was family.

Karen brought two cups of hot tea into the den and set them on the coffee table. "Where do we go from here, Mark? You never said." She lent him whipped green-and-brown eyes.

Mark knew what Karen meant. She was asking if he intended to continue their sexual relationship. She had a right to know. Her heart was vulnerable, hanging out there to scar.

"The other night was a mistake, Karen," Mark couldn't bring himself to look her squarely in the eyes. Instead, he dissolved the herbal teabag in his cup with a spoon, retrieving the slice of lemon swimming aimlessly in the dark liquid. She didn't respond.

"Your mother is right about my being too old for you, Karen." Mark made eye contact. "Can't we just forget about what happened between us and go back to being friends?"

Mark cast his eyes toward the window. It was a sunny day, perfect weather to drive out to the country club and play a few holes of golf. He wanted to think about anything but the present.

"But you love me?" Karen blinked tears. "I know you do." She reached out and touched Mark's arm, wanting him to hold her and fulfill a romantic dream that controlled her thoughts.

"Yes, I do, honey." Mark patted her hand, "but not in the way you want." He slowly took a sip of tea, daring to make eye contact again. Karen's disappointment was obvious, but he couldn't help how he felt. He had loved Victoria since the tenth grade in high school. As always, he'd languished in Jeffrey's shadow, though the man had been dead a quarter of a century. When would Jeffrey's ghost leave everybody alone? *When?*

"Then why did you sleep with me?" Karen asked.

Mark set his teacup on the table. "Because I'm a man, because I'm weak, because I'm lonely." He was all too aware of his shortcomings. No one despised his self-serving choices more than he did. But in the long run, Mark James always acted in ways that benefited himself. Today was no different. He was, after all, characteristically a selfish manipulator like Dick Branson.

"And because I was there," Karen said with disgust. "I understand completely. And I made it so . . . easy for you."

"Saying I'm sorry won't help, will it?"

"Nope." Karen plopped down on the sofa and crossed her lanky legs covered in a pair of dirty gray sweats she'd run in before a breakfast she had barely touched. "I guess this is the end."

"Karen? Don't take the news so hard," Mark said. "You've always known I love your mother. Nothing's really changed." He questioned if that were the truth. Victoria was gone.

Brooding over Mark's revelation, Karen was confused over how much loyalty she owed her mother. Wasn't it her time to claim happiness? And, indeed, did her mother care one iota?

Mark regretted having let Karen spend last night at his place, though she'd slept in the guest bedroom. In the future he should be careful not to encourage her. She would be studying his every gesture, looking for any sign that he wanted her.

He shrugged at the obvious: where Karen was concerned, lust shouldn't rule. It was irresponsible. *No, stupid.*

Maybe, it was impossible to continue a benevolent role as Karen's mentor after experiencing intimacy. So what was he to do? Abandon her in the worst possible hour? He couldn't.

"We can't let one night destroy our friendship. We need each other," Mark said, hoping to bridge the widening gap. Hadn't Karen proven loyal in the past, regardless of her quirks?

"I suppose we do," Karen replied as a bitter spirit manifested itself on her pretty face. Life had always been difficult. Mark would eventually come to his senses and realize that Vicki wasn't coming back to him. Then he would turn to someone else.

I will be there for him, Karen determined. *Whatever is required to earn his affection, I will unashamedly do.*

The phone rang and Karen leaped to answer it. "Yeah?" She waved Mark away. "Who is calling?" he mouthed.

"It's Sheriff Grimes calling from Nashville," Karen whispered. "Thanks for calling, Sheriff," she said to Andy. "Did you find my mother?" She impatiently listened to the chief officer walk her through the bizarre scenario that had occurred earlier that morning at the Green Gables care facility.

"What?" she interjected periodically. "Disappeared?" Karen used one-word phrases like a first-grader. "How?" The conversation continued in a lopsided fashion then was suddenly over. "Okay, bye." Karen hung up the phone

"What?" Mark grabbed Karen by the shoulders. "Tell me."

"Mother's gone and done it again!" Her seething gaze melted Mark to the core. "I can't believe the trouble that woman gets in!" She had never felt such frustration.

"What now?" Mark worried Victoria had been caught and would have to face a murder trial. Truth had the power to rescue her, but dare he defy Dick? Karen might wind up dead, too.

"She's busted my grandmother out of Green Gables and has done her disappearing act again. If I didn't know she believed in Jesus Christ, I'd swear she was a witch." Karen smiled at the idea of her mother taking a pin and sticking it into a rag doll that resembled Mark. It wouldn't hurt him to suffer for his mistakes.

"What? You're smiling at this news? Did the sheriff say anything else?" Mark barked. "Why did Vicki take Kimberly with her?" The idea of her acting so irrationally stunned him.

"Don't ask me to explain Mother's motives."

"Surely Vicki is aware that she cannot properly care for her sick mother while on the run." None of the above made any sense. Assessing the *whys* walloped Mark.

"Mother didn't want my grandmother to participate in *voluntary cessation*. I knew she wanted to remove her from the facility, but I didn't think she would act on her impulses."

"But she did," Mark concluded.

"Actually, I didn't think the authorities would let my grandmother leave. But who am I to say anything's impossible?" Karen settled her emotions, caving in to reality.

"So do the authorities have any idea where Vicki is?" Mark worried he might never see his beloved again. How would he face the future without her? He would be hopelessly lost.

"No. I'm afraid the trail is cold again."

4

Memphis, Tennessee

Georgie Hendricks returned Devin Baldwin's motorcycle late Wednesday morning. It had been five short days since she'd talked to Victoria Tempest at O'Charley's Restaurant.

They were seated side by side in Devin's basement on a pile of lumber the attorney planned on using to repair his damaged wooden deck. Above the rafters, banging pans said his wife Melanie was on a mercy mission of cooking breakfast.

The Baldwin's sleepy shepherd out back fussed at passing cars. Devin seemed overjoyed at having his motorcycle back, though he'd showed little enthusiasm at seeing Georgie again.

"So what's up, detective?" he broke the ice.

"Quite a lot," answered Georgie.

Trusting Devin with her life, she told him what she'd learned from Gloria Gordon in Florida, including every spicy detail down to nailing his bail-jumper. Mortified, his mouth hung open.

"Wow," Devin said over and over until it irritated Georgie.

"Can't you say anything but wow?" she finally asked, pulling a pack of Virginia Slims from her shirt pocket. "Smoke?"

"Why not?" He acted like a nervous sneak in accepting the forbidden cigarette from Georgie's gritty hand.

"So what will you do now?" Devin asked, coughing as the smoke seared his lungs. Having quit the habit numerous times, he periodically resumed his bad habit like it was comfort food.

Georgie really had not expected Devin to put his life on the line for her, but she had hoped for his professional input to help make what she planned on doing a little easier.

"I'm not asking you to become personally involved with my quest," she cleared the air. "I don't want to endanger you."

"I know . . . but you've taken on a lot, you realize. Proving Victoria's innocence and all. I'd hate to be in your shoes."

"Well, if I'm to learn why Dick Branson bombed my apartment and stole my life, I can't just sit around and expect the answers to fall into my lap. I never did have good luck!"

"You aren't seriously thinking about returning to Fernwood?" Devin cranked his head sideways, thinking that Georgie had more gumption than the average run-of-the-mill detective.

"That's exactly what I'm gonna do." Georgie had an idea solidifying in her mind. "This is the deal. People think I'm dead, so who will expect me to show up at Branson to apply for a job?"

"Right." Devin choked on his own saliva. "That one act alone could prove fatal." He eyed the PI with curiosity, snuffing out his sizzling cigarette butt on the plank he was sitting on.

"But you already know that," Devin added. It beat him how Georgie came up with solutions most people preferred to ignore.

"I have to take the risk," she said. "I guess you saw on the tube how the police have Victoria cornered at a federal assisted-living facility in Nashville." Georgie yawned from fatigue.

"Yeah, too bad. I liked the gal," said Devin. "When she's caught, they'll hook her up to a lie detector and make her spill her guts. You think she won't tell on you, you're mistaken."

"Won't matter if she does. I'm like a ghost. Nobody's going to find me unless I want them to." Georgie had successfully survived her childhood, both sexual and physical abuse.

"You always were a good detective." Devin was masterfully stingy with compliments. "You've got savvy and more guts than any guy I know." Georgie was special in his book.

"I like you, too, Devin." She heard footsteps on the stairs above them. "Should I go? Is that your endearing wife?" She knew the wedded pair weren't experiencing marriage bliss.

"No. Sit tight and I'll go see what's up." Devin made his way over to the stairwell. "Honey, is that you?" He waved Georgie back in case Melanie ventured into his domain.

"Yeah," a lilting voice came back. "I need your car. The engine keeps dying in mine."

"No problem," Devin said. "My keys are in the right top drawer of our dresser."

"What are you doing down there so long?" Melanie inquired.

"Getting the lumber sorted so I can work on our deck this weekend," Devin called out.

"Oh. Well, don't be too long. Danny's playing a computer game and you need to take him to the doctor at eleven if I don't get back." Devin heard Melanie's footsteps retreating.

Danny was Devin's nine-year old son. He had early signs of MS, a disease Devin refused to discuss with anyone. He looked at Georgie. They were alone again. "Anything else?"

"Yeah." Georgie's eyes were turquoise daggers. "I need a new identity, to move around Fernwood with ease."

"As in a CIA-type used for the witness protection program?" Devin's voice quickened. "You're askin' a lot."

"I was thinking if I could get hold of some credit reports and identify persons who haven't used their credit cards for, oh say, eight months to a year, I could borrow one of their social security numbers." She left the door wide open for Devin's creative input.

"And?" He listened with no clue where the conversation was headed. "Don't be bashful. You never were."

"Okay." Georgie's eyes enlarged with speculation. "Say a gal gets kidnapped, or left her house for the grocery store and never came back. She'd be missing, maybe even dead." Georgie plotted her new life. "The government can't find this person."

"So you become her," Devin said. "There's a problem with that scenario. It won't work. Missing persons remain on lists for years. When you assume someone's identity and start using their private credentials, you'll be tracked down and the jig will be up. You gotta come up with a better idea than that, Georgie."

"What about a homeless person? I understand only a small percent of homeless people report to help centers. Large numbers are teen runaways, mentally impaired from alcohol and drug abuse. Maybe I could just reappear and apply for a social security card." Georgie thought it was a winning idea.

"Daddy!" a child's voice called from above. "Can you come up a minute?"

Devin put his finger to his lips signaling for Georgie to be quiet. "Yeah, son. I'm almost done down here."

They waited a minute before saying anything more.

"The homeless person idea . . ." said Devin, "it might work. But how will you get hold of the names of homeless people if they're not plugged into the government's system?"

"Maybe I don't need a name," said Georgie. "Maybe I just invent my past. That's something I'll have to work on before I apply for a job with Branson." She knew who might help.

***

Sarah Boswell had heard the precinct gossip. It appeared that Sheriff Andrew Grimes was on a tare to bring Victoria Tempest in for questioning. New evidence had turned up suggesting that the fugitive had hired the thugs who killed her husband in 1989.

Preposterous! Sarah scoffed to herself. *Victoria doesn't have a devious bone in her body.*

Still, Sarah questioned her ability to judge Victoria's motives, regretting her slight involvement with the troubled debutante the time she got a parking ticket. The woman was unpredictable and usually left behind a trail of bloody friends.

Why should I risk my neck for someone I barely know?

Although sympathetic with Victoria's just cause, the last thing Sarah wanted to do was endanger the lives of people she cared about. A smile developed and curled on her lips.

Maybe Dick Branson had messed with the wrong person this time. If Victoria had the guts to stand up to the man, she might reconsider lending a helping hand. *Maybe.*

"Sarah?" A voice broke through her concentration.

"What?" Sarah spun around and saw Josh Tenny standing close by with a report in his hand.

"Can you handle this? I've got Sheriff Grimes on the horn."

"What does he want now?" Sarah flippantly asked. "I thought he was in Nashville chasing the bad guys?" She knew this was a big catch for the sheriff and his good friend, Dick Branson.

"He is," Josh said. "Seems the gal they were looking for ain't nowhere to be found."

"Oh?" Sarah lifted an eyebrow. "And how did that happen?" She nearly laughed.

"Nobody knows. The fugitive was last seen going into Green Gables around nine a.m. this morning. The police surrounded the facility and searched every corner inside and out."

"And what did they find out?" Sarah asked.

"The Tempest woman wasn't there," said Josh. "Neither was her mother. Ain't nobody got a clue how the two of them got out without being seen. Sheriff's hopping mad, he is."

"I bet," said Sarah, suppressing a snicker under her breath. *Good.* Somebody pretty smart had helped them escape.

"Too bad," Sarah told her cohort. "Should you keep the sheriff waiting on the phone line?" Josh often got distracted.

"Oh, yeah." He handed Sarah the report and scurried across the room to get the phone.

So Victoria got away again. The gal had ten lives. Sarah chuckled. She was starting to believe Jeffrey's widow was getting help from the Almighty. *Maybe I should pray more.*

THURSDAY, MAY 22

5

Somewhere in Canada

Victoria and her mother Kimberly Ann had been living on the premises of GloryVale for the past eight days. Kimberly resided in a one-bedroom permanent unit while Victoria used an efficiency apartment designed to accommodate short-term guests.

The CPA's elegant senior citizen apartment complex was part of a planned community that sponsored a hospital and a village with stores operated by business entrepreneurs. Glory Gorge ran right through the middle separating the complex from the town.

Offering the most advanced around-the-clock medical care available, the healthcare facility where Kimberly Ann lived was fully staffed with qualified personnel and structurally designed to therapeutically assist residents in achieving a higher quality of life.

Nature walkways strategically placed throughout the complex provided opportunity for residents to exercise regardless of the weather conditions. The building's atmospheric conditions—both physical and emotional—were as wholesome as Texas promised.

As far as Victoria could discern, no one had a reason to be bored or depressed with the variety of daily activities offered by the capable staff. Senior citizens, mentally and physically capable of working, found employment in the village nearby.

Pleased with her mother's new setting, Victoria would not have minded staying on a while longer had she not been involved in a murder drama more real than the big screen might portray. Until proven innocent of killing her husband, she expected there would be no sense of normality in her life, no true rest, no peace, until the real perpetrators had been caught and prosecuted.

Like it nor not, she would leave Canada as soon as Texas came to get her. *Hurry Texas.* It had been difficult saying goodbye to her capable hero and trustworthy friend. She inwardly smiled. *Wasn't there something more between them than friendship?*

Jon Branson had thought so. Hadn't he said it was love at first sight for Texas? And hadn't she known from the moment she laid eyes on the tall, handsome fellow that he was to become somebody special in her life? Why else would Texas have risked his life to rescue her from Green Gables? Smitten with the media specialist, Victoria had to ask herself, "So what now?"

"Honey?" a voice addressed Victoria from behind.

"What?" She turned around and noticed her mother standing at the threshold of the door. "Oh, hi, Mother." The nostalgic mood was broken. Time would tell, as her mother had said.

"Your door was unlocked so I let myself in. Hope you don't mind?" said Kimberly Ann.

"No problem. Make yourself at home."

Victoria was still in her pajamas, comfortably seated on the windowsill of a picture window that offered a breathtaking view of Glory Gorge below. The scenery reminded her of "North to Alaska," a film she and Jeffrey had viewed together a lifetime ago. Memories were like still clips from the past.

"Aren't you feeling well?"

"A little melancholy today, but I'm fine." Victoria smiled, welcoming the company. She needed to get her mind off Texas anyhow and start thinking about how to clear herself of a murder charge. "You look nice, Mother. Where are you headed?"

"Down to the village to buy some fresh vegetables. You want to come?" Kimberly asked, eyes wide and sassy.

"Sure." Victoria loved that her mother looked so healthy. Moving her to GloryVale had been the right decision.

"Then get dressed." Kimberly noted the starry gaze in her daughter's eyes. *Texas.* She grinned at the prospect of Victoria's newfound love, recalling the sweet touch of her own husband.

"Sure." Victoria hopped down from her window perch and headed to her bedroom to get dressed.

"I didn't mean to hurry you, dear. Take your time," said Kimberly. "Did you hear from Texas yet?"

"Not yet," Victoria called back as she left the room.

Kimberly liked the young man. While seeming genuinely concerned for her daughter's welfare, Texas wasn't the type to be easily led by wild whims. Principally, she believed he was strong in Christian character, and that was what truly mattered.

"Do you know why he hasn't called?" Kimberly pried.

"Texas has important work," Victoria answered from her bedroom "He doesn't have time to think about me." She hoped it wasn't true, a little concerned he hadn't called in over a week.

Did that mean he'd had a change of heart?

If so, Victoria huffed to herself, surely he'd be gentlemanly enough to say so. She pushed aside the fear of rejection.

Go slow, she reminded herself. *Take a breath.*

Texas was just busy. Like her, he was constantly in danger of being apprehended. In fact, on any given day, he probably took more risks than she did. Hadn't he said he would be conducting Christian services on the California beaches?

Quit worrying, Victoria told herself. *He'll call.*

"A penny for your thoughts," said Kimberly as Victoria returned to the room. "Your silence says quite a lot."

"I was just wondering why Texas hasn't called."

Kimberly chuckled, knowing she was interested in the man.

"What?" Victoria noted the expression on her mother's face.

"Oh, I really don't think you should be worried, dear. It's my opinion that Texas considers it his top priority in keeping up with you." Kimberly was not so old she couldn't call a spade a spade.

"You think?" Victoria felt encouraged.

"You should have declared the man taken the moment you laid eyes on him." Kimberly laid a bony finger against her daughter's nose, a gesture borrowed from years ago.

"*Taken?*" Victoria blinked dreamy brown eyes, considering how Texas would receive so rash an action.

"He's sweet on you," said Kimberly. "Just like your father was on me. That kind of devotion is God-sent."

Victoria's cheeks felt hot. Why was she even thinking of telling Texas how she felt? The timing was off. There was no room in her life for romance. To think otherwise was foolish.

"Why don't you read a magazine while I clean up in the kitchen and turn off the coffeepot?" Victoria handed her mother a current issue of *Home Life* on her way into the kitchen.

What about Jeffrey? She couldn't just abandon him.

"Darling? Don't take Texas for granted like you did Mark James," Kimberly warned. "Good men are hard to find."

Humph. "Aren't you just full of advice today?" Victoria came through the kitchen archway, glancing around the apartment to see if she was forgetting something.

"Pay attention. I've lived longer and experienced more."

"Mother! Texas is nothing like Mark."

"I agree. Let's go," said Kimberly."

Victoria locked the door as they left. She was warmly dressed in a pair of jeans and sweatshirt. Exiting the complex together, they were met by a brisk invigorating wind in the fifties, feeling icy cold mixed with the mounting humidity. Victoria drew in a quick breath of the mountain air, slapping her arms with her hands.

"What a marvelous place to grow old," she said.

"I agree," Kimberly replied.

From what Victoria had been told, the CPA complex was environmentally safe with its drinking water drawn from a system of deep springs in the mountains. One had only to breathe deeply to appreciate Canada's clean air, free of chemical pollutants.

"And the best part is that I don't have to grow old alone," Kimberly added. "And there's no voluntary cessation here."

"Thank God," said Victoria. "And that's why I feel safe in leaving you." She squeezed her mother's hand. "I love you."

"You've only been here a week, dear. Already missing that handsome Texan? I see the restlessness in your eyes."

Victoria tossed her mother a leave-it-alone glance.

33

"That bad, huh?" Kimberly teased. "I've been there and done that before. Falling in love rocks the emotions."

"Mother!" Victoria hustled down a stone pathway leading to the railway station. "I don't want to talk about Texas."

Victoria and Kimberly took the railway tram over to the village twenty minutes away, crossing Glory Gorge.

"So you really like your apartment?" Victoria made light conversation, hoping her mother wouldn't bring up the subject of Texas again or question her about how she planned to avenge Jeffrey's death. For the next few hours, she just wanted to play.

And shop, shop, shop, Victoria inwardly giggled.

"Of course I do," Kimberly replied. "Best of all is the freedom I have. Thank you for letting this old bird out of a cage."

"Freedom, it's so important." Victoria cringed at the idea of being locked behind bars. "It shouldn't be taken for granted."

"Don't worry so much, dear," said Kimberly. "Everyone who loves you knows you're innocent." She could always tell when her daughter was troubled. "The truth will win out."

"I pray." Victoria felt like her thoughts were audible since her mother seemed always to know what she was thinking.

"I'm awfully glad the architects included a kitchenette in my efficiency apartment," Kimberly said on a lighter note. "I do enjoy shopping for groceries and cooking my own meals."

"I suppose you didn't do much that gratified you at Green Gables." Victoria patted her mother's wrinkled hand. "I'm sorry I ignored your needs for so long." *Why was I so busy?*

"It wasn't so bad as long as your father was living. We went down to the main hall and played cards with friends we'd made. But one by one they all died . . ." her voice trailed off.

"How old were these friends?" Victoria inquired.

"In their late seventies to mid-eighties. Come to think of it, people who lived at Green Gables didn't last much longer."

"Mother." Victoria's eyes misted tears. "I'm so sorry about what happened to Dad. You know he was saved and Jesus forgives sin. I believe he was cleverly led into assisted suicide."

"I know. And I signed those same stupid papers, believing I'd rather go on to Heaven than live a lonely life." Kimberly regretted her decision. "I hope God understands."

"Count on it," Victoria replied. "Your thinking was impaired because of medication. Taking massive doses of prescription drugs isn't good for anyone. Good food, exercise, and vitamins are a much better way to maintain health."

"I believe that, now that I'm taking fewer pills and feeling so much better. I don't expect to live forever, though."

"And Mother, about daddy's death, please don't let guilt hinder your future happiness. All right?"

"I'll try not to," said Kimberly, sounding tentative.

Victoria understood all too well. Hadn't she had trouble forgiving herself and in trusting God's grace to cover her sins?

"But what about the overpopulation of the elderly and the financial burden it puts on young taxpayers?" Kimberly voiced concern. Propaganda for choosing early death called upon the elderly to act unselfishly since a person outlived their usefulness.

"What about it?" Victoria listened with an open mind as the tram rumbled over the tracks toward the village. "You know that nature has a way of controlling overpopulation. The Bubonic Plague during the 1800s took hundreds of thousands of lives."

"To be honest with you, honey," Kimberly made eye contact, "sacrificing my life for others isn't a big problem for me. How many years do I have left? Five, ten, at most?"

"Mother!" Victoria exclaimed, the rippling of water flowing beneath the tram becoming magnified. "You can't be serious!"

"That was how my doctor put it to me when he asked me to sign the voluntary cessation papers," Kimberly admitted. "I didn't think of it as suicide, more as a gift to others."

"Your doctor told you that?" Victoria would like to get her hands around that doctor's throat, quickly realizing that her violent human nature was just as sinful. Living a Spirit-filled life in Jesus Christ involved continually seeking God and obeying Him with a devoted heart. There was no room for revenge.

But wasn't that what she wanted when it came to getting even with Dick Branson? Isn't it right that he should pay for his crime?

"Can we talk about something else?" asked Kimberly "I grow weary of the past. I sense the topic upsets you, too."

Victoria sighed, glancing out the window.

The tram stopped and let them off. They walked across a bridge and entered the village resembling a huge mall beneath a two-way reflector glass roof. Hidden from the normal eye, aircraft pilots flying overhead would never suspect that a CPA complex lay nestled in the green terrain below. Like Texas had said, the facility was a masterpiece, a place of hope and new beginnings.

"You have a great future here at GloryVale. Don't forget that, Mother," Victoria commented. "The opportunity is a gift."

"I know, dear. And I am thankful."

"I understand a research center has been set up in one wing of the hospital to work on cures for Alzheimer's and Dementia." The prospect for eliminating age-related diseases was exciting.

"Yes," Kimberly responded. "The researchers have found new ways to genetically engineer human cells without the use of stem cells." She still kept up with the latest health advancements.

"I'm afraid you've lost me, Mother. *Stem cells?*"

"I hated the idea of scientists using tissue taken from human fetuses. God forgive us for the millions of babies that mother's have aborted! And the researchers who used the tissue."

"Where did you hear all this?" It was news to Victoria. *Human embryos used for scientific research?* She had her head stuck in the eighties and this was astounding news.

"I like to read scientific magazines. I used to teach school as you recall." Kimberly's thin pale skin wrinkled at the corners of her dark eyes. "I'll lend you my materials."

"Thanks." Victoria smiled, pleased that her mother was still ambitious at seventy-eight and kept up with technology.

"I'm so proud of you, Mother." Victoria realized her self-centered effort in solving Jeffrey's murder and appeasing Mark James had left her mother in third place at the end of the line.

"I'm proud of you, too." Kimberly smiled.

"After we finish shopping, I want you to tell me about the newest developments in science. And about my son, Daniel."

Victoria realized she couldn't hide in the past forever. God had prepared an exciting future for her, without Jeffrey.

"I was wondering how long it would take before you asked about your son," said Kimberly.

"I'm asking *now*, Mother."

"Daniel is in Europe working for the International Peacekeeping Taskforce. He's absolutely brilliant, the most decent young man you'll ever meet. Any parent would be proud."

Victoria paused in front of a deli and inhaled the flavor of brewing gourmet coffee beans. She wanted to ask about her deceased son but didn't. The subject of Paul was too painful.

"Anything else you want to know?" Kimberly asked.

Victoria's eyes filled with tears. "Daniel is twenty-five now? Is he married?" She prepared her heart for the truth.

"Not yet." Kimberly stepped inside the deli behind Victoria. "You were pregnant when your horrible automobile accident occurred. The doctor wanted to abort Daniel because you were in a coma and not expected to live, but Mark wouldn't hear of it."

"My Mark?" *Chalk one up for him*, thought Victoria.

"Yes. He adores you and loves Daniel like his own son."

Victoria cleared her throat, unwilling to discuss her broken relationship with Mark. "From what I've been told, I came out of the coma after ninety days. After I was released from the hospital, did I live with you and Dad?" So many questions were surfacing.

"No," said Kimberly, "our house wasn't equipped to handle a wheelchair. At the psychiatrist's request, Karen and Paul resided in your Tudor home with Patricia Norris, a full-time nanny. When you left the hospital, you moved in with Mark and Beverly James, in their new home on the Hatchie River."

"What?" Victoria flushed with surprise.

Mark had designed a handicapped house to include her?

"Wait!" Victoria exclaimed. "You're saying that Mark and Beverly included me in designing their dream home? Why?"

Had Mark been romantically interested in her while still married to Bev? How far would he go to earn her affection?

"It's true, Victoria. Mark always believed you would fully recover, though Beverly had her doubts. Anyhow, it seemed wise to include wide entrances should they later decide to sell."

"When did Pearlynne Blackstone enter my life?"

"Mark hired the nurse to take care of you when you got out of the hospital," Kimberly explained. "Later, when you were up to handling the children, you returned home."

"Handling my children?" Victoria was puzzled. "What does that mean?" Surely, she cared about her family.

"You didn't remember Paul and Karen, Victoria. I know you can't recall how confused you felt now that your memories have switched again. I'm sorry, but it was a terrible time for all of us."

"What happened to the nanny, Patricia?"

"She got married and moved away," said Kimberly.

"So what did Beverly think of my living under her roof?"

Victoria knew if it were Jeffrey she would not approve of him devoting his time to another woman, under any circumstances.

Was Bev jealous? Is that why she later divorced Mark?

"Mother, I know you're not going to like this idea," Victoria interjected, "but I'm going to ask Texas to take me to Colorado as soon as he phones." Sitting around wasn't getting her answers.

"Why on earth would you want to go to Colorado? I thought you would set your sights on Europe first, to look for Daniel. I'm sure Karen can help you locate him. They stay in touch."

"Of course, I want to see my son," Victoria replied. "But first, I must talk to Beverly." She would figure out how Mark fit into the night Jeffrey died and evaluate the level of his guilt.

"I understand, really I do." Kimberly's kind eyes focused on her daughter. "But isn't running around the country asking a lot of questions dangerous?" She sat down at a table.

"Yes, Mother." Victoria took a seat and ordered two hazelnut coffees. "Every step I take from here on out will be dangerous. Get used to it." There was no room for discussion.

FRIDAY, MAY 30

6

Dick Branson stared at the phone for the longest before picking up the receiver. He was thinking of calling Mark James to pick his brain. Here it was the last of May and nobody had seen hide or hair of Victoria Tempest for over two weeks.

Where was the pesky woman and what was she doing?

Up to no good, no doubt, Dick surmised, keenly aware how very upset Mark was over his *Little Vicki's* absence.

Jake, Dick's PI, reported how the popular doctor had shown up at the country club bar after work most every day to drown his sorrows in booze and let his complaints fall on the deaf ears of uncaring strangers. The man seriously lacked courage.

Dick rang Mark's cell, wondering if his confidante had parted ways with Karen Tempest. *If so, what did that mean?*

W*hy* worried Dick the most. He listened impatiently as the phone rang and rang. Oh dear, he had a terrible premonition. Had the fool doctor confessed his sins to Victoria's daughter?

Dick slammed his fist on the desk. Whatever Mark had discreetly shared with Karen about her father's death was bound to be incriminating. He was no saint in anyone's book. No sir.

But getting Mark to admit he had broken confidence would require a face-to-face confrontation. Give ol' Dick a little time and he'd squeeze the truth out of Mark's alcoholic fed brain.

Dick heard a click at the other end of the line.

"Yes?" It was Mark's voice.

"Oh hi," Dick said, "Glad I caught you." He jacked up his slouchy pants, vowing to buy a bigger belt next time he had Marjorie shop for him. He might even hire a personal shopper.

"Hello, Dick. What's up?"

"You sound in a hurry. Headed out somewhere?"

"Kind of," said Mark. "I'm on my way over to pick up Karen and go out for a little supper." He slipped on his sports jacket.

"Oh, that's nice. How's she holding up, with her mother still missing and all? I really feel sorry for the girl."

"Yeah," Mark sarcastically said. "You didn't call to chit-chat, now did you, Dick? So what can I do for you today?"

"Well, actually I did need to see you. How 'bout a late nightcap? Oh say, nine thirty at the country club?"

Dick had to be certain of Mark's loyalty, whose side he was taking. Confessing his sins to Karen after all these years would be a colossal mistake. But then, guilt did that to weak men.

"Make that nine forty-five and we got a date." Mark held the phone by his chin in the process of gathering his things to leave his office. "Have to go now." He was taking Karen to a new seafood restaurant located next door to the new mall site.

"Hot date?" Dick pried.

"Are we done here?" Mark asked.

"Fine, but don't be late getting to the club," Dick ordered. "Marjorie likes me home before midnight."

"Since when did you have a curfew?" Mark shut off the lights as he walked out the door and caught the elevator going down.

"Gotta stay on the wife's good side, you know, to insure a hunky-dory trip to Rome. Comes with the territory."

By *hunky-dory*, Dick meant keeping Marjorie happy. Tough as the gibbering old tyrant was, he had an itching for spontaneous romance. Who could fault a man for that?

"Are you there, friend?" Dick pressed the phone tightly to his plump ear so he could hear better, scratching his mustache.

"Yeah, I'm here, Dick. When you call me *friend* I get nervous. Makes me wonder if you got something up your sleeve."

Dick chuckled. "Naw, nothing like that. Just thought we'd get together and discuss our Rome trip, to make sure we've got all our ducks in a row. Friend to friend, you know."

"Speaking of the Rome trip, I should arrange for someone to cover me at the hospital. Allen can't possibly handle all my scheduled surgeries while I'm away. We probably oughta take on a new partner. Means less money, but we're both overworked."

Dick cleared his throat. "Well, now that we got that little matter straight . . ." he was uninterested in Mark's problems at work. "See you at nine forty-five, the country-club bar."

Clunk. Mark didn't bother to say goodbye because Dick had already hung up. He made a quick stop at the men's restroom to gargle with mouthwash before leaving the building.

His yellow BMW was where he left it, in the parking space marked "Reserved for Doctor." He loved that old car. Bought it from a junk dealer and restored it in 2005.

Somehow the car was symbolic of his younger years when he'd been footloose and free, unencumbered with guilt. Why, back then, he'd had a different woman rooting for him every night when he gambled on the Gulf Coast. Those had been wild and wooly days. And they had reaped nothing but trouble.

Mark stretched his tired body and breathed in the fresh spring air, thick with sumptuous odors. It promised to be a great evening with a full moon rising. His heart ached for Victoria.

As of late, Mark had been shopping for a new car, thinking the old one reminded him too much of his romantic interludes with Victoria. In many ways, he was a changed man because of her influence. She was the most decent person he knew. And although he didn't view God the way she did, he respected the depth of her faith because it brought beauty into everyone's life.

Memories of the love he had shared with Victoria in that Jackson apartment now seemed more like a dream. He should try to forget about licking his wounds and get on with his life.

Goodness! He might even treat himself royally to one of those brand new hardtop convertibles with all the electronic gadgets. *Red.* Didn't he deserve some happiness in his old age?

But how could he forget what the past had meant to him when Karen incessantly talked about her mother?

I can't. Vicki owns my devotion.

The drive over to Karen's took less than twenty minutes despite the hectic late-afternoon traffic. Victoria's daughter came to the door looking remarkably beautiful in her mauve crepe dress trimmed in tiny seed pearls. Light reflected in her wide hazel eyes.

"Come in, Mark." She motioned with a hand.

"Hi." He grinned and stepped inside the condo, his lusty eyes busily scanning Karen's slender figure pressing against her tight-fitted dress. *Meant to tease him no doubt.* He grunted.

Unlike Victoria, Karen had a daring quality about her that intrigued him. For the past week he'd steered clear of her sexual overtures, hoping tonight wouldn't ruin his perfect score.

"Thank you for accepting my invitation." Karen handed Mark her cape. "Help me with this, please?" She turned her back to him as he draped the knit sweater over her shoulders.

When they faced again, Karen peered deeply into Mark's eyes, her luscious lips gently parted, as if waiting to be kissed.

Mark chuckled. Karen was definitely after his affections. Missing Victoria so terribly, he restrained himself from grabbing the girl and groveling in lust. Instead, he took a step back to put some distance between them. "Are we ready to go?"

He probably should not have agreed to have dinner with Karen, not as strong in character as he pretended, being a rejected man. After sampling the product, he yearned for seconds.

"Don't look so downhearted. This isn't a formal date. I asked you. And I have two free dinners, so you don't have to pay." Karen was unclear why she had said that. Mark wasn't short of cash. He had no response to her outburst.

"I'm sorry, Mark," she apologized, privately wondering who was paying her mother's way out on the streets.

"Paying the tab is no problem, dear." Mark centered his gaze on Karen's troubled face. "You know how much I enjoy your company. I'm afraid I've neglected you," he lied to spare her feelings. "Forgive me?" There was some room for tenderness.

Rebels In Paradise

"I don't know what's got into me lately," Karen said. "I didn't want to attend the company dinner party alone tonight."

"I know," Mark empathized.

"Most of the other commercial agents are married and will bring along their spouses," she explained. "Sometimes I feel like a fifth wheel. Anyhow, I've missed you."

Karen's dreamy hazel eyes silently fell on Mark. "I've missed you, too, Karen," he said, feeling hollow and awkward.

"I've been too forward, haven't I?" Karen read Mark's expression like a psychologist. "I'm not myself these days."

"Maybe a little. You all but dragged me to bed."

Karen softly laughed. "It's just that I love you so much."

"We just need to find you a good-lookin' fella young enough to keep up with you." He was no match for Karen.

"I had one of those, remember? I killed him," Karen said rather stoically. "And you bravely rescued me." She reminded Mark of his allegiance to her.

Mark tugged at his bow tie. "Like my new suit?" He hoped Karen's maudlin mood wouldn't ruin the entire evening. For dessert he was swallowing Dick Branson's bull.

"Here, let me help you look presentable." Karen straightened Mark's tie. "You look fine. Great!" She ran her fingers down the lapel of his suit, hungry eyes tracing Mark's moist lips.

"I hope this event is not going to take more than two hours. That's all the nice I have left in me," Mark bluntly remarked.

Rudeness beat making a mistake he was sure to regret.

"Why? Do you have a late night date?" Karen had sarcasm down to an art. "You can stop with me, you know. Why take your love to all the wrong places? I'm here and willing."

Mark swallowed hard. Karen didn't mince words. That she wanted him romantically was perfectly clear. There was no reason he shouldn't tell Karen about his meeting with Dick.

"Actually Dick invited me to join him at the club for a drink."

"You could take me along. I promise to be good."

"Dick didn't invite you, Karen. We're discussing the Rome trip. Details, you know." He wanted to touch her pug nose like a

43

father would a daughter, like he'd done a thousand times before one indiscreet night of romance changed everything.

But he couldn't. Mark clinched his fists. "I'll get the lights."

"Wait! Let me make sure I have my house key." Karen searched through her purse. "Guess I'm ready now."

"By the way, can you see your way clear to come along to Rome?" Mark dreaded asking Karen, but dared not leave the girl home alone to fend off lurking danger.

"I might as well!" Karen locked the door behind them.

"Why the attitude?" Mark took Karen by the elbow and led her toward his BMW. "One minute you're sweet, the next," he needn't say more. "Your emotions are all over the place."

Anger bubbled in Karen's gaze. "Mother's not coming back or I would have heard from her by now. Not one e-mail, mind you. Or phone call." She took off walking to her side of the car like a rat after cheese. "Guess I know where I fit in her life."

Mark didn't know quite how to help. He was the rock Karen leaned on, her point of reference. He couldn't let her down now.

"Don't be so hard on your mother, Karen. And please don't take your wrath out on me. I'm still your friend."

Considering Mark's statement, Karen ran her hand over the hood of the BMW. That she was upset was a given. *Friend?*

"Interesting choice of words." Karen stared into the dark spaces of heaven where glittering stars struggled to shine through the dark clouds. "Friendship."

Mark was at a loss. What *more* could he say?

"Don't sell this car," Karen remarked. "I like it." She scooted into the passenger seat and secured her seatbelt. "It feels more like an old friend than—" she stopped, smiling.

"Than I do," Mark completed Karen's sentence, wincing over her scared opinion of him. One night of spontaneous romance had ruined a perfectly wonderful daughter-father relationship.

"Can we just drop the sarcasm and get on with the evening?" *What am I supposed to do?*

"I'm sorry that life has been so hard on you, baby," he tried to make it better, climbing into the driver's seat.

"I'll get over it," said Karen, lips pouting.

Too bad Karen had made so many unwise choices in her life, Mark thought to himself. And now she was living with guilt while suffering the consequences. Still, he wouldn't abandon her.

"Too much change is not good for anybody," Karen said. "Not even you, Mark." She was not only talking about his BMW. The doctor had poorly handled his relationship with her mother, his current unrest a result of years and years of unwise choices.

"As far as the car . . ." Mark grunted. "Don't get too attached to this old relic." He thumped the dashboard with his right hand, thinking he had outgrown its usefulness.

"Why?" Karen peered at him.

"Because I've already talked to a salesman about ordering a brand-new red BMW convertible to the tune of a hundred and fifty thousand." Spending money was a diversion from heartache. And he badly needed a new toy to replace his unchained lust.

"Mark!" Karen exclaimed. "I don't make *that* much money in real estate in one year. Isn't that kind of extravagant?"

"Hey, kid! Do I tell you how to shop?" He ignited the engine. "You have money, so why should I feel sorry for you?" Mark revved the engine, feeling the power of being in control.

"I don't care about money, anyhow," Karen said.

Mark laughed. "That's because you have it, honey. Try living without it." He thought back to the time he had gambled away all his savings and owed his soul to Dick's company store.

"Are we set to go?" Mark tired of babble, recalling the enormous amount of blood money he'd earned for making one stupid phone call. The act of betrayal ended his best friend's life.

"Talking about spending money, it makes me wonder how Mother's getting by." Karen drew in a breath as Mark rammed the pedal to the floorboard, whipping the BMW into the street.

"Vicki? You think she's living like a homeless person?" The thought had never entered Mark's mind. "She's obviously getting help from someone. We just need to figure out who and why."

"I've been over this scenario a *jillion* times," Karen said. "Mother doesn't have any close friends. Other than your ex-wife, and they parted ways years ago. I know Mother went to see Beverly right after she regained her former memories," Karen recalled. "Beverly told her that you gambled in the eighties. Did you? Is it true?" Karen stared at Mark.

"What if it is? That's all water under the bridge. Besides, Bev would say anything to hurt me. She's the get-even type. Maybe someone else is helping your mother."

"I can't imagine who." Karen shook her head.

Mark took the entrance ramp to the interstate. "It puzzles me how a person can just drop off the planet without a clue."

"Trust me, she hasn't!" Karen declared. "If I know my mother, she's out there running around trying to nail the criminals who killed my father! She won't rest until she does."

"What?" The idea of Victoria learning the truth unnerved Mark. "Karen, your mother has no resources, no friends that we know about, and by now the police have plastered her picture over their crime network and in every U.S. Post Office."

"So?" Karen reacted.

"So Vicki can't go anywhere without being recognized by some do-gooder who will report her to the police."

"You're forgetting something, Mark. Mother won't look like herself," Karen replied with confidence. "She's moving about in a disguise, just like she did in Fernwood. I'm sure of it."

"But, of course, you're right. She was posing as Tina Banks when she worked for the cleaning company. And she had the credentials to prove she was Tina. How did she do that?"

"My mother is *very* clever. She'll find a way to outsmart the police and nail the lid on my father's killers. God help the person who gets in her way." The idea brought a smile to Karen's lips.

She's right, thought Mark. Victoria was the most determined individual he'd ever known. When she got an idea in her head, and believed she was right, there was no stopping her.

"So where do we start looking? And what are her chances of survival without us?" Mark blinked, swerving past a car.

"Oh, I think her chances are excellent," Karen replied. "I also believe that my mother knows exactly what she's doing and when she's ready for us to know her agenda, we will. There's the restaurant up ahead. Don't miss the exit."

"You think this is all a game to her?"

"It's no game, Mark. And you can count on Mother's showing up one day with the goods in her hands."

"What goods?" Mark asked, growing worried.

"You know—the information Mother needs to convince the police that she's innocent of planning my father's death."

"How can she, when the police failed?"

"I don't know. But when she does . . ." Karen peered into the vast universe as the moon broke through the darkness, "light will shine brightly on the truth, and the truth will set her free."

"What? I never thought of you as a philosopher, Karen."

"Turn now, Mark," Karen instructed. "Call me foolish, if you will, but when Mother's truth hits home, how will you fare?"

"What do you mean?" Mark rolled the BMW into the Seafarer's parking lot, guilt lodging in his throat like a boulder.

"I guess I'm asking if your hands are clean of dark deeds?" Karen lifted an eyebrow. "Because if they're not, and you know something more about my father's death than you're letting on, you'll never survive my mother's wrath." *Let him chew on that!*

7

Dick was seated at the country club bar Friday evening when Mark arrived fifteen minutes late. *Let the dictator see how it feels to wait on someone.* Mark stood loosely behind his so-called friend.

"Hi, Dick. Sorry I'm late." Mark made his presence known. "You drinking all alone these days?"

"Huh?" Dick craned his head around to view Mark. "You're late." He'd specifically asked the doctor to be on time.

"So what are you drinking?" Mark climbed on the barstool beside Dick. "Karen and I had supper earlier."

"Oh," Dick said. "I'm drinkin' Scotch." His gaze remained impersonally focused forward. "She doin' okay?"

"Karen? Fine." Mark noticed the sexy barmaid carrying a tray of drinks. Clad in black hoes and a skin-tight leather miniskirt, her scooped white blouse left little to wonder about.

"Cute, ain't she?" Dick seldom missed a trick. "She's new, and married. I checked." The mover-shaker rocked around in his swivel barstool, giving Mark the once over. "Interested?"

"No, and why the scrutiny? I'm not carrying a piece." Mark raised his hands, feeling betrayed by Dick on many levels.

The meatpacker chuckled, then belched. "Just checkin'."

"About the barmaid, I didn't notice," Mark lied about his lusty reaction to the sensuous woman. Why let Dick have the last laugh? *So I'm a liar.* "Why did you summon me tonight?"

"Fill 'er up," Dick told Nell. "Wanna talk, that's all."

"Talk? Sure." *Motive* was Dick's middle name. "I need something cold to drink." Mark glanced around for Nell, his mouth dry as feathers from the salty salmon he'd eaten earlier.

Like Karen thought, the office get-together had been a couples' affair and not the most pleasant of evenings. They had eaten heartily to avoid answering personal questions about Victoria's disappearance, eyeing each other for support. When he failed at socializing, Karen suggested they leave. He agreed.

Dick heartily slapped Mark on the back. "I'm paying, so what'll it be? I know you've had dinner, but how 'bout dessert?"

"I'm full, thanks anyhow," Mark answered. "My belt won't expand another notch, but I could use a drink." Why did he feel like the buttered-up gingerbread man waiting for the fox to have a bite? "I'll have ice water," he decided, ready to get Dick's agenda behind him and end the uncomfortable evening.

"Hey, Nell!" Dick called out. "One bottled water over here!"

Embarrassed, Mark's neck turned red around the collar.

"Calling me your friend earlier, what does that mean, Dick?"

"Huh? You think I got an agenda?"

"I know you do. Is this about extra privileges?"

Dick chuckled. "I swear you always could make me laugh." He clubbed Mark's shoulder with a hand. "I need some comedy in my life. Gets rough sometimes when the heat's turned up."

"What kind of heat?" If Dick was talking about Victoria's disappearance, it wasn't a bit funny. Mark's sullen mood was a dark contrast to Dick's light banter. Water and fire don't mix.

"Lighten up, fella. Too much stress and you'll have a stroke."

"Gotta little question for you, Dick." Suspicion flooded Mark's expression. "Did you have *anything* to do with Victoria's mysterious illness or disappearance from the hospital?"

Dick spewed out a mouthful of Scotch. "Goodness, Mark! I already told you I didn't!" He slammed down his cold glass on the polished cherry counter. "I'm not a common criminal."

"No, there's nothing common about you," Mark said. "Before all this is over, it's going to get a whole lot less common."

"All right, all right." Dick defensively put up a hand. "Truce, man. Please. I don't want to argue with you. Hear me out."

"Water." The head bartender placed a Perrier in front of Mark. "If you don't mind, guys, tone it down a little. We like to make a good impression 'round here at the country club."

"Sorry," Mark apologized, seeing Dick was about to explode with indignation, ready to remind the bartender who owned the club and that he could pretty much do as he blamed well pleased.

Dick shook his head, making eye contact with Mark. "You'd think these Fernwood bimbos would eventually learn who's in charge around here." He felt the impact of alcohol, caring less and less what others might think.

"So you say, buddy." Mark swigged on his water, reminding himself that he needed a clear head to outwit Dick.

"Another Scotch," Dick ordered. "And bring us some salty peanuts to munch on. We're takin' our drinks over there." With a plump finger, he pointed across the room, climbed off the barstool, and staggered a few steps. "Coming?" He glanced back.

Mark shrugged and trailed Dick over to a table under the shade of a palm, dreading what the meatpacker had to say that was too private for others to hear. The old drunk coot plopped down in a chair, belched, and pompously glared at Mark.

"What?" Mark winced at Dick's bad breath, laden with stale tobacco. He wasn't up to the aggravation. Over supper, Karen's real-estate coworkers had rudely grilled him about their relationship. Teasing, of course, nevertheless irritating. He'd politely tiptoed around the details to save Karen the embarrassment. At least, the lobster bisque was good.

"Have you told Victoria's daughter anything you shouldn't?" Dick said in a hushed voice, leaning across the table.

"And what's *that* question supposed to mean?" Mark reared back indignantly. "Karen is her name. Say it. *Karen*."

Dick shook his head disparagingly. "I can always tell when your mushy conscience starts to cloud your good judgment."

The bomb in Mark's subtle glare threatened to ignite.

"It's you and me, buddy. So let's come clean here," Dick laid his cards on the table. "No secrets, you hear?"

"If you think I have formed some secret pact with Karen against you, you're way off base," Mark declared. "You know I wouldn't betray *us*. Haven't I remained loyal all these years?"

Dick leaned back, hooking thumbs in his belt. "You sure?"

Mark winced a smile. "All right, I admit I gave some thought to telling Karen the truth," he confessed. "But I didn't."

Dick coughed and spewed out whiskey.

"I realized my confession would help no one."

"Well, bravo! My guy said—" Dick's thought got cut short.

"Your guy?" Mark reacted. "Your PI, you mean?"

"Well, yeah. Jake's been keeping an eye on you for me. He says you leave your office early and drink way too much."

Mark blinked, anger mounting.

"A man who loses touch with his brain takes too many risks," Dick drove the knife in deeper. "You could be out at some bar, airing your personal problems and sayin' something you'd later regret. Then a whole bunch of trouble would descend—swoop down like a demonic vulture and devour our future."

Dick was his usual dramatic self, thought Mark.

"Can't let that happen, Mark. Am I making myself clear?"

"What?" Mark had swallowed all Dick's bull he could stomach. "What happened to trust?"

"Did I say I didn't trust you?" Dick squinted his red eyes, toying with his empty liquor glass. "You're a smart man. You understand why I'm worried. With Karen all upset and playing on your emotions, I was uncertain. Tonight was to make sure."

"Okay, let's get one thing straight." It was Mark's turn. "I did a job for you years ago and you paid me. Since then, I've paid plenty in regret, but I'm not about to bury us. Got that?"

Dick hit the table with a fist. "Good! Marjorie and I leave for Rome in a week, and I want you and Karen on the plane with us. That way I can keep an eye on the both of you," he said. "Don't even try to protest. I've already purchased our tickets."

Why argue with Dick when he'd already decided to go?

"I need to take care of a few details at work before I can leave," Mark said. "What if Vicki comes home?"

"So what?" Dick was unsympathetic. "Let the police do their job, I'll give my cell number to Andy. If anything happens with Victoria, he'll phone us in Rome. Meanwhile, we'll kick up our heels and have some fun." Dick put on his jacket in preparation to leave. "Meanwhile, you need to lighten up a little."

Maybe a vacation will do me good, Mark reasoned.

8

Memphis, Tennessee

Nearly two weeks had past since Georgie had seen Attorney Devin Baldwin. During the interim she had kept a low profile on Memphis city streets, hiding out in cheap motels, doing her homework at the public library, and sometimes praying.

Imagine. Ask her any question about homeless people and she knew the answer now that her life hung by a short boot string.

She'd sure like to *boot* Dick Branson off the planet.

As for Devin, he was a family man and it was time to cut him loose. He'd been a super human being and gone all out for her beyond expectation. Not being family, he owed her nothing.

Besides, expecting Devin to keep secrets from his wife was a terrible imposition. No friend did that. How could PI Georgie live with herself if anything bad happened to Devin or his family?

Nope. From here on out it was a solo flight.

It was Friday afternoon, and Georgie was waiting for Marisa Straus to come home from work. Recalling where her former client hid the emergency key, she had used it to gain entry.

Marisa's condo was much nicer than Georgie's demolished apartment before it was bombed. If she were a normal person—which she wasn't—she'd like to own one like it.

Shoot! She might even buy a high-definition TV and watch it occasionally. *Who was she foolin'?* Georgie slid down the kitchen wall into a dark corner and listened to her disturbing thoughts.

During uninterrupted moments of loneliness, like this, weird images of Georgie's childhood pressed in to distract her focus. She was a worm crawling into a cocoon hoping for rebirth.

Shoving away painful memories of a terrible childhood, Georgie attempted to concentrate on the case at hand. Victoria Tempest was in grave danger and needed help, but outsmarting Dick Branson wasn't a piece of cake, by no means.

Aw, nothing ever is. Georgie sulked in the shadows of the dying day. At least, her visit to Florida had proven successful. In a few days she had learned enough about Dick's unholy kingdom to do some serious damage, thanks to Gloria Gordon.

As soon as Gloria heard that Beverly James had been run out of town the same weekend that she had, her ruby lips flew open like a flytrap. Like anyone who knew anything about Dick's business practices, Gloria was sick of the evil *chameleon* slithering through life with changeable shades of truth. That did not mean she wasn't afraid, or that she would testify on Victoria's behalf.

One day somebody's gonna kick Dick Branson out of his plush green garden of success and expose his lies. It would be my pleasure.

When Gloria started talking, she hadn't known when to quit. It seemed she knew more about what went on in Fernwood than any gossip columnist. Gloria said it was because she'd worked at the Olde Soda Shoppe half of her lifetime. People came to eat and drink and they talked. About everybody and everything!

A smile curled Georgie's lips. *Everything.*

Terrance Wilson, Tanya Mason's brother, died from leukemia in February of 1988, five years after working on a cleanup crew for Hearty Meats, Inc. In January of 1989, his mother Elizabeth approached Attorney Jeffrey Tempest about her son's premature death. After hearing about the improper cleanup of the toxic barrels of oil, Jeffrey agreed to gather data in order to file a complaint against the company for environmental negligence.

"Why wait so long?" Georgie had asked Gloria.

"Elizabeth didn't suspect foul play until she learned that two other boys on Terrance's crew had died," she had replied.

When Mrs. Wilson came to see Jeffrey Tempest, the existence of toxic substances on Hearty property was only a theory. Because the files had been stolen from Jeffrey's office, no one knew what evidence he had collected over the months before he died. It was inconceivable that the travesty had happened.

Why didn't city hall halt the company's activities when they failed to do proper soil tests? Who had interfered with protocol?

Someone powerful and well connected, Georgie realized. Like others residents of Fernwood, Jeffrey Tempest must have found it difficult to believe such an event took place.

Licenses and permits were required, weren't they?

The shock of the aftermath played havoc in the lives of those who had access to incriminating information. Terrance Wilson for one, barely twenty-three years old when he prematurely died. By then, the company had hurt many honest, hard-working folks in their quest to reach the top of Fernwood's food chain.

"They oughta pay plenty for their mistakes!" Georgie had agreed with Gloria. But the bad guys didn't always get caught.

That injustice existed in Fernwood was no big surprise. Life had taught Georgie that money wielded power. And Dick Branson apparently had plenty. But why was he perpetuating the cover-up if he wasn't responsible for environmental negligence?

What is the man hiding that I don't see? Georgie pondered the situation. *No,* Dick had acquired his wealth from doing something more lucrative than just packaging raw meats. *What?*

Georgie needed proof of wrongdoing before contacting the FBI about an investigation. Like Victoria, she was after the unedited truth. Danger would track her like a hound for the rest of her life if she went after Dick Branson. And death was final.

Gratefully, the soil samples she had collected on Branson property proved that PCBs still existed—unless Dick had already cleaned up the toxic sludge. *Then what?*

Georgie groaned at the uncertainties plaguing the Tempest case. The murder investigation was like a giant puzzle with many scattered pieces. When found and placed in order, the bigger picture would logically appear. Then she would know exactly what steps to take next. *But*—there was always a "but" to tarnish every good scenario—without Elizabeth Wilson's testimony to back up her evidence there was no case against Branson.

Terrance Wilson's mother had received a note the night Jeffrey died containing a hundred grand and a note telling her to leave town. *Coincidence?* Not in Georgie's book.

Elizabeth Wilson died in a freak automobile accident two years later. *How convenient for Dick.* She'd say so, hands down.

With available witnesses having dwindled over the decades, Georgie desperately needed for Victoria's friends to testify on her behalf. Too bad, Gloria didn't want any part of the notoriety that came with a big trial. And Sarah Boswell had made it crystal clear she would not testify. Tanya Mason was as skittish as a wild filly, unpredictable even if she decided to take a legal stand.

"Why won't Sarah testify?" Georgie had asked Gloria.

"Won't do any good!" Gloria had exclaimed. "Anything Sarah has to tell is second-hand. Hearsay is inadmissible in a court of law, ain't you heard, girl?"

Some things are best left unsaid. Georgie thought she understood the three women's dilemma. Fear was a factor in any unsolved murder. In this case, Dick Branson was the fear-maker.

Oh yeah, PI Georgie had once backed off from the case—the stormy night Victoria was hospitalized and almost died. Standing in the hall shadows, she had questioned the sanity of being involved with a woman she barely knew. Feeling unqualified to make judgments, PI Georgie had walked away.

Leaving the hospital feeling guilt-free, she had headed back to Memphis. No amount of money was worth risking her *only* neck. Then, a couple of hours later, someone had the gall to bomb her apartment. That was when Victoria's business suddenly became hers. And now there was no turning back.

What's keeping Marisa? Georgie glanced at her wristwatch, stretching her tired body, rubbing her aching calf muscles. She now knew that there were two other plaintiffs joining Elizabeth Wilson in filing an environmental complaint against Hearty

Meats—relatives of sick boys who had worked alongside Terrance and later died from their weird illnesses.

The garage doors groaned and lifted as a car entered. A few minutes later, Georgie heard a key turn in the backdoor lock.

"Who's there?" The owner was sensitive to an intruder.

"It's me, Marisa," Georgie replied, coming to her feet and stepping from the shadows. "Don't be frightened."

"Oh, wow!" Marisa Straus stumbled backwards a few steps. "I thought you were dead!" The color in her face washed out.

"I'm not dead, as you can see." Georgie flipped on the kitchen light. "It's me. No ghost. Flesh and blood."

"You scared me half to death!" Marisa peeled off her suit jacket and dropped it on the floor. "What happened to you?" She came closer to Georgie. "Why are you here—how can I help?" Questions rolled off her tongue from a stunned brain.

"Slow down, gal!" Georgie put up a hand. "Obviously, I survived the bombing of my apartment. You might say my life hung by a thread. A yellow one." If she hadn't noticed the broken string across the threshold of her doorway, she would likely be dead, floating out in space without a body, headed to where the unbreathing go before they decide what to do next.

Oh, Georgie realized her statement of faith was a poor excuse for a religious philosophy, but it was the best she could muster at the moment. Maybe Victoria would enlighten her someday. Forces of evil against good, she understood. God, she didn't.

"I don't suppose you'd like to explain." The Spanish girl pulled a soda pop from the refrigerator. "Lime is all I have. Want one?" She eyed Georgie with suspicion. "Are you in trouble?"

"Yes, on both accounts." Georgie reached around Marisa and grabbed a lime soda off the top shelf. "Trouble's always been my stalker." She erected herself. "I need your help."

"I was afraid you were going to say that." The one-hundred-five-pound, twenty-eight-year-old divorcee found her spongy legs and wobbled over to the kitchen table. "Is it bad?"

Georgie leaned her weight against the table. "I wouldn't be asking for help if I had another choice."

"I know," Marisa commiserated. "Sit down and tell me what you have in mind." How could she refuse the private eye who had negotiated a lucrative divorce settlement with her ex?

"Thanks," Georgie straddled a straight chair backwards. "What I'm going to ask you to do won't get you into any trouble, I promise." She felt her shirt pockets for a loose cigarette.

"Nobody will know but us?" Marisa's inquisitive chocolate eyes widened. "I don't want any trouble with the law."

"You won't." Georgie continued her search for cigarettes.

"I keep a carton of Camels in my cabinet for when my boyfriend comes over," Marisa said. "Help yourself." Her olive complexion was ghostly pale, her expression cloaked in worry.

"Thanks." Georgie opened a cabinet door, retrieved her find, and returned to the table. "This is the gig."

"What gig?" asked Marisa.

Georgie took her time lighting up the Camel, resuming her slumped posture with elbows resting on the maple tabletop.

"I can't tell you the whole story, Marisa . . ." Georgie drew smoke into her lungs, "but I can tell you everything we say here tonight must be kept confidential. I'm dealing with some bad dudes who would skin us both alive if they knew I was here."

"The ones who bombed your apartment?" Marisa was a quick study. "I don't see how I can help you."

"You will." Georgie leaned over and parted the window blinds, scanning the front yard. A purple car drove by, turned around and came back. "Are you expectin' company?"

"No," said Marisa, taking a peek through the blinds. "The car belongs to a fifteen-year old kid down the street. He's practicing to get his driver's license."

"Are you ready for my tale of woe?"

"I guess," said Marisa, nervously fidgeting.

"I was doing work for this gal, you see, who happens to be in a heap more trouble than I am," Georgie vaguely informed Marissa. "I uncovered certain illegal facts for her."

"Because this person is your client," Marisa said.

"Exactly." Georgie leaned her elbows on the table. "The guy my client is exposing is powerful, and the information I have can pull down his financial kingdom." Turquoise eyes narrowed.

"I see," said Marissa. "So this *bad* dude found out you were working for this gal and came after you." A question crossed her face. "Why didn't they go after your client?"

"Unfortunately, they did," Georgie replied. "The same night, a few hours before my apartment was bombed."

"Oh, dear. I don't think I want to hear this."

"Like I said, Marisa, you're safe as long as you don't talk."

"And your client, how is she doing?" Marisa wanted the rest of the story. The can of soda was shaking in her hands.

"She's safe. I met with her two weeks ago and we talked. The police have turned up evidence suggesting that my client hired thugs to do in her husband. She's wanted for murder."

Marisa gasped. "Not that rich debutante from Fernwood?"

"Exactly," Georgie admitted, thinking she might as well reveal the whole sordid tale. "This is how it all came about . . ."

When Georgie had finished her story, Marisa's brow was covered in beads of sweat. "Any questions?" she asked.

"No," said Marisa.

"Sorry to involve you, but as I said, I really need your help."

"What do you want me to do?" Marisa was trembling like a scared kitten. "I'll do it as long as it isn't illegal."

"I'm coming into your office to apply for a social security card, and you're gonna help me." Georgie peered at Marisa. "I'll be posing as a homeless person, so you won't recognize me."

"Wait! How is that going to work?"

Georgie winked with her left eye and pulled her right ear with her right hand. "That's the signal, so you'll know it's me."

"What else? And how do you plan to pull this off? Picture I.D, home address, person next of kin, are all required."

"I'm homeless, remember? I've been on the streets since I was twelve. My parents are dead and I've never been plugged into the system, never had a social security card, or a home address, or been to a homeless shelter for help. It's doable, trust me."

"Do people really do that? Live on the streets without help or a paycheck?" Marisa asked, astonished.

"Yep." Georgie peered out the window, checking the yard again. "I did some research at the library and discovered that the Social Security Department is less likely to run background checks on homeless applicants than any of the other agencies."

"Really?" Marisa reacted. "I thought the government did away with *those* kinds of folks. You know, if they can't be rehabilitated, last resort they are put out of their misery."

"And not so voluntary either, I'd say."

"Yeah." Marisa grimaced.

"Don't look so worried, dear. I'm worth rehabilitating." Georgie flashed a grin. "As far as the government knows, I died in a gas explosion." She offered Marisa her right hand. "Meet Jaycee Moore. It'll work fine, trust me."

"I don't see how you're going to pull this off, but I'm game," said Marisa. "Can't see how I can be blamed for your lies."

"Don't look so worried. My plan will work."

"Are you hungry?" Marisa asked. "I could make us burgers."

"Sounds wonderful." Georgie's stomach was a sinkhole.

"Why don't you tell me the rest of your scheme while I cook?" Marisa got out of her chair. "I have to change clothes first. Would you like to take a shower? And if you need fresh clothes, my sister's are hanging in the guest bedroom."

"Sure." Georgie glanced down at her worn flannel shirt and torn jeans purchased at a second's shop.

Rebels In Paradise

SUNDAY, JUNE 1

9

Just ask, and Victoria could tell you the exact time Texas Holmes had phoned. *Who could forget an answered prayer?*

It was Sunday, June 1, 6:00 p.m. Pacific Time. She had been praying all day long her handsome hero would call so she could ask him for a lift to Colorado to find Beverly James.

Not ten minutes before she'd been obsessing over how she had fallen victim to a chain of unbelievable circumstances that made her feel responsible for Jeffrey's death. Worse, how she'd been falsely accused of his murder and labeled a common criminal. Would she ever be able to stop running from the law?

How did life get screwed up so fast?

Gratefully, the information Georgie Hendricks had recently gleaned from Gloria Gordon in Florida helped identify what questions Victoria ought to ask Beverly when they next met. Like, had Mark mentioned anything about a pending environmental complaint against Hearty Meats? He was there, after all.

Surely, the clever doctor had suspected something was amiss when the meatpackers flew into town and plopped down on the old tannery site with no questions asked. As workers became ill in the following years, didn't the locals complain, gossip, and make wild conjectures? Or had Dick pulled the wool over the eyes of every resident of Fernwood? If only she could recall the past.

Take Mark, for instance. He had to know that the tannery process left behind deadly solvents. What was the EPA doing all this time? Who was protecting the citizens of Fernwood?

If Mark had been aware there was an environmental problem and said nothing, didn't that mean he was involved in the cover-up and partially responsible for Jeffrey's death?

Victoria prayed he was innocent, but what were the chances of that? Mark had been keeping secrets from her for years. Could she expect anything less than deceit from him *now*?

Just before Texas called she had grabbed a warm wrap from the hall closet and was about to leave for the vesper service to be held in beautiful Christmas Gardens overlooking the GloryVale Gorge. While switching off the lights, the phone had sounded.

"I can't talk now, Mother," Victoria had rushed to say in anticipation of who was calling. "No, it's me, Victoria."

"Texas!" she had exclaimed, his baritone voice sweet music to her ears. Slipping off her sweater, she'd collapsed on the sofa, so full of what she wanted to say, and so overjoyed, that she hadn't known where to begin. "Thank goodness, you called!"

"Why? Is something wrong?" He'd picked up on Victoria's apprehensive excitement. "Did I call at a bad time?"

"Goodness, no! I just need a lift to Colorado," she'd replied. "When are you coming to get me?" Assuming that he would be eager to help. After all, Jon had asked him to take *good* care of her.

Texas had laughed. "I wanted to give you time to visit with your mother before I horned in. GloryVale is such a great place to live, I thought you might decide to stay," he'd said.

"Don't be ridiculous, Texas! I don't want to stay here! I have too much to do." She hadn't cared if he thought her a bit forward. "I have a friend in Denver I need to see immediately."

"Immediately? Like tomorrow? Is this friend a Christian fugitive in danger?" Texas always looked at the bigger picture.

"No, I don't think so. Beverly was—Texas, stop! Take two. I can't explain this complicated situation over the telephone. I can tell you that I'm hoping to learn something to help me prove my innocence." There, she'd been blunt but made her point.

"Oh," Texas had said, static beginning to interfere.

"Well, are you going to help me or not?" Victoria was aware that her freedom hung in the balance. If she didn't come up with a justifiable defense, she would be tried and convicted of murder.

"Of course, I will. See you early tomorrow morning."

"Really?" Victoria's heart had swelled.

"Pack a bag so you can leave with me later in the day." Texas had said. "I won't be in Canada again for at least another month."

"Not a problem." She had been elated at the idea of running off with Texas again. "Thank you."

"No problem. I—" the line had fallen dead.

The conversation had taken place a few minutes before. No telling how long Victoria had held the receiver before hanging up.

Was Texas going to say I love you?

Overcome with joy, Victoria put on her jacket, ran out the door and down the hall into to her mother's apartment without bothering to knock. "Mother! Where are you?"

"In here," a lilting voice called out from the bedroom.

"You'll never believe *who* just phoned," Victoria exclaimed. "Texas! He's picking me up tomorrow and we're flying in his helicopter to Colorado. I'm so excited. What shall I wear?" In a dither, she wrung her hands like a schoolgirl on a first date.

Kimberly stood in the bedroom doorway, eyebrows cautiously raised. "Did Texas say that, or did you just *assume* he would follow orders?" Victoria often presumed too much.

"I can't be worried about that!" Victoria took exception.

"Well, you should be. Don't push the man too much." Kimberly came into the living room, rubbing her hands with fragrant lotion. "Men don't usually like assertive women."

"I didn't come here for a lecture, Mother."

"You don't want to let this one get away." Kimberly offered some motherly advice. "Texas is fine specimen."

"I know that," Victoria answered, "but this is not about romance, it's about solving a murder and I need his help."

"It's always about relationships, dear."

"Mother? I'd rather you didn't interfere."

Kimberly glared at her impetuous daughter.

"I suppose you told Texas all *that*. I'd think he has more important things to do than to chase after fantasies." Kimberly believed Jeffrey's killers had left a cold trail impossible to follow.

"I'm glad you're better, Mother, but I *don't* want your advice."

"Honey, I don't mean to meddle, but please think before you act!" Kimberly said. "Don't mess up your future by clouding it with the past. Live for today. That's all any of us have."

Victoria relaxed on the sofa. Kimberly Ann joined her.

"What you just said about living for today—I fully agree. But there's more to it than I've told you." Victoria thought her mother should be aware of the situation.

"What, dear?"

"An enemy—whom I won't name—has cooked up evidence to make me look guilty." Victoria ventured on to explain how Jeffrey had taken out a life insurance policy two weeks before he died, and why she had signed for him on the bottom line.

"Perfectly legal. Folks do that all the time," said Kimberly.

"Except the police believe I plotted Jeffrey's murder for the money, to benefit myself with a grander lifestyle."

"My word, Victoria!" Kimberly's narrow lips pursed with anxiety. "How much money are we talking about?"

"Two million dollars. Jeffrey arranged for the policy, not me. He phoned me around eleven on a Thursday and said he was due at the insurance company to sign some legal papers and couldn't make it. Would I go in his place? I just did as I was asked."

"You think Jeffrey suspected he was in danger?" Kimberly inquired, now emotionally involved. "Did he say so?"

"No," Victoria replied, exasperated.

"Well, I must admit, " Kimberly concluded, "according to many of the crime novels I have read, the finger of guilt does appear to point at you, dear. And only you."

"Mother! I didn't hire thugs to kill my husband!"

"I know you didn't, sweetness." Kimberly patted Victoria's hand. "You wouldn't hurt a fly. But follow the evidence—Jessica always did. You know, in that TV program, *Murder She Wrote*." Twentieth century mystery reruns were Kimberly's favorite.

Kimberly's assessment of criminal reality chilled Victoria to the bone. She had learned something new about her mother: She was also a detective at heart. "So that's where I am today."

"Then you must prove your innocence," Kimberly wisely said, pointing a bony finger. "Whatever it takes."

"Exactly," Victoria agreed, feeling vulnerable. "That's why I must go to Colorado to consult Beverly James about the matter."

MONDAY, JUNE 2

10

Texas set down his Bell helicopter on the green tarmac a quarter mile from GloryVale, Canada. Killing the engine, he reflected a moment on his chancy relationship with Victoria Tempest. Were his strong feelings real, or temporary?

A few minutes before, he talked to Tom Bates in the radio tower to let him know he'd arrived. The sun was barely peeping over the mountains, framing the outline of the army jeep coming over the rise to pull his bird half a mile to the aluminum hanger.

GloryVale, a Christian Protection compound, maintained the highest possible security to protect its fugitives. With religious freedom restricted in these last days, many believers had congregated in safehouses around the world to pool their resources and escape society's harsh criticisms regarding their faith in Jesus Christ. These were desperate times.

Although excited about seeing Victoria Tempest again, Texas had been cautioned by Jon Branson to take it easy on romance. Suffering from a twenty-five-year gap in time, the lovely debutante was still grieving over her husband's death. Given time, Jon believed Victoria would adjust and continue on with the living.

As a man in love, Texas sure hoped so.

The trip over to the hanger took about ten minutes.

The June morning was experiencing temperatures in the mid-fifties. And on the eastern horizon, the sun blazed a trail of red. Canada's cool summers sure beat the dry heat southern states in

America experienced. When Texas left the Chicago airport hours ago the winds were erratic and a storm front was forming. Thankfully, he'd lifted off before all aircraft was grounded.

Grabbing his backpack, he climbed out of the helicopter. Tom Bates was waving at him through the window glass of the air-traffic office. His friendly smile was a welcome sight.

"Hi, Tom, beautiful day," Texas said as he entered the compact office equipped with a sophisticated electronic control panel and a kitchenette large enough to accommodate a small table with two chairs. "How's it going?" He set his gear down.

"Fine. You?" Tom asked.

Texas nodded, thinking that Tom always said a lot with fewer words than any man he knew. He usually made it a point to hang around and chat with the former Delta pilot before taking care of business. In the late nineties, a sudden stroke had forced Tom into early retirement. They had met at NASA when Tom decided to humble himself and apply for a janitor's job.

Life sometimes slammed folks in a corner.

"What brings you back to GloryVale so soon?" Tom eyed Texas with his hazy blues. "Got a fresh pot of coffee brewin'." He motioned for Texas to sit. "Wanna cup?"

"You bet." Texas sat down at the table and studied Tom in his mid-seventies, still able to get around pretty well despite impaired reflexes. He was married to a great woman, Mimosa.

"Ain't changed the way you like your coffee, hav' ya?"

"Nope," said Texas. "Cream and a sugar, please." He removed his bomber jacket and kid gloves, laying them aside. "Looks like Mimosa's been here." He glanced around the place.

"You noticed, huh?" Tom chuckled and coughed. "Fanatic about cleanliness, that woman!" He slapped his thigh and glanced out the window. "Notice anything else new?"

"Yep. I see you have a new radar tower."

"Complete with telescopic lens for visuals. Don't want nuthin' sneakin' up on us." Tom handed Texas a mug. "Hope the coffee's good, like you want it."

Texas took a sip of the strong chicory brew. "Ah! You still make a great cup of coffee." He sat down his mug. "I guess you like this job better than your janitor position at NASA."

Tom grinned, aware that Texas was teasing. "You betcha! Get a load of this." He went into a series of physical gyrations to prove his agility. "Ain't I doin' good, huh?"

"Wow! I'm impressed. You're moving around a lot better." Texas watched Tom lift his right hand over his head and wiggle his legs in a little jig. "Proud of you, man!"

"'Course I take a lot of medicine," Tom admitted.

"Nothin' wrong with that," said Texas. "Treating problems is what medicine is for." He drank his coffee, hot and fresh.

"Guess so." Tom chuckled. "After my stroke I questioned whether I'd ever use my right arm again. But with therapy, and a good wife to stand by me, I've done all right."

The janitor's job at NASA had been Mim's idea, to get Tom out of the house. "I never saw myself as sweeping material, but I enjoyed the camaraderie. Don't hurt to clean up a little dirt now and then." He brushed his hands together. "When Mim says."

Texas laughed. "Can't fault her for that, can I? Taking Mim's advice worked well for you, didn't it?" He recalled how Tom had fallen into deep depression following his stroke and forced retirement from Delta Airlines. At sixty-two, he'd been indebted to an expensive beach house and maxed-out credit cards.

"Gotta admit, lotta time women know best."

"Yeah, guess they do," Texas agreed.

"S'cuse me a minute, partner." Tom walked over to the electronic board and communicated with the postal pilot arriving with the weekly mail. The conversation lasted five minutes.

Texas watched Tom safely guide the CPA postal plane onto the tarmac. GloryVale residents received their mail at a PO box address in Toronto. Twice a week, the mail was picked up and delivered to the compound. E-mail correspondence took place between the hours of 10 p.m. and 6 a.m. Transmitted via CPA satellite, the service was paid for by Christian financiers and operated by a valid Internet provider. Personal cellphones were allowed with secure numbers. Still, breaches happened.

"So how is Mim making it?" Texas asked.

"She's great, just perfect." Tom sat down at the table.

"Good." Texas recalled that Mimosa Bates had attended a Bible class led by his wife, Joann. With permission Mim had used Joann's study materials to form her own class in Boca Raton, Florida. Interest in God's Word had grown so rapidly, small study groups soon formed across Florida in a matter of months.

When PEACE FIRST came about in 2012, Mim secretly continued to supply Bible study groups with new original materials she had written. Eventually, the classes were infiltrated with well-meaning citizens who reported to the authorities that the instructors taught that Jesus Christ was the only way by which a person could be saved, a philosophy contrary to international law.

Caught and fined, Bibles were confiscated and the group of Christian ladies fearfully scattered over the incident. Too bad, the national news media made a big thing out of the sting and bashed Christians for their narrow-minded religious opinions.

Like the Bible had predicted, *interfaithism* prevailed.

Seeing that Mim was in trouble with the authorities and about to be prosecuted, Tom had approached the CPA about moving to a safer location where they could freely worship Christ.

At the time, Texas was an atheist and believed in the natural context of a happenstance universe. Had he been a Christian and taken positive steps to protect his wife Joann, as Tom had Mim, life may have turned out differently. But there was no going back.

"Mim would sure like to see you." Tom brought Texas out of his thought fog. "'Course we're growing older, y' know, but we both got responsible jobs and enjoy working. She volunteers at the hospital children's ward. And we still teach a Bible class together on Sundays. Can't beat that with a stick, can you?"

Texas raised an eyebrow at the mention of children. "Kids live here? I didn't know."

"Yeah, you heard me right," Tom said. "A few lucky folks have obtained custody of their grandchildren and are raising them in GloryVale. We even got a new school s'posed to be built next year." He looked at the board. "S'cuse me, got another aircraft comin' in." He scurried over to his command post.

Texas helped himself to another cup of coffee.

"I'm pleased the Christian Protection Agency has the foresight to see that children will carry on the work when we older ones are gone," Texas said when Tom returned.

Nobody liked to think about dying, but it was inevitable. People had no choice in birth parents or their moment of entry into the physical world. Neither would they select their time to die, unless they committed suicide. Texas was of the opinion that God saw all lives from beginning to end. In that, he took great comfort. Life had purpose, unless the individual wasted it.

"Gotta say, I wouldn't mind at all if Jesus came back today. It's my opinion that Bible prophecy has been fulfilled, and the Rapture could come at any second. Lotta folks won't be ready."

"You're right," said Texas, "but I guess God sees how hard we're all still working to spread the gospel, or else He wouldn't have sustained this sin-sick world by grace for this long."

"What about all those Muslims left in Iraq?"

"Israel hasn't come to their senses, either."

"Guess we got a ways to go yet," said Tom.

"We can pray for the lost," Texas pointed out.

Back at the turn of the century, US intervention in Iraq had brought a measure of democracy to the country. But the old feud that had existed for twenty-five hundred years between the Arabs and Jews perpetuated conflict, until PEACE FIRST arrived.

"We still have a lot of people to reach with Christ's message," Texas pointed out. "Millions of people are born every year. Who's gonna tell them about Jesus if the churches can't?" His emerald eyes possessed a sincerity of truth that defied argument.

"Can't fault a man for wantin' to meet Christ in the air," Tom professed. "Can't say I'd mind exchangin' this sick human body for a heavenly one in the twinkling of an eye. Folks who don't believe in Jesus don't know what a ride they'll be missing!"

Texas smiled. "You bless my soul, partner." He patted Tom on the shoulder. "Guess I'll be going now."

"Until we meet again," Tom said with a firm handshake.

"I hope before the roll is called up yonder!" Texas chuckled. "If you don't mind, have your mechanic check the oil in my helicopter and gas her up. We've got a long flight ahead of us."

"*We?*" Tom smiled. "You gonna take off later today with that pretty Tennessee lady? A fine specimen, that one."

"Which one?" Texas knew two fine gals.

"Take your pick," said Tom. "I like 'm both."

"Has Victoria been giving folks any trouble?"

"Model citizen," said Tom. "Have a great day, you hear?"

"I will." He was anxious to give Victoria a big Texas hug.

11

Victoria heard a knock on her apartment door. It was mighty early for her mother to come calling. *Who is it?*

Texas Holmes hesitated a moment. *Where are you, Victoria?*

About to decide she was either not yet up or out, he turned around to leave. A few steps down the hallway, he heard a door open behind him and a woman's melodic voice call out.

"Texas! You beat the roosters up this morning, didn't you? Come back right now and see me," Victoria said.

Spinning around, he caught sight of her peeking around the open door, head towel-wrapped in turban fashion, and on her face a big smile that jiggled his heart. "Texas! My goodness, I was in the shower." She didn't deliberate the issue of whether it was proper to invite him inside. And he knew her boundaries.

Didn't he?

"Well, are you just going to stand there?" she asked.

At the thought of a door standing between them, Texas' pulse leaped to attention. He was a man in love, whether it was the right time or not. He wanted to tell this beautiful woman exactly how he felt, but was she so wrapped up in solving her husband's murder she might not take him seriously.

"Shall I come back later?" he asked.

"Gracious no! Give me two minutes to get to my bedroom then come inside. I won't be long. If you like we can go to the cafeteria for breakfast. I'm starved, how 'bout you?"

Texas heard the sound of Victoria's feet pitter-patting across the carpet. Resetting his watch to Pacific Time, 5:15 a.m., he pushed open the door and stepped inside the apartment.

His face flushed at seeing Victoria's presence was all over the place—the odor of her perfume and her lilac shampoo. From the kitchen drifted the pleasant aroma of brewing coffee.

Being here with Victoria felt like coming home.

Texas walked around the living room looking at family photos in ornamented silver frames. Next to the corner fireplace was a cushy red recliner just his size. Papa bear would have loved it. A lazy fan spun overhead, purring gently like a happy cat.

Pretty swell, he thought, taking a seat to wait for his date. *Did Victoria think of him in a romantic way as he did her?*

Doubtful—though he hadn't missed her seeking eyes testing the waters. Like Jon suggested, he'd give her some time.

Ten minutes later Victoria appeared at her bedroom door, clinging to the frame like she was afraid to let go. Shocks of short curly dark hair framed her pretty face. He was stunned.

"Hi, Texas," she sweetly said. "Thanks for coming." A lump formed in her throat.

"Hi." Texas swallowed the rest of what he wanted to say and came to his feet, clinging to his cap like it was going to keep the whirlwind of love from blowing him over. She was wearing a form-fitted pantsuit the shade of mink. A thick gold chain encircled her slender neck, matching her double-looped earrings. The best of Victoria's lovely features was a pair of magnificent brown eyes set aglow by shards of morning light.

"I missed you," Victoria said. Her confession came so easy it was surprising. With the grace of a stately angel, she glided across the room toward Texas, glossy ruby lips nervously trembling.

Empowered by strong emotions, Texas could do no more than open his arms to receive Victoria as she embraced him. "You look lovely and smell even better," he said.

"Oh, it feels so good to have your strong arms around me again." Victoria tilted her head to view his face, to revel in her excitement. *Could Texas feel all she was feeling?*

As natural as opening his eyes in the morning, Texas leaned over and kissed Victoria on the lips. The depth of passion contained in a single kiss surprised both of them.

"Oh!" Victoria drew back, touching her lips. "I'm sorry."

"I'm not," Texas said with a grin. "That was amazing."

Victoria grinned. "Grace is amazing, don't forget?" She reminded him of a conversation they'd had in the secret gardens of the old state mental hospital. "But it was . . . nice."

Victoria blushed and took a few steps backward.

"*Nice?* I thought it was second only to grace." Texas brilliantly smiled. "Want to try again?"

"Shall we sit and talk?" Victoria was embarrassed over her impulsiveness. Of course, she'd asked for the kiss. What was she thinking? Walking straight into his arms like that?

"Sure." Texas reached out and drew Victoria's right hand to his lips. "I'm quite fond of you, but you already know that." He led her to the sofa and they sat down together.

Blushing, Victoria said, "We're not kids, you know." She thought about telling him of her recent involvement with Mark James. "There are things you should know about my past."

"I thought you didn't recall your past." Texas peered at Victoria, wondering if she had recovered her full memory. "Has something changed?" He lent her his cool green eyes.

"I've learned quite a lot about myself from other people." She hesitated to plow dangerous ground.

"What things?" he asked.

"Want some coffee?" Victoria asked, anxious to take the spotlight off her past. He might not understand.

"Sure," Texas answered. "Can I help make the coffee?"

"No, it's ready." She hurried into the kitchen and brought back two coffees. "I put extra cream and a scoop of sugar in yours, if I recall correctly." She handed him a warm mug.

"Perfect. Thanks." Texas was already wired with caffeine and took only a sip. "About the past—we've all made mistakes." He didn't want to destroy the beautiful moment in progress.

Victoria sighed. "You're already aware that I had amnesia for twenty-five years." She gazed at him. "After hearing the fatal shots that killed my husband I lost control of my Mazda and crashed in a ravine. It was a terrible night, stormy with tornadoes forecast." Those memories were all too vivid.

"I know. Jon told me. He said he was there. Isn't it strange how God works?" Texas thought of his wife, Joann.

"You mean, like, putting people together before their lives have meaning to one another?" Victoria inquired. "Jeffrey and I were like that. From the beginning, we were children in love."

"Exactly. My wife and I attended the same high school. We were best of friends, though not in the least bit interested in dating. I was already out of college and working when I ran into her at a restaurant in Seattle. Imagine that? She was teaching public school and I was a budding pilot."

"And romance happened." Victoria wouldn't expect Texas to fill in the details. And now God had arranged for *them* to meet, finding common ground in their uncommon grievances.

"Yes," said Texas. "We were married for thirty years, until Joann died three years ago. A lot happened during those years, some good and some bad, but we stayed together."

"I was three years younger than Jeffrey. He first asked me out on a date at the beginning of his senior year. Back then I was a sophomore and cheered for the Fernwood Tigers' football team." Victoria paused, sighing. "Mark James and Jeffrey were best friends. I thought they still were when Jeffrey died in 1989."

"You have doubts?" Texas raised an eyebrow. "You've mentioned Mark James' name before. Is he important to you?"

"He's been in my life for a long time," Victoria admitted. "We grew up together. Our families were close. Mark later married Beverly Yates, my best friend from college."

"The gal in Colorado?" Texas asked.

"Yes. About Mark—my mother said he faithfully visited me every day at the hospital when I was in a coma. He took care of me while I was recouping. Our history is involved, Texas. I was engaged to Mark nearly four months before I awakened on April 14th of this year. After my memory switch, I returned his ring."

"You didn't love him?" Texas wondered.

"I don't know. Anyhow, if I did, I don't believe it was an enduring love. Our relationship just wasn't meant to be."

Texas held Victoria's hand tight, aware how difficult it was for her to share the past. "You can stop here if you like?"

"No, I want to tell you all of it," she passionately declared. "Until recently I had no idea that Jon Branson was the person who called 911 and reported my automobile accident in 1989. If it hadn't been for him, I might have died. Jon became my son Paul's best friend. Life has so many unusual twists, doesn't it?"

Texas nodded, interested in her drama.

"When I was exposed to a toxin and was hospitalized a few weeks ago, Jon saved me once again." Anger surfaced. "Too bad Dick Branson doesn't have his son's good ethics."

"From what I understand, Dick has not had a personal encounter with Jesus Christ. Jon has read the Bible and the Holy Spirit has changed him. He admits that he and Paul were as wild as they come when they were young and sewing oats."

"You're saying people can change," she responded.

"I believe so," Texas replied. "After Jon rescued you from the hospital, he carried you to Safehouse #36. We met, and here you are. Rather, here we are." He was talking about chance meetings. Some were significant, others not so.

Victoria walked over to the window and peered down at GloryVale Gorge, a jungle of green, thoughts scattered and confused, feelings playing havoc with her heart. Turning around to face him she said, "It's difficult not knowing who I was before April 14, or how I lived during those dark years."

Texas came to his feet and joined Victoria at the window.

"Honey, I'm so sorry." He wrapped an arm around Victoria's waist and peered into her lovely face. "We both have *stuff* we'd like to forget about, more than enough baggage to bog down our futures. I don't know about you, but I want to live in the present, let bygones be bygones, if at all possible."

"Me, too." Victoria swallowed hard, looking up at Texas, half a foot taller and rock solid. "During those lost years I acted in ways I regret. My daughter filled me in on my past and it wasn't pretty. Karen thinks that my mental condition is psychological."

"What does your doctor say?" He gently rubbed Victoria's arms, yearning to tell her to lean on him.

"I don't know," she said. "I was out of it after I received the mysterious package left on my front porch and was hospitalized."

"Exactly what happened?" he asked.

"I was living with my daughter when the incident occurred. After selling my condo in February, I moved in with Karen in anticipation of marrying Mark in June."

Texas attentively listened.

"I heard a knock at the front door," Victoria recalled. "It was late Tuesday afternoon, April 29th, when I glanced outside and spied a brown-wrapped package on the porch."

"What did you do?"

"Thinking the package was something Karen had ordered, I brought it inside the condo and tossed it on her desk, in no mood for surprises." Victoria insecurely hugged herself. "I'd been a little depressed earlier in the day."

"You didn't immediately open the package?" Texas reacted.

"No, not at first. Karen arrived home from work around 5:30 in a terrible mood, more depressed than I was. I should have realized in my spirit that something bad was happening."

"Yes," Texas frowned. "My sensitivity to the Holy Spirit has spared my life more than once when danger approached."

"Karen brought home a bottle of chilled wine and was bent on drowning her miseries. When I asked her to stop drinking, she retaliated by accusing me of being a bad mother."

"I wish I'd been around to lend support," Texas said. "You must have been terribly upset."

"I don't recall all that we said, but Karen let me have a dose of truth, her version. After we had hashed out some mother-daughter issues, she noticed the brown package on her desk."

Texas led Victoria by the hand over to the sofa where they sat down. "And then what happened?"

"Karen suggested the package might contain the makeup I had ordered over the Internet. Actually, I didn't order makeup," Victoria revealed. "I lied to get her e-mail address so I could contact my friend, Beverly James."

"You did that?" Texas reacted, surprise on his face.

"I did, and I'm so ashamed. Lying seems to come natural for me when I'm in uncomfortable situations. Pray for me?"

"You bet." Texas' face relaxed into a smile. "Beverly James appears to be a key player in your life. Why?"

"Bev was my sorority sister from the University of Memphis. We stayed in touch after I married Jeffrey and she came for a visit. I introduced her to Mark James soon after he began his medical practice at Hardeman County General. Mark's father was a practicing physician there at the time and had connections."

Humph. Texas absorbed the information.

"Anyhow," Victoria continued, "Mark and Bev had a zany whirlwind romance before getting married. The four of us were great friends, inseparable for years." The rest of the story was sad.

"Then Jeffrey died and things changed for you."

"Drastically." Tears crouched in the corners of Victoria's dark eyes. "After being in a coma for ninety days, I revived and didn't recognize the people who loved me most. Frightened and depressed, I couldn't recall one fact about my past."

"Amnesia," Texas said. "I'm so sorry," he empathized.

"Recently I learned that I was six weeks pregnant when my accident occurred. I gave birth to a second son, Jeffrey Daniel, late that fall." Victoria wrung her hands. "When my memories switched on April 14th of this year, I forgot about Daniel. Can you imagine? How can a mother forget birthing a son?"

"My word, you've been through it, woman!"

"Yes, I have." Victoria struggled to maintain her composure. "But according to Karen, following my accident, I bounced back beautifully and eventually became a selfish bridge-playing, golf-putting debutante involved only in pleasing myself."

"Oh?" Texas raised an eyebrow.

"Karen blames me for Paul's wretched life and early death."

"Your son, Paul? But surely you weren't responsible for the chain of events that led to his death," Texas defended Victoria. "It wasn't your fault, honey. None of this is your fault."

"That's what I'd like to believe." Victoria lent Texas glossy eyes. "Anyhow, skipping over twenty-five years . . ." she grunted, "on April 14th of this year, my memories switched and I suddenly recalled that frightening night of April 13, 1989."

Texas waited patiently for her to complete the story.

"The kicker was that I didn't know what had happened moments before. It was like being born all over again."

"You didn't recognize Karen or where you lived?" Texas attempted to internalize the mystery. "What did you do?"

She let out a half hysterical laugh. "I stood in the middle of the street not knowing what I was supposed to do next until Karen called to me from the balcony of her condo."

"Wow!" Texas shook his head.

"Karen coached me inside and offered me coffee." Victoria chuckled. "I recall thinking my daughter was an imposter. I was convinced that my husband had hired the woman to play a joke on me for our fourteenth wedding anniversary. Nothing that was taking place at the time made any sense."

"How awful for you."

"It was pretty bad. Mark James came over and I didn't recognize him either. I was in a daze the rest of the day. I soon realized something was drastically wrong with my memory. My amnesia had somehow flip-flopped, creating all the confusion."

"I see," said Texas. "That's why you didn't recall being engaged to Mark or living in the condo with Karen."

"Correct. Bits and pieces of my past began to surface. I recalled hearing gunshots over my car phone while talking to Jeffrey at his office prior to meeting him in town for our fourteenth wedding anniversary supper. I wanted to know where he was. I wanted my family back. But I soon learned that he died seconds before I crashed my Mazda. It made me livid."

"So what did you do?" Texas asked.

"I vowed to bring his killers to justice. I even hired a private eye to help me with the investigation. All of this, I did in secret because I trusted no one," Victoria explained.

"You hired a PI?" Texas realized he'd hardly scratched the surface of this woman's intricate mind. There were many beautiful layers to her personality, both satisfying and scary.

"And that brings me to today, why it's so important for me to talk to Beverly James. I need her input to solve this crime."

"You want me to take you to Denver?"

"Yes," Victoria replied. "I have so much I want to tell you, Texas. But foremost, I need to explain my relationship with Mark James." She could not rest until the truth was out.

"You said you and Mark were friends. I don't need to hear more. I'm just grateful to God that you're here with me."

"I recently learned a disturbing fact about myself."

"Disturbing?" His suntanned forehead wrinkled.

"Yes." Victoria drew in a deep breath, dreading to reveal her intimate sexual relationship with Mark. "Before I got my memories back we were sleeping together."

There, she'd said it. "Do you think less of me?"

Stunned, Texas searched for the right words to reply to the courageous woman. She could have lied and he might never have known. But she hadn't. She had told the truth.

"Oh, Texas! I'm so sorry!" Victoria squeezed his hand. "Can you ever forgive me? I was out of my right mind. I had no memory of my Christian background and I did stupid things."

"Of course, I forgive you. Friends don't judge."

Texas embraced Victoria, offering a warm hug.

"Worse," the tears were slipping down her cheeks, "I forgot I was a child of the King with moral responsibility. I asked God to forgive me and He did." She peered up into his lovely eyes.

"Jesus always does when people truly repent." He was glad she had confessed. "How 'bout breakfast now? I'm hungry."

"You're okay with this?"

"Sure. If Jesus forgave you, I do, too. He pulled Victoria to her feet. "We'll eat, then we're off to Colorado."

"Oh, thank you, Texas." Victoria threw her arms around him and planted a big wet kiss on his lips. "The cafeteria has a great buffet. How does country ham, scrambled eggs, and buttered biscuits with preserves sound to you?"

"Like the perfect way to start a day," he replied.

12

Fernwood, Tennessee

Dick arrived at his office early Monday morning around seven thirty. Not knowing where Victoria Tempest was or what she might be doing deeply disturbed him. The woman was out of control and unpredictable. He'd once taken the bull by the horns and sent her a pack of Lady Havana Cigars to solve his problem.

Unfortunately, that hadn't worked! He inwardly scowled.

According to his spy, a giant had stood guard at the threshold of the woman's hospital room. Preposterous, of course! But neither could he deny that Lady Luck had been on Victoria's side.

Around midnight, after the lights at the hospital had blinked out because of a storm, some do-gooder had helped Victoria out of bed and whisked her safely away from the hospital.

It wasn't accidental that someone had shown up with an antidote to counteract the lethal drug attached to the Havana Cigar wrapper. Dick groaned, not wanting to embrace the facts. He now knew Victoria's hero was likely his very own son, Jon.

Who else had free reign to his house and his office?

After Paul Tempest was found dead in the back of a gay bar in 2012, his rascal son had drastically changed.

Why was that? Had Jon blamed himself for Paul's death?

The boy had actually shaved and reported to work on time, didn't curse anymore, and was probably kind to little ol' ladies crossing the street when his daddy wasn't looking. So unusual was the change in Jon that his wife Marjorie even noticed.

Ah . . .so what was a dad to do? *Graciously applaud his son?*

Too busy with work, Dick hadn't asked the right questions about what had caused Jon to change. His inability to share intimacy was coming home to roost in his own castle.

No longer should he assume Jon was the faithful son.

Dick jerked up his baggy pants, a size larger than he'd formerly worn. Weight gathered on his bones like trials and tribulations. *Bring on the donuts!* Didn't a man have more important things to think about than looking like Bruce Willis?

Dick's detective, Jake, recently followed Jon to an apartment in Selmer, Tennessee. The boy was living with a beautiful Spanish woman. That was good. At least he still cared about women.

Half the time Jon wasn't there, so where did he go? And what nonsense was he in to? *Living a double life?* Dick fondled an unopened box of Havana Cigars. Jon wasn't packing meats, so how was he earning a living? Didn't his son realize he was first in line to inherit the billion-dollar meatpacking industry when his old man kicked the bucket? Dick flicked his Bic lighter.

The boy appeared uninterested. *Why was that?* Everybody loved money, didn't they? It bought fame, power, and loyalty.

Dick kicked back in his swivel rocker like he did every other day of his life and torched an expensive Havana. He enjoyed burning money. It was his to throw away if he wanted.

And more was coming down the pike when the Arab countries opened up to receiving his meat shipments containing drugs. Just think! The Iraqis could dream again.

The younger George Bush's *War to free the Iraqis* had ended the reign of Saddam Hussein and disrupted his terror network in 2003, setting the stage for a democratic Iraq. Unfortunately, the fundamentalist Muslim Iraqis didn't want democracy anymore than they wanted the Jews to own Palestine. They wanted Allah to bless them, and in return they would assassinate the infidel.

But even democracy costs, Dick thought. *Nothing in life is free.*

So how much would it take to earn Jon's loyalty?

Maybe he could talk some sense into that Spanish woman shacked up with Jon. It was worth a try. He'd just drive over to Selmer and knock on the door and see what happened.

Dick parked his cigar in a gold-plated tray and looked up the number for Anthony Vorices, his Mafia contact in Miami. While he took care of personal business with Jon, Anthony could track down Victoria Tempest and bring her home.

The Fernwood police was deft when it came to getting the job done. Twist a few people's arms and they would gladly spill their guts. He could start with that PI gal from Memphis.

What was her name? Dick winced. *Georgie Hendricks.*

People believed that Victoria's private eye died in the apartment bombing, but he knew better. Finding the gal's body burnt to a crisp, unrecognizable, was entirely too neat.

To get the real story Dick sent over a sweet young detective to speak to Aunt Ginny, the old gal who lived across the hall from Georgie. The old bag was the nosy type, you know—kept up with her neighbors—and always so grateful to have company. In less than twenty minutes, Ginny spilled the beans about Georgie.

Of course, Beth Ann had promised never to tell a soul about what really happened to her first cousin. It would be their secret.

"Anthony? This is Dick Branson. I need a favor."

***

GloryVale, Canada

Kimberly Ann Martin was delighted to see Texas Holmes seated in the cafeteria across the table from Victoria. GloryVale hadn't seemed the same without him. He'd come to take her daughter away, but that was okay, she adored him like a son.

Enchanted with her new flame, Victoria hadn't noticed her mother's arrival. Looking like she was going to fracture, she was engrossed in every word that fell from Texas' lips.

"Hi, dear. I'm glad I caught up with you," Kimberly said, smiling at Texas as she took a seat at the red vinyl-top table.

"Hi, Mother," Victoria said, a slight chill in her tone.

"Kimberly!" Texas stood up and hugged the elderly woman.

"It's so good to see you, Texas." Kimberly hugged her hero back. "Am I interrupting a private conversation?"

"No," said Texas. "We were having a farewell breakfast."

"You weren't leaving without saying goodbye, were you?" Kimberly turned to Victoria, warm sunrays filtering through the reflector-glass and splashing color on her pale face.

"Mother!" Victoria reacted. "I wouldn't do that."

Kimberly's eyes drifted to Texas. "So you're gonna take my daughter to Denver, Colorado?" She snapped her fingers, her gaze flickering to Victoria. "Just like that!"

"This is *not* any of your business," Victoria said to her mother, cautiously eyeing Texas for his disapproval over her quick tongue. "You want to take me, don't you?" she asked him.

"No way, I'm not getting in the middle of a family squabble. You two have at it!" He swiped his mouth with a napkin.

"Texas?" Kimberly eyed her daughter's suitor with suspicion. "You're not letting my Victoria run the show, are you? She's got ideas that will take you on wild goose chases. Beware!"

"Mother!" Victoria exclaimed. "Please! If you don't mind, this conversation is between me and Texas."

Victoria's molten-lava eyes scorched Kimberly to the bone. "Oh, all right," she relented, unloading her tray. "If you don't want my opinion, I suppose that's your right. I just don't see any need in wasting good time chasing after fantasies. The Bible says we're to live for today and let tomorrow take care of itself."

"Thank you, Mother, for that slice of reality, but we really don't need your advice. Texas and I are leaving for Colorado later today." Her bag was packed and she was ready when Texas said.

"Kimberly . . ." Texas patted her frail hand, "will you trust me with your daughter? Victoria will be safe. That's really what this discussion is about, isn't it?" He understood the concern of a parent for a child, though he had born no children of his own.

"Texas is right," Victoria interjected. "I'll be fine, Mother."

"We'll phone you as soon as we land in Denver and let you know what's happening. This is a business trip."

"Monkey business?" Kimberly remarked, spreading her paper napkin over her lap.

"But necessary," Texas replied.

"I see," Kimberly said. "You know I'd rather have Victoria here at GloryVale with me, safe from harm's way." Her inky black eyes, big as quarters, slid sideways toward her daughter. "I hope you realize what a jewel you have in this man."

Victoria affirmatively nodded, eyes downcast over her mother's bold assessment of Texas, her usually quick tongue super-glued to the back of her throat in this case.

"Don't let me stop you gals from expression your opinion," Texas remarked with a chuckle, somewhat embarrassed.

"So, Mother, what are your plans today?" Victoria asked.

"Well, after breakfast," Kimberly sipped from a cup of decaffeinated chicory coffee, "I'm gonna hit the spa for a swim. Mim is meeting me there and we're getting our hair done later this morning." She wiped her thin lips with a white paper napkin.

"Mim?" Texas reacted "Tom Bates' Mim?"

"Yep," said Kimberly. "Best Christian couple I ever met. 'Course I miss my friends in Nashville, but the opportunities for wholesome living is far better here."

"You're a brave lady," said Texas.

"Mim told me about your wife," Kimberly said, embarking on a disturbing personal subject. "You're been through a lot, like my Victoria. I'm proud of you for being a Christian."

Victoria sighed. Now that her mother was back to her old self . . . she would likely be meddling in everyone's affairs.

A lump formed in Texas' throat. At the mention of Joann, familiar hurt flooded in, drowning him once again in remorse. When would she let him go? How long before the hurt stopped? When could he go forward without looking back?

"Don't worry, son, I'm not going to ask you any embarrassing questions," Kimberly reassured Texas. "We all got things in our past that hurt. But God is our great healer."

"Well said, Mother. Shouldn't we be going now?" Victoria peered at Texas. The conversation was taking on a life all its own, revisiting old hurts. "I'm finished with breakfast if you are."

"Sure." Texas lifted sea-green eyes, sad from hard wave-tossed years, yet so full of devotion to his wife's memory that it astounded Victoria. He had no illusions of the risk involved in transporting a fugitive. The police would have Victoria's profile, and likely be watching Beverly James' place, anticipating her visit.

It's a contest of wits, thought Texas. *But God is on our side.*

"I need to stop by my apartment." Victoria came to her feet first and tossed her napkin aside. All she had to do was retrieve her travel bag, switch off the lights, and lock up.

"Did you clear your departure with the apartment manager?" Kimberly asked, liking all the loose ends neatly tied.

"I asked Henry to store my things until I return," Victoria replied. "You'll water my plants, won't you?"

"Sure, dear." Kimberly became a little emotional over Victoria's leaving. "You will keep in touch?"

"Of course," Victoria replied, giving her mother a hug.

"The weather looks favorable for flying," Texas said. "We'll see you in a month, Mama." He leaned over and tenderly hugged the senior citizen, kissing her lightly on the cheek.

"You take care." Victoria squeezed her mother's hands as the cellphone attached to Texas' belt tingled.

"It's Tom Bates. He says the bird is set to go."

"Great!" Victoria kissed her mother on the cheek. "Don't worry about us. We'll phone you when we land in Denver."

"I won't," said Kimberly. "Be safe."

When Victoria turned away, tears wet her cheeks. "I hope I'm not forgetting something." She laid fond eyes on Texas.

"Flight time to Boise, Idaho is approximately four hours." Texas looked at his Seiko watch set into a wide black-leather band.

"What?" Victoria responded.

"Oh, I forgot to tell you that I had a couple of stops to make on our way to Denver. I'm in the microchip business, don't forget." He eyed Victoria for approval. "Is there a problem?"

"No problem." They took the elevator up to the second floor and entered her apartment. "I don't want to interfere."

"You're not. When we reach Denver we'll check into a hotel under assumed names and order in a nice meal. Then we need to seriously talk about a matter." He wouldn't go into the details.

"I don't suppose it would do any good to—"

"Ask? No, it wouldn't." Texas picked up her bag.

Victoria turned off the lights and locked the door, grumbling to herself as they exited the building. She would die from curiosity until Texas revealed the subject he wished to discuss.

"You okay?" He was sensitive to her unrest.

"I'd feel better if you'd tell me what it is you want to discuss."

"No." His word was final, Victoria could tell.

They rode over to the village in the tram and took a cab to the airport. Texas could tell that Victoria was torn with leaving her mother behind, but didn't ask why. Neither did she query him again about what it was he wanted to discuss when they arrived in Denver. Was she speculating he would declare his love for her?

That wasn't it. The long silence finally took its toll.

"You're mighty quiet, dear." Texas glanced over at Victoria.

"Maybe we should e-mail Beverly and tell her we're coming. I still remember how to get into the Senior Citizen's Chatroom where we first communicated. What do you think?"

"No. The element of surprise is in our favor."

The cab came to a bumpy halt and Texas climbed out his side of the vehicle, opening the door for Victoria. They ventured into the airport hanger and peered up at the Bell helicopter.

"Say something," Victoria lent Texas perky brown eyes.

"Something," he teased. "Get in, woman. Mercy, you're a handful even for an experienced man." He picked Victoria up like a sack of potatoes and loaded her in the helicopter.

"Experienced? As in with other women?" She peered down at her handsome suitor. *Is that was he was? Her suitor?*

Chuckling, Texas tossed their gear in the back seat, walked around the back of the helicopter, and mounted the pilot's seat.

"No comment," he said, buckling up.

Seconds later, the jeep pulled them from the hanger. Half a mile away, Texas manipulated the computer panel until the engines were purring and the helicopter rotors spinning.

"You all set to leave?" he asked his passenger.

Victoria nodded. "I hope Mother isn't mad at me." She thought of her emotional outburst in telling Kimberly to butt out, still having trouble taking motherly advice. Not an age thing, either. It was pure stubbornness, inbred in her defiant spirit.

"Kimberly knows you're full of it," Texas said, not about to empathize. "You're a good kid at heart. Your mother can't stay miffed at you for too long for telling her to get lost."

"I did say that, didn't I?" Victoria giggled.

"Un huh."

"What I said to Mother was disrespectful and unkind. No, rude!" Victoria grimaced. "Granny Martin used to wash my mouth out with soap when I got too frisky," she recalled. "Shoot, I feel like swallowing a whole bar of Palmolive right now."

"You!" Texas reached over and grasped Victoria's hand. "Who can keep from loving you?"

Did he just say he loved me? Victoria was starry-eyed, bubbles tickling her stomach as the helicopter effortlessly lifted.

13

Attorney Devin Baldwin was working in his home office late Monday evening when he heard a tap at his door. He had just ripped June 2 off the calendar, hoping the third would prove better. Thinking it was probably his secretary who had forgotten something Devin raced over to the door, unlocked and opened it.

He stared into the face of a stranger. "Yeah?"

"Attorney Devin Baldwin?" A man, wearing a suit and built like the FBI type, stepped inside his house without being asked.

"I'd say come in, but you've already done that." Devin pushed the door shut, cursing himself for his stupidity. "What can I do for you? Am I in trouble?" He eyed the big fellow.

Wondering if he'd filed the late form to delay paying his income taxes, Devin uncomfortably shifted his weight from one foot to the other, waiting for the noose to drop.

"Depends." Suit motioned for Devin to sit. "On what you tell me." He adjusted his tight collar like he'd burst his neck muscles if he didn't. His biceps matched his demeanor.

Devin followed instructions and took a seat at his desk.

"Look, if you're from the IRS you can contact the gal who does my taxes. I'm covered in case of a technical mistake," Devin explained. "I have a lot of work to complete tonight."

"It's not about your taxes," Suit said, the bulge in his coat pocket looking like he might be packing a pistol.

"So why are you here?" Devin asked.

"It's about another matter."

Devin swallowed, then grinned. "My wife didn't hire you to do me in, did she?" It was a joke, but not very funny.

Suit's blond eyelids flickered

"No, nothing like that," he said. "I'm looking for a gal. Georgie Hendricks is the name. Seen her lately?"

Devin took the fifth and cleared his throat.

"I hear she does investigative work for you." Suit spread his feet and crossed his arms over his massive chest.

Devin shook his head "no," busy digesting the request while staring into the man's golden eyes. Suit's mouth was set into a wide jaw like the Rock of Gibraltar, reminding Devin of Dick Tracy. The surgically implanted glint behind his black pupils suggested intelligence. Over six-feet-six, weighing in excess of two hundred fifty pounds, he wasn't a man easily outmaneuvered

Swallowing hard, Devin lied. "Georgie's dead."

Immediately realizing that he had pounced on the answer too quickly, Devin decided to expound on his answer.

"The detective died in her apartment. A gas explosion, the newspapers reported, but you probably already know that." Devin's fragmented sentence was a testimony to his flighty heart.

Suit wasn't the FBI, so who was he?

An amused smile tugged at the bully's lips.

"Who do you represent, Sir?" Devin respectively asked.

Alone, with his wife and son away spending the night at her mother's, anything might happen when you let in a stranger.

"I have a few questions for Miss Hendricks, that's all. We have proof that she's alive, so why don't you make it easy on yourself and cooperate?" Inflicting pain was the last option.

"What proof?" Devin suspected Suit had been a party to the bombing squad that took a hunk out of Georgie's apartment.

"I'm not at liberty to say," the intruder replied. "Let's make this easy for both of us, okay?" He patted the piece inside his coat pocket. "Tell me where Georgie is and I leave. Deal?"

"I saw her a few days ago." Devin was suddenly loose-lipped, owing loyalty to no one but himself. "She's planning to change her identity. You'll never find her." It was true.

"So she's still in Memphis?" Suit's hard-core gaze fell on Devin's desk. "You have her address in that book?" He knotted one fist, cracked his knuckles, and flexed his biceps.

Devin swallowed hard. "Leave Georgie alone. She doesn't know anything. She's homeless. You won't find her." He peered up at Suit, a lather of sweat gathering under his arms.

"You already said that," Suit grumbled, his mannerisms signifying he was running out of patience. "Let me make that determination if you don't mind." He grew more agitated.

Devin took a couple of seconds to determine his options. He could lie and send Suit on a wild-goose chase.

But when he came back...

"Like I told you, I don't know where she is," said Devin. "Last time I saw Georgie was a week ago, at my house."

Humph. "Does she often visit you?"

"Occasionally." Devin squirmed, worms crawling up his spine. "When she needs to borrow money—she's unpredictable."

"Thank you, Mr. Baldwin." Anthony Vorices grinned at the frightened attorney. "Resume what you were doing, I can take it from here." He turned around and walked out of Devin's office.

Well, have a nice day, too, Devin thought to himself.

TUESDAY, JUNE 3

14
Germantown, Tennessee

Around 10 a.m. Tuesday morning, a homeless person walked into the Germantown Social Security Office and approached the counter where a Spanish girl was helping with applications.

When it came Georgie Hendricks turn, she winked her left eye and pulled at her right ear. Prim-and-proper Marisa Straus immediately recognized the signal, glancing down at her paperwork to hide amusement. Hands folded neatly on the counter, she lifted her pretty face and looked straight into Jaycee Moore's contact-layered gaze. "May I help you, Sir?" she asked.

"Yeah, I need a social security card," Georgie replied, aware of those standing within hearing range—the woman on her right with a kid, and a small man on her left—applicants like herself.

"You lost your old one?" Marisa asked a routine question, coughing to hide a chuckle. One brown contact lens had slipped off center, making Georgie's eyes appear weirdly crossed.

"Ain't never had one," the detective answered, casting a chilly warning for Marisa to get serious. "Just got a job, but can't go to work 'til I git a card. What I gotta do to get one?"

Marisa sobered, nervously fidgeting with her pen. "Can you read and write?" She smacked her full pink lips together and followed protocol. "If you can't, don't be embarrassed."

Georgie shook her head no.

Marisa nervously glanced around for her supervisor. Stay out of her way and she'd get the job done in record time. *Uh oh.*

"What's the problem?" Charles Tidworthy barreled out of the adjoining room, causing Marisa to jump like a nervous fish caught on a sharp hook. "Is this vagabond causing problems?"

"No." Marisa made eye contact with her supervisor. "This guy wants a social security card. Says he's homeless and never had one," she hurriedly explained. "I was explaining the procedure."

"Oh?" Tidworthy glared at Georgie. "Everybody has a social security card. Why don't you have one? Are you an alien?"

Is that of the Third kind? "Never had one." Georgie peered crookedly at the wiry man with an inflated governmental ego. "Ran away from my foster home when I was twelve. Been on the streets ever since. Ain't never needed no card until now."

How many negatives make a positive? Georgie evaluated her sentence structure, thinking that speaking bad English was hard.

"You never once attended public school or drew a government paycheck or visited a health clinic?" Mr. Tidworthy asked, flabbergasted. "How did that happen in our country?"

"Don't know, Sir, but it did." Georgie expertly played her part. "All I know is I gotta chance to work for this garbage company an' the boss tol' me to come here and ask for a card."

Humph. Tidworthy tapped his pen on the counter, aware that a line of applicants was building behind Georgie.

"Fill out a card for the fella and get a mailing address," he ordered Marisa. "We can't spend all day fooling around with a homeless person." Tidworthy rushed back to his cubbyhole.

"That was quite impressive." Marisa hurriedly pulled out a blank form for Jaycee Moore, success gracing her pretty face.

"Can I have a card now?" Georgie asked with a wink.

"What address shall I give?" Marisa asked, rather enjoying the act of pulling the wool over her supervisor's prudent eyes. "We have a nice Germantown shelter. Will that do?"

"Fine by me." Georgie leaned across counter. "Just hurry."

THURSDAY, JUNE 5

15
Fernwood, Tennessee

Dick Branson had a light Thursday morning work schedule at the plant and decided to drive over to Selmer to confront his son Jon about Victoria's disappearance from the hospital. All he wanted was the truth—which required interpretation in a world framed with cautious minds. But first, he'd stop by his house.

"Marjorie?" *Where was the little woman?* "Oh, there you are, honey. I just wanted to let you know I'll be out of town today. Be home for supper around six. What're we having?"

She walked out of her bathroom-sized closet wearing a fuchsia-colored pantsuit with matching pumps. "Ribs and baked potatoes," she said. "I thought we'd bypass dessert tonight."

"Why? I like dessert." Dick patted his obese stomach.

"Okay. I'll pick up a pie on my way home later." Marjorie towel dried her damp hair. "I'm playing bridge with the girls at noon. Oh, and Kathryn Billingsly asked me to pick her up on my way over to the club. It seems her car engine died this morning."

"Does she ever hear from Victoria Tempest?"

"Not since the woman skipped town. I don't think they're friends anymore," Marjorie offered an opinion. "After lunch, I'm going to the salon for a perm. Where are you headed off to?"

"Why you diddle with that frumpy librarian is beside me," Dick said, not wanting to disclose where he was going. "You don't have to fraternize with the locals, you know. We have plenty of friends in Miami and abroad. Kathryn's a vicious gossip." He'd once needed her to tattle on Victoria, and she had.

"Dick! Don't speak to me about friendship. Your friends are never around when you need them," Marjorie retaliated. "Besides, I like Kathryn and we both enjoy bridge. As far as socializing with the locals, don't forget Fernwood is *our* hometown, too."

"Oh, all right. I guess I do get on my high horse sometimes."

"Besides," Marjorie fussed, "you cater to Mark James and that pretentious daughter of Victoria's." She didn't like Karen. "The girl is too involved in Mark's life for his own good."

"Well . . ." Dick knew when he was losing the battle, "I'll be going now. Have a nice day. Tell all your good friends hello."

There was no use messing up a perfectly swell marriage with an unpopular opinion. And his bone to pick wasn't with his pretty wife. It was with his naughty son who had helped Victoria.

Marjorie pecked Dick's plump jaw with glossy red lips. "Be careful, Poopsie." She used a Kleenex to wipe away the red smudges on Dick's cheek. "And don't drink while driving."

"I will," said Dick. "And I won't." He was half way out the door and climbing in his brand-new, lime-colored Jaguar, thinking he would do exactly as he blamed well pleased, like always.

Punching the garage gizmo, he let up the door. When the sunlight hit him in the face, he punched a button to automatically collapse the metal top. Spring was radiant outdoors. The temperature was moderate, the wind brisk. He was in a good mood, though unsure of the reason. Maybe it was his new toy.

The drive over to Selmer took about forty-five minutes. Dick's new sports car performed to perfection on the highway.

Too bad he couldn't control the affairs of other people, especially the stupid ones who believed they could somehow dethrone him. Let them try. He always came out on top.

Having no trouble locating Jon's apartment complex, Dick whipped his steel-goddess into a parking spot and locked up.

The climb up the stairs was a challenge. Jon lived in a two-bedroom apartment on the second floor according to the superintendent. And he had a roommate. No surprise, again. Jon had always loved women. He was a man's man all the way.

Dick reached the second landing huffing and puffing every step of the way. One day he would exercise—on another planet, in another life. Apartment 208 was clearly marked.

Dick's fist was poised to knock when it occurred to him that Jon had chosen to live in poverty. He had plenty of money in his bank account, so why didn't he use it? The boy was worth millions, yet he had traded a life of luxury for a boring work-a-day routine and a dump to live in like Somerset Apartments.

To each his own, Dick thought as he tapped on the door and waited for a response. "Probably nobody home middle of the morning." He peeked though the window.

A woman's scream brought Dick to attention as he stumbled back a few steps when the door swung open. A young Spanish beauty rushed outside and pronounced a parade of words that sounded like she was cursing him, though Dick wasn't sure.

"And you would be?" He matched her glare.

"You *peeking* Tom!" She raced toward the telephone attached to the kitchen wall. "Help! I call police now!"

"Wait!" Dick stepped inside the apartment. "Is this Jon Branson's apartment? Don't call the police. Please!"

The woman spun around, receiver in hand, confused. "Who say you are?" Magnetic brown eyes the size of purple plums came to rest on Dick. "Say so quickly, or I call Super."

"No! Don't call anybody. I'm Jon's father. I'm looking for him." Dick straightened his suit, a civil gesture.

"Oh," said the feisty Spaniard. "You wan' me to call Jon?" Latisha Mangosa placed the receiver in its cradle.

"If you don't mind," Dick said in a hushed voice, exhausted by the antics of the hyper woman. "I'll just sit down and wait."

Surveying the sparsely furnished den, Dick recalled that Jon's old apartment in Fernwood had twice the spice as this dump.

The next few sentences out of Latisha's mouth were foreign. "English, please," Dick calmly requested.

"My name *e'ss* Latisha Mangosa." She had to be careful not to divulge Jon's undercover name: Benjamin Bolt. He had said *never* tell anyone, especially not his father. Jon relied on privacy.

"So where is my son working now?" Dick spied a large bowl of leftover spaghetti sitting on the kitchen counter. Actually, inside the apartment was much nicer than the complex's outward appearance. Strange, it was the exact reverse with human beings.

"Are you two . . . ?" Dick's face twisted into lines of worry.

"Lovers?" Latisha giggled. "Why it matter?"

"Of course it matters!" Dick exploded, hustling to his feet. "Are you two serious?" He got up in her face. "Oh, I hope there isn't a little bambino on the way. I'm not the grandfatherly type."

Latisha defensively leaped to her feet, spurting rapid Spanish, forgetting her guest couldn't understand a word. "Jon and me, we good friends, Mr. Branson. Share rent, tha's all."

"Whew! That takes a load off my mind." Dick swiped his wet forehead with a clean white handkerchief and sat back down.

A few seconds of silence passed.

"Will you kindly give my son a message?" Dick didn't need to write down so simple a request. "You won't forget, will you?"

"What you wan' me say?" Latisha asked.

"You say—tell him his daddy said to come see him, that he has important news." Dick laid a crisp green bill on the counter. "Just a little something to help out with the groceries."

"*Gracias*," Latisha replied, never turning down money.

"I'll be going now." He would invent some astounding news to announce. What he really wanted was to bribe the lad with an early inheritance. Oh say, a million to come back to Branson.

FRIDAY, JUNE 6

16

Karen Tempest had a bad day at the office. She'd lost a big real estate commercial listing. Overpriced, and the owner knew it but didn't care. She never should have taken the listing in the first place. It had cost a pretty penny to advertise and now some other agent would likely reap the profits. Her anger boiled.

Never mind, she was going home and get drunk. How could she concentrate on work when she hadn't heard a word from her mother in weeks? Besides, she didn't feel well. Home. *Yes.*

Anyhow, she needed to think about what clothes to carry on the Rome trip. Mark said they were leaving on Friday and flying Delta to New York. The timing seemed wrong but hadn't she promised Mark? And Rome would be fun. Maybe even life changing. She was about to put her phone on hold when it rang.

"Yes?" Karen quickly answered, heart chasing after rabbits.

"It's Mark, honey. What's going on?" The girl sounded in a dither, frazzled, not unusual with the stress she was under.

"Nothing. Everything. I lost my big commercial listing."

"I'm so sorry. You'll get another one." What else could he say? Loss was loss, and it was never pleasant.

"I don't care anymore. I can't think. I need a drink."

"Please don't, honey. We both have been boozing too much and too often. It won't bring your mother back to us." He was about finished up at the office.

"Will you meet me at my condo?" Karen asked. "I need a little comforting. Otherwise, I don't know what I will do. I'm going out of my mind, Mark. Nothing is working in my life. Nothing." She had no one else important in her life but him.

Nothing? Was Karen referring to her romantic involvement with him? It was only one night, a huge mistake and definitely not an act of love. Then there was the matter of her mother.

"I don't know, Karen. Maybe it's not a good idea." He was uncertain if he could keep Karen at bay. He was, after all, human.

"You can help me pack for Rome. I don't know what to take. I've got all these cocktail dresses to choose from, and can't find a thing I want to wear. Please?"

"Typical woman," teased Mark. "Okay. If you add a steak and potato to the offer, I'll come over and help you pack." He wanted to go over Dick's tentative plans for them, anyhow.

"Can you be at my place around six? I still need to grocery shop." Karen suddenly felt better. Mark did that for her. "Am I allowed to drink wine if I promise not to get drunk?"

"Two glasses max," said Mark. "I'll stick to the quota, too."

"Good," said Karen. "See you later."

***

Dick was at home, perturbed his PI in Denver had phoned to report that Beverly James had not spoken to anyone but her regular cosmetic customers or met with anyone suspicious during the month of his surveillance. What was he going to do now?

"What about her e-mail?" Dick had asked Jim.

"E-mail's hard to monitor," the private eye answered.

"Well, can't you check her garbage can?"

Dick had reminded the investigator to watch out for a tall, right-handed woman. Anything else about Victoria Tempest could be different. She was tricky and clever with disguises. But Jim was positive the fugitive had not come anywhere near Beverly.

Paying Jim more money wasn't a problem, thought Dick. But the longer the murder case remained open and unsolved, the more likely something could go wrong. He could not afford for anyone who had information about Jeffrey's death to show up and support Victoria's testimony. Too much was at stake.

Ever since Victoria hired that nosy Georgie Hendricks, trouble had knocked. Like Victoria's toxic tongue, a quagmire of environmental contaminants had surfaced at the back of Branson property, bubbling up through the soil. Hopefully, nobody important had noticed. But he couldn't count on that.

Anyhow, in order to avoid future prosecution Dick had personally employed an environmental crew to clean up and properly dispose of the barrels of toxic oil found on his property. As far as he knew, nobody had filed a complaint with the EPA.

"What?" Dick turned around. It was Marjorie.

"I said have you packed for Rome? You know we're leaving on Friday." Her husband was sometimes a procrastinator.

"Of course, I'm packed," he barked. "I'll buy more clothes in Italy if I need them. Stay off my case, will you?"

"Oh, Jon phoned," Marjorie casually added.

"What?" Dick was uncertain he heard correctly.

"Your son called." She paused, half turning to lend Dick her eyes. "Jon wants to see you as soon as possible."

My son wants to see me? Dick had almost forgotten about his surprise visit to Jon's Selmer apartment earlier in the week.

"Here's the number." Marjorie handed Dick a piece of paper with the number. "Is something wrong, he sounded concerned?"

"No. I'll make the call from my office." Marjorie didn't need to know everything that went on with him and Jon.

Holding the number tightly in his hand, Dick hurried down the long hall, smooth-soled shoes scuffing the polished hardwood, and entered his private home office through the library. In a tare, he slammed the door and trotted over to the phone.

Hand poised in mid-air, now that Dick was about to talk to his son, what would he say? He was supposed to have come up with a clever financial offer that Jon wouldn't think about twice.

But bribes wouldn't work with the boy. He should appeal to Jon's softer nature, play on his sympathies. Yeah.

Dick dialed Jon's number. He would let the cards fall where they would. "Jon, here," a smooth, confident voice answered.

"Oh hi, Son." Dick's mind was searching for an angle.

"Latisha said you stopped by the apartment. Did you need to see me about a matter?" Jon asked.

"You took your time in getting back to me!" Dick failed to keep his impatience from showing.

"So what did you want to talk about, Dad?"

"What are you doin' in Selmer with that Spanish girl?" Dick couldn't help himself for asking. Nice wasn't his forte.

"As compared to why aren't you working at Branson?" Jon knew exactly where the conversation was headed.

The boy was too smart for his britches.

"Look, Dad. I don't mean to be rude, but I've got business at hand. What can I do for you today?"

"Why are you working at a gas station for minimum wage? It breaks my heart to see my own son stoop so low. I thought I raised you better." Dick knew he had blown it royally.

"Gotta go, Dad," said Jon. "When you feel better we'll talk."

"Wait! Actually, that's the reason I phoned." Dick had an idea. "I'm not feeling so well—got a doctor's appointment." It was the truth, halfway. He had to get shots before going overseas.

"What's wrong? Are you in pain?" Jon worried over his father's salvation. He could no longer afford to put off telling him about what Jesus had done in his life, why he had changed.

"I thought we might have a bite of lunch together one day soon and talk things over." Dick swallowed his pride. "You know I run a big business, and you are my only heir."

"I'm not interested in running Branson, if that's what you are suggesting. Can you meet me somewhere on Tuesday?"

"How 'bout the country club?" Dick suggested.

"That's not good for me," said Jon. "I prefer Lindsey's." Let his dad stoop a little. It would do him good.

Humph. Dick hated the idea of dining with the locals.

"Bud Lindsey's, it is." If that was the only way he could get to his son face to face . . . so be it. "Eleven thirty, okay?"

"Until then."
Well that didn't go so well, did it?
But it could have gone a whole lot worse, Dick thought as he hung up the phone. He had a few days to consider what it would take to get Jon back working for him.
The ol' ticker wouldn't last forever.

***

Preparations for supper had been made. Outdoors, the sun slowly slipped down the horizon leaving a dusty trail of purple. The Chardonnay was in the refrigerator chilling, and Karen's heart was quite warm with memories of her romantic evening spent with Mark, erotic thoughts sending sweet signals to her body.

After arriving home from grocery shopping, Karen had taken a hot bath and donned casual clothes. She was mixing the dip when she heard a knock at the door. Mark had arrived.

"Sorry I'm late." He slouched into the foyer barely taking notice of her, and collapsed on a barstool. "I need a drink."

"Is the quota thing still on? Or can we indulge?"

"A drink of water," Mark clarified. "It's hot outside, and I'm thirsty." His eyes wandered around and landed on Karen.

"Oh." Karen pulled a bottle of spring water from the refrigerator along with a salsa dip she'd whipped up a few minutes before he arrived. The chips sat on the bar between them.

"So what type clothes are you carrying to Rome?" Karen fingered a chip. "I suppose it depends on our agenda."

"Coupl'a suits with matching shirts and ties—casual pants and some short-sleeve shirts. And shorts. A bathing suit, in case we decide to try out a spa. The usual stuff." He dipped a chip into the red-hot salsa. "Yum . . .Karen, this is delicious."

"What? No tuxedo?" she teased.

"That, too." Mark brushed salty crumbs from his hands.

"Well, at least it gives me some idea of what to take with me to Italy. I'm not the fashion buff my mother was, you know." Karen immediately regretted bringing up a torrid subject.

"I'm so sorry your mother's absence continually haunts you," he said. "By now, Vicki could be residing anywhere in the world and starting a brand new life." Her absence left a big hole in life.

"Without us," Karen added, her eyes cold and vacant.

"Shall I put on the steaks?" Mark realized that worrying was futile. It cycled the mind, bruised the heart, and confused options.

"They're in the frig marinating."

Mark's comment about her mother starting a new life left Karen feeling abandoned. How could she do this?

"I'll take out the steaks while you start the grill," Karen said.

"Mark dragged his tired body from the barstool, walked through the den and slowly opened the glass sliders. A brand new grill stood on the patio. With no forethought of how he would be affected, he walked over to the wood railing and looked down at the street where Victoria had stood the morning she forgot who he was and how she felt about him: a tragedy too sad to plot.

A love story with no ending, Mark mused as he lit the gas grill and flames shot up. It seemed to him that life was just as explosive, hot and furious, burning bright, yet so easily snuffed out.

A few minutes later Karen brought out the marinated steaks along with a couple of glasses of wine.

"It's been a beautiful day," she said to make conversation. Actually, it had been lousy. "How are you making it?"

"Barely," he replied. "At least the weather's holding up nicely for June, warm but pleasant." Mark hoped Rome's weather would treat them as royalty. "The trip must've cost Dick a mint."

"About Dick and Marjorie," Karen said.

"What about them?" Mark stabbed a steak and seared it on the grill. "Rare?" Dick certainly was when it came to planning.

"Rare is good," replied Karen. "Marjorie makes me feel uncomfortable. If you don't mind, I don't want to spend all our time as a foursome." She sipped wine from a long-stemmed glass.

"Fine by me," said Mark, flipping Karen's steak. "Are the potatoes in the microwave?" He made eye contact.

"Set for fifteen minutes. Marjorie doesn't like me."

"You don't know that for sure," Mark argued.

Rebels In Paradise

"When she looks at me, I feel the daggers."

A couple of minutes passed.

"Steaks are almost done. Why don't you finish up inside and we'll eat soon." Mark was hungry. Gaining weight around the middle, he had been indulging in alcohol too often at the country club and failing to exercise at the gym. His heart wasn't the best. *Consequences of old age,* Mark thought with a shrug. *A lot of people needed pacemakers. Irregular heartbeat didn't kill you, did it?*

MONDAY, JUNE 9

17

Denver, Colorado

Texas Holmes set the whirlybird down on the tarmac around 4p.m. Monday at a private airport located thirty-five miles out of Denver, Colorado, owned and operated by a Christian couple. Cutting off the engine, he climbed out and stretched his limbs.

Rugged terrain of steep mountains cloaked in velvet green artistically etched the backdrop of a royal blue sky. Deeply inhaling, he took fresh oxygen into his lungs. The weather was gorgeous, the air crystal clear, bringing his tired body to life.

Victoria was waiting to be helped out of the helicopter. The trip from Canada with all the required stops had taken exactly one week. Claiming she hadn't minded, Texas was certain that wasn't the case. She couldn't hide her sense of underlying urgency regarding the use of time. And he understood. The woman had many good traits, but seldom complaining topped the list.

Besides his scheduled stops to deliver microchips, Texas had been summoned to New Hampshire to repair a damaged satellite system. Along for the ride, Victoria had urged him not to worry about her and to take care of business first. He had.

Twice since leaving GloryVale, they had communicated with Victoria's mother by cellphone. Kimberly Ann was a trooper and told them not to be concerned about her. She loved GloryVale and was making many new friends. The news was comforting.

Victoria had proven the perfect companion—reclusive when Texas was working—sensitive and talkative when they were in flight. Landing periodically to rest and refuel, they often shared a delicious meal in some quaint out-of-the-way restaurant.

Texas was getting to know Victoria pretty well, he thought. Her spiritual depth and perky personality were phenomenal assets.

And she was beautiful. He had not failed to notice.

So here they were in Colorado, looking to find Beverly James and meet Victoria's goals. Texas jogged around the helicopter.

"Thank you for bringing me here."

Arms reached out for him, a smile defining Victoria's perfectly formed red lips. Seeing her dark brown eyes sparkling with appreciation, Texas didn't miss the powerful connection, both exciting and frightening. "No problem," he said.

"I hope I wasn't any trouble." She sailed down into his arms, a breath away from kissing him. *I dare you.*

"No, it was wonderful having company on the trip," he answered. Victoria made no effort to pull away from him. "This feels pretty right, you know. Mind if I keep you here in my arms for a while?" He inhaled her womanly freshness, intoxicated with love emotionally overflowing. He was not lonely anymore.

Victoria's stepped back and gazed into Texas' big aquamarine eyes, unable to think straight. A funny tingling curled her toes. *Is this true love?* She brushed the wrinkles from her denim skirt and glanced around at the breathtaking scenery.

"This doesn't look much like Denver," she said.

Texas laughed. "It's close, though."

The terrain consisted of rugged mountains and acres of fields planted in corn and hay. "Where exactly are we?" She lifted her face to meet Texas' gaze. "Are we going to walk?"

He smiled. "No, we'll probably bum a ride into town."

"Oh," said Victoria, never having hitchhiked.

Texas removed their gear from the helicopter and escorted Victoria over to the tower. "Nice day, huh?" He squeezed her hand. "I hope we won't have a problem finding your friend."

"Bev?" Victoria peered into Texas' glistening eyes. "I have some ideas how to find her." For a week she had been planning.

Texas had prearranged a ride for them with a trucker taking a refrigerated load of vegetables into Denver. "Hope you don't mind," he said to Victoria. "If we encounter road blocks, we can hide in the sleeper." That was unlikely since the police were probably still scouring the Nashville area for their fugitive.

"Hmm. A ride in a truck?" The prospect was exciting.

"Mind?" Texas pinned Victoria against the door, his strong arms supporting his body as he leaned close enough for a kiss.

"A truck ride? No, it's a first for me." She laughed, ducking under his arm and climbing aboard like a trooper. Once seated in the cab, she gave the horn a honk. "Whoopee!"

Texas laughed at Victoria's childish antics, glad the trip had been fun and had taken away some of the horrible tension of running from the law. He saw the driver approaching.

Raymond Bailey scooted into the driver's seat as Texas got in the passenger side, sandwiching Victoria between them.

"Hi, folks call me Ray," their driver said.

"I'm Victoria." She shook Ray's hand and launched into all kinds of questions about how he came to drive cross-country and where he got his fresh vegetables. His answers were to the point.

"Do you travel twenty-four seven?"

"Four days on the road, three days at home," the trucker answered. "My wife travels with me sometimes."

"Where do you live?" She wasn't finished.

"Aren't you askin' a awful lot of questions?" Texas asked

"Well, yeah! How else is a girl gonna learn?"

Texas and Ray looked at each other and guffawed.

"You'll get used to her before long. She's kind of different," said Texas, patting Victoria's hand. "Aren't you, honey?"

"I am not!" Victoria protested. "I'm plain American with no extra spice." Ray eyed Texas and burst out laughing again.

"Not in my book," said Texas. "Why don't you take a nap, dear? We have a lot to accomplish when we arrive in Denver."

"You just want me to shut up, I know," she teased. "But a nap sounds nice." She crawled over into the back, curled up in the sleeper and closed her eyes, hoping for sweet dreams.

Rebels In Paradise

When Victoria woke up the truck was rolling into the parking lot of a motel. The lighted sign said CROSS-COUNTRY INNS.

"Are we in Denver?" She scrubbed her eyelids. "What time is it?" She rolled to a sitting position and looked out the window.

"A few minutes after five," Ray answered, climbing down from the rig and removing their duffle bags from the back of the truck. "Let Benny know when you need a lift back." Benny Jones ran the small private airport where Texas parked his helicopter.

"I will," said Texas. "And thanks, Ray. Hope we didn't put you off schedule too much." The truck was headed to Wal-Mart.

"No problem. Enjoyed the company." Ray got in his rig and pulled the truck away from the curb, waving goodbye to Victoria with his hand stuck out the window. "Good luck!"

"I really like Ray!" Victoria exclaimed and waved bye.

"Me, too." Texas wished they had an escape plan should someone recognize Victoria and report her to the Denver Police.

However, it was unlikely the authorities would be looking for a couple, Texas considered as he accompanied Victoria across the parking lot and into the office. He paid for their rooms in cash and gave assumed names. The office manager looked Victoria over pretty good, but Texas thought it was because she was pretty.

"Room 205." Texas handed Victoria an electronic key when they reached the third level. "I'll be next door. If you need me, call, or just knock three times on the wall," he said with a big grin.

"If I want you?" She recalled the old country song.

"Right into your arms, sweetheart."

Victoria flushed, embarrassed over how fast human thoughts skittered out of control. If she were the main character in a novel, she would know exactly what to do next: fall all over the man she adored and let the obvious happen. But as a Christian, she was responsible to God for her actions. Moral behavior counted.

"Why don't I order Chinese and bring it over to your place in a little while," suggested Texas. "Then I'll tell you what I wanted to say a week ago." He hoped she would receive his words well.

"Oh." *Why was he being so secretive?*

Is he going to talk about our future? Victoria was torn between devotion for Jeffrey and a burning in her heart for Texas. *Is it possible to have two great loves in one life?*

Alone in her motel room, Victoria switched on the television and caught the evening news. Nothing eventful had happened.

No news regarding her whereabouts was good news, wasn't it?

Victoria relaxed a bit and let hope chase away her fears.

Dusk had nearly snuffed out the sunlight when Texas showed up with a Styrofoam tray of Chinese carryout. The packaged food sat on the table for fifteen minutes while they talked strategy.

Agreeing it would be best to contact Beverly James the following morning after they'd rested, Victoria suggested they eat.

"I'm famished," she said. "Are we done talking?"

He nodded. "Yeah, we'll do our business tomorrow."

With that decided, they dove into the food like deprived vultures. The appetizer was egg rolls, and fabulous.

Victoria sat in the middle of the bed Indian fashion, devouring a paper plate of noodles steeped in lobster sauce and oriental vegetables. Eyeing Texas, she raved over supper.

When Texas finished eating, he switched on CNN, fuming over how the liberal media had painted the spiritual awakening occurring among the homeless in America. The reporter had labeled "born again" believers as narrow-minded bigots.

Disgusted, he switched off the television. "I hate the way the news bashes the Christian movement," he declared. "They are tactfully labeling us as rebels. Freedom in America is a myth."

Victoria agreed, based on her limited experience with the media. The interfaith movement to consolidate religions had been mentored by the Vatican and embraced by the majority.

"I don't know about you, but if Earth is Paradise, I'm definitely a rebel. And I don't care what anybody else thinks. Hooray for the homeless! May they praise Jesus forever!"

"Bravo, Sister! Well put." Texas joined Victoria on the bed. Leaning over, he took a bite of her fortune cookie. "Yours taste better than mine," he said, kissing the ends of her fingers.

"So what did you want to tell me?" Curiosity ruled.

"It's about your son," Texas said.

"Daniel?" Victoria was taken back. "Isn't he working somewhere overseas? What about him?"

"You want to see him, don't you?" Texas traced his right forefinger down the bridge of Victoria's nose.

Do I? She questioned the wisdom of opening a new can of worms when she had her plate full.

"Of course, I do," she said to appease Texas. "After I've spoken with Bev and cleared my name with the police."

"And what if you never clear your name?"

"Then I suppose I'll approach my son incognito."

"I thought you'd say that." Texas smiled. "So how would you like to go to Rome?" He pulled Victoria to her feet in a tight embrace. "With me, to see Daniel?"

"What?" Her mind did flips. "Italy?"

"You can view the moonlight sparking on the Mediterranean Sea, experience the culture of great Italian food, and dance with me like a princess in a palace." His gaze was intense.

Huh? "What are you talking about, Texas?"

"The CPA wants me in Rome next week to report on the bash the Big Whigs are throwing for Alexander Luceres Ramnes." He peered down at the lovely woman in his arms.

"The Antichrist! You want to take me to a party thrown for *him*?" Victoria separated herself from Texas, shaking her head.

He blinked, seeing she wasn't finished.

"You want me in the same room with the scoundrel who blended religions? The cad who took away Christian Bibles?"

"Yes," Texas replied.

"Not a chance!" Fury flew all over her.

"Daniel's coming to Rome." Texas hoped to dissuade Victoria from missing the event. "The International Peacekeeping Taskforce is being honored at the final banquet on Friday."

"What?" Victoria spun around to face Texas so quickly she nearly lost her balance. So much had already happened, so much change, how would she feel seeing a son she'd forgotten?

Can I emotionally handle it?

But here was a chance to see Daniel, talk about a past they had shared and she had forgotten, get some issues settled in her mind. "I—" words were lodged in her dry throat.

I can't face the Antichrist, I can't.

"Everyone in the world who is important will be there," Texas embellished his proposal. "Here's your chance to rub arms with the world's dignitaries, dine with kings and queens."

Victoria wasn't yet convinced. Her friend, Old Fear, stirred the murky waters. "What do you think?" he asked.

"I don't know if I can do that," Victoria replied.

"Of course, it's a given we'll go disguised," said Texas. "You can see Daniel up close and personal without his knowing who you are. You'll be safe with me, I promise." He reached for her hand. "I'll teach you my tricks—how to stay safe in scary places."

You're already too quick for me. Victoria took a deep breath and mulled over the idea, then said, "Rome, Italy. It does sound . . ."

"Romantic?" Texas eyebrows danced. "I can handle that."

"You're positive no one will recognize me?" A corona of light encircled Victoria's pupils as her heart skittered a little and she nervously envisioned standing beside Texas in Rome.

"Absolutely. When we're done here, I'm taking you to my ranch in Texas. The CPA is sending over a prince of a makeup artist. When he's finished with you, well . . ."

Victoria was enticed by the idea.

"Then you'll be my date to Rome?"

"Why not?" She laughed.

"Now that that's settled, how do you plan to find Beverly?"

"I have a few ideas to run by you."

"Oh?" He lifted one eyebrow. "I might still have a surprise or two for you, too." He kissed her lightly on the lips.

TUESDAY, JUNE 10

18

Early Tuesday morning Texas rented a used Volvo from a local car dealer. Victoria accompanied him to the dealership, but waited outside while he signed the rental contract. Wearing her hair tucked under a baseball cap and an oversized plaid shirt loosely hanging over baggy blue jeans, she leaned over and secured the ties to her ragged pair of tennis shoes.

No use tripping over my own shoestrings if I have to run.

Victoria's wary eyes scanned the busy street like she was guarding the joint while Texas robbed it. As a squad car cruised past, she faced the plate glass window to avoid making eye contact with the driver. Through the window glass she saw him pass.

Don't mess with me, buster, unless you wanna bloody nose!

Victoria was starting to get into the part. On the bridge of her nose was perched a thick pair of drugstore spectacles, which twitched because the false mustache tickled her upper lip.

Despite her attempt to portray a guy, Texas insisted that she looked as cute as a bug about to drag off a fly twice its size. The bubble gum swelled between Victoria's lips and loudly popped.

She hated the putrid-green Volvo Texas selected. Its fender was badly bent and the rickety old motor threatened to quit any second. Texas argued that it was a cheap rental and the model was not a choice the police would expect a debutante to drive.

Right, Victoria popped her gum. *Let's get this show on the road.*

Like every good high-profile sales agent, Beverly James had advertised in the *Yellow Pages*, making public her whereabouts.

She'd even listed her home phone number and given an e-mail address. A web site was set up to show her cosmetic products.

Bev had nothing to fear anymore, so she thought.

"You ready to roll?" Texas came out the door with the car key and headed down the aisle toward the rental vehicles.

"Yep." Victoria loudly popped her gum and climbed in the passenger seat. "Cops came by. Took one look and drove on by. Guess I passed inspection." She felt a sense of accomplishment.

"You really get off on this detective stuff, don't you?"

"It's not all that bad—even fun, sometimes."

"Well, you're about the cutest fugitive I know. If I were the sheriff, I would arrest you just so I could watch you in jail."

"Oh, you . . ." Victoria punched his right arm with her fist.

Texas drove slowly past Beverly's apartment flat looking for signs of any life stirring beyond the window blinds. *Zilch.*

"So what do we do now?" asked Victoria. "Park the car and wait for Bev to return?"

"*Unnk!* Bad idea." Texas pointed to the vanilla-colored van parked down the street with CARPET CLEANING painted on the side. "It's a surveillance van. Your friend is being watched."

"Because . . . of me?" Victoria's voice shattered.

"Probably. I know no other reason why someone would have her activities monitored. She's not a Christian, is she?"

Victoria shook her head no. "Actually, I'm not sure," she confessed. "I've known Bev most of my life and I don't recall asking. Some friend I am. Now she's in trouble because of me."

"It's all right, honey. We all make mistakes."

"Not big ones! Why is it that everyone who tries to help me gets into trouble? I can't possibly be that important."

Seeing Victoria's distress, Texas knew he needed to say something positive. *What?*

"Who knows? Maybe God has you in this special place in time for a specific purpose," the words fell out like prophecy.

"My mother once said that." Victoria folded her hands in her lap, her glossy brown gaze floating on Texas. "I find *that* difficult to swallow." What great skill did she have to dedicate to God?

Victoria Tempest couldn't carry a tune in a bucket, or play a musical instrument. She had no oratorical skills. She was always getting into trouble and bringing others with her. It wasn't much to offer The-Lamb-That-Was-Slain for saving her soul.

"God doesn't expect perfection, Victoria," Texas kindly said, wisdom filling his mind. "Only commitment. You have an overdose of that, my sweet. Use it and thank Him."

"Do I?" Victoria loved the way Texas said "my sweet," like candy melting on his tongue. She liked his wide chiseled jaw, the way his blue-green eyes secretly frisked her when he didn't think she was looking. She loved how he smelled and walked.

She loved him?

"What? You're blushing, my dear." Texas gripped the steering wheel with his strong hands. "Penny for your thoughts? I'd love to know what's going on behind those mysterious eyes?"

"Nothing to speak of," said Victoria.

"Okay," Texas said, "this is plan B." Plan A had failed when they didn't find Beverly at her apartment. "We go into the public library and you get on line with the Senior Citizens Chatroom. If we're lucky, Beverly will respond." His eyes targeted Victoria.

"And?" She sensed his reservation.

"And be advised, your encounter with your friend should be in public and brief. Someone might be watching."

"Otherwise . . ."

"Otherwise we may get caught," said Texas. "And you don't wanna miss Rome." He reached over and patted her hand.

"Exactly," said Victoria, her thoughts wandering to Daniel.

19

Back in Tennessee

Georgie Hendricks quit her garbage job at the end of two weeks. She'd given a lame excuse, asking to be paid for her time. Looking miffed, the foreman had paid her wages in cash, reminding Jaycee Moore he needed to be more committed to work if he intended to thrive in today's society. *La-de-da.*

Regardless of how others viewed her, Georgie had to move forward with her plan. She had things to do and people to see.

Using the money she earned from garbage plucking, Georgie had purchased a fourth-hand motorcycle from a second-hand Harley dealer. Fifteen hundred bucks swung the deal.

First stop was the Fernwood Police Precinct. She marched through the front door with confidence that nobody would recognize her. "Can I speak to Sarah Boswell?" she asked.

"Sarah ain't in," said a co-worker manning the desk.

"Is she expected back?"

"Nope. It's Friday and she's got the weekend off," said the lady attendant. "Is this police business? I can he'p you?"

"No, it's personal."

Georgie hurried outside and climbed on her motorcycle. Seconds later, she followed the one-way flow of traffic around the courthouse, hoping that Sarah was home and had a kind heart big enough to include a bed for the night. Unfortunately, until Jaycee Moore acquired a job at Branson Meatpacking Company, she could not afford to buy a meal, much less rent an apartment.

But life would soon improve. It had to.

Georgie impatiently waited in the old rocker on Sarah's front porch. By noon it had grown hot and she was thirsty. Fifteen minutes later, the officer turned into her driveway and gaped at her uninvited guest. Georgie came to her feet and gaped back.

"Excuse me, buster!" Sarah sassily rolled down the window of her Buick. "What are you doin' loitering on my porch?"

"It's me, Georgie Hendricks—in disguise."

"Well, well . . ." Sarah let out a snicker, turned off the engine and got out of the car. "What brings you back to Fernwood?"

"What's in the frig good to eat?" Georgie asked, hungry from not having eaten in hours.

"Strange but I don't recall asking you to lunch!" Sarah unlocked the car trunk and reached inside for a sack of groceries.

Georgie leaped into the yard. "Can I help?"

"Sure. Grab hold of a sack," Sarah replied.

While removing the grocery sack from Sarah's navy blue Buick, Georgie took a whiff of California sourdough bread.

"Smells yummy," she said, inhaling the yeasty aroma.

"Fresh baked at the Kroger deli. Come on in, sister, and we'll see what suits your appetite." Sarah aggressively mounted the front porch. "I'm flexible. I take it you haven't eaten all day."

"No, I haven't." Georgie trailed Sarah down a long hallway into the kitchen. Plopping down the sack of groceries on the breakfast bar, she asked Sarah. "Got somethin' cold to drink?"

"Help yo'rself." Sarah pointed to the refrigerator, proceeding to unload the canned items and placing them in the cabinets.

"I'll get lunch goin' in a sec," Sarah said, dumping a handful of fresh vegetables in the sink. "You like your salad loaded?"

"Everything and the kitchen sink," Georgie quipped, removing two cherry colas from the top shelf of the fridge. Popping a lid, she handed the first cola to Sarah before snagging one of her own and guzzling it down in record time. "Ah . . ."

"Did you let down the car trunk?" Sarah asked.

"Yep," said Georgie, grabbing a second cola from the fridge.

"So why are you here?" Sarah drank half her cola in one long series of swigs. "Hot outside, ain't it?"

Before grocery shopping, Sarah had been searching through the police archives for Victoria's missing accident report. She didn't find it, which made her wonder who had checked it out.

"I'm here to find work at Branson Meatpacking Company," Georgie said. "Had some time on my hands, so I came here."

"Oh?" Sarah's interest piqued. "Doing what for Branson? Murder ain't legal. Leastwise, not in the state of Tennessee."

"Anything the company will hire me to do," Georgie said. "Meanwhile, I need a place to stay. I was hoping I could count on your help. I'll pay you rent when I get my first paycheck."

"Did I ask you for money?" Sarah haughtily reacted. "My friends don't pay for a place to crash, got that?"

"You're all right, Sarah. No wonder Victoria likes you so much." Georgie knew she had chosen the right side of the law.

"You seen her lately?" Sarah grabbed Georgie by the collar before she thought. "Sorry. Old habits die hard."

"Not since we had supper at O'Charley's a few weeks back. If I know Victoria, she's doin' just fine," Georgie said, opening a new pack of cheese Doritos. "I'll share," she teased.

"Well, I'm not doing fine!" Sarah snapped, grabbing a chip. "I don't like what I've been hearing at the precinct. Word has it there are people willing to finger Victoria as the person who hired the thugs that broke into her husband's office the night he died."

"That doesn't surprise me," said Georgie. "In my opinion, Victoria is incapable of murder. Obviously, she's being framed."

"Somebody's gotta take the murder rap so Dick Branson can walk," Sarah raised her voice. "That makes me mad."

"Me, too. That's why I'm not just sittin' by and letting it happen," Georgie confessed. "I'll get proof Victoria is innocent."

"I suppose you found Gloria Gordon in Florida."

"Yep," said Georgie, munching out of the Doritos sack.

"Don't think you're going to get outta here without telling me what happened in Florida." Sarah stored the milk in the refrigerator. "I gotta stake in this, too." Her life was tied up in knots with the past. People she loved were either missing or dead.

"What do you want to know?" Georgie asked.

"Let's start with your plan of action," Sarah replied.

"Sure." Georgie took a seat at the kitchen table. "I might ask you the same question," she remarked. "As an officer of the law, are you in a better position to obtain information than I am?"

"Possibly," said Sarah, slamming a can of coffee on a shelf.

"Oh?" Georgie raised an eyebrow.

"Actually . . ." Sarah collapsed in a chair across the table from Georgie, "I've already been doing a little investigating."

"Yeah, what?"

"Been rummaging through some old police files all afternoon lookin' for Victoria's accident report from 1989." Sarah shook her head. "I tell you, it ain't there—which makes me wonder if Dick Branson has a mole at the precinct working on his behalf."

"The proof is in the pudding," Georgie deducted.

"Uncle Rhe-mus—God rest his soul—was the officer who wrote up Victoria's accident report. It's police procedure to deliver a copy to the insurance company." Sarah's global eyes were black as a starless midnight. "All that information is on Victoria's report somewhere, if I could only find the blame thing!"

Sarah hopped to her feet and paced the kitchen.

"The report could've been checked out," Georgie said.

"If so, it wasn't recorded." Sarah eyed her guest.

"I'm not at all surprised the report is missing." The PI came to her feet and leaned taut hips against the kitchen counter for support. "Dick could make the Holy Ghost disappear."

"That's not funny, Georgie!" Sarah snapped.

"Sorry," Georgie said, supposing Sarah was a Christian. "The case against Victoria is solely built on the premise that she plotted Jeffrey' murder to collect on his life-insurance policy. Without access to Caldwell Insurance files, we can't disprove it."

"Looks like the creep responsible for the break-in at Jeffrey's office has neatly tied up all the loose ends," Georgie remarked.

"Except for Victoria," Sarah pointed out.

"Who was mentally impaired and no threat for years, mind you," said Georgie. "No one expected her to recover memories."

"And now that she has . . ." Sarah's thoughts drifted. "Hey, do you think it's possible another insurance company took over Caldwell's files, like banks are governmentally insured?"

"I don't know," Georgie replied. "But you can bet your bottom dollar Dick Branson knows and is not telling."

"Probably." Sarah sighed. "He was certainly in town and on time to participate in the robbery scheme. What was it? 1984 when Hearty Meats opened its operation in Fernwood?"

"Yeah," said Georgie. "Branson came on board as manager at the end of '87. By 1991, he had acquired enough money to purchase the company for a buck. And that makes me curious."

"1991 . . ." Sarah rubbed her chin. "That was the same year Mark James divorced Beverly and paid off his debts. Seems to me both Dick and Mark acquired a lot of money over a two-year period. The question is . . . was their wealth acquired legally?"

"That's what I'm wondering," Georgie said. "And don't forget the popular doctor was named executor of the megamillion Gift Trust Fund awarded to Victoria Tempest's family."

"Is it a coincidence all of this took place simultaneously?"

"Not to my way of thinking," said Georgie. "While Victoria was in a coma, who conducted business for her?"

"Mark James never left her side," Sarah said.

"You think the doctor knows a lot more about Jeffrey's death than he's letting on?" Georgie asked.

"It's possible," Sarah remarked.

"What we really need is proof that Victoria did not apply for the insurance policy in question," the detective concluded.

"Which we can't get because the company went belly up in 1989," Sarah pointed out. "All a jury will look at in a trial is verifiable evidence and the testimony of reliable witnesses."

"I guess it's up to me to get hard evidence."

"All this speculation gives me a headache." Sarah laid a large T-bone steak on the counter and covered it in pepper and salt. "This one has your name on it, Georgie." She smiled.

Rebels In Paradise

"I've landed in Heaven." The PI drooled over the red meat, her stomach growling like a mad puppy.

"Let's eat before we continue this discussion."

"I'll crank up the gas grill." Georgie noticed a new one on the back porch. "Any kind of dessert will do."

"You don't expect much, do you?" Sarah chuckled. "I'm a great host, so I don't mind."

Before the day was over, Sarah planned on telling Georgie about her *other* uncle's involvement with Hearty Meats.

20

It was 5 o'clock p.m. according to the wall clock in the Denver Public Library branch. Tuesday was going fast. Victoria had been surfing on the Internet for hours, talking to everyone and his uncle. If Beverly James was roaming around in the *Senior Citizens' Chatroom*, she was not responding to Victoria's cartoon character.

Failure was discouraging. "Let me fax Beverly a coded message," Victoria suggested to Texas, taking her last option.

"What kind of message will you send?"

"For whatever reason, Bev isn't responding. Chances are good she'll check her phone and fax machine messages when she gets home." *If she gets home,* Victoria privately grimaced.

Texas listened, unconvinced.

"If Bev doesn't respond and come to the library by closing time, I promise we'll leave. Please, Texas. Let me at least try."

"What will you say?" He was positive the people in the tan van lurking outside Beverly's flat were monitoring her personal correspondence, but he didn't say so. Victoria was so hopeful.

After consideration, she jotted down a few words on a clean typing sheet. This." She handed the paper to Texas.

TONGUE TEASER FOR WORLD PLEASERS: UP FRONT AND WATCHES HER BACK, A PRODIGY OF SHERLOCK HOLMES WHO CAN'T COME BACK. HINT: THE ANSWER IS AT YOUR LOCAL PUBLIC LIBRARY AMONG VOLUMNS OF INFORMATION.

Texas read Victoria's words and smiled. "Do you think it will work?" he queried. "Will Beverly respond and come to *this* library looking for you?" If this effort failed, they were finished here.

"I'm counting on it." Victoria approached the fax machine and dialed the number given in the telephone advertisement ad.

***

Branson Meatpacking Company

Georgie had been waiting patiently for two hours to speak to someone at Branson about a job. Paying close attention to the conversation, she learned the big fish was leaving town on Friday.

Good. Dick Branson was sharper than his submissive staff.

4:30 p.m. by her watch, today's window for opportunity was almost gone. Getting up, Georgie stretched and eyed Jeannie.

"Sorry for making you wait so long," the redhead apologized again to Georgie, a.k.a. Jaycee Moore. "Wanna Coke?"

"No thanks." She peered at Dick's secretary in her tight-fitted blue mini-dress, as fit as her impeccable manners.

"I'm so sorry Mr. Branson is unavailable," Jeannie said, uncomfortably. "He usually interviews every applicant we hire."

Why doesn't that surprise me? "Your bulletin board says you need more packers," Georgie went on to say.

"Uh, we do." Jeannie lifted spacious auburn eyes, flipping her fiery-red curls to her left shoulder and returning to her work.

"Look! I just came into town, and if I don't get a job I won't have a place to sleep or eat," Georgie said in a husky voice.

Jeannie glared at the applicant, who seemed slightly familiar. Tall and lanky, Jaycee wore mighty expensive shades for a pauper. Wearing his bleached hair short, his mannerisms were effeminate.

"Have we met?" Jeannie had to ask. "Something about you seems so—never mind." She glanced down at her work.

"No, we haven't." Georgie was grateful her dark sunglasses disguised her tale-tell turquoise eyes. She'd remember to put in her colored contact lenses next time, if she got hired.

"Hey, it's not that I'm unsympathetic with your need to work," said Jeannie. "I fully understand. Money pays the bills."

Georgie offered no comment.

"It's just that my hands are tied when it comes to hiring," she explained. "Maybe Jerry Loafer could help you. He's the night foreman and has been complaining for over a week that he was short-handed." She grabbed a ringing phone.

Jerry Loafer? Georgie pinched herself to keep from laughing.

"Where can I find Jerry?" Georgie inquired. "All I'm askin' is for someone to give me an interview. I'm a hard worker."

Trust me, Jeannie.

"Ask Mr. Loafer if he'll see me," Georgie pushed for an interview. "Tell him I'll work on a trial basis. If I do good, Mr. Branson can approve my application later."

"Well," Jeannie thought a moment, "I guess it wouldn't hurt to ask." She barely smiled, appearing uncertain.

"I'd be much obliged. I'll owe you."

"We are kind of short-handed." She gazed at Georgie. "I'll buzz Jerry and see if he has time to come up front." She picked up the phone and punched in an extension.

Georgie waited, a "yes" on the tip of her tongue.

"Jerry? Gotta guy here who wants to talk to you." Her expression turned blank. "Mister . . .?" Eyes fell on Georgie.

"Moore," Georgie stated "Jaycee Moore."

"Is that J period, C period?" asked Jeannie.

"Spelled J-A-Y-C-E-E." Georgie cracked her knuckles.

Jeannie looked up startled, like she remembered something.

Great! Georgie grimaced over her mistake.

"Fifteen minutes. I'll tell Jaycee." She hung up the phone, a puzzling expression on her face. "I'm certain we've met."

"No," said Georgie. "Thanks for getting me an interview, Jeannie. Like I said, I'll owe you." Wasn't it lucky that Dick was out of the sheep pen hobnobbing with the other foxes?

Jerry Loafer came up front to meet the anxious applicant.

Georgie tried to say everything right and was invited to visit the warehouse. As Jaycee, she followed Jerry down a hallway listening to him explain how Branson's packing system worked.

"Every morning between six and ten, fresh meats arrive via refrigerated trucks from slaughterhouses all over the mid-south. Tennessee, Kentucky, Arkansas, Alabama and Mississippi," Jerry said. "Three work shifts cover the 24-7 time span."

"Question. Does Branson exclusively pack beef?"

"Exclusively." Jerry observed the applicant closely. "Trucks roll away from the plant every four hours and the packaged meats are transported to large warehouses owned by name-brand companies such as Kroger and Sam's. From there, the meats are distributed to local grocery stores and sold to customers."

"It's not a difficult job," Jerry told Jaycee. "We're automated for the most part. But the work requires staying focused."

"I see." Georgie stepped briskly to keep up with the long-legged Loafer. They entered another building.

"As you see in this part of the plant, the meats are delivered to a conveyer belt either sliced or ground," Loafer explained. "Machines precut the wrapping paper to the right size and automatically plastic wrap the meats. Our workers check to make sure the wrap is secure and place a stamp of approval on the packages. Here's the stamp for that." Jerry showed Georgie one.

"That sounds easy enough. Makes me wonder why applicants aren't knocking down your door. It ain't easy finding steady work. Trust me, I've tried," Georgie commented

"We screen our applicants pretty carefully," Jerry said. "Like I'm doing now. You only get one chance to prove yourself."

If Georgie was right, there was a select crew in the plant including drugs in some of the packages. Too much money passed through Dick's hands to be entirely legitimate.

"So, how many people work on a shift?"

"Depends on the volume. I'll introduce you to a few of our packers." Jerry sliced an identity card through the security pad. Electronic locks popped and the double doors jolted wide open.

"You first," Jerry said to Jaycee. "Down the hall and to the right." He lagged behind. "Any questions yet?"

"No. I'm impressed and ready to work."

"Good. I like you, Jaycee. I'm short of packers, so you can start tonight, on the red eye shift. Eleven to seven a.m."

That quick?

"Thank you, Jerry." Jaycee shook the foreman's hand. "I won't disappoint you, I promise."

"Oh, before you leave, Jeannie will fix you up with a security card. You can't access our buildings without one."

"Sure." Georgie took a few minutes to greet a few of her coworkers before returning to the front desk.

Jeannie gave Jaycee a coded card and congratulated him.

"I'll be back," she said, thinking of Arnold Swartzenegger.

Getting into places where Georige had no business going would prove easier with a legit access card. And she wanted to view every inch of Branson's lucrative establishment.

21

The afternoon traffic had picked up in Fernwood by the time Georgie left Branson Meatpacking Company. She was on her way over to Sarah's to tell her about landing the packing job. In the perfect spot to get the goods on Dick, danger was a given. No way would she let fear deter her. This was sweet revenge.

Easing her motorcycle into the garage beside the cop's Buick, Georgie shut down the motor and closed the door.

Seconds later, she raced around the side of the house, leaped on the back porch, and peeked through the window glass. The officer was in the kitchen cooking. Deciding to go on in without knocking, Georgie bolted through the doorway.

"So you're back!" Sarah's eyes chased after Georgie.

"Goodness, girl! You oughta keep this screen door locked! What if I had been a burglar, or worse, a serial killer?"

"What?" Sarah turned down the high-powered rap on the radio and raked Georgie over with her dark eyes. "Since when do I need to be afraid? Since you showed up. Right?"

"You never know when Darth Vader will step on your turf, Sarah." Georgie swiped her sweaty forehead with the back of her hand, welcoming the cool drafts of air sputtering through the vents. "It's not a safe world. Trust me, I know from experience."

"Yeah. Well . . .guess I'm the old-fashioned type who still believes in trusting folks—unless they give me reason not to." Sarah was intent on her preparations for supper. "Any news?"

"Other than the world's not a safe place to live?" Georgie pulled her heavy set of keys from her back pants pocket and laid them on the kitchen counter. Her mind whirred with scenarios regarding how to prove Branson was a drug-peddler.

"I hope you like hog jaw and sauerkraut." Sarah made eye contact. "If you don't, you won't like what else goes with it."

Georgie had no opinion.

"Anyhow . . ." Sarah waved a big stainless steel fork at Georgie. "As you expect, we country folks enjoy our heritage foods." She set a large bowl of creamed potatoes aside.

"I'm not particular, Sarah. Any kind of food with calories sounds good." Georgie had lost eight pounds in two weeks and her body was crying out for nourishment. "Can I help you?"

"Yeah!" Sarah waved the dangerous forked utensil. "Stay outta my way so I can get done here." She moved like superwoman around the kitchen, hands flying in all directions.

Feeling at home, Georgie grabbed a soda from the fridge.

"You should know I'm expectin' another guest. Tanya Mason." Sarah rolled wide eyes over on her guest.

"She's coming here?" *Wow!*

"I tell you this now, because I don't want you interrogatin' the woman the second she walks through my door."

"I promise," Georgie replied. "Did you tell her I was here?"

"No way! She'd cancel her trip and I'd miss seeing her."

"Yeah, I can't imagine she'll be happy to see me." Georgie sat down at the kitchen table with her soda. "By now, Gloria Gordon has probably told her I was in Florida asking questions."

"I expect Tanya will have a few questions of her own."

Sarah handled the vicious knife like a gourmet chef as she sliced and diced fresh vegetables for the salad.

"I'll answer hers, if she'll answer mine," Georgie said.

"No, you won't." Sarah put down her weapon, eyes pointed like daggers. "You will keep your mouth shut. I mean it! I know how you investigators work. Press, press, press."

"Whoa girl." Georgie raised both hands to signify defeat. "I'm not a friend-slammer. "However you want, I'll play it."

"Good. Now that we got that settled." Sarah resumed her cooking. "You just zip those thin lips and give Tanya some time to get used to the idea of you being here." Sarah poured a stringy sour concoction into a glass bowl, sampling a loose piece of meat off the top. "Lordy mercy, this is topnotch stuff!"

Georgie laughed, couldn't help but. "What is it?"

"Por' and 'our k'aut." Sarah mumbled, her mouth full.

"Pork and sour what?"

"Kraut? Sour cabbage," Sarah explained.

"Oh." Georgie had no idea how the dish tasted.

Of all the diverse cultures she's been around—and Chicago had them all where she grew up—the most interesting was the Southern Black with its unique dialect and culinary preferences. Every minute she spent with Sarah was an adventure.

"What?" Georgie caught Sarah staring at her.

"Oh?" Sarah raised an eyebrow. "That's all you got to say for my effort?" She planted one hand sassily on a hip.

"I'm sure the dish is wonderful." It smelled awful.

"You'll love it," said Sarah, licking the spoon.

"If it's okay with you, I'm hitting the showers before supper." Georgie dashed into the hall, then stopped to relay her news. "Oh, by the way, I landed the job at Branson."

"Whut? You walk in this door and don't tell me this news?" Sarah's black eyes danced. "What's wrong with you, girl?"

"I start tonight," Georgie said. "At eleven o'clock."

"Hurry up, supper's almost ready." Sarah scurried around the round oak table, slamming down plates and silverware on rosy-patterned place mats. "Go on, an' git your shower."

"Did you leave me some hot water?"

"Get outta here." Sarah threw a wet dishrag at Georgie.

***

Denver, Colorado

Victoria was still at the library waiting. She nervously looked up. It was almost nine o'clock according to the wall clock.

Where are you Bev? It's almost closing time.

Had Beverly received the urgent fax message, or was she out of town? The prospect of failure capsized Victoria.

Texas had left a little while ago to run an errand, not saying exactly where he was headed or what secret mission he was on.

Feeling alone, surrounded by strangers, Victoria grew paranoid. Suspicious eyes were aimed her way. The librarian glared, definitely questioning her reason for loitering. A little boy wearing a blue ball cap stuck out his pink tongue at her when she stared back. A tall angry-looking baldheaded man with exploring eyes constantly stalked her. *Was he FBI, or a pervert?*

Oh, dear. Victoria self-consciously slipped from her chair at the library news table and uneasily paced the long aisles between the tall rows of historic paperbound books. *Where are you, Texas?*

Victoria nearly screamed when a security guard came around the corner and bumped into her. "Uh, excuse me," she said in a tenor voice, lips dry and tasting salty. "Guess I wasn't watching where I was goin'." It was evident he was unhappy she was here.

"Oh, it's *you*," Tall-and-mean said with disdain.

Victoria swallowed hard, her gaze hitting the multi-colored Berber carpet, unsure how to react, or what to say in response.

"I've had my eye on you and that friend of yours—where did he go anyhow? What are you up to, lad?" The guard glanced down the aisle. "Get your business done and leave, you hear?"

"Yes, Sir." Victoria struggled to make eye contact.

"The library closes at ten and I'll expect you outta here long before then." Goliath placed a big hand on his wide belt equipped with a set of silver keys and a leather club. "Don't cross me."

"I was waitin' for my cousin. I don't have a ride. I won't cause no trouble, I promise. It doesn't look like he's coming—" Victoria lost her concentration when she spied Beverly James walking toward them. "Looks like my ride is here."

Victoria ducked under the security guard's arm and hurriedly returned to the library table where she had left her things. Acting as if she hadn't seen Beverly coming, she scribbled a few words on the perimeter of a daily Denver newspaper:

Bev's baby blues washed over the message, *Meet me in the restroom,* and in acknowledgment, made eye contact with Victoria.

Yes! Victoria brushed past her friend and briskly walked toward the front of the library, aware of the security guard's hot eyes on her back. *Texas, you sure picked a fine time to leave.*

Victoria ducked into the women's restroom beside the water fountain, heart pounding and about to take flight. Standing at the sink, she peered at her tawdry image in the mirror. Hot and flustered, sweat poured from underneath her arms. She was close, so close, to success. If only the guard hadn't followed her.

Turning on the faucet, Victoria removed her glasses, bent over the sink, and doused her face with a handful of cold water. Hopefully, Bev would arrive before the guard popped in and arrested her for loitering. She went over in her mind again what she wanted to say to Beverly: *I'm sorry I involved you in my mess?*

Inadequate, Victoria knew. She would apologize anyhow and give Beverly the directions to the motel. There, the three of them would talk privately without any irritating interruptions.

If she didn't get herself arrested first.

Victoria dried her hands with a wad of paper towels and sighed. If Texas wasn't back soon, she was leaving the library.

Thank God, Bev got the fax.

22

Victoria leaned against the bathroom wall of the public library praying that a stranger wouldn't enter and freak out over seeing a guy—which she wasn't. Just in case, she ripped off her baseball cap. Waiting for Beverly James to arrive was pure agony.

This could be a fine moment. Don't blow it, Victoria.

Crazy as it sounded, she was considering telling Bev the unedited truth, the nitty-gritty facts surrounding Jeffrey's death as Georgie had relayed them to her after speaking with Gloria Gordon in Florida. His death had touched many innocent lives. Because of the deceit, fear hung like a thick veil over Fernwood.

Possessing a life philosophy that "some things are best left unsaid," would Bev believe the truth if she heard it? Hadn't she run before? What did that say about her reliability?

Victoria was counting on Mark's ex-wife filling in the obvious blanks in a sketchy trail of disorderly facts. By examining the evidence together, they might develop a clearer picture of what really happened the stormy night Jeffrey died. With answers, life for Victoria would drastically improve. Why, she could go home and straighten things out with the police and get her life back.

Justice would be served. Dick Branson would get his just desserts and spend time in prison for his crimes. Karen would forgive her for running away, and maybe she and Mark could get back to being friends again instead of enemies.

And everyone would live happily every after. If the world were a perfect place in which to live—which it wasn't!

"Hi," Bev casually said as she stepped into the restroom. "Are we alone?" She leaned over and peeked under the closed doors of empty stalls. "Yep. Just you and me, chickadee."

Chickadee? The endearing term touched Victoria deeply, reminding her the picnic she and Mark had at Chickasaw State Park. They had once been very close, until Jeffrey died.

"So, Victoria, here I am in living color. What do you want with me?" Bev leaned slender hips against the fake-marble sink, pulled a cigarette from her purse, and boldly lit it up. "I have to say, you almost had me fooled in that outfit."

"Put that cigarette away! You'll set off the smoke detectors!" Victoria grabbed the weed from Bev's lips and snuffed the flame out in the sink. "I didn't come thousands of miles to get caught!"

"Don't be so testy! I know the guard."

"I don't want to talk in here. I'm staying at the CROSS-COUNTRY INN on Runnels Street—off the northern loop around the city. Room 205. Meet me there as soon as possible."

Victoria was already walking out the door when she hollered back, "And make sure you're not followed."

Luckily, the guard was not around. Retracing her steps to the library table, Victoria confiscated her copy of a Denver City map and notepad, deeply troubled that Texas was nowhere in sight.

Had he been picked up for questioning by the police? Fear knotted in her stomach. Even so, he would never divulge her presence in Denver. *I'm leaving now.* She made the decision.

On her way out of the library, she spied the public payphone beside the water fountain and decided to try Texas on his cell, dreading calling a cab and going back to the motel alone. She dropped fifty cents change in the meter. *Where are you, Texas?*

"Young man?" Someone from behind tapped Victoria on the shoulder. Startled, she spun around to see who it was.

"I don't want to alarm you, but the police have just advised me they believe a fugitive is in the library. If I were you, I'd make my friendly call somewhere else," a well-meaning woman said.

Victoria glared at the library patriot, feeling sick at her stomach. "What?" she reacted, knees turning to putty as strobe lights crossed the periphery of her eyes. *Are they looking for me?*

"You look ill, lad. Shall I call a doctor?"

"No, I'm fine," Victoria squeaked an answer—shaking so hard internally she was uncertain if she could walk.

Head for the door. Now!

The soles of Victoria's shoes felt coated in lead as she struggled to put one foot in front of the other. Her eyes remained focused on the EXIT sign. Just keep walking, she told herself.

The air in the library was muggy, thick like water, making it difficult to breathe. Victoria's heart was beating so fast she was hyperventilating. *Lord! Show me what to do!*

"What now?" Victoria stopped dead in her tracks in front of two policemen stationed at the exit door. The short cop was chatting with a third party over his two-way radio.

Victoria peered through the window glass of the revolving doors and saw a wash of blue. The police were out in droves.

My God! She felt weak and dizzy. *I have to go out that door.*

A buzz of concern echoed through the library as people got out of their seats and discussed the presence of a dangerous fugitive. Victoria took a few steps toward the policemen to hear what the officer using the cellphone was saying.

"No green Volvo parked in the lot. Yeah."

They are after me. Did someone recognize her at the car rental agency? She'd better leave the building now, if possible.

"Excuse me, Sir." Victoria boldly stepped between the two policemen. "My mother's outside waiting for me."

Their eyes slid on her in slow motion.

"Really, I have to go to work," she lied with the commitment of a criminal. "Is it all right if I wait outside?"

Bending the truth with such ease frightened Victoria worse than getting caught. Had she come to accept the world's behavior, doing whatever it took to get by? Acting as unethically as Dick Branson, or maybe worse? Was it time to quit running?

She could just as easily have said, "I'm the fugitive you're looking for." The chase would be over. She was, after all, innocent, and surely the American justice system still worked.

Victoria waited for one of the officers to answer her.

"Sure, boy. You're free to go. A good job is hard to come by these days. Don't linger in the dark parking lot."

Free to go. Did she want to do that, or go home and see Karen? Victoria floated through the revolving doors and noticed a gray Buick pulling up to the curb. The driver at the wheel honked. *Texas? My hero.* Her eyes raced to the officer closest to her. "It's my daddy," she said. "Guess Mom couldn't make it."

She skipped across the sidewalk, and seconds later, leaped inside the Buick. Somewhere in the process of self-evaluation she had decided that running away from the police was a whole lot smarter than being awarded her own private jail cell.

"You've got good timing, cowboy!" Victoria tossed her partner-in-crime a gratifying smile as she waved at the two officers guarding the doorway. "How did you know?" Eyes were wide.

"Call it a hunch." Texas exited the library parking lot before elaborating. "Actually, I noticed how the guy at the rental place kept staring at you out the window. Later, I decided that guessing what he was thinking wasn't good enough, so I decided to return the Volvo and rent this Buick from another dealer."

"My mug's been all over the tube." Victoria grimaced.

"You're getting more popular every day. From now on, we won't be renting any vehicles except from qualified dealers," said Texas. "I'll get an international list from the CPA."

"And here I was thinking my disguise was so perfect."

"You have a beautiful face and that's difficult to disguise. Those magnificent brown eyes are hard to miss. Maybe you should get colored contacts." The car whizzed down the road.

"You think? Oh, by the way, Bev showed up at the library. She's probably on her way over to the motel as we speak." Victoria considered if Bev had alerted the police to her presence.

Texas sped the Buick onto the interstate loop circling the city of Denver and peeled off at the Runnels Street Exit. The S letter in the CRO S-COUNTRY INNS sign had blinked out. He hopped out of the car and opened the passenger door for Victoria.

"Go up to your room alone and wait for Beverly. I'll be next door. When you're certain everything's on the up and up with your friend, knock three times on the wall."

"Do you think Bev tattled on me?" The idea of betrayal by a friend hurt. But somebody had recognized and reported her.

"We'll soon know. You gave her the address of the motel and your room number, didn't you?" Texas piercing algae-green eyes reflected the streetlights bathing the dark parking lot.

"Yes." She climbed out of the car and they embraced for thirty seconds. "What will happen if the police show up?"

"I'll think of something," said Texas. "Now get going."

The popping of Victoria's tennis shoes on the black asphalt reminded her of a clandestine scene she had viewed decades ago with Jeffrey. Tom Cruise running from the bad guys through the streets of Memphis in the big movie smash, *The Client*. Though not an actor, she was definitely a hot item, and on the run.

Upstairs in her motel room, Victoria locked the door and tightly closed the curtains. Taking a long breath, she flipped on a lamp and limped into the bathroom. It had been a grueling day.

Afterwards, when Victoria's breathing evened out, she turned on the coffee maker, guessing it was going to be even a longer evening. It was comforting to know Texas was a few steps away.

Bev would come, wouldn't she?

23

Alone in the motel room, Victoria listened to the coffee brew, inhaling the sumptuous odor. She might as well settle down. It was going to be a long night. *Don't be frightened. Texas is nearby.*

It was ten thirty before a knock rattled the door.

Praying it was Beverly James and not the police, Victoria parted the window curtains to see who lurked there.

"Well, it's about time." She jerked the chain, opened the door, and pulled her wiry friend inside the room.

"Easy on the hands, okay?" Bev's big baby blues targeted Victoria. "I worked hard getting here without being followed."

"What happened?"

"Some guy in a van has been tailing me for over an hour." Bev tossed her purse on the bed and kicked off her designer Madonna sandals. "I don't suppose you have anything to drink stronger than water." She laid eyes on Victoria. "I'm pooped."

"No, but there's drink machine on the first floor."

"Never mind. I'll survive. The police were all over the place looking for you," Bev said. "They want you pretty bad."

Victoria nodded. "Yeah."

"I thought they were going to bed us all down for the night at the library. You must have slipped out just before the hoopla started." Bev testily walked into the bathroom and slammed the door behind her, mumbling obscenities.

"I was fortunate to have escaped," Victoria hollered loud enough for Bev to hear her through the paper-thin walls.

The commode flushed and Beverly reappeared.

"Well, I wasn't that lucky, honeychild. So why did you come to Denver?" Bev sashayed over to the bed and collapsed on it like it was hers for the night. "I've had a long day. Can't we put off our discussion until morning? I'm at my best when I've rested."

"No," said Victoria, banging on the wall three times.

"Knock three times if you want me . . ." Bev began singing, her hands comfortably placed behind her head. "What's this? We're having guys over?" She giggled. "You've changed."

"Shut up, Bev!" Victoria had had enough of her smart mouth. "I was signaling to my friend Texas."

"Testy, aren't we?" Bev gazed at Victoria. "So we *are* having a guy over. Anyone I know? You never used to settle for one-night stands. You've come a long way down, baby."

"Whatever." Victoria didn't argue the point. Obviously, she had fallen from man's grace, though she didn't recall how.

Did it really matter? Situations changed, and so had she.

The tap on the door told Victoria that Texas had arrived. Just the same, she flipped off the lights and peeked through the window curtains to make certain. Then she let him in.

Looking remarkably handsome, Texas nearly took Victoria's breath away when he stepped through the door. Using his time wisely, he'd showered, shaved, and changed into a pair of fitted blue jeans and a western-styled plaid shirt. Taller than Victoria remembered, his eyes appeared cobalt blue in the dim-lit motel room, his gaze flaming with intelligence and curiosity.

And he smelled better than a dozen red roses.

Bev hadn't failed to notice Texas, either. Dropping her jaw in awe, she came to her feet as the lanky Texan walked over and shook her hand. "This is your friend?" Bev gulped.

"Yes, I'm Texas Holmes." He smiled, showing a mouthful of even white teeth. "And you must be Beverly James."

"Exactly." Bev blinked, swiveling her head toward Victoria. "Why didn't you tell me you had a handsome guy hidden away? I might have come a whole lot sooner." She was drop-dead serious.

"Texas is a friend of . . . a friend." Victoria decided not to mention Jon Branson's name. "He was kind enough to give me a lift to Denver so I could talk to you about Jeffrey's murder."

"Oh, that's really peachy of him!" Bev plopped down on the bed again, still barefoot and gathering her skinny legs beneath her. "I'll take that cup of coffee I smell. *Now.*"

Victoria walked over to the coffee maker on the bar and filled two Styrofoam cups with coffee. One cup she served black to Bev, the other she doctored and offered to Texas.

"None for me," he said. "I just had a Coke. You drink it."

"Thanks." Victoria gulped down the hot liquid like it was a cure for fear. Texas pulled a chair up to the small round table and sat down. A nod of his head said she had the floor.

"I—" Victoria was uncertain where to begin.

"I have the proof I believe you're looking for," Bev said, her lazy blues eyes sliding on Victoria. "Here. In my purse."

"Huh? What kind of proof?"

"You already know that Mark received a large sum of money the summer of 1991, and that he used those funds to pay off the IRS and a huge gambling debt he accumulated while patronizing the casinos on the Gulf Coast. What you don't know is how he came by the money," Bev said, pausing to reflect.

"I'm listening." Victoria eyed Texas with renewed hope.

"Oh, Mark told me some cock-and-bull story about being handsomely paid by a physician in Argentina for teaching him the tricks of the cosmetic-surgery trade. When I asked him where and when, he was evasive. But the sum was substantial."

"Go on," Victoria urged.

"I didn't believe Mark then, and I don't now. I knew he was lying, but we were fighting and I didn't care as long as he paid me alimony when the divorce came through."

"I'm so sorry," said Victoria.

"Anyhow," Bev continued, "I recently found proof to verify my suspicions. I hope it will help you in some way."

"What proof?" Texas leaned forward in his chair, rubbing his smooth chin with interest. "You have this proof with you?"

"Yes," Beverly directed her answer to Texas. "I have copies of the bank statements Mark received after depositing the money in his account. Money I suspect came through a Swiss account."

Bev's gaze skittered to Victoria. "Of course, Mark's Argentina story was pure fabrication. I had also heard from a reliable source that he'd been sleeping around, but I didn't want to believe it. Mark had friends in high places and lied like a pro."

"I'm so sorry," said Victoria, meaning it.

"I used to think it was you who took my place in his bed," Beverly said to Victoria. "I now know that wasn't true."

"What?" Victoria was appalled. "No, I wouldn't have—"

Would she? What about all those lost years since her accident? And the Jackson apartment she had shared with Mark?

Karen had said she acted like a different person after her accident. Maybe she was guilty of adultery. *What else?*

The horror on Victoria's face stimulated a wave of kindness in Beverly's expression. "Don't be so hard on yourself."

"I wish I could change what happened," Victoria said.

"It wasn't you, Vicki, I had Mark followed." "Anyhow, let's not drag up old grievances. So guys . . . any questions?"

"Yes," Texas said. "How did you come by those bank statements? Surely Mark wouldn't leave something that important lying around the house." His eyes flitted to Victoria.

"No, he was too smart for that. I came by them accidentally when I visited his office one day. Out of curiosity, I opened his mail to see how much he was worth," Bev explained. "I walked over to his copy machine and made myself a copy, put the statement inside the envelope and resealed it. Mark never knew."

"Smart girl." Texas shifted in his seat. "If the Argentina doctor didn't pay Mark, who did?"

"Dick Branson, of course!" Victoria chimed in.

"Got anything to eat?" Bev asked, needing nourishment. "I haven't had anything since lunch." She was sinking fast. "Today's been a drainer. Help me out, here."

"Texas," said Victoria, "will you order us a deluxe pizza? I'm hungry, too." She reached over and patted Bev's hand.

"Sure, honey." He walked over to the phone and looked under the table for a copy of the *Yellow Pages*.

Honey? Bev's lips formed the words as she made a face.

"Why didn't you tell me about the bank statements?" Victoria asked, disappointed their friendship had disintegrated.

"I actually forgot," said Bev. "After I had moved to Denver and started unpacking, I found a bunch of old papers in a box." She paused to reflect. "I've got it pretty good here, Vicki—my own cosmetic business and enough money to splurge on occasions. I hope you don't mess things up for me."

"That's not what I'm trying to do."

"I'd like to put Fernwood behind me if I could."

It was a plea for freedom.

"I understand. What about the Gift Trust Fund?"

"What about it?" Beverly yawned. "I might need to take a nap." She patted the bed. "Just a few while the pizza's coming."

"Not on my time," Victoria was adamant. "Texas and I are leaving soon. If you know anything else, tell me."

"You're a slave driver!" Bev said. "If I recall correctly, the gift fund was established in January of 1991."

"Hearty Meats paid my bills up until then."

"Yes." Bev collapsed in the bed, her curly blond head sinking deep into the folds of the soft feather pillow. "So much has happened since." She closed her eyes in retrospect. "Too much."

"Something else disturbs me," said Victoria, pacing the room. "Why would I move in with you and Mark when I got out of the hospital instead of staying with my own parents?" She was a mystery to herself, a phantom with a ghostly life of its own.

Bev's eyes shot open. "Because Mark wanted it." She sat up. "He said he felt responsible for your recovery and I believed him. Anyhow, I felt sorry for you. We made it just fine, didn't we?"

"Yeah, I suppose. Did you always do what Mark asked when you were married to him?" Victoria had never thought of Bev as a wimp. "Where did Mark get the money to set up my trust fund? Why didn't you ask questions on my behalf? I was in no shape to—" she stopped mid-sentence. "I'm sorry, it's not your fault."

"That's your job now," Beverly coldly said, referring to Victoria's engagement to Mark. "Don't count on me to dance at your wedding. I'm not *that* forgiving." Anger surfaced.

"Bev! I'm not marrying Mark. *Ever!*" Victoria thrust her hand forward. "I broke off the engagement. See, no ring."

"Good for you!" The blond stared at Victoria's left finger. "I knew there was a good reason I still liked you." She swung her skinny legs off the side of the bed and took in a deep breath.

"The pizza's on its way," Texas interrupted the tense conversation. "Mind if I ask one question, Beverly?"

"Any time, handsome." She gave Texas her full attention.

"Victoria told me that Jeffrey took out a large life insurance policy a few weeks before he died. What do you know about it?"

"Nothing," Bev answered. "Why?"

"Victoria's signature is on the policy. The police believe she planned the break-in at his office and had him murdered."

"No . . ." the word lingered on Bev's tongue before dying.

"Only because Jeffrey asked me to," Victoria said in her defense. "I had no idea he was in danger. We were the ordinary family living in a small town. We went to church every Sunday. We had no known enemies." Victoria's eyes were filled with tears. "I didn't even know the amount on the policy."

"Which was two mil," said Texas.

"The exact amount of the Gift Trust Fund," said Beverly. "Well, I'll be. That smarty pants!" She could add two and two.

"Which smarty pants?" Texas inquired.

"Dick Branson, of course. He financially arranged everything through his company. A benevolent fund for Victoria, so he had said, because Mark was his *good* friend," Bev recalled. "The jerk."

"Yeah," Victoria sarcastically remarked. "You'd have thought that Mark would have collected the insurance money on my behalf and given it to me." More questions were coming to light.

"That's a thought," Bev remarked. "Mark had power of attorney for you and Jeffrey at the time."

"Victoria was in no shape to file a claim," Texas interjected. "There's no way we can prove Mark collected the money."

"All I know is what Mark told me, that Dick's company was footing Victoria's bills until the trust fund came about."

"Mighty nice of Dick Branson," said Texas, privately contemplating if Victoria's own money was used to set up the trust fund. Was Mark trying to protect Victoria from becoming a murder suspect? And why did Dick cooperate?

"Man, I wish I had some way to find out if Jeffrey's policy was cashed. I could use those funds for my criminal defense."

"Karen still draws from the trust. Why she bothers working is beyond me." Beverly picked at the loose curls on her forehead.

"My Karen?" Victoria blinked. "How much do I get?"

"My word, Victoria, you're a rich widow!"

Widow? Victoria would take poor any hour of the day to have Jeffrey back. What good was money without happiness?

Beverly glared at Victoria, born with a silver spoon in her mouth. One extra makeup sale could make the difference in affording groceries. Still, given the opportunity to trade places, she wouldn't for all the money in the world. What a cross to bear!

"I want my money!" Victoria peered at Texas. "I can pay my own way and I'm going to the Fernwood Bank to get it."

"No," Texas said. "Bad idea."

A knock came at the door. The three of them froze.

Texas put his finger to his lips. Switching off the table lamp, he walked over to the window and parted the curtains.

"You gals can relax, the pizza's here."

A ripple of sighs blew through the room.

24

Jon Branson was not happy with the way he'd left things with his daddy when they last spoke over the phone. Unfortunately, he had to cancel lunch on Tuesday because of pressing business at the safehouse. Eventually, he would tell his daddy why he left the company and what had changed him. It should be soon.

Used to being in charge, Richard Branson the Third had been livid that something came up more important than having lunch with him. "I haven't seen you in weeks," his daddy had said.

"I can't help it, Dad," Jon had apologized. "I'm sorry. We'll reschedule next week." But that wasn't good enough.

"Can't," Dick huffed. "I'll be out of town. "Call me the first of the month and we'll talk about a time."

That was how it was between a son and a father who embraced different gods. Only Jesus could bridge the gap.

Jon had heard that his daddy was invited to the elaborate festivities taking place in Rome the last week in June. Oh, to be a little fly on the wall and hear what Alexander Luceres Ramnes had to say when he accepted his International-Man-of-the-Year award for chairing the International Religious Ethics Committee. He'd be the first to stand up and boo him in protest of PEACE FIRST.

News forecasters had reported that the international celebrity was slated to chair the Reorganized Economic Common Market Committee. The committee's goal: to devise a plan that would unify the world's unstable currencies.

Ha! Luceres probably had enough gold stashed away in a Swiss bank account to prop up the entire world market.

The rich got richer, the poor . . .

Daniel Tempest would also be attending the conference. He and his team of young peacekeepers were going to be recognized by the United Nations at the final banquet on Friday for their skilled diplomacy in snuffing out potential wars around the world.

Eventually, Jon would hear firsthand what had taken place at the banquet when Texas Holmes reported the details to the CPA Board of Trustees in July. Thinking of Texas led Jon to wonder how Victoria and her mother were getting along at GloryVale.

Supper at the safehouse had been an hour ago. When Jon finished his lengthy e-mail correspondence, he was going over to see his mother at her house. Marilyn Branson was in failing health, plagued by leukemia that was slowly sapping her life.

Most comforting was to know that she trusted Jesus to see her through a nasty death, should it come to that. Nearly as stubborn as his daddy, she had refused to sell the home she'd lived in for fifty years and move into a nursing facility.

But Jon couldn't fault his mother for that. Owning property debt free was a rare freedom. His cellphone rang, startling him.

Jon punched a button and said, "Hello."

"Hi, it's me," said Texas. "We're wrapping up things here." *We* meant he had someone with him. He didn't say *where*, either, knowing Jon was gearing up the Global Satellite System to track his location. "Next stop is my ranch. We've made progress."

"Is she with you?" Jon asked about Victoria.

"Yes."

"Your identities are in place. By the time you get home, the details will be there. Let me know if I can do anything else."

"Good," said Texas and hung up.

It was pitch-dark outdoors when Jon departed Western State Hospital. His mother was dying and his daddy didn't know it.

Would he even care?

The drive over to Marilyn's house seemed brief in the light of the heavy burden Jon carried—how to effectively witness Christ to a father who dismissed soul matters. Jon might well be a CPA star, and run a successful safehouse, but he had miserably failed as a son. Dick Branson was lost as a goose in the middle of a vast ocean of sin. Lost, and didn't know it, in darkness, without light.

Dear God, how can I make a difference?

Marilyn Branson lived in a declining neighborhood of small homes constructed in the 1950s. The city was trying to force the residents to sell so they could install a condominium development just like every other low-rent complex built inside the city limits.

Of course, like other residents, his mother was uninterested in moving. Laws were still in place to protect ownership rights without governmental interference, and she believed Jesus was returning to earth before she died, the hope of every Christian.

Jon prayed she was right, but there were no guarantees the Rapture would happen anytime soon. Only God the Father knew when, so he relied on good doctors to care for his mother.

It was a twenty-minute trip over to Marilyn's house. Jon drove his motorcycle into a narrow gravel driveway, shut down the motor, and approached the side door. Tapping lightly on the windowpane, he peeked inside and saw no light in the parlor.

No one rushed to answer the door.

So where are you, Mother?

A moment later the door swung open. A woman wearing a scowl peered at Jon. "What is it?"

"Where's my mother?" he bluntly asked the lady in a crisp white uniform. "And what are you doing in her house?"

"I'm sorry, but your mother fell ill late this afternoon and passed out," the nurse replied. "You need to go, I'm busy."

"Wait!" Jon protested, strong-arming the door. "I just talked to her a couple hours ago. Why didn't someone call me?"

He shouldn't have put off so long in coming.

"She isn't here," said the nurse. "The ambulance left with her a few minutes ago. I was just gathering a few of her things to take over to the hospital. I don't know any of the details."

"My mother is in the hospital?" Jon's mind leaped back to a time when he was young and she had held him in her strong arms. On his tenth birthday, she had thrown him a big party. He could still see the dozen colored balloons floating overhead, the ice-cream cake dipped in chocolate syrup, and all the presents. She was the best mother a little guy could have. *I need to help her.*

Marilyn Branson had refused to buy health insurance, had no driver's license, or state medical card required for hospital registry. She had purposely slipped between the cracks to keep the government ignorant of her meager existence. In particular, that she was a Christian. Believers had to be extremely careful.

"Is there something else you want, young man?"

"No," he told the nurse. "I'll gather the rest of my mother's things and take them over to the hospital." He didn't want her stumbling on his mother's Bible. "Thanks for your help."

"I'm afraid that's impossible," Nurse Gray answered.

"No, it isn't." Jon stepped inside the kitchen and instructed her to gather her things and leave. She frowned, but complied.

Not until Nurse Gray was in her car and driving away did Jon finish packing, lock up the house, and leave for the hospital.

***

Denver, Colorado

Around midnight, after Texas and Victoria had bid a fond farewell to Beverly James in the parking lot of CROSS-COUNTRY INNS, they slipped out of Denver unnoticed. Texas had telephoned Benny Jones and arranged for a cab to pick them up at an Exxon station across the street from the Buick rental.

The trip to the private CPA airport took an hour. Let out in a cornfield a half a mile from where Texas had parked his Bell helicopter, they walked the rest of the way to the airport, enjoying the cool evening and fantastic view of the moon.

Victoria inhaled the refreshing mountain air, a far cry from the moldy-smelling motel room in Denver. Walking side by side, they privately assessed Beverly James' information. She was the first to break the silence. "Do you feel good about the evidence?"

Texas knew she was referring to Mark James' bank statements. "Is it enough to prove he did something illegal?"

"I don't know," Victoria replied, shoving aside the tall green cornstalks as she maneuvered down a narrow dirt row with no end in sight. "I feel bad for Bev."

"Why is that?" Texas peeked over a tasseled stalk. "Because she had a bad marriage, a raw deal in the divorce, was run out of town on a whelm, and forced to start over at fifty-six?"

"Well, yeah." Victoria considered his accurate assessment of Beverly's circumstances. "It wasn't exactly the fairy-tale life Bev had envisioned when we were college students."

"It was a bad wrap any way you slice it."

"I wish I could do something more to help her."

Two rows over, Texas said, "Bev will be fine. I think she's proud of her new life in Denver. I also think she told you everything she could about your husband's death."

"Yeah. Deep down, the gal has a really good heart."

"Listen." Texas paused to hear the singing katydids and moaning owls. "I love the countryside." His white teeth gleamed in the moonlight. "God did a beautiful thing when he surrounded mankind with wildlife and natural beauty."

"Happy, aren't they?" The confusion inside Victoria twisted like a knife. Would life ever be sane for her again?

"And I adore the way your eyes glow in the dark," Texas said with a grin. "Makes me wonder what you're thinking."

Victoria blushed deep within. *So intimate, yet so subtle.*

"Well, a gal can't tell all, can she?"

Above them, the moon swelled in the sky, bathing the valleys in a melon glow. Every movement beneath Victoria's feet signaled a creature on the prowl. She couldn't recall a time in her life when she was more confused over what action to take next, yet so grateful to be with a man who genuinely cared about her.

I wonder how Mother is doing at GloryVale.

"Penny for your thoughts." Texas tried again as he clawed through the brambles entangling the cornfield, his eyes chasing after Victoria with interest.

"My thoughts are more expensive than that!"

"So? I'll pay a little more."

Rebels In Paradise

"I was thinking of my mother and how we escaped Nashville in your helicopter. What really grabs my heart is how you so easily witnessed to Beverly about her eternal salvation," Victoria shared.

"I love sharing my faith in Jesus Christ."

"I wish I could have witnessed to Bev. But the stuff that's gone down between us—" Victoria choked up.

"Oh, honey." Texas wanted to leap over the cornstalks and dry her soupy eyes. "Nobody is truly qualified to deliver the gospel message, or understands the miracle of salvation taking place at the soul level. But we can be assured, when the Holy Spirit is at work, people receive *new life* and hope of eternal life."

"I love the way you express your faith, Texas."

"Hey, you've got as much faith as I do. Share it."

"I'm still working through who I am," she admitted. "With half a memory, I don't feel qualified to help others."

"You're hoping you'll recover from amnesia?"

"Yes. My condition is pretty unnerving."

"Look! There's the clearing up ahead."

"Where?" Victoria ran effortlessly alongside of Texas, feeling as if her two feet were mounted on angel's wings, offering a prayer of gratitude for God's sending a caring man her way.

Arriving at the airport, they took a moment to catch their breaths, giggling like school kids at the end of a race. The walk in the moonlight had been romantic and stimulating, minimizing any discomfort from the moist chilly night air.

That Texas cared for her deeply was even more evident. It was Tuesday morning, 1:30 a.m. Mountain Time, when the Bell helicopter became air-born and pointed toward Fort Worth, Texas. "I thought you said you lived in Dallas," Victoria said.

"Dallas/Fort Worth are sister cities, you hardly know when you leave the city limits of one and enter the other," said Texas.

Victoria nodded.

"I tell people I'm from Dallas so they won't look me up." He peered at his passenger. "It isn't that I don't trust you."

"I understand. It's a dangerous world."

"My ranch is south of Fort Worth, about thirty-five miles. I own six hundred acres, left to me by my paternal grandfather. My parents are deceased, and I have no siblings. Anything else you want to know about me, ask." He eyed her. "I totally trust you."

Victoria felt the same way. Staring into Texas' caring eyes, glimmering like sunlit seas, she believed that her mother had been correct in saying that he was indeed special.

"Is there anything you want to know about me?" she asked.

"Yes," Texas shifted uncomfortably in his seat. "Are you still in love with your husband?" He spoke of Jeffrey Tempest as if he were alive. Indeed, it felt that way.

Victoria was caught off guard by the question. Yes, she had feelings for Texas that were—unexplainable.

"Do you believe in predestination?" she suddenly asked.

"Yes. And no," said Texas. "I once heard a preacher say that all of mankind was contained in the physical embodiment of Adam and Eve." He glanced over at Victoria, spacious brown eyes filled with curiosity, her lips as supple as velvet. *Kissable.*

"Anyhow," Texas continued with a lump in his throat. "The message this preacher was conveying suggested that God viewed His entire creation in the personages of Adam and Eve."

"Now, you've lost me," said Victoria.

"Genetically speaking, God envisioned men and women living out their lives in the span of time given them. Our creator saw alpha to omega all at once."

Texas realized the philosophy sounded pretty strange.

"Okay." Victoria was willing to give the idea a chance, eyes rolling and widening. "God is Omnipotent, all knowing."

"Yes! Think of it this way, Victoria. With God, there are no time boundaries. He perpetually exists in the past, the present, and the future. Nothing new happens on this earth."

"Oh," said Victoria. "I'm starting to get it. When God looked into the faces of Adam and Eve, He saw you and me there. Our lives, our choices, and how it would all end."

"Exactly," said Texas.

"Does that mean freedom of choice is nonexistent?" Victoria was uncomfortable with the idea of predestination, thinking that prayer and good works had a positive effect on peoples' lives. "Isn't that a rather Calvinistic attitude?"

"All I'm saying is that God knows our choices before we make them, but I believe He still gives us the freedom to choose."

"Which comes first? The chicken or the egg?" Victoria smiled. "What does any of this have to do with you and me?"

"Just this," said Texas. "When I first saw you, I felt I knew you—deep down in my soul. Like we fit."

The breath caught in Victoria's chest.

"I felt the same way," she admitted.

"Did you feel that way with Jeffrey?"

"Yes," said Victoria. "He was the love of my life."

"Me, too—with my wife, Joann."

"You think God allows two great loves in a lifetime?"

"It appears He does," Texas replied. "I must admit my attraction to you is much stronger than it was with my first wife. I wonder if we had met . . ." Texas measured how much to share.

"If we had met before we married other people, would our lives have been different?" Victoria completed Texas statement. "I don't know. We didn't. But here we are now."

"Yes," said Texas. "Here we are now. And I do love you with all my heart. I just wanted you to know."

Breathe, Victoria told herself.

WEDNESDAY, JUNE 11

25

Except for two breaks, Georgie Hendricks had worked nonstop all night stamping approval on Branson's packaged meats. Every worker on her shift was beat when daylight came. Almost instantly, she'd come to admire her hard-working blue-collar associates who were daily devoted to the same menial tasks.

Georgie ached all over. Neck stiff, the crick was no help—not to mention a headache the size of Godzilla. When she closed her eyes, packages of meat whizzed past at the pace of the Roadrunner. When would she find time on the job to investigate Dick's business practices? The answer was obvious. *Never!*

No, to get at the truth, PI Georgie would have to nose around Branson on her own time. And she only had one week.

Clocking out, Jaycee Moore bid Jeannie goodbye.

"See you tomorrow," Dick's secretary cheerfully said. "I'm free Friday night if you want to grab a hamburger before work?"

I'm not, thought Georgie. "We'll see. I'll let you know."

"I hope you don't think I'm being too forward, but you really seem like a nice guy," Jeannie said. "I'm not flirting. Really."

"I know," said Jaycee. *Really!* "It's just that I have a pretty full week. Could we think about a later time?" *Not a chance.*

Georgie left Branson in a tailwind, crossing town in record time. She parked her motorcycle in the garage and used the key Sarah gave her to enter the house through the back door.

Promising not to make trouble, Georgie pushed open the door and refrained from screaming, "I'm home, honey."

Rather meekly, she limped down the hall into the guest bedroom and fell headlong across the bed.

Hours later, Georgie awakened to noises coming from the kitchen. It was afternoon: 12:30 p.m. She'd slept for five hours fully dressed—the best rest she'd had in many days.

After a steamy shower, Georgie donned a clean pair of jeans, which Sarah had so kindly laundered, and a gray T-shirt with a blue Branson logo—a gift from pretty Jeannie.

"Hi." Georgie stepped into the kitchen. "What's that I smell cooking?" She inhaled deeply. "For sure it ain't sour."

"Nope!" Sarah eyed her guest. "Black-eyed peas and ham hock. Gonna make us some cornbread to go with it. Got slaw in the fridge, and about to finish whipping the hot taters."

"Sounds yummy." The detective, a non-cook, watched Sarah rake the creamy buttered potatoes into a Corning Ware casserole bowl and lick the wooden spoon clean. "Yummy. Wanna a lick?"

"No, I can wait." Georgie laughed. "I'm starting to like the way you talk, Sarah Jane Boswell. Your cookin's pretty swell, too. Maybe I should plan to stay on for a spell. Been years since I've been pampered by a mother as attentive as you are."

"A mother?" Sarah indignantly exploded. "I ain't old enough to be yo'r mother, girl. Don't go dating my years like that!"

"It was a compliment, Sarah. You're a good hostess. And my mother's dead. I wish I'd known someone like you growing up. My life might have taken more positive turns."

Sarah tilted her head sideways and sighed. "So how was the job?" The attitude fell away like the butter from her spoon.

"Busy. I worked hard. Branson's setup is pretty impressive. The assembly line operates like clockwork." Georgie ventured over to the coffeepot, poured the hot murky liquid into a slender green mug and took a sip. "Aw, this hits the spot."

"Explain clockwork," Sarah requested, hands busy.

"Branson's got automated machines wrapping the meats."

"Yeah?" Sarah raised an eyebrow. "So what'd you do?"

Georgie laughed, choking on the hot coffee. "I stamp my approval on wrapped meat packages. No easy feat I can tell you, if you manage to keep up with the blame conveyor belt."

Sarah chuckled. "What job is easy?"

"Don't laugh!" Georgie scolded. "I must've stamped a million pounds of beef last night. At least it seemed like it. And I've grown to appreciate Tylenol a whole lot more."

"So you worked for eight hours at Branson and learned absolutely nothin' about our crooked friend!" Sarah grew serious. "Like I said, getting the goods on slippery Dick won't be easy."

"Hey! It wasn't a total waste of time. I did learn how the meatpacking industry works." Georgie placed her empty mug on the counter. "Give me time. I'll find out what Dick is up to."

"Which means you'll have to nose around where you're not wanted without alarming the guards," Sarah said.

"Exactly," Georgie replied.

Humph. "Explain how you're gonna do that and not git caught, girl. You'll be one more dead person on Dick's hit list."

"I'll find a way," said Georgie. "Count on it!"

"Now, wait a cotton pickin' minute, detective! I don't want you taking unnecessary risks here," Sarah fussed.

"Risks are necessary," Georgie professed.

The hostess ripped off her dirty apron and tossed it aside.

"Now you listen good, woman!" Sarah pointed her finger. "If Branson has high-tech equipment like you say, you can bet your boots he'll have the latest surveillance cameras operating—all tied into the Fernwood Fire Department and the police station."

"I know, and I'm not at all surprised," Georgie replied. "If my suspicions are correct, Dick is peddling a far more expensive commodity than meats." Stone-cold turquoise eyes fell on Sarah.

"You're talkin' about drugs," Sarah surmised. "If that's true, Dick Branson has a lot at risk. He won't mind killing you to keep his secret. *Or me.* And I've gotten pretty used to my skin."

Georgie smiled, weighing the pros and cons. She really liked Sarah, her concern noted. But Victoria was the one who would end up dead or behind bars for life if somebody didn't step up to the plate and knock Dick's ball out of the court. PI Georgie wasn't superwoman, but she had guts. And right was right when it came to justice. "I'll take my chances," she said.

"I don't think you should do it," said Sarah. "It's far too dangerous." There was honest concern in her voice.

"I have to," Georgie replied. "My client's life depends on decoding the secrecy. For decades, this company has been lawlessly running rampant. Don't expect me to ignore the fact that Dick Branson is operating his business on land soaked with toxic chemicals. I don't think so." She had her priorities.

"You're talkin' about chemicals left behind by the old tannery before EPA laws were created," Sarah said. "So . . ." she rolled her hand. "Enter PI Georgie and solve the problem?"

"Don't get cute, Officer! Somebody tried to kill me, don't forget. This bone I'm picking with Dick is not only for Victoria. Nobody messes with Georgie Hendricks and gets away with it."

"Bravo!" Sarah clapped. "One brave fool left standing in Fernwood. We'll put that phrase on your epitaph."

Sarah's cold reality rattled Georgie. "Right or wrong, insane or not, I am going to get proof of wrong-doing and nail Branson's fat *patoot* to the wall. "Are you in or out, Sarah?"

***

Southwest of Dallas, Texas

Texas had to land the Bird in Amarillo for necessary repairs, something about a blinking light on the control panel that concerned him. By the time they were circling over his ranch, sunrise was spinning a thin web of light over the countryside.

"Look, Texas!" Victoria pointed to the emerging sun.

As if God were announcing His holy presence, the bloody sun exploded on the horizon and spread light like molten lava over the dull-gray countryside. Out the window, she saw the helicopter's shadow dancing across the emerging fields of green.

As dawn turned into day, the powerful rotary blades seemed to whip the color out of the tall, wheat-colored grasses.

Awestruck at the beauty of the morning, she sighed in retrospect of God's mercy. How long could a planet maintain its natural beauty when its residents were so brutally destructive? When would God's Son return and make all things new on Earth?

"It's breathtaking, isn't it?" Texas reached over and took Victoria's left hand. "I love the early morning."

"Words can't describe it from the air. I had no idea . . ." the lump in Victoria's throat closed off the words forming in her mind. There were certain moments in time that were sacred.

The weatherman had promised a beautiful day, the highs going only into the low eighties. Still in awe over how powerfully Texas had moved her with his declaration of love, Victoria wondered what had kept her from sharing her feelings.

But last night, she hadn't. *No, couldn't.* To say "I love you" would somehow betray Jeffrey's trust in her commitment to solve his crime. The time for moving on wasn't yet right.

Furthermore, she had been downright rude. While dwelling on the difficult concept of predestination—where she and Texas fit into the scheme of things—she had fallen asleep.

But now that she was fully awake and thinking more clearly, Victoria wondered if her inability to say those three little meaningful words boiled down to pure stubbornness.

Was she so determined to solve Jeffrey's murder that she would not let anyone or anything get in her way?

Regardless of the reasons Victoria's psyche might list, to deny her feelings for Texas seemed an injustice to the living. Her husband was dead. Under God's law, she was free to marry. And if she did so, it certainly would be to Texas Holmes—who must be related to *Sherlock*. She smiled, allowing herself to daydream.

"Down there," said Texas, jarring Victoria into the present. "That's my ranch house nestled in that clump of trees."

"Wow!" she said, meaning it. The rambling one-story with a clay-colored tile roof looked like it covered half an acre. Behind it was a clear blue swimming pool that glistened like diamonds in the sunlight. Acres and acres of pastureland, fenced in for horses and cows, surrounded the house. "I'm impressed."

"Me, too. At God's goodness." Texas lent Victoria those seaworthy eyes that thrummed her heart. "About what I said last night," he stammered. "You're not making this easy on me."

Victoria knew Texas meant about loving her.

"I can't give you an answer yet," the words slipped quietly from her lips. "But I do care for you deeply."

"I understand." His face expressed disappointment.

Did he really? Victoria wondered.

Texas set the Bird down on a narrow strip of green tarmac between two rows of tall trees. Switching off the engine, he climbed out his side, walked around the copter, and offered Victoria a lift down. Sailing into his arms felt as natural as breathing, which was difficult for Victoria to do in the moment.

"Daddy, Daddy!" a young boy around eleven loudly screamed as he ran between the trees and grabbed Texas' neck with a bear hug that probably hurt. "You're home!"

Victoria realized the lad was speaking in Spanish and she understood what he was saying. *How?* Had she once studied the language? She was dumbfounded and it showed on her face.

"What?" Texas noted her distress. "Meet my adopted son, Lucas," he said. "Lucas, greet Ms. Victoria Tempest."

"*Buenos dias, senorita Tempest.*" Lucas grinned.

"*Mucho gusto, senor Lucas,*" Victoria replied in perfect Spanish.

"You speak the language? You never told me."

"You never asked." She confidently smiled.

"The house is a short distance through those woods." Texas gathered their gear and led the way. Lucas followed, short and skinny for his age, and dark-skinned because he was Mexican. His glossy hair, plentiful and long, shined like black diamonds. The lad also limped, his left leg having been trampled on by a bull.

While walking over to the ranch house, Victoria conversed with Lucas. She learned how he came to live with Texas, who in her eyes kept getting better and better. Texas listened, speaking very little Spanish, amazed how well the two of them got along.

"Why, Texas, this is absolutely gorgeous!" Victoria entered the ranch-styled house from a side door, its interior walls, floors, and vaulted ceilings constructed from polished woods.

"I agree," he said. "But I can't take credit for building it. I inherited the house from my grandfather. I would be penniless if it weren't for him." He set down his gear.

"How long ago?" Victoria asked.

"Two years. Soon after I became a Christian and started working for the Christian Protection Agency. My grandfather died suddenly from a heart attack. I was his only heir."

Texas led Victoria into the massive vaulted den. "The fireplace is beautiful when it's lit. Maybe I'll turn down the AC one evening so we can have supper by firelight."

Victoria's emotions raged. A firelight dinner with Texas and he would set her shoes on fire. How could she keep from declaring her love any longer? She had to think of Jeffrey.

"What?" He didn't miss the emotion hiding behind her eyes. Tracing a finger along her full lips, Texas embraced Victoria and kissed her longingly. "One day I'm making you mine."

"I'd like to see the rest of the house," she swallowed hard, trembling with locked feelings she refused to release.

When I am free, she thought to herself.

Texas showed Victoria through the house, which took about forty-five minutes, explaining the details of construction required to heat by solar-powered energy. Of course, she absolutely loved the kitchen, always her favorite in any house, great or small.

Texas' study was no slouch, furbished with high-tech satellite equipment and beautiful mahogany desk furniture. Climbing the walls was a collection of resource materials fit for a scholar.

"Seems to me, you're a guy with everything."

"Not everything," Texas said, kissing the back of Victoria's hand. "A woman's touch would make all the difference."

Did he just ask me to marry him?

FRIDAY, JUNE 13

26

Friday had arrived and Dick Branson was anxious. He'd taken time off work to pack and get his house in order before leaving for Rome. Nothing this week had gone right. Worse, he was at odds with his son Jon, who was taking the enemy's side.

With Victoria Tempest running free, no telling what evidence she had gathered to convict him of Jeffrey's murder. While the Italy trip had the power to financially bless him, her meddling could end his lucrative career and change his life forever.

"Hurry, Marjorie, or we're gonna miss our plane," Dick barked, running on a sugar high. "I've already put our suitcases in the car. My word, you're taking a lot of unnecessary things."

It was five o'clock, Friday the thirteenth.

"I hope nobody tries to bring a black cat on the plane," he hollered up the stairs, overly suspicious when it came to destiny.

"I'm coming, I'm coming," Marjorie declared, hurrying down the stairs. "I think I have everything I'll need while I'm gone." She peered into the dark eyes of her chubby, somewhat lovable husband. "Did you drop the cat off at the vet's? I hope you remembered to pick up your tuxedo at the cleaners this morning."

"Got it," said Dick impatiently. "Are you ready? We still gotta swing by Mark James' place." He glanced at his gold watch.

"Wait a minute—I think I left a light on in the bathroom."

"Don't go back up!" Dick held up a hand. "I'll do a last minute check around the house and lock up."

"Goodness! You're testy today!" Marjorie scolded.

"So I am! And don't dare tell me that you forgot somethin' when I get back. Get in the car. I'll join you soon."

Dick ran out of the hall like a chicken with his head cut off. "Because I'm not lingering another second," he mumbled to himself, aware that Marjorie couldn't hear him.

In less than three minutes, Dick toddled into the garage and climbed into his new jade Jaguar, which he planned on leaving in valet parking at the airport Marriott because he wasn't taking a chance on it's getting dinged in the public parking lot.

"Did you turn up the AC?" Marjorie asked.

"Yes, woman, I took care of everything. Quit complaining. Who do you think I am? Some peon?"

"I sure hope you calm down a bit before you get to the airport or you're going to rattle everybody's cage. There's no reason for you to be so stressed over a vacation!"

Dick sucked in his response as a smile trickled across his bulbous lips. "Of course, you're right. I've been in a dither all day. Just wanted everything to come off as planned."

Marjorie kept her eyes forward as Dick backed out of the three-car garage. "Did you call the post office to stop the mail?"

"Marjorie!" He gasped.

"Sorry."

"Forgiven." Dick wanted to be on good terms with his wife, so they could have some honey-making time alone in Rome.

Marjorie lent him mint-colored eyes. "How can I stay mad at you, Poopsie? So you're a hornet with a bad sting. Yet you treat me like a queen. Let's try to concentrate on having fun."

"I can do that," said Dick with a chuckle.

***

Fernwood, Tennessee

Tanya Mason was late arriving at Sarah Boswell's on Friday because she had stopped by a local bakery and purchased a carrot cake, Sarah's favorite. She climbed out of her yellow Ford Taurus, removed her suitcase from the trunk, and entered the yard.

Rebels In Paradise

While waiting, Sarah became worried that Tanya might become upset when she discovered Victoria's private investigator was there—not that Sarah had invited Georgie for a visit, mind you. But never once had she turned away even a stray puppy.

So how could she have refused to help Georgie?

The detective had reassured Sarah there was no reason for concern, that she would not make trouble and keep a low profile. Besides, Georgie would be leaving for work shortly, her third night in a row to certify packaged meats at Branson.

Sarah jumped when she heard a knock. *Tanya?* She flew to the door and greeted her good friend from Birmingham, Alabama, with hugs and kisses. "Come on in, girlfriend!"

Georgie hid in the kitchen like a common criminal, listening to the women's conversation as best she could through the walls. Sarah and Tanya's reunion took fifteen minutes, words flying ninety miles an hour. "I have someone I want you to meet," Georgie heard Sarah tell Tanya. "Come on in the kitchen."

Footsteps fell down the hallway.

Georgie cleared her throat and stood tall, preparing for the confrontation. It was worse than she anticipated, seeing a ghostly white wash over Tanya's dark face before turning to crimson.

"*Her?* What is this? Please don't tell me this is—" anger swelled in Tanya's expression. "Sarah Boswell! How could you do this to me?" She let out a parade of obscenities.

The woman, like Sarah, was venomously quick-tongued.

"Hold on! It isn't Sarah's fault I'm here," Georgie defended the hostess, sticking out her right hand. "Truce?"

"Forget the handshake!" Tanya fussed. "I'm goin' home!"

"Aw, Tan. Don't act like that!" Sarah pleaded.

"Please, Tanya. I kind 'of crashed Sarah's pad a few days ago with no place else to go. Hear me out, why I'm here, and I'll leave if you're still uncomfortable." Georgie dug in for the long haul.

"She will, too," said Sarah, meaning it.

"The least you could've done was warn me," said Tanya.

"Like I said, Tanya, Sarah didn't invite me."

"Look! For all I care, you two can have a free-for-all over who's right. But first, we're gonna eat," Sarah declared. She pulled the warm food from the oven and sat it on the table.

"So sit, girls." Dark eyes swept over Tanya and Georgie. "Eat until you bust, but don't either of you dare ask one question about anything until you're finished. Got that?"

"Yeah." Georgie took a seat at the table that demonstrated true devotion to Martha Stewart. Sarah had gone to a lot of trouble to prepare a tantalizing meal and arguing shouldn't ruin it.

"Bow your heads while I bless the food," Sarah said.

Tanya glanced at Georgie out of the corner of her eye then closed them. After the prayer, Georgie loaded her plate, and tore into the sumptuous country dishes. "This is a *fine* meal."

"Thank you, Georgie. How is yours, Tanya?" Sarah asked.

"The same." Tanya, still miffed, played around her food in the plate like a dog waiting for a reward biscuit.

"Look, Tanya . . ." Georgie couldn't stomach the standoff.

"Shut up, Georgie!" Sarah snipped. "You're not through eating yet. I tol' you we'd talk about our differences later."

"Yes Ma'am." Georgie zipped her lips and cleaned her plate. Food had not been a high priority with danger lurking at every turn. Feeling a measure of success in landing a job at Branson, she had actually begun to relax and enjoy the debatable company.

Dessert was apple pie—the best Georgie had ever put in her mouth. "Hey, Sarah. Why don't you open up a restaurant?"

"No, thank you," the cop passed on the idea.

When the three of them had finished eating and cleaned the dishes, Sarah invited Georgie and Tanya into her living room.

"Talk," Sarah ordered. "And no fist fightin'!"

Georgie grinned. "Ladies first, Tanya."

Humph. Tanya's clandestine gaze glided to Sarah, lingering for a long second before coming to rest on Georgie.

"You've already talked to Gloria and know my brother Terrance died of leukemia because he was exposed to a poison while working for Hearty Meats." Tanya came right to the point.

Georgie affirmatively nodded.

"My mother was paid to leave town the night Jeffrey Tempest was shot to death in his office. April 13, 1989. Her cooperation didn't change a thing. The people who paid her later took her life anyhow." The chill in Tanya's voice cooled the room.

"Wow! You believe your mother's death wasn't accidental?"

"The people responsible are still watching my house," Tanya revealed. "Ever so often I see a strange car cruising down my street and get those old déjà vu feelings, like the nightmare is about to happen all over again." Tanya wilted in her chair.

"I'm sorry," Georgie said.

"I got a husband I love and two great kids."

"I understand, and I don't want to involve you if I don't have to," Georgie returned. "But Victoria's life is at stake."

"What's that rich stuck-up woman ever done for me?" Tanya bolted to her feet, on the defensive. "She's lived like a queen all these years while I've been hidin' out like a criminal."

"I get your point, Tanya." Georgie shifted in the antique maple rocker. "There were two other people involved in the law suit against Hearty Meats. Do you know who they were?"

Tanya bent her head, glanced at Sarah, and sat back down.

"I'm afraid I'm the one keeping things from you," Sarah said, feeling guilty. "You haven't met Rhe Muscle-Shoal Hornsby, but Victoria did. He died recently from lung complications."

"Uncle Rhe-mus, the cop who wrote up Victoria's accident report?" Georgie clarified. "Why mention him now?"

Sarah eyed Tanya, both appearing stressed.

"Well I think you oughta know he is my real uncle, my mother's brother, so that makes Katsy Hornsby my first cousin"

Huh? "Go on."

"Katsy phoned me right after Victoria's surprise visit to Rhemus all upset, complaining that Victoria was after information, specifically were there any other witnesses to her accident."

"I know all that," Georgie said. "Victoria told me. So what's the point to your story?" She glared at Sarah.

"Uncle Rhe-mus was too sick and too scared to cooperate with Victoria, afraid that someone might be watching."

"Wait!" Georgie began connecting the dots. "Are you telling me somebody has been running surveillance on all three of you for twenty-five years?" The depth of the cover-up was staggering.

"Yes," Tanya chimed in. "Not every week, but ever so often. I had the feeling a bug was planted somewhere in my house, but never found it. We all were pretty undone over it."

"It's illegal to run a sting in America without cause," said Georgie, thinking she'd better do a bug search on Sarah's house.

"Forget legal," said Sarah. "Dick Branson has the police in his pocket. He and Andy Grimes are as thick as thieves."

"Yeah," Georgie sighed. "It's no big surprise."

The room was quiet except for the cool air rushing through the AC vents. "So we're at a dead end," Georgie concluded.

"Not quite." The curve in Sarah's lips suggested a smile.

"What?" Georgie queried.

"My *other* second cousin, James Hornsby, worked for Hearty Meats alongside Terrance Wilson in 1984. James was another victim to die after exposure to environmental toxins."

Georgie blinked with comprehension.

"Johnny Hornsby and Uncle Rhe-mus were brothers. My mother, Mary, was the youngest sibling," Sarah revealed. "James suffered from a degenerative nerve condition that caused a massive stroke. He passed in 1986. Our family was devastated."

"So Johnny Hornsby, your uncle, was one of the three plaintiffs who hired Jeffrey Tempest to investigate Hearty Meats."

The company's travesty was a family affair.

"Yes." Sarah's eyes welled up with tears. "James was barely twenty-six when he died. It wasn't fair, but our hands were tied."

"Too bad." Georgie realized Dick's choices had left a trail of tears. "I wish I had been around to help. Somebody should have taken legal action against the company then and there."

"My Uncle Johnny tried, but when his attorney died . . ."

"He was terrified," Georgie completed Sarah's sentence. "Is Uncle Johnny still living?"

"Yes," said Sarah. "That's the good news."

"What's the bad?"

"He has advanced Alzheimer's."

"Maybe there's still a way to apply justice in this situation," Georgie said. "If the two of you would testify in a court of law to what you've just told me, it would create enough interest to get the FEDS involved." Troubled eyes swept from Sarah to Tanya.

"Our testimonies would show that Hearty Meats had motive for the break-in at Jeffrey's office," Sarah said.

"Exactly." Georgie believed she had them convinced.

"We ain't testifying!" the girls exclaimed in unison.

27

Mark picked Karen up at her condo at 4:30 on Friday and drove her over to his place. Dick and Marjorie Branson were picking them up there and chauffeuring them to the airport.

His condo was spotless, thanks to the maid. And he could go to Rome in peace knowing that Allen was seeing his patients.

"How about something cold and wet?" he asked Karen, glancing at their four suitcases parked at the front door. "Our ride will be along soon," he said. "Did you have a difficult day?"

"Every day is difficult. A glass of wine sounds inviting."

"I'll get us each a glass. I could use a drink, too."

While Mark was in the kitchen, Karen recounted the events of the morning. Having neatly tied up her real estate affairs at the office, she had left two capable agents in charge of her business.

"Do you have something for a queasy stomach?" she asked when Mark returned. Butterflies had plagued her tummy all day.

"What? Are you nervous about flying?" he asked. "Maybe you should take Benadryl to calm you. Just a sec." He set two glasses of wine on the bar and took off walking down the hall to retrieve the compound for his skittish traveling companion.

At the mention of antihistamine, Karen's mind shot back to the day her mother ventured outdoors to get the morning paper and returned a changed woman. "Give her two Benadryl," Mark had said when he learned of his *Little Vicki's* confusion.

Her mother had acted like an alien landing on a new planet. It had been the most frightening moment Karen recalled ever experiencing, outside of dealing with her husband Teddy's death.

Like always, Mark had come over and handled the unsettling situation like a pro. What would she ever do without him?

"Here is an effervescent compound. This should settle your stomach. Forget the wine. It's acidic." He handed Karen a glass of fizzing Alka-Seltzer. She drank it down in one big swig.

"What about the Benadryl?" she asked.

"You can take it when we get on the plane."

"Thanks, Mark. I don't want to be a burden on anyone."

"Dick should be here at any moment now." Mark walked over to the front door and peered through the glass insert.

"What time is our flight?"

"Seven," Mark replied. "Are we clear that you are not to bring up your mother's name to either Dick or Marjorie?"

"Yes." She didn't feel like arguing.

"I've said all I'm going to about Vicki, and I'm satisfied that Dick isn't responsible for your mother's disappearance. We're going on a vacation to have fun. Let's not make waves."

"You make *fun* sound so easy," said Karen. "You think I won't worry about my mother while I'm away in Rome? For heaven's sake, Mark! I'm her daughter. I'm supposed to worry."

"Now I didn't mean to ruffle your feathers." Mark snuggled Karen in his arms. "I know Vicki will be on our minds and in our hearts. I just don't want us to talk about her while we travel. Trust me on this one, Karen. You don't know who might be listening and use what we say to cause Vicki more trouble."

"Wait." Karen processed his remark. "You think my mother has enemies that will be in Rome the same time we are?"

"Anything's possible," replied Mark. "The less information we give out about Vicki, the better. Who her friends are or where she might have gone. It's just safer not to say anything."

"I hope I can be civil to Marjorie Branson. She's in Mother's bridge club. *Was.* The woman knows a lot about our stormy history. What if Marjorie confides in the wrong people?"

"I don't think we can worry about that, honey. We can't control every situation. I guess Vicki is in God's hands."

Mark couldn't believe he had professed in God's ability to watch over Victoria. But she believed it, didn't she? And certainly her faith counted for something in the scheme of life.

The doorbell sounded.

"That's them," said Mark. "Are you set to leave?" He wasn't talking about her packed suitcases.

"As much as I'm ever going to be," answered Karen. "Let's get this show on the road."

***

South of Fort Worth, Texas

Today was Friday. Victoria had arrived at Texas' ranch early Wednesday morning, two days before. The better part of the first day she had spent conversing with Lucas in Spanish. Whether she had learned the language through classes, or it was a God-given gift, she was unprepared to discuss the phenomenon with Texas.

With growing admiration for Lucas, Victoria could not recall ever meeting a boy so young with such a level head on his shoulders. He had to be one of God's exceptional creations.

Texas had stayed busy catching up on the ranch chores most of Wednesday and all of Thursday. Cloistered in his home office, he had taken care of CPA business and arranged the details for their Rome trip. Thursday evening, he skipped supper and went straight to bed. Feeling a little neglected, Victoria had retreated into the guest bedroom and used the extra time to record in her diary, read Bible scriptures, and pray for the trip ahead of them.

On Friday, at breakfast, Texas apologized for being so busy. He found the time after lunch to teach her how to ride a horse while showing off his six-hundred-acre ranch. They had laughed and cried and shared until she felt she knew him inside and out.

Both views were beautiful.

When dusk fell, as promised, Texas lowered the AC in the den to sixty-five and set a glowing fire in the hearth. Lucas had supper in his bedroom opting to watch a CPA-approved 1960s flick. And Alice, who ran the affairs of the house, prepared a scrumptious meal of roast beef, scalloped cheesy potatoes, and a Caesar salad before leaving for the day. They were totally alone.

When Victoria walked into the den she discovered a large tray of food on the massive coffee table, hand-carved from a cross-section of California Redwood. Texas soon joined her, freshly shaved and smelling clean like soap. They briefly embraced.

In deep thought, Texas sat on the sofa next to her holding a glass of cold tea in one hand and staring into the flames leaping wildly from the hearth. She was content to watch the last rays of light sift through the windowpane as the sun dwindled away on the horizon. The evening couldn't have been more perfect.

"Texas?" she uttered. "Are we going to eat anytime soon? I'm starved." All she had for lunch was a tossed salad.

"I don't know," he replied with a smile, peering deeply into Victoria's spacious eyes. "I kind of like sitting quietly here with you and watching the sun go down." She had no argument.

Texas sat his tea glass on the table and wrapped a warm arm about Victoria's shoulder. "Having you here feels so right."

Victoria smiled. "I confess I haven't felt so safe in a long while. I really like your house. And Lucas. We speak the same language. You wonder where I learned to speak Spanish."

"Yeah, I guess I do. You continue to amaze me with your talents. Just when I think I know you, you go changing on me."

Victoria frowned. Mark had said the same thing about her.

"The atmosphere here at the ranch is great." She embarked on another subject. "It's so beautiful and peaceful. Does the sun perform like this every evening?" She lent him her eyes.

"When it isn't cloudy," Texas answered. "But out here in the open, even storms are nice. Lightning puts on quite a show."

"Lucas said you rescued him from the streets of Los Angeles," Victoria said. "How did that happen?"

"Seven months ago I was in California—at a night revival meeting on the beach. We were ministering to the street people, praying over them to be delivered from demonic influences." He thought back to that moonless night in December, cold and blustery, ocean waves loudly slapping the shoreline.

"I first saw Lucas running along the beach," Texas revealed. "The kid was barefoot, kicking up the sand, running back and forth flying his box kite. Imagine! In the cold of December."

"At night?" Victoria interrupted.

"Street people love the night. They sleep during the day to avoid being picked up by the police and taken to an institution." He turned turbulent eyes on her. "America has changed."

"According to my daughter, Karen, there are few homeless and elderly—because of voluntary cessation." Victoria grieved over the loss of her father. "I want to phone my mother."

Texas handed her his cellphone. "Have at it."

"Thank you for understanding." Victoria made eye contact. "You never question my actions, though sometimes off the wall."

She flipped open the cellphone and punched in the number.

"It's after six in GloryVale, so you're legal," Texas said. "Tell Kimberly Ann we're fine and miss her, but don't reveal where we are—in case this line is not secure. We have to be careful."

Victoria nodded as the number in Canada rang.

"Mother? It's Victoria," she said. "How are you?"

Texas listened to the one-sided conversation and saw the delight spread over Victoria's beautiful face. Kimberly was doing fine and loved her new location. She missed them, but they were not to worry because Mim and Tom were taking good care of her.

Victoria said she would call again soon. No, she hadn't heard a word how Karen was doing. No, she wasn't going back.

"I have to go now, Mother. I'll call soon," Victoria said and hung up. "Mother said tell you hello and to make me behave."

Texas laughed. "I gather Kimberly is doing great."

"Better than great." Tears formed and dripped down both cheeks. "She is so adaptable. I'm proud of her."

"Me, too." Texas removed two white linen napkins from the tray, unfolded one and placed it over Victoria's lap. "It will all work out, honey, I promise. Shall we pray over our food?"

Every time Texas said "honey," Victoria melted inside. Seeing him bow his head, she followed suit.

His prayer of thanksgiving was so moving Victoria opened her eyes to watch. When he finished, he lifted his head and looked deeply into her soul, evoking powerful emotions.

"Texas, that was beautiful," she said.

"Thank you."

Victoria picked up her fork and bit into the roast beef.

"Remind me to tell Alice that she's the best cook in the world," Victoria said. Texas promised that he would.

28

Fernwood, Tennessee

Friday night rolled around like clockwork. It was pitch-dark outdoors with not a sliver of moon showing, a great night for sneaky folks to move around town without being noticed.

Georgie Hendricks departed Sarah Boswell's house around 10:20 p.m. needing to stop and gas up her motorcycle before reporting to work at Branson Meatpacking Company.

Whizzing past houses, she thought about her conversation with Sarah and Tanya Mason. The details they shared regarding Jeffrey Tempest's environmental lawsuit against Hearty Meats had effectively painted a picture of why Dick Branson was motivated to erase all opposition. Although he wasn't on the scene at the time, his company had been so anxious to open the doors for business in 1984 they had by-passed governmental requirements.

Why? Georgie pondered the critical question.

Thinking like a private eye, she believed Hearty Meats, Inc. was involved in an illegal activity so lucrative the risk had been worth taking. In her mind, that involved drugs.

And *now* PI Georgie was about to uncover their dirty secret.

In 1983, when the company leased the land, management had not anticipated a problem. How could they know that the tannery had buried the barrels of toxic transformer oil years before?

Before 1969, government guidelines were non-exist regarding the proper disposal of dangerous materials. The environmental mishap had occurred while a work crew cleared the land for

Hearty Meat's buildings to go up. The employees involved were only following instructions when they relocated the barrels to the back of the property. After being exposed to toxins, some of the crew began to suffer health consequences. A few complained.

The only way for the company to protect their business interests was to cover up what happened and compensate the sick young men, hope the problem wouldn't reach the ears of federal watchdogs, especially the Environmental Protection Agency.

But the parents of three deceased boys weren't about to let the company off the hook. They secretly approached Attorney Jeffrey Tempest and asked him to file a complaint against Hearty Meats, Inc. for gross environmental negligence. Time passed.

Then came the night of the break-in at Jeffrey's office.

So did Dick's plan involve only stealing pertinent files? Or had Jeffrey's death been ordered from the beginning?

Twenty-five years went by and nobody protested what happened in 1984? Was that because all the members of that work crew were dead? Or was it because their families had been paid big bucks to leave town and keep their mouths shut?

All of the above applied.

Georgie yawned. If she had it her way, Dick Branson would not get away with the environmental cover-up or his part in Jeffrey Tempest's death. If he peddled drugs by packing them in his meats, he would go to jail on both accounts.

Was it fate she had gone to Sarah's house?

Georgie thought so. Tanya Mason and Sarah Boswell had part of the missing puzzle pieces she was searching for.

As for Tanya, she'd been abrupt on the start but had proven most helpful. Polishing off her fourth cup of coffee when Georgie left the house, Tanya was high on camaraderie, sharing memories with Sarah over a big bowl of salty popcorn. In time, maybe they'd come to see the need to testify on Victoria's behalf.

Where are you, Victoria? There are developments in the investigation you need to hear about.

Georgie eased the Harley into a quick-stop gas station and climbed down. After feeding the engine its required diet of gasoline, she ventured inside and paid her gas tab in cash. Before leaving she purchased a Coke and candy bar for energy.

Outside, she placed a call to Devin Baldwin's cell number.

"Yeah?" the attorney was quick on the draw.

"This is your gal." Georgie didn't say her name.

"Oh, hi, so glad you called!" Devin sounded funny. "I'm so sorry I didn't get back to you sooner. A stranger showed here asking a lot of questions about your friend—you know, the gal who died in that apartment explosion."

Devin was under some kind of duress. "So?"

"So my visitor didn't believe your friend was dead. He had some wild theory she was out on the streets, so he sent someone over to talk to the lady who lives across the hall."

Aunt Ginny! I knew she couldn't keep her mouth shut.

"About your first cousin—she stopped by asking for you."

"Yeah?" Georgie had no cousins. "She doin' all right?"

"As well as possible under the circumstances."

Who was the stranger looking for her?

"That's about it," said Devin. "Don't bother with coming by my house again. Your cat died."

My cat? So the plot thickens.

***

En Route to Rome

The massive Delta Boeing 747 headed for Rome was filled to capacity. Dick Branson had purchased four reclining seats in First Class, positioned directly in front of the big screen TV. Each seat had cost an extra ten thousand bucks, but Dick wasn't concerned over spending the money. In another few days he would be expanding his business to encompass the Mid-East.

Governments had interfered with politics in Iraq and paid mercenaries to kill off the unsavory rebels who opposed UN policies and rejected democratic principles. In return, the thugs had gained permission to harvest opium. What Dick was doing wasn't any worse. He was just adding a new product to the line—cocaine. Whatever it took, Peter Coates would work a deal.

Mark was seated beside Dick, satisfied that he had made the right decision in going to Rome. Hopefully, it would be good for Karen, too. She needed to get away from Fernwood and familiar surroundings, quit grieving over her mother's absence. To compensate, Karen had focused her affections on him. Her hormones were raging, and he wouldn't be her cuddly teddy bear.

Karen noted that Mark was in his own private world, perfectly fine with her. He probably thought she was sleeping because her eyes were closed. Though her stomach felt queasy, she was not going to complain and cause him concern.

The team of Delta flight attendants running the air show seemed efficient and polite. Soon after the plane had taken off, a steamy meal rolled out from nowhere. Everyone seemed ready to eat, eager beavers washing their hands with square wet white napkins in anticipation of dining. Mark read a business magazine while waiting to be served. The food smelled sumptuous.

Seated next to the aisle, Karen gratefully received her tray and tore into a generous portion of plump pink prime rib. Gratefully, Marjorie was on the other side of Dick. But after dinner, all that changed. At Dick's insistence, Karen switched places so she could visit with Marjorie, a dumb idea. Sandwiched between fat Dick and his loquacious wife, Karen had everything to lose. *Oh brother.*

Meanwhile, Marjorie was uncommunicative, happily curled up in her reclining seat and taking a nap while Karen viewed a CNN news clip on the big screen. It was a rerun of an interview with Alexander Luceres Ramnes, the author of Peace First.

Poised like a bronzed god before the reporters, the world leader was dressed to kill in a gray Italian suit, white shirt, and a black tie that featured miniature redbirds. *Why not doves?*

Microphones hung on every prophetic word out of Luceres' mouth. He was enjoying the attention, and Karen couldn't help but recall her mother's comment regarding the young politician:

Satan will indwell the Antichrist and rule the world. Many will be deceived and lose heart. But Jesus Christ will come back for His Bride, His church.

This is crazy! Why was her mother's voice playing in her head? Karen wasn't a religious person anymore. For all she cared, the entire world could go to a Christian hell as long as she and Mark carved out a safe place for loving. *Selfish?* You bet.

Her mother's ideas were antiquated and had little bearing on the golden present. Because of her memory problem, she had forgotten that PEACE FIRST bridged the gap between old world religions. Interfaithism had paved the way for greater tolerance.

A close-up camera shot captured Luceres' unusual eyes, the slate color of a lizard's, but nevertheless beautiful and striking.

"So, dear, what do you think of that man?" Marjorie's milky-green gaze came to rest on Karen.

"Huh?" How long had Marjorie been staring at her?

"Well . . ." Marjorie had an opinion. "I think Luceres is a dreamboat. With his clout, some girl will be lucky to hook him."

"Clout?" Karen reacted. Yeah, she supposed he would wield a powerful influence in the world's political arena. Maybe she should talk to the world leader about her mother's situation.

***

Back at the Ranch

The food that Alice had prepared was delicious and Victoria had heartily partaken. The chef would have to teach her a few tricks regarding the Mexican seasoning she had used.

Brushing the breadcrumbs from her hands, Victoria said to Texas: "Dinner was great!" She came to her feet and stretched her lithe body. "I couldn't hold another bite of anything."

"Wait, Alice has a frozen dessert in the freezer. Her feelings would be hurt if you didn't at least taste it." Texas rushed off to the kitchen and came back with chocolate parfait loaded with sticky pecans, most appealing and difficult to turn down.

"Maybe we could just sit and talk for a while, let what we've eaten settle a bit," Victoria suggested.

"No problem." Texas set the desserts on the coffee table. "I'll get our coffee. Two creams and a sugar?"

"Yes." Victoria smiled.

Texas retraced his steps into the kitchen.

"Can I help?" Victoria called out to him. "I'm pretty good with cleaning up." With all the pampering she would grow lazy.

"No." Texas appeared in the doorway, a dry towel in his hands. "Why don't we sit on the patio and talk for a while?"

"Sure." Victoria came to her feet, walked a few paces, pushed open the double patio doors, and stepped outside.

The sun had withered on the flat horizon. A pleasant odor of honeysuckle mingled with mint from Alice's herb garden sifted into her nostrils. The humid air had pleasantly cooled down from a warm eighty-five degrees into the seventies.

A breeze swept across the patio stirring the metal chimes. Inhaling Stetson cologne and strong coffee, Victoria became aware that Texas was standing behind her and smiled.

"Cream and two sugars, doctored to suit," he said, stepping to Victoria's side. "Starbucks. I hope you like it."

"Great! I love any kind of coffee. She took a sip of the hot liquid. "So smooth, and you do have a talent in making it."

The admiration for her in his eyes was genuine.

"I swear," Texas chuckled, "if you didn't just describe yourself." He made a deep throaty sound, both sexy and teasing.

Victoria smacked him hard on the stomach. "Watch it!"

"Ouch." He spilt a little of his coffee on the stone patio.

"Mind your manners, Texan. You're with a lady." She tossed him a sobering look, using a napkin to wipe up the liquid.

"And I might add, a lady with a strong right arm. Have you ever considered boxing?" He stepped back to protect himself.

"You've made your point. Sorry for the roughhousing gesture." She gazed into the sky. "Isn't the evening magnificent?"

"I don't need a star show to delight me, I have you." He reached out and grasped her empty hand. "I have an idea." The love in his eyes peeled away the mask over Victoria's heart.

"What? Dare I ask?" Her pulse leaped at his nearness.

"Marry me."

"What?" Had she heard correctly?

Victoria's mind went into a tailspin. Suddenly dizzy, a flash of something silver crossed the periphery of her gray matter. Weak in the knees, her memory sharpened on an image of her son, Paul. He was a mature man standing on the portals of her mind calling out to her. This was not a childhood memory.

"Are you ill?" Texas asked, concerned.

"What?" Victoria became aware that Texas had steadied her so she wouldn't fall. "I—" words escaped her mind.

"What is it, Victoria? Is something the matter?"

"I can't—" Victoria's words were lost in a black fog as she plunged forward and hit the brick patio floor with a thud. Somewhere in the distance she heard her named being called but couldn't answer. It was her son Paul, telling her that Mark was responsible for his father's death. "No. . . ." she was screaming.

29

Georgie reported to work at Branson Meatpacking Company Friday evening for the third night in a row. Working hard to impress her hardworking supervisor, Jerry Loafer, she took her breaks seriously and listened in on every whispered conversation.

Unfortunately, Georgie had not heard one bit of gossip suggesting that anything illegal had happened under Dick's sanitary roof. It appeared Sarah was right. Catching Dick Branson at mischief was going to be a monumental challenge.

Tanya Mason had expressed regret over refusing to testify in Victoria's behalf, claiming that the stakes were just too high. Georgie thought she understood their point of view. Fear was a factor. But with a personal vendetta to settle, quitting was no option. All her life she'd taken chances. The risks of dying young came every day. You might drop dead from a stroke or heart attack at any moment. Living with the threat of death was around every corner whether people liked it or not. It just was.

When two a.m. rolled around, Georgie took a much-needed break. Instead of going into the Relief Room, as it was called, she went outside into the parking lot to smoke a cigarette.

"We ain't got enough packers to get the job done 'fore daybreak," complained a man with a sour expression.

"Yeah. We're a couple men short tonight. The merchandise has to go out on the morning truck or it won't make it to the port in time," his partner said, lingering in the shadows, flicking ash.

Georgie's pulse leaped as she realized they were talking about packing drugs. Was this the time to intervene?

"Pardon me," she said, "but I couldn't help overhearing you needed another packer tonight." She leaped into the conversation with no forethought of danger. "I'm on the assembly line in Building Two, but we got enough workers. Don't mind switching jobs if it'll help you guys out." Jaycee Moore made a firm offer.

"What'd ya think?" Al peered at Glen. "We can clear the change through Jeannie in the morning. Boss won't know."

"Whatever you say. Ain't my neck on the line." Glen shrugged his big shoulders. "We gotta do what we gotta do."

Georgie was more positive than ever the men were doing something illegal by the way they were talking.

"What's yo'r name, fella?"

"Jaycee Moore," Georgie replied. "Just a sec. Let me tell my supervisor I'm leaving. Where can I meet you?"

"We'll wait on ya, jest hurry," Al said.

Jerry Loafer had already left Building Two, and Mary Jo wasn't sure he would approve of Jaycee's skipping out, but she said to go on anyhow, that she would explain it to him later.

"Make sure you're on time tomorrow night if you wanna keep this job," Mary Jo warned Georgie as she exited the side door.

Al had waited for Jaycee like he promised, lingering in the shadows. The man named Glen wasn't there. Together, they walked around the back of the main warehouse and entered Building C through a coded door that required Al's access card.

At the end of the passageway was another door, which Al opened with a key. They walked down a flight of stairs and Al used his card again to get them into a large basement room where half a dozen men were hand-wrapping some prime-rib steaks.

Georgie glanced around the room, trying to get a feel of the situation. The fluorescent lighting was adequate, but not bright like in other parts of the plant. The packers didn't look like other employees, more like thugs. They talked, joked, and cursed profusely. Nobody noticed Georgie until Al commented.

"This is Jaycee Moore," Al said. "Treat 'im right."

"Jaycee?" the guy with a scar on his right cheek addressed Georgie. "Is that two letters or all one word?"

The men guffawed.

"One word. J A Y C E E," Georgie spelled the name.

"Hey, you look like a clean-cut fella. You sure you wanna do this thing?" The speaker's eyes were dark and hard.

"Yes, I need the work," Georgie replied.

"Al, has Jaycee been cleared?" Hardeyes glared at his boss.

"Why don't you shut up, Tony, and git to work. What I say goes down here. The boss is outta town, and we got a job to do. Jaycee is an extra hand, so let's get to it!"

"Over there." Al pointed to a table.

Georgie joined a man called Hank. She watched him pick up two large steaks from a metal tray and insert a flat plastic package filled with a dusty white powder slap-dab between them.

Cocaine? Georgie was sure of it. *Now what?*

"Top of the shelf," said Hank, licking his finger from a slashed package lying on the sidebar. "The best Columbia has to offer. The boss don't care if we sample the stuff, now and then."

Al cursed. "Did you go and drop a package on purpose, Hank? I swear, Branson will have your tail if he finds out."

"Whoopee!" Georgie acted like she was a user, and stuck in her finger. "I hope you saved some out for me." Swiping her pants leg to remove the white power, she placed her finger to her tongue and pretended to taste it, yelping crazily afterwards.

"So whut, Al. We accidentally bust a few bags now and then." Hank laughed. "Goes with the territory." He touched his tongue to the fine powder. "This drug's gotta real punch."

Hank's eyes glazed over, shoulders slumping as he relaxed and enjoyed the impact of the drug. "Yeah. Nice and smooth."

Al picked up the cocaine package and put it in his pocket. "Git back to work men! I want the job finished on time."

Everyone centered on the work at hand, Al keeping his eye on the wall clock to make sure his team met the packing quota.

Georgie learned that the batch of meat was headed to Canada to a warehouse owned by a Mafia lord from Colombia. There, it would be distributed for street use. To her disadvantage, she had trouble staying focused, wanting to grab the cocaine out of Al's pocket and split. But that would be a huge mistake. What she had seen tonight would be her word against the other packers.

Besides, one wrong move, one error could put Jaycee Moore six feet under. Nobody would come looking for him.

Time went by. Shortly before dawn, Georgie offered to help out Monday night if she was needed. If her scheme worked, afterwards, she would not be returning to Branson. So far, the undercover sting had gone more smoothly than she ever dreamed.

"Al? Need to take a leak." Jaycee hollered across the room. "Where's the restroom?"

"Take five. Out that door." Al pointed.

Georgie stepped into the shadows of the hallway. Removing a small camera from her pocket, she began randomly snapping the packing process going on in the room. With names to match faces, she should be able to convince the Federal Bureau of Investigation to open a formal investigation into the matter.

Of course, PI Georgie would include the lab results of the soil samples taken from the sludge she found on Branson's property showing dangerous levels of contamination. The pack of the cocaine stuffed inside her pocket was solid evidence that Dick was peddling drugs. And she had photos to prove it.

Georgie's plan was ironclad. No fault, like the spray in her crisp Branson shirt. All she had to do was get through another hour. Once she clocked out, goodbye and good riddance to Dick.

***

Fort Worth Hospital

Victoria woke up Friday evening, thirty minutes short of midnight. Her head thrumming like a druid was inside playing a discordant tune on a base tuba. Images of her son, Paul, flashed through her mind like slivers of lightning, bits and pieces of conversations she was certain were memories. Prepared or not, lost memories were starting to emerge.

"Ruth? Can you hear me?" Victoria shook her head no.

"My name is Dr. Ian Denouski. You are in the hospital, at Fort Worth General Hospital. This is the ER."

Victoria strained to focus her vision. The doctor's face appeared ghostly white in the bright overhead lights. His eyes were blue, the folds of flesh beneath them steeped in shadows.

"You fainted a few hours ago and your friend brought you to the hospital. We've all been pretty worried."

Victoria nodded, barely moving her lips. Words formed in her mind, but she could not speak. Out of the corner of her eye, she caught sight of Texas, who was shaking his head. She blinked her eyes twice, to signify that she understood.

"Ruth just needs rest," Texas told Dr. Denouski. The fear tucked away in his expression alarmed Victoria.

My name is Ruth Matthews, Victoria reminded herself. *My hair isn't red anymore. I need to get it cut.* She felt for her body, naked and cold, to see if she were truly awake. The fine line between reality and fiction, life and departure, grew fuzzier by the moment.

Is this death, Lord?

The doctor spoke up.

"I've ordered an MRI. It should show if there is an obstruction that caused Ruth to faint," he said to Texas. "Let's not assume the worst until we know the facts."

The worst? Victoria was grateful the doctor was at least thinking positive. Her condition was probably a case of the jitters. *Everything will be fine,* she told herself, praying for God to help.

"Are tests necessary, Doc?" Texas asked, hoping to remove Victoria from public view as soon as possible. If the media got wind of a patient with amnesia, the worst might actually happen.

"I think it is," Dr. Denouski replied. "Ruth's pupils are dilated—which may indicate that she has pressure behind them."

I have a brain tumor? Victoria leaped to a chilling conclusion, awake enough to process what was being said about her and feel the throbbing pain in her skull. Mark had tried to convince her to check into the hospital for tests and she had refused. He believed basically the same thing, that something was wrong with her brain.

Victoria had meant to see a doctor about her weird flip-flopped amnesia, had even allowed Mark to schedule hospital tests for the following Wednesday. Then Tuesday April 29 happened. Next thing she knew, Jon Branson was rolling her out of Hardeman General on a gurney and into a chaotic life of running.

One thing for certain: she had to leave the Fort Worth hospital *now*, before the police came calling. Her mug shot was plastered all over everywhere, and she had no murder defense.

"Miss? Don't try to get up, please!" A nurse restrained Victoria's arm. "You have to lie still. We'll give you a sedative to help you relax if you are in pain. Then you'll be taken down to X-ray. Don't worry, you're going to be fine."

Gee, everyone keeps saying that like they believe it.

As much as Victoria wanted to resist treatment, she could not. "No" lodged in her dry throat blocking her breathing. A sharp silver needle gleamed in the light, headed for her right arm.

A minute later, it didn't matter.

Time passed like it didn't exist. When Victoria awakened it was morning. The sunlight filtered through the blinds into the hospital room, brightening the colors of the walls and lifting her spirit. She was alive. Or was she? *God, is this Heaven?*

Then she noticed Texas patiently standing by her bed.

"Hello, sweetheart, welcome back. How do you feel?" The pressure of his cold hand felt good on her forehead.

Victoria nodded and blinked her eyes.

Texas looked a little ragged, tired around the eyes. Probably he'd been up all night guarding her like a watchdog.

"I've had better days," Victoria found that she could speak, her tongue no longer Super Glued to the roof of her mouth.

"Did the doctor find out what was wrong with me?" She pulled the sheet tightly to her throat, feeling chilled in the cold room, "I'm thirsty. Is there a glass of water somewhere?"

"Sure." Texas grabbed a glass from the portable stand and filled it with ice water from the decanter. "Here. Drink this."

The glass felt cold to Victoria's parched lips. She drank like a camel about to go across the desert. Or had she already crossed one and forgotten? This morning, her mind felt quite fuzzy.

"It appears you have some scar tissue that has accumulated in an old wound," explained Texas.

"On my brain?" Victoria reacted, struggling to sit up in the bed. She failed and plopped down on her soft downy pillow.

Texas crossed his arms over his chest and peered down at Victoria. "Don't try to get up before you feel steady." He shifted his weight from one foot to the other.

"About the scar tissue, will they do surgery?" she asked, afraid the police would get wind of the procedure and investigate. "Did you tell the doctor I had amnesia?"

Texas shook his head no. "The less we say about you, the better. We should get you released from the hospital as soon as possible." He squeezed her hand. "A CPA doctor can take over from here and do whatever is necessary. Surgery might be the only answer." He could tell the idea chilled Victoria to the bone.

"Not before I go to Rome and see Daniel," she passionately declared. "Please, Texas." She propped herself up on one elbow.

"You're a stubborn woman."

"I know," she gave him that.

"I'll do the best I can to make Rome happen for you, but no more fainting spells allowed, you hear?" A smile materialized on his rugged unshaved face. "Can't lose you now that I found you."

Victoria understood. Life kept changing on her, too.

SATURDAY, JUNE 14

30

The feisty Fernwood foursome en route to Rome arrived in New York at 12:02 a.m. Eastern Standard Time for a brief layover. When the jet taxied to the Delta gate and the seatbelt light was turned off, Karen freed herself from the restraints.

Stowed in the overhead bin was her Liz bag, stuffed with a computer laptop, compact makeup case, and a change of clothes should the airline misplace her luggage. She reached up.

"Can I help?" Mark looked at Karen.

"Get my bag for me, will you? Up there, in the bin."

Karen stood up the best she could and waited for her chance to push into the aisle. Mark opened the overhead bin and pulled out the Liz bag. She repressed the urge to retrieve her computer and check her e-mail messages to see if she had new business.

Later. She'd only been away a few hours. *Let the agency handle it*, she argued with sudden impulses. An impertinent kid wanting off the plane gave her a nudge. *Hey buster*, Karen pushed back, grabbed her Liz bag from Mark and moved forward in the aisle.

Behind Mark, Dick stumbled into the aisle, so obese one had to question how he boarded the plane in the first place.

"You ready, baby?" The business guru grabbed Marjorie's arm and shoved her into the aisle in front of him, plugging the way so nobody else could pass. Seconds later, his cellphone rang.

"Yeah?" Dick gruffly answered the call.

Karen glanced back at Dick as he hastily retrieved the phone from his coat pocket, wondering who was calling him so late at night. "You coming?" Mark nudged her forward.

"What's this about? I told you not to call me unless it was important." His phone had been on during the flight against Delta policy. *Rules were meant to be broken, weren't they?*

Dick listened to Jerry Loafer's request. His night foreman wanted approval to officially hire a young man who had been living on the streets and badly needed a job. They were shorthanded with packers because several people were out sick with viruses. Jaycee Moore was working out just fine.

Anyhow, Dick didn't want to deal with hiring procedures now. He had fun to do. *Rome is waiting.*

"Fine, by me," he gave his approval, wanting to get on with his vacation. If the guy turned out to be a dud, he'd fire him later.

"Anything else?" Dick listened. "Good. Bye."

He slapped the phone shut and wiggled out the narrow door of the plane. Marjorie was waiting for him up ahead.

"Comin', sweet pea!" he hollered. "Wait on big daddy." Dick tunneled into the main terminal like a squirrel after nuts.

***

Fort Worth, Texas

The hospital wasn't so bad, Victoria decided. It had been a very long night, not that she remembered much.

"So did you convince the doctor to let me go?" she asked Texas, pulling on a robe as she stood up. Her fainting spell had occurred twelve hours before, the symptoms now gone.

"Do you think it's a good idea to get out of bed?" Texas assessed Victoria's condition. The whites of her eyes were bloodshot and she appeared unsteady. "Maybe you should wait for the doctor to give his approval. I don't want you to fall."

"Texas? I remembered something important last night." Victoria perched on the edge of the bed, feeling queasy because she hadn't eaten. It was nothing that breakfast wouldn't cure.

He swung his head in her direction. "About your accident?"

"No. About my son, Paul." She shivered at saying his name.

"I don't understand. I thought you had lost all memory of events in your life since your accident." Texas walked over and closed the hospital door. "After Dr. Denouski signs your release form, a nurse will take you downstairs in a wheelchair."

"I can walk," Victoria said.

"Hospital policy," Texas noted. "I brought you to the hospital in my old work truck. Looking poor and ignorant is a clever cover-up—like insisting on taking you out of the hospital against the doctor's advice. No easy feat, mind you."

"Oh," said Victoria, distracted as she viewed her hair in a compact mirror. "I look terrible. Did you bring a brush?"

"You look wonderful to me," said Texas.

"Really? You have a way with words, as I've said before." She knew how bad she looked. "Just get me out of here and I'll be forever grateful—cook for you, wait on you."

Most anything you want, she thought.

"I'd just settle for an explanation—about what happened yesterday. I know what the doctor thinks. What's your take?"

"Can we talk about this later?" Victoria asked. "Will you help me remember to thank Alice for the nice meal last night?" His housekeeper would not be retuning to the ranch until Monday. "Never mind, I'll tell her myself tomorrow."

"That won't be possible." Texas gazed at Victoria. "We'll be in Tennessee on Monday, and on our way to Rome before we see sunset on Tuesday. Do you think you're up to flying?"

"I'm up to *anything* that will get me to Rome to see Daniel. Now that I remember Paul, I have a lot of questions I want to ask my other son." She trembled, glimpsing Texas through teary eyes.

"I'm getting my memories back," she admitted. A door of fear opened. "I'll explain later, when we're in the air."

The nurse hit the door with a hand and rolled in the wheelchair. "Miss Ruth Matthews?"

"Yes," Victoria answered. "You're free to leave the hospital. Dr. Denouski is sending you off with a copy of your MRI and a sharp warning not to wait too long about having surgery."

Not asking why, Victoria imagined there was danger in delay. "Is my condition critical?" *Please, God, not now!*

"I'm not at liberty to discuss your condition, Miss Matthews." The nurse scooted the wheelchair close to Victoria and invited her to step aboard. "I'm sure you'll be just fine."

Great bedside manner, thought Victoria, eyeing Texas. The threat of an aneurysm or stroke posed potentially devastating consequences, if death did not first occur. She could be paralyzed for the rest of her life with no way to communicate her love.

Her worst nightmare could still lie before her.

***

Jon Branson was at the Hardeman County General Hospital around 8 a.m. Saturday morning to visit his mother. Marilyn Branson had been there a couple of days, free gratis of The Cancer Society. In a last ditch effort to extend her life, the doctors had ordered blood transfusions. Jon was reading a sheet put out by Hospice when she opened her eyes and noticed him.

"Hey, son." She weakly smiled. "Thanks for coming."

"Mom. You gave us all a scare. How are you feeling?"

"Not the best—but I'll live.

"Why didn't you tell me how sick you were?" he asked, feeling guilty. "I could have come over sooner."

Jon peered into her sleepy eyes, the fruity color of lime, and realized she had genetically gifted those orbs to him.

"Don't digress on the negatives, dear." Marilyn patted her son's hand, adjusting her frail body in the bed to achieve more comfort under the sheets. Her eyes were gaunt with dark circles underneath. The cancer tenaciously hung on despite her prayers.

Jon couldn't help but grin. "You never were a pity-party maker, were you, Mama? I know it must have been hard on you when Daddy left you for another woman." He'd never spoken so frankly before. The curl on her thin lips said he'd gotten his facts wrong. "What? Is there something I'm missing here?"

"I'd expect your father to tell you his version. Dick's got an overdose of pride. The truth is, I dumped him, Jon. Not for another man, but for Jesus Christ. I became a Christian soon after we married. Richard didn't like the change in me at all. He didn't want me keeping a Bible in the house or going to church."

"I never knew," said Jon. "I guess I never asked either of you enough questions. The prodigal son, you know. I still have things I want to say to both of you." He had many regrets.

"What things?" Marilyn asked, feeling some better from the transfusions and the drugs. "Ask away."

"A couple years ago, when Paul Tempest died, I began to do some soul searching," he said. "I didn't like what I saw. In a rash moment, I returned to the site where Victoria Tempest's accident occurred—to get something I had stolen and buried."

"I don't understand," said Marilyn. "What was it, son?" She retrieved a glass of ice water from the bed stand and drank all of it. "I'm so thirsty. It must be the strong medication."

"The doctor says you're doing great." Jon patted his mother's hand. "I pray you'll recover from this disease." He had faith Jesus could do it, just didn't know if He would.

"Anyhow, to continue my story. The stormy night Victoria crashed her car out on Highway 64, I was there on my motorcycle. I witnessed her Mazda tumbling over an embankment. I was the one who dialed 911, Mama. And I never told anyone but Dad."

"Ha! I would expect your father to tell you to keep your mouth shut and not get involved."

Jon smiled. "That's exactly what he said to me."

What did you do after you dialed 911?" asked Marilyn. "Did you go back to the wreckage and try to help Victoria?"

"When I saw her bloody head pressed against the screaming horn, I knew I couldn't help," Jon recalled. "But I did something terrible, Mama. I stole Victoria's Bible while she lay there dying."

Guilt had a back slap that took the grace of God to salve.

"You did what?" Marilyn said in disbelief. "Why?"

"The holy book—it was lying on the front seat of the car. Untouched, like it hadn't ridden down the ravine in the same spot. I thought it was some kind of miracle, special, so I broke out the window on the passenger's side and stole it."

Marilyn gasped. "What did you do with the Bible?"

"Took it home with me, kept it."

"I bet your father didn't approve," she said, winching from pain as she rolled over in the bed. "Or did you tell him?"

"About the Bible, no. But I did tell him about witnessing the awful crash and anonymously reporting the accident. He said in no uncertain terms that I was not to become involved with the accident. I should never tell anyone what happened. *Ever.*"

"And you were scared, weren't you?"

"I was, Mama. I didn't know what to do, so later that evening I returned to the crash site and buried Victoria's Bible in the woods." The nightmarish scene replayed in Jon's mind like it had a life of its own. His mother glared, making no judgments.

"And then what?"

"And. . . .I'm so sorry." Jon's eyes filled with tears.

"Shouldn't you tell Victoria that?" Marilyn always had the right response. "Confession is good for the soul."

"I have, Mama, and she's forgiven me."

"And you told God, too," Marilyn made certain.

"Yes, but there's more to my story." Jon clasped his hands together between his knees as he collapsed in a padded plastic chair beside his mother's bed. "Following Paul Tempest's death I was troubled over the way he died. Paul wasn't gay, yet he was found overdosed in a gay bar. He smoked marijuana sometimes, but he didn't do hard drugs." Jon gazed at his sick mother.

Marilyn's eyes widened as she punched her pillow and sat up. "Go on, Jon, I'm listening."

"I went back to the crash site and dug up Victoria's Bible. I read the New Testament, Mama," Jon revealed. "The prophetic words made me realize I was living in sin, so I accepted Jesus Christ as my personal Savior. And it—" he couldn't go on.

"And it changed your life." Tears wet Marilyn's pale cheeks. "I suspected something like that had happened but I didn't ask. It could have been that you had new priorities after Paul died."

"I wanted you to know, Mama, because I love you very much. Thank you for praying for me all these years. I'm living with a group of Christians now who can't function normally in society anymore. Fugitives like Victoria, and others who have been falsely accused of crimes. We are good friends now."

"Friends? You're telling me this now because you think I'm dying," said Marilyn, smiling. "Don't count on it." She had some perkiness left in her. "I won't give the devil an inch."

"I know miracles happen, I just haven't seen one," said Jon. "I wish I could. I hear about them all the time." Jon realized he was saying too much. "Anyhow, that's how it is with me now."

"I'm so proud of you, Jon. Does your father know about your salvation experience?" Marilyn groaned and lay back down.

"Not yet, but I plan on telling him soon. I don't want Daddy to go out of this life without hearing the truth from my lips."

His mother looked tired and old beyond her years.

"Thank you for sharing, Son." She closed her eyes.

"Get some rest and I'll be back to pick you up in the morning and take you home. Hospice wants to talk to us about home care." Jon was uncertain if she would go along with the treatment.

"Do you think it's a good idea?" asked Marilyn. "Hospice."

"I think anyone looking after you is a good idea."

"I'll think about it." Marilyn produced a radiant smile.

31

En Route to Rome

During the trip over to Italy, Karen hadn't napped well on the plane due to blinking TV lights. Although sound was conveyed through individual earphones, all the annoying snores, grunts, and shuffling about had run interference.

Mark and Dick were kicked back in their seats, out like a light. No guilt, no worries, or conscience to hinder rest. It would require months of psychotherapy for Karen to fall asleep so easily.

Ah . . . but with men, it appeared to be innate, a natural defense against predators who would steal sleep to slay corporate dragons. Karen widely yawned and peered at Marjorie, currently wrapped up in a romance novel. Well, here she was, cloistered in a plane with the elite from Fernwood, unhappy as a mole in mud.

"What's the matter?" Marjorie folded the pages and wedged the book between the armrest and her slender body.

Karen nodded, eyes red and bleary. "The flight won't be much longer." Marjorie patted Karen's hand. "I think I'll try to get some shuteye, and you should, too."

The kind gesture took Karen by surprise. Knowing she was too pumped to sleep, she closed her eyes anyhow. Flashes of Paul scrolled across her mind—not that Karen welcomed the images of her deceased brother. The memory was about a conversation they had five days before Paul met death by overdose in a gay bar.

Paul was upset the night he came over to Karen's condo, babbling about a phone conversation he'd accidentally overheard between Dr. Mark James and Dick Branson. "Doc said he was sorry about his part in daddy's death," Paul revealed.

"I'm sure you misunderstood, Paul," Karen had responded, hearing him out while thinking he was delusional. Smelling alcohol on his breath, she'd sent him home to get some rest.

Lately, she had begun to question Mark's integrity, finding herself easily upset when her father's name came up. What if Paul was right and Mark knew more about their father's death than he was saying? Her mother certainly questioned his innocence.

Not wanting to hurt Mark's feelings, or alienate him because she loved him so deeply, Karen pondered the situation. It was odd that Mark never offered a defense to any of her queries.

His silence on the subject said something, didn't it?

Mark, always clever and cunning, changed the subject, or left quickly on some urgent task he'd forgotten to do.

Didn't that confirm Mark was hiding something?

And what about his ongoing friendship with Dick Branson over the years? The wealthy meatpacker was rude and bullish, suave as a pig in a dress shirt. Mark was a physician, socially apt. Putting the two together was like mixing oil with water.

So what was she doing here on a trip with *them*? It was totally daft to camp out with her mother's enemies. What was Mark thinking? That she could ever let bygones be bygones.

Not a chance!

Going to Rome sounded like the dream vacation. Mark had convinced her it wasn't safe to stay home alone.

The question was, safe from what?

Weary of chasing thoughts, and dragged down by air travel, Karen closed her tired eyes and drifted off to sleep. Not until the Boeing 747 had touched down at Fiumicino Airport in Rome, Italy, did she awaken. "Are we here?" Her eyes flew wide open.

Gazing out the window, Karen spied the rising sun spinning a web of light on the eastern horizon. It was six hours earlier in Tennessee, Central Standard Time. The lengthy flight felt more like three grueling days of hard labor. She yawned, having slept little, worried much, and often checked her office messages.

Avoiding Marjorie like the plague, she had spent most of her waking time in the plane watching the depressing tube. There was one disturbing clip about her mother that appeared on late night news. The high-profile fugitive from Fernwood was spotted near a car dealership in Denver, Colorado. *What did that mean?*

Come to think of it, Karen recalled that Beverly James had moved away from Fernwood in April. So had her mother gone to Denver in pursuit of her friend? *If so, why?*

"Mark?" Karen nudged him. "Wake up, we've landed." Dick was snoring like an old bear hunkered in for the winter.

"Huh?" Marjorie's dreamy eyes opened. "We're here?"

Karen guessed she was the only one who had a miserable trip. Hopefully the day would get better. Just putting her feet to the ground sounded like a real winner. Jet lag was more like carrying a heavy anchor on her back, making it difficult to stay afloat.

Mark jumped up and glanced out the window at the rolling green hills glistening in the morning sunlight. "We're in Italy?" He had the expression of a child on Christmas morning.

"On the ground," said Karen. "Did you know Mother was in Denver?" She gathered her purse and magazine from the seat.

"Huh?" Mark jerked his head toward Karen. "Where did you get an idea like that? Vicki doesn't know anybody in Denver."

"From the news I saw last night, I'd say she might." Karen had a monumental headache and felt miserably tired.

"I can't think about your mother now. What time is it?" Mark glanced at his watch. "Eight-0-three Rome time."

Karen yawned. Mark appeared perky, sickeningly refreshed.

"I assume you didn't rest well." He glanced over at Karen.

"It was a long trip." He yawned, shaking out his tight shoulders.

"You assume correctly." Karen attempted to organize her stiff bones in order to walk. Like a shrimp in a can, she'd been squeezed into her seat far too many hours. "Let's deplane."

Mark reached in the overhead bin and discovered Karen's bag was missing. "Where is—"

"Right here." Karen patted her Liz bag. "Let's get out of here. I am in bad need of some fresh air and strong coffee."

"Are you still feeling sick at your stomach?"

"Sick of flying? Yes," Karen said. "Otherwise, I feel fine." It was an effort to move forward with people crowding the aisle.

Mark considered Karen's remark regarding the news. "So what did the media have to say about Vicki?" he asked, following Karen into the jam-packed aisle filled with deplaning frequent-flyers. "Are you positive they identified Vicki?"

"I'll tell you more about Mother later." Karen pushed toward the exit, stomach rumbling like a stalled train. If she didn't get some breakfast down her, she was going to puke.

"Fine." Mark sighed, despising that he cared so much.

After deplaning, they went through customs, their passports in impeccable order as expected. Dick fussed because it had taken so long, complaining it was wasting his vacation time. Marjorie, on the other hand, was surprisingly congenial and talkative.

Uninterested in anything that Marjorie had to say, Karen had nodded to keep the conversation in motion. Up ahead of them, she spied an Italian pub and pointed it out to Mark. "By chance, are you interested in a cup of coffee and muffin?"

"Sure," he replied, "I could use a little nourishment myself."

Sensing the odd couple trailing behind at a distance, Mark glanced back and spied Dick Branson tottering down the terminal toward the escalators, half dragging Marjorie by the arm. Out of respect, he paused before stepping on the rolling stairway.

"Don't wait on that creep." Karen floated down the escalator to Level 1. "Don't worry, they'll catch up with us at the hotel."

"I can't just leave them behind. Dick will be beside himself." Mark stepped on the escalator. "We should include them at breakfast, don't you think?" He hoped Karen would agree.

"Whatever." *Why argue?* The trip over was supposed to have been fun, an adventure. *It wasn't.* She walked with attitude.

Messing up the day even more, Karen recalled how Marjorie had taken every opportunity to reiterate every scandalous act in which her mother had been involved during the past five years. To top it off, Marjorie had condemned Mark's *Little Vicki* for breaking her engagement two months before the wedding.

All irritatingly true. Karen had offered no defense because there was none. Hadn't her mother pulled every trick in the book? Like, pretending to be a maid when she'd secretly returned to the condo, and in a fit of anger left her engagement ring on the stem of Mark's razor with a hurtful note. The least her mother could have done was confront Mark. All water under the bridge.

Karen beat Mark to the sidewalk restaurant. Tapping her toe—not to music—she shook her head, in a terrible mood.

"Did you take a sedative to help you sleep?" Mark asked as he caught up with Karen. "You seem . . ."

"Upset," said Karen. "I am. And tired."

"You should have taken two sedatives, knowing how nervous you get when cramped up." Mark swiped his face with his handkerchief. "Hinds sight, you know. Sorry, dear."

"It's not your fault." Karen walked into the breakfast pub and waited to be seated. A stylish girl in a long skirt and high heels that were made entirely of straps handed them a menu and walked them over to a table. "The food smells good," she noted.

"It's been a long flight. Jet lag has us in its grips."

Karen nodded, gripped by more than jet lag. The waiter rushed over and spouted off the menu selections in Italian.

"Did you understand him?" she asked.

"No, but I can point to the picture." Mark smiled.

Karen smiled back, sorry for taking her displeasure out on him. She pulled the computer *thingy* that translated language phrases from her purse. Besides Italian, the mixed culture of Rome residents spoke German, French, Slovak, and Albanian. Greek was a common language used by Sicilians and Sardinians.

Mark pointed to a picture of a frothy cup of liquid on the front of the menu. "*Si*," said the waiter. "*Latte macchiato*."

Karen pointed to the muffin. *Give a moose a muffin and . . .*

The slender male waiter hurried away and came back with their orders in record time. Karen took a sip of the European blend of strong coffee and cream, and immediately excused herself. "Be back in a second." She was going to throw up.

She ran into a stall and emptied the contents of her stomach. Jet lag. That had to be it. She wet her forehead and waited for the wave of nausea to pass before returning to the table.

"What was that all about?" Mark asked when she returned, having polished off his bran muffin and coffee.

"Sorry," she said. "Jet lag."

***

The hotel in Rome where Dick had booked rooms was fit for royalty. A bellhop in a black suit trimmed with red-and-gold braiding opened the limousine door for Karen and escorted her into the lobby, heels clicking pavement as he briskly walked.

Mark and Dick tagged along behind Karen. Marjorie was fascinatingly attached to a young handsome Italian as he filled her brain with compliments. Karen was convinced she couldn't understand a word he was saying—which didn't seem to matter.

Amused, Karen watched people coming and going while Mark registered them with the front desk. Marjorie began conversing with an American woman wearing a long mink.

Located in the heart of the city, the J. W. Marriott was a mock version of the ancient Roman coliseum. Designed by world-class architects, the building was a round structure ten stories high with a large vaulted atrium at the center.

Magnificent would be an apt description of the hotel's interior décor. Gold-and-red embossed wallpaper climbed the walls above beryl paneling. Sparkling chandeliers, swirling with tinkling glass beads, swung from the sculptured ceilings.

The floor beneath Karen's feet was constructed of gleaming-white marble. Paintings of the art masters rampaged the walls, simply there to be admired and appreciated by hotel guests.

The furniture was a mixture of Mediterranean and French. Lamplight on tables glistened through stained glass shades. Opulence ruled everywhere in the eye of the beholder—even in the toilets where attendants vied to hand out delicate sheets of toilet tissue to the guests. It was a different world from America.

"Aren't you glad you came?" Mark blew in Karen's ear, a gesture of a lover, not a friendly mentor.

"Are we sharing a room?" Karen tingled inside, wanting to be held in Mark's arms again. *In a different world, they might . . .*

"We have a suite, with a living room in between." He clearly drew the line. Karen glared, unconvinced he meant it.

"Ha! A couple of doors won't keep me away from you, Mark James." Karen was surprised at her bold invitation. "I'd consider it an honor to share your bed." She might as well say it. *Fools jump in where angels fear to tread*, as the old saying went.

"Keep talkin' like that, kid, and you'll get into a lot of trouble," Mark made light of her statement, even chuckling.

I'm already in trouble, Karen thought, *more than you know*.

They reached their destination on the fifth level before their suitcases arrived. Mark used his electronic key, opened the door, walked though the living room, and flung open the double doors to the balcony. There sat a small wrought-iron table and chairs.

"Wow!" He peered down at the bubbling fountain on the ground level. "What a great opportunity to commit suicide."

"Mark! What a terrible thought!" Karen stared into the abyss, her mother's chilling words surfacing: *Satan will rise from the Abyss and be loosed a thousand years.*

"What?" Karen realized Mark had said something.

"I asked why the troubled face? Where were you, dear? For a second I thought you were going overboard."

"Mark? Do you know much about the Antichrist?"

"All I care to know," he said. "Shall we go inside the room and have a drink?" He was uninterested in Bible prophecy.

"Mother says the Antichrist is evil like Satan. He will oppose all that is holy and rule the world. I guess I wonder—do you think Alexander Luceres Ramnes could be the Antichrist?"

"Karen!" Mark reacted. "I can't believe you just asked that!" His expression reflected displeasure. "We come all this way to praise the man because he has brought peace to the world, and you accuse him of being the devil? What are you thinking?"

Karen swallowed hard. "No, not me, my mother."

"But she isn't here," said Mark.

"She might be. You can never tell about Mother." Karen looked at the gardens below. "I think I feel her presence."

"Don't let your imagination run away with you, dear."

"Without my dreams, I would be nothing."

"Is that a quote from Shakespeare?" he asked.

"No. It's the essence of my life."

"Oh," said Mark, no further comment.

32

Karen loved their Marriott hotel suite, reminiscent of the old Hotel Peabody in Memphis, Tennessee. A cozy living room furnished with a wet bar and a corner fireplace separated her bedroom from Mark's, but fortunately, only a short walk.

Wondering what he was doing, Karen opened his bedroom door and stepped inside. "Mark?" she announced her presence, feeling preciously alone with him. "Where are you hiding?"

"Here, in the bathroom." He stepped through the opening with a wet towel wrapped around his waist.

"Oh, sorry." Karen suppressed a giggle. "Shall I come back when you're dressed?" He blushed like a teenager.

"Suit yourself." Mark traipsed into the walk-in closet and slammed the louvered doors. "Doors were made for knockin'," he loudly remarked. "You should try it sometimes."

"Don't be mad." A smile unfolded as she tested the agility of the queen-sized bed. "I just wanted to see your part of the world." Her eyes traced the beautiful sconces on the wall.

Although decorated with a masculine flair, Mark's bedroom was the exact size as hers. Embossed wallpaper in a twisted blend of tan and gold stretched up the ten-foot ceilings. The cathedral ceiling featured a stunning glass chandelier with hundreds of sparkling glass beads. Karen lay back on the satin pillows.

Mark stepped from the closet fully dressed. "I thought we might go downstairs and have a bite to eat. The trip over was long and I need more calories to keep going. Are you hungry?"

Karen sat up in the bed, canvassing Mark's trim body with her lazy hazel eyes. "You've lost weight. Did losing Mother cause that, or did you decide to diet?" *Why did she say that?*

"Karen!" Alarm flooded Mark's expression.

"Either way, you look *real* good." She came to her feet and mussed her hair. "I'll get ready. Give me a few."

She was walking out of the bedroom when she heard Mark whisper thank you. I am counting my calories."

"I'm sorry for being so . . ." she turned around.

"So *you*," Mark said. "I don't want an apology."

"Whatever." She turned and walked away.

Mark hadn't told Karen that his heart was bothering him. A little out of rhythm, the ol' ticker was acting up again. He wasn't an old man but neither was he young. And with all the stress . . .

Karen hurried across the living room, uncomfortable with the bloating in her stomach. Maybe she needed a fluid pill. She returned to her room, ran a brush through her hair, and retrieved her purse from the dresser. Mark was waiting for her.

"I'm ready. Let's go exploring," she said.

They exited the suite through the door leading into the interior hallway where the fifth-floor elevators were located.

Karen stepped aboard and viewed the open atrium below through the elevator's glass wall. People were drawn like magnets to the gigantic bubbling fountain, eyes exploring the exploding water splayed with colored lights. Children tossed in shiny coins with hopes of future dreams coming true.

Moments later the elevator doors yawned open.

"Where did all these people come from?"

"From all over, by invitation only," said Mark. "You should thank Dick for including us in his party."

They stepped off the elevator.

"Thank you, Dick," Karen sarcastically remarked. "Have you seen the pair of ducklings lately?" She glanced around the atrium.

"No, but trust me, they're around." Mark led Karen through the crowd, spying a popular Italian restaurant. "I hope lasagna sounds good," he said, the food he had at the airport long gone.

"I'm keeping my eyes open for Daniel," Karen said. "Do you think he's arrived yet? I'd like to check the front desk."

"Your brother is coming here?" Mark raised an eyebrow.

"Yes. Didn't I tell you? The Peacekeeping Taskforce is receiving recognition this week. His cell must be turned off."

"How nice." Mark gently nudged Karen through the arched entrance of the restaurant, people speaking Italian all around him. "We should have hired a translator," he remarked.

"Did you forget I have an electronic one?" Karen retrieved the computer from her Gucci purse. "It translates common phrases at the touch of a button. Progress, huh?"

"That's great. Ask your calculator to tell the maitre d' that we want a table with a view of the fountain," Mark asked as a young woman with midnight black hair approached them.

"*Buon sera*," the hostess cheerfully said.

Karen punched in the message and read the translation.

"Good evening to you, too. Do you speak English?" Karen asked. "May we have a window seat, if at all possible?"

"Sure. We'll have a table for you shortly," the maitre d' replied in perfect English. "Wait here, please."

"See, that wasn't so hard." Karen chuckled.

"About Daniel . . ." said Mark, "he probably cut off his cell for some R & R." Their table was ready. "Let's go." He held to Karen's elbow until she was seated. "What a nice view."

"Daniel knows my number, Mark. He could call me." Karen daintily unfolded a pink linen napkin and laid it across her lap. "But you're probably right. He's already here and in meetings."

Mark picked up the menu and stared at it. "What kind of meetings? How do you know that?" he curiously asked.

"*Che ne dici di una bottiglia di Chianti?*" the waiter asked, pen in hand ready to take their orders.

"*Perfetto!* A bottle of Chianti sounds nice," Karen answered.

"I'm going to have the lasagna," Mark said.

"Make that two orders, and bring fresh bread," Karen added.

The wine and two glasses were promptly delivered to the table along with a bottle of Balsam Vinaigrette containing the ingredients of *olio di vinacciolo, pepe rosa* and *peperencino e alloro,* which translated into English as virgin oil, pink peppercorn, chili pepper and bay leaves. *Presto!* A basket of fresh assorted breads arrived moments later. The odor of food was delightful.

Starved after having emptied the contents of her stomach at the airport, Karen tore off a piece of yeasty baked bread and dipped it into the balsamic Italian condiment. "Yum. Great!"

"Bring us bottled water, too," Mark ordered, impressed with the service. "Oh, and a wine list." He wanted to look it over in the event he wanted to purchase a case and ship it home.

A sommelier came over to the table to talk to Mark. Karen looked over the extensive wine list on the back of the menu and said, "Bring me a glass of *Vichon Mediterranean Syrah.*"

"Karen, we already have a whole bottle," Mark said.

"I want you to taste this particular wine," she replied.

"*Si,*" the sommelier bowed and left.

"It's a fruity blend made in France," Karen explained. "From grapes grown in the sunny Mediterranean climate of the *Languedoc* region where the hearty vines have been cultivated for over two thousand years." She wiped her lips and peered at him.

"And you know this because?" Mark said from across the round table, busily devouring the hot bread.

"I'm not stupid, Mark."

"Well, I am when it comes to wines," he admitted. "Guess I've lived in Fernwood too long. How did you get so smart?"

"Actually," she smiled, "some of the guys I work with at my office brought a bottle to the office to celebrate the closing of a sale. I couldn't read the wine list either. What's wrong with pretending, if it gets the job done?" Hazel eyes searched his.

Mark sensed a greater meaning underlying Karen's remark.

"Nothing, I suppose," he replied, thinking it was his modus operandi most all the time.

"I have to tell you I'm upset Daniel isn't responding to my calls." Karen's thoughts turned elsewhere. "What if I had an emergency?" She needed to tell her baby brother their mother was missing. For that, a face-to-face discussion was required.

"Enjoy lunch and forget about him. He'll contact you soon."
"About the secret meetings going on with the peacekeepers?" Karen peered at Mark. "Have you heard any gossip?"

"Alexander, ur, Luceres—as the mastermind prefers to be called—has been summarizing his future plans for keeping peace around the world," Mark explained. "According to CNN."

"And the news is never rosy." Karen grimaced. "I wish Mother would call and tell me what's going on. I'm afraid something terrible will happen to her in Denver."

Mark smacked his lips together in thought. "When Vicki phoned you—the day she escaped from Green Gables—was she using a cell? Or was she on a payphone?"

"I was the one who phoned her," Karen reminded Mark.

"Oh," said Mark. "When we get home I think we should have a trace put on your phone. We need to find her soon."

"But won't the police know, too?" Karen whispered.

"I'll ask Dick to help us. He knows more about surveillance than I do. The police won't have to be involved."

"Good. I want to find Mother, but I don't want her caught until she is ready to face the murder charges filed against her."

"Oh, there you are!" a familiar voice chimed from behind Karen. Whipping her head around, she saw Marjorie Branson and her frog-smiling husband, shaved and dipped in French cologne.

So goes the intimate lunch . . .

"I told Marjorie it was you!" Dick exclaimed. Without asking, he pulled up a chair, hiked up a leg, and covered it. "Over there, Sweetpea." He pointed to a seat. "I hope you don't mind."

Marjorie scooted past Karen, plopped down, placing her large purse on the floor. "We've been looking everywhere for you."

"Hi, folks." Mark stood to be polite until Marjorie was seated. "We've been busy getting settled in our rooms and came down for a snack. Did you try to call us?"

"Twice," said Dick. "Good thing you got here early. There's a long line forming outside. I'm so hungry I could eat a cow. Do they have prime rib on the menu?" He grabbed Mark's.

"I doubt it," said Marjorie. "As in Rome, do as the Romans do," she uttered, glancing around for a waiter.

"What are you having?" Dick's saucy gaze fell on Karen. "Is the flavor good?" He reached for Mark's glass of wine and sampled it. "Excellent. Let's get two bottles."

"We're having the lasagna," Karen answered for them.

"Lasagna sounds divine," Marjorie agreed. "This is a great view of the atrium fountain. I love this place."

"Yes, it is," said Mark. "What's on the agenda tonight?"

"Oh," said Dick-the-control-freak, standing slightly to jack up his size 52 designer slacks. "I thought we'd walk around the hotel, get a little exercise then rest a while in our room before dinner."

"This is our dinner," Marjorie reminded her husband.

"Actually it's lunch," Karen interjected. "The Italians eat again mid-afternoon and have dinner around nine. I'm certain to be hungry by then." She folded her hands neatly together.

"We've been invited to a private fundraiser for the Peacekeeping Taskforce tonight, if you wanna go," Dick said.

"What about it, Karen?" Mark peered at his companion.

"Sure, it might be fun," she answered.

"You know, nothing is free in this world." Dick slapped a napkin in his lap, ignoring Karen like she didn't exist. "It'll give us a chance to wear our tuxes, Mark."

Karen placed a hand on Mark's arm. "Do you think Daniel will attend?" She preferred not going with Dick and Marjorie.

"Possibly," he whispered. "But don't count on it. He didn't return your call. He might not even be here yet."

"Oh no," Dick chuckled. "Only the rich and famous will be attending—not the peons who run the show for the Taskforce." He yanked off a piece of Italian bread and dipped it in the condiment. "Mmm, this is good. What's it called?"

"What do you mean, *only* the rich and well-known are going to the party tonight?" Karen took exception.

"Oh no, dear. You're with us," said Marjorie. "We have the money, so don't worry, you don't have to be rich or famous."

Karen couldn't believe her ears. "Maybe Mark and I will take in a movie. They do have theatres here, don't they?"

Marjorie patted Karen's hand. "We're scheduled to see a live play tomorrow evening, so why don't you and Mark join us?"

Karen wilted under Mark's gaze. "Sure, why not?" She might as well get with the program Dick was orchestrating.

33

After walking around the hotel mall, the Fernwood foursome opted to rest the remainder of the afternoon in preparation for the fundraiser banquet scheduled later Saturday at 8 o'clock.

Dick had been correct in his assessment. Daniel and his pack of young international peacekeepers had not been invited to the banquet. In fact, Karen suspected that she was probably the youngest one in attendance, and likely the least wealthy.

Seasoned veterans of diehard fundraisers, the elderly ladies were dressed to impress, weighted down in precious jewels of diamonds, pearls and rubies. The men were no less eloquent, wearing expensive tuxedos and wry arrogant smiles, typical of high society types who believed that goods purchased happiness.

"Over here." Dick scooted around a table and found their nameplates. "You sit here, Marjorie. Mark and Karen, over there," he directed, pompous and flittering like a moth.

Karen sighed. It was Dick's nickel, so to speak. Let him orchestrate, she didn't care. Just get her some food, please.

"Are you all right, Karen? You're mighty quiet," Mark observed. "Did you rest well this afternoon?"

"Yes, but I'm still feeling a little drained. The plane trip did me in." The news clip about her mother didn't help, a matter left to ponder. Why ruin the evening by discussing the fugitive?

Karen glanced around the ballroom, unconsciously fondling the diamond necklace borrowed from her mother's jewelry box full of antiquities. *She'd chosen poverty over this?* The idea of jewelry "left behind" reminded her of a Christian novel series that had been published around the turn of the century dealing with the "rapture," a future event when Jesus promised to remove his church from the world in the blinking of an eyelid.

Karen hadn't read the series but she'd heard about it from others. Although fictitious, supposedly the story lined up with the Book of Revelations and Daniel. What if the writers were correct in their assumptions and the Bible proved true? What if the Antichrist was already born and rising to power right now?

What if the world had it all wrong and Jesus was it?

"Look! They've got Tennessee blackberry cobbler as a choice of dessert." Mark nudged Karen out of her thoughts.

"I heard that famous chefs from around the world were preparing the meals," Karen remarked.

"Lindsey's makes the best cobbler I've ever eaten. I wonder if Bud's chef is here?" Mark cranked his head in all directions.

"I don't know." Karen's stomach suddenly turned queasy again. She should be in bed giving her self a few more hours to recoup instead of gorging on food. Tomorrow they were touring Rome's fabulous old buildings and she wouldn't miss that.

"We're supposed to designate which entrée we prefer." Mark picked up a pen and studied his choices. "The fresh Atlantic salmon with green beans and mushrooms sounds delicious."

"Uh huh." Karen glanced around the ballroom.

The tables were quickly filling with hungry patrons. Languages she didn't understand bounced off the walls and reached her ears in a cacophony of whispers. Her head was spinning like her stomach. *Oh . . .* she felt so nauseous.

"Look at the menu, honey. You have to decide soon." Mark patted Karen's arm. "And don't look so sad, like you aren't enjoying this. Rome, Italy. Who wouldn't want to be here?"

"I'm sorry, Mark." Karen gazed into his captivating eyes, deep blue as winter pools. "I'm sort of out of it tonight."

"Jet lag?"

"Probably."

"Let's get this party rolling!" Dick signaled a waiter to bring on the drinks, clucking like an old hen directing his brood.

Karen leaned over and whispered in Mark's ear: "Thank you for being my handsome date and putting up with my moodiness."

His reticent smile said volumes—that he much preferred picturing himself in the comfortable daddy/mentor role rather than embracing the bewitching idea of a suitor.

Tough. The night Mark slept in her bed changed their relationship. He would have to live with the consequences.

The food came in courses, nine in all, prepared by the finest chefs in the world. Karen ate heartily, hungrier than she believed possible as the fatigue and nausea lifted. If she kept this up, she would lose whatever waistline she had left. Was she indulging in food to abate depression over her mother's departure?

Whatever. She put her distraught thoughts to bed.

"I've never seen you eat so much," Mark noted. "I thought you didn't feel well." She was acting strangely. Why?

"I'm fine now," she said. "Guess I just needed to put some solid food on my stomach." She winced, embarrassed over her indulgent spree. "You did pretty well at cleaning your plate, too."

"Well," he wasn't dieting while in Rome, "I'm headed off to the restroom before the speaker begins his appeal. Coming?" He offered Karen a hand, a smile curling his lips.

"To the men's toilet? No, thank you," she teased. "But I will go powder my nose in the ladies'." She got out of her seat.

Mark chuckled. "Touché."

As soon as most people had taken a fifteen-minute break and been seated again, the announcements from the main table began.

Sir Lancelot Galalahan, a name sounding like it had leaped off a medieval page in history, approached the podium and loudly cleared his throat. "Good evening, ladies and gentlemen."

A round of applause sealed his welcome.

After a few personal remarks, Sir Lancelot explained how a large portion of the money collected that evening would be appropriated toward the efforts of International Peacekeeping Taskforce. Settling conflicts among Third World nations didn't come cheap. The remainder would go into a slush fund used to sponsor future high-level meetings between national leaders.

"How much money do you think Dick will give?" Karen's lips barely moved, revealing her thoughts.

Mark shook his head then said, "Depends on whom he wants to impress." He chuckled and shifted positions in his chair. "I'm making a small contribution myself. How about you?"

"Undecided," she replied. *Why the hesitancy to participate?*

"There are envelopes on each table," Sir Lancelot pointed out, surveying the crowd with dreary dishwater-gray eyes, his noble British background enthroned in his mannerisms and speech. "Write a check, or simply give your credit card number along with the amount you want to donate, and place your offering in a sealed envelope. All donations are tax deductible."

Why did Karen feel like she was in a Baptist church?

"We'll be sending some lovely ladies around to collect the gifts." Lancelot motioned for the couriers to come forth.

"That sounds easy enough," said Karen. "Mark, why don't you cough up a cool million? By now, you ought to have an overflow in your bank account—with what Dick has paid you."

Mark spewed coffee from his lips. "What are you babbling about *now*, Karen?" His wary eyes narrowed in disbelief.

She blinked, unsure where the sarcasm had come from.

"Why are you attacking me?" Mark began wiping the stain from his white shirt with a linen napkin.

"Every time I ask you about my father's death, if you know anything about it, you manage to take the fifth. Is that because Dick has purchased your silence?" Mark was right, she was angry.

Dick abruptly scooted his chair away from the table, came to his shaky feet and rudely belched, leaving the room in a hurry.

"Is this a discussion we have to have *now*?" Mark asked.

"Absolutely!" Karen exclaimed, out of nowhere feeling in a destructive mood. "You never said what you and Dick were discussing the night Paul overheard your disturbing conversation."

"Shut up!" Mark grasped Karen's wrist so hard it hurt. "We're leaving now." He glanced around to see if her outburst had drawn attention. "You have no idea how much trouble you will stir up if Dick overheard your accusations. He's not a man to diddle with. Now get your purse, because we're leaving."

Karen's eyes skittered to Marjorie then back to Mark.

"So it is true," she said, a blank expression stalking her pretty face, hurt to the core of her being. "You betrayed my father."

"Get up, Karen. Like I said, we're going."

SUNDAY, JUNE 15

34

Karen woke up Sunday morning and ran into the bathroom. Upchucking half the digested food she'd eaten the night before, she cursed the fact that jet lag had upset her semicircular canals to the extent she was experiencing the effects of vertigo.

That was all it could possibly be, wasn't it?

Around eight thirty, Mark tapped on Karen's bedroom door.

"Come in," she said, in no mood for chitchat. The room was circling around her like vultures about to attack.

"I thought you'd be up by now and wanting breakfast the way you guzzled the food last night." Mark was surprised to see Karen still in her pajamas and lying in the bed like a frail invalid. "What's wrong with you?" He walked over and felt her forehead. "No, temp. You think you caught a virus or something?"

"Maybe." *Something.* "I don't know," Karen grumbled. "I threw up a few minutes ago for the third time this morning. Guess the trip over didn't agree with me. If you don't mind, I'll skip the breakfast buffet. Why don't you go on down and make my apologies? I just need to get a little more shuteye."

"If you insist." Mark needed a strong cup of coffee, absent of Karen's sly remarks. However, he was pleased that she had apologized for her critical remarks regarding his association with Dick. Did she know how close she had come to the truth?

"Can I bring you anything? Fruit or a pastry?" Mark asked.

"No thanks. Just go." Karen sank under the covers, thinking she might die. *Please, dear God, don't let this be what I think it is.*

Thirty minutes after Mark had left, feeling some better, Karen sat up in the bed and dialed Daniel's cellphone number. Surprisingly, he answered this time. "Hey, little brother, where have you been? I've been trying to reach you for nearly a month."

Karen was uncertain how to tell him about their mother's unusual memory switch, failed engagement to Mark, sudden departure from Fernwood, and reclassification as a criminal.

"Climbing the Himalayas, among other things," said Daniel. "Where are you calling from, Sis?"

"I'm at the Marriott in Rome, with Mark James. We're guests of Richard Branson and his wife Marjorie." Karen paused to let a wave of nausea pass, worry nagging in the back of her mind.

"Are you having a good time?" Daniel asked.

"Actually, we had a bumpy flight over and the time change is a real challenge for me." She placed the receiver to her other ear. "What's that noise I hear in the background?"

"I'm involved in a tennis match. I'll have to cut this short and get up with you later. What's your room number?" Daniel privately mumbled something to his partner.

Karen told him. "Who's there with you?" She plugged a finger in one ear. "It's hard to hear. Can you speak up?"

"I'm with Daria Langstead. You know, the girl from Holland I told you about. We're together now." The plunking noise of balls clashing with racquets persisted in the background.

Together? "Is it serious?" asked Karen. "Mother won't like being left out of the loop. Have you told her yet?"

"Speaking of Mom, have you talked to her lately?"

"You know our mom, she's always busy," Karen replied.

"Yeah, I tried calling her cell but it's been disconnected." Daniel continued a side discussion with Daria. "Sorry, Sis. What did you say?" He refocused on their conversation.

"I said I need to talk to you about Mother, face to face. I hear you are coming to Rome to receive an award."

"Yeah, we're arriving tomorrow morning. What's Mother done now?" He could hear the concern in Karen's voice.

"I don't want to talk over the phone. Play your tennis game and enjoy your vacation, but make time to come over and see me at the Marriott. Oh, say . . . around four on Monday."

"Why are you in Rome with Dr. Mark?" Daniel asked with his usual forthrightness. "Is Mother ill?"

"Her situation is too complicated to discuss over the phone."

Karen dreaded telling Daniel about their mother's recent memory episode. More unbelievable was how Mark's Little Vicki disappeared from the hospital without a trace until it was determined she was posing as Tina Banks, a Handymaid.

Their mother: the undercover detective.

"See you soon," Daniel said.

"Call me on Monday." Karen hung up the phone, sauntered into the bathroom, and drew a tub of hot bubbly water. As soon as she felt better, she would order breakfast sent up to the room and decide how best to tell Daniel about the fugitive's situation. Intelligent, unemotional, and trustworthy, he would surely have some idea how best to locate their run-away mother.

Besides, Karen thought, *I want to hear more about the young woman who stole my brother's heart.*

***

Back in the USA

It was 2 a.m. Sunday morning, and Victoria could hardly believe that she was in the air again, flying with Texas on yet another high-risk mission. She had hoped to remain on his ranch for at least a week to catch her breath, but duty called. However, with Texas nearby, she could feel safe wherever they ventured.

"How much farther is it to Safehouse #36?" she asked.

"As the crow flies, it's about two hundred more miles." His gaze was directed forward, but his right hand was holding hers.

"Wings are nice," Victoria noted. "Birds should thank God." She was anxious to see Jon Branson again, to get the low-down on what was happening with Karen, if he'd seen Mark lately, and if he knew what nonsense Dick Branson was cooking up on her behalf.

When could she get to the bank to claim her money?

"You're mighty quiet, lady." Texas made some adjustments on the computerized panel causing the helicopter to tilt and turn slightly. "What's going on in that inventive mind?"

"I was just wondering what Karen was doing, how her life was going without me around," said Victoria.

"According to Jon, she's off on a trip with Mark, guests of Jon's wealthy papa. I don't think she's missing you much."

"What?" Victoria's eyelids nervously fluttered. "I don't approve of Karen traveling with Dick Branson. And Mark James has busy hands, not to mention a calculating mind."

"Isn't that being a little judgmental?" Texas noted.

Humph. Victoria placed her hands in her lap, mouth pouting.

"Forget I said that." He observed Victoria's dour expression. "Karen can take care of herself. It's likely we'll bump into them while in Rome. How will it make you feel, seeing them together?"

"Ha! I'd like to punch out the meatpacker! Give me a few seconds alone with Mark and I'll straighten out his priorities."

Texas chuckled. "You won't do any of that, dear."

"What if Karen recognizes me?" A lump formed in the back of Victoria's throat, insecurity ruling as reality set in.

"She won't," said Texas. "When the professional makeover artist is finished with you, our Heavenly Father will hardly recognize you." He smiled. "I'm more concerned about your health than your looks. Are you truly up to the task?"

"Hopefully," admitted Victoria. "I pray I don't have a fainting episode while in Rome." Which made her think of her weird brain anomaly. "Any idea where I should go for surgery?"

"Jon is working out the details with the CPA. He'll give us a report when we arrive at the safehouse. The lad has your best interest at heart. You should be pleased by his concern."

"I am." *Despite the fact his father is running interference with my investigation into Jeffrey's murder.*

"I don't want you worrying about the overseas trip. Let me take care of the details. Okay?" He glanced over at Victoria.

"Okay," she replied. "I see doubt in your eyes. Why?"

"I'm concerned that we aren't making a lot of headway in proving you are innocent of murdering your husband."

"What?"

"Admitted, your friend Beverly James was quite helpful in providing the copies of Mark's bank statements showing that he received a sizable amount of money in 1991." Texas lent her his eyes. "But do the statements prove he did anything wrong?"

Victoria swallowed hard, suddenly feeling vulnerable. "And I was beginning to feel pretty good about our evidence." She squinted her eyes to hide the tears about to explode.

"I don't mean to burst your bubble, dear," Texas patted Victoria's cold hand, "but chances are good that Mark has a real doctor friend in Argentina who will vouch for him."

"Gee, you sure know how to make a girl feel better." Victoria sighed. "Shall we buy the rope and get the deed over with?" She pictured herself hanging in a dark dungeon.

"Don't despair yet." Texas noted the dark fear crouching in Victoria's gaze. "I still have a few ideas to explore."

"I'll try to be positive." The maelstrom forming in the pit of her psyche threatened to capsize her. Despair was not an option. Faith had to win out or she would miserably fail. *Help me, Lord.*

"Didn't you say you had a PI working on your behalf?"

"Uh hmm."

"I'd like to talk to the investigator and see what she's found out. We're not finished with this investigation yet, not by a long shot." He noticed storm clouds gathering on the horizon.

Was that a sign of trouble rising?

35

Back in Rome

Around one on Sunday, Karen joined Mark, Dick, and Marjorie for a leisurely stroll down the Marriott promenade of stores and restaurants. She hadn't ordered breakfast sent up as planned, trusting that fasting would stave off the bacteria inhabiting her stomach. The nausea wasn't pleasant.

Mark held Karen's hand tightly as they trekked behind the Bransons, who were acting like school kids on their first picnic.

To Karen, Mark seemed more attentive than usual, probably because he was concerned over her frail health. That he loved her, or thought of her in any other way than a daughter, would certainly come as a surprise. In time, that might change.

Marjorie spied a pair of Italian sandals on window display and insisted that Karen accompany her inside to purchase a pair. About to decline the offer, Mark pulled out his Master Card and told her to buy them. Dick heartily approved of the purchases.

Karen grinned. She had to admit that the leather shoes were classy and way too expensive for a small-town girl. But because they were a gift from Mark, she would always cherish them.

"Thank you, Mark." Karen pecked him fondly on the cheek. "For being you." Her escort was chockfull of delightful surprises.

As, no doubt, she was.

"How terribly sweet!" Dick remarked. "For being you."

Around three in the afternoon, Karen grew weary, the time change catching up with her. She told Mark that she wanted to go back to the room and rest. He agreed, so they bid Fernwood's financial guru and his feisty wife farewell until another time.

Karen dragged her tired body up to her room and pulled the bedspread all the way down to the cool satiny sheets. Nearly falling into bed, she thought of a time long ago when she was a small child on her father's lap. He had been reading a bedtime story to her in a soft husky voice. Through sleepy eyes rimmed in green, she had spied Alice slipping down the Rabbit's hole into Wonderland, a fanciful place where she had dreamed of going.

"What happened to Alice when she came back up?"

"She went back to doing what she always had," her daddy had said. "What was that?" Karen had asked. "Living from day to day, ordinary things," he returned. "That's no fun," young Karen had balked. "I want adventure. I want to stay down the hole." *I want to stay down in the hole. I want to stay down in the hole . . .*

Karen opened her eyes and sat up. Mark was shaking her. "What hole, dear?" he asked. She didn't answer him.

Back to the ordinary, though not quite!

Rome, Italy, was as amazing as her companion, Dr. Mark James. Maybe Karen had already leaped down the Rabbit Hole and was about to learn something important. With Mark beside her, weren't the possibilities endless? She smiled at him.

"What were you dreaming?" he asked.

"You wouldn't understand." Karen rubbed sleepy bugs from her eyes. "Have I been asleep long?"

"A couple of hours. You were tired."

"You should have awakened me sooner." She still had to bathe and dress for dinner, no easy feat for a princess in distress.

Mark's image was impeccable. He had showered, shaved, and donned his black tuxedo and red bow tie, claiming Dick had insisted that he put on the dog and spare no expense. Tonight, they were putting Fernwood, Tennessee, on the global map.

"You need to dress for dinner," he reminded Karen.

"I know." She climbed from the bed and gazed at her frumpy figure in the mirror. Her hair was a mess and she needed a frost. Eye makeup was smeared around her tired eyes, and one cheek had too much blush. "Get out and I'll see what I can do to make myself presentable." She shoved Mark out of the bedroom and closed the door. For the night's event, she would wear a sequined emerald after-five cocktail dress cut low in the bodice and showing plenty of leg. Hair was another matter to tackle.

"Are you ready yet?" Mark tapped on the door.

"Almost," she said, reviewing her image in the full-length mirror and admiring her long legs in the short cocktail dress, a genetic blessing. *Where are you, Mother?* Karen rigorously brushed her hair, staring at her hazel eyes through the tunnel of the mirror, aware that the lovely orbs belonged to her father. *His gift.*

Daniel has his daddy's eyes, too, Karen recalled, wondering how her mother would react when she faced the son she had forgotten. Would she freak out again and have another memory switch?

Karen opened the bedroom door and ventured into the living room. Mark was nowhere in sight and his door was closed.

Probably locked . . . to keep out bad girls.

Love made a woman act foolishly, Karen thought as she stepped outside on the patio and viewed the lush green gardens below. The flowers were afire with color as the evening light diminished. A cool, refreshing breeze was astir. Moments later, she became aware of Mark's presence as he stood behind her.

Karen inhaled his mint cologne, and felt weak in the knees. Did he have this affect on her mother? She was breathless.

"Baby? Are you ready to go?" Mark placed his hands on her shoulders, turning her slowly around until they faced.

Baby? In Mark's arms, Karen felt a renewed sense of belonging, keenly aware that she was alive in a world of death.

"You look nice tonight," she said, a lump in her throat.

"Thank you." He smiled. "Actually, you are beautiful."

"Actually . . ." Karen's thoughts crystallized, "I've been wondering how Mother will react when she sees Daniel. You do realize he looks exactly like my father did at age twenty-five."

"That's not likely to happen anytime soon," Mark replied. "But if it did, are you worried she will go into shock and have another memory lapse?" They should not limit possibilities.

"Maybe it would be a good thing for Mother to recover her full memory. She wouldn't act so high and mighty around her family and friends if she recalled her shortcomings. I'm still upset she didn't treat you fairly." Karen peered into his blue eyes.

"You sound bitter, dear." Mark let Karen go. "It's getting late. Perhaps we should head out to the banquet hall. Dick and Marjorie are probably already there and searching for us."

"I don't care—thinking about them makes me want to forget about going tonight." Karen couldn't shake the assaults of Fate.

"We are going, and you look spectacular."

"I do?" Karen was blown away, so full of sappy love she could hardly contain her emotions. If she were only Mrs. Mark James . . . she peeked down the Rabbit hole . . . they could face the mean Queen of Hearts together, grow larger with love and see their world more clearly. It would be a fairy-tale ending.

"I see that mind working. What?"

Karen chuckled. "You don't want to know."

36

Late Saturday in the States

The helicopter ride became bumpy as a storm front diagonally formed from West Tennessee to the Gulf Coast.

Texas skirted the whirlybird around the billowing cloudbank the best he could. Lightning zigzagged across the dreary sky as wind whipped the aircraft like it was a toy. Victoria hugged her stomach, sick from the rocky motion, and praying for deliverance.

"Texas? What will we do when we get to Rome?" she asked through her headset, privately concerned that they might crash.

"Are you worried about bumping into your son?"

"Yes and no. I really do want to see Daniel."

"I sense a *but*," said Texas.

"Yeah, well, I'd like for Daniel to know it's me when we meet." Victoria made a face. "Under the circumstances, I don't think that's possible." The same went for Karen and Mark.

"I understand your apprehension, but we have a job to do for the CPA. We need to give the appearance that we're enjoying ourselves like the other guests attending the festivities."

"Except we're not like other people, are we?" Victoria reacted. "I'm trying to cope with my situation. Really."

"This is *not* a game, Victoria. Undercover work is dangerous business, and we must stay alert to our surroundings in order to gather accurate information," he reminded her.

"What kind of information?" She was new at spying.

"As you may realize, a strong political candidate requires financial support. In today's world arena, the folks putting their nickel behind Luceres want something in return."

"Oh?" Victoria lifted an eyebrow. *Must life always boil down to the exchange of currency?* She was once high on the commodity, and even now, privately miffed that she couldn't get at her own funds.

Texas took a moment to communicate with a small airport located south of Shreveport, Louisiana. "Ten-four," he said to the air-traffic controller. "Our destination is the Shelby County Airport. Arrival expected within the hour." He gave their exact location. "Yeah, the weather's no comfort."

Victoria listened to the one-sided conversation, holding her stomach through the air bumps, a question forming on her lips. When Texas shook his head no, she didn't dare ask.

"I have business in Memphis," he said. "GyroDynamics is a computer-chip company located in California." He paused for a response. "I'm delivering supplies to Bakersfield Electronics." Texas winked at Victoria. "Yeah, you too. Over and out."

"What was that all about?" Victoria inquired. "And why are we flying into Memphis when we are going to Fernwood?"

"I don't want to alert the authorities that our final destination is Safehouse #36. We'll rent a car in Memphis and drive over. No, you can't get your money out of the bank while we're there."

"I—" Victoria's protest was interrupted when Texas pointed out the side window at a perfectly arched rainbow forming against a dewy backdrop of cumulus clouds.

"Pretty, isn't it? God's sign that He would never destroy the world by water again." Texas hoped Victoria would view the rainbow as God's promise to guide them through the trip.

Victoria swallowed her pride. Texas knew his Bible well. *Her too.*

"And you shouldn't go back to Karen's condo either."

"I hate it when you know what I'm thinking. It takes all the joy out of surprise." She meant it, although appreciating the endearment resting in his fond gaze.

"Why is going back so important?"

"Oh, I don't know," said Victoria. "To wander through the place where I once lived, to feel my daughter's ambiance. Maybe pick up an extra dress or two." She missed Karen terribly.

"I understand, and if you want—"

"No, it's a bad idea—what you said about the suspect Antichrist," Victoria revisited a disturbing subject. "What do his supporters want in return for their money?"

"You're familiar with Bible prophecy, particularly Daniel's exposition regarding a fourth kingdom rising on earth."

"Yes," Victoria replied as Texas banked the helicopter and readjusted their flight path. "It will be different from all others."

"Some 500 years before Christ's birth, King Nebuchadnezzar had a disturbing dream about a statue with a head of gold, chest and arms of silver, belly and thighs of bronze, legs of iron, and feet partly of iron and clay. Daniel explained the vision when no one else in the Babylonian kingdom could."

"The king didn't know what to make of the statue falling apart in his dream, its ash dispersed by the wind."

"Bible scholars believe the statue was symbolic of future earthly kingdoms: the gold representing Babylon; the silver, Media-Persia; the bronze, Greece; and the iron, Rome," Texas expounded on the Scripture. "The feet, a mixture of iron and clay, represented the final world government under Gentile rule."

"A government led by the Antichrist," Victoria said. "The ten toes depicting the nations who will follow his leadership."

"Yes," Texas said. "It will be a government stemming from the old Holy Roman Empire, a liaison between church and state."

"But God will, of course, prevail," Victoria professed.

"Not until the seven years of tribulation have played out on earth," Texas said. "In the 17th chapter of Revelation, John the disciple again mentions the ten kings who will receive authority to rule with the beast." He fondly glanced over at Victoria.

"The beast being the Antichrist," Victoria clarified. "What will the ten kings do?" she asked, referring to the land that would be divided by the world leader and entrusted to ten caretakers. How that would all come about remained a Biblical mystery.

Rebels In Paradise

"As individuals of authority, *these* ten men will give their allegiance to the beast, Satan's choice boy."

Victoria listened attentively.

"On Earth, it will be a time of unprecedented persecution for Christians. Satan hates Jesus Christ because of His elevated position in Heaven as the one and *only* Son of God."

"And the people who trust in Him," Victoria interjected.

"One more thing concerning the subject: once a powerful angel highly honored in Heaven, Lucifer became jealous of God's authority and convinced a third of the angels to rebel. Cast down to earth for a season, Satan plans to make the most of his fury."

"His first evil deed occurred in the Garden of Eden."

"Yes, when the Serpent tempted Eve to disobey God by tasting the forbidden fruit," Texas continued.

"But God loved mankind and sent His Son Jesus to Earth to die on the cross and make things right again between the creation and the Creator." Victoria lent Texas her sincere gaze.

"Correct. And that's why Satan rages against God's elect—all those who have professed to believe in Him and have been born again in the Spirit. It's a wonderful concept, yet difficult to comprehend—God's unique Oneness in three personalities."

"It took grace." Victoria shook her head in amazement.

"At the end of Daniel's seventieth week, Jesus will return to Earth to judge sinful people for their spiritual choices."

"At the Great White Judgment Throne," Victoria interjected. "God will send Satan to a place called Hell, along with everyone who chooses evil over good. All those who had rejected Jesus."

"Exactly." Texas peered at Victoria.

Victoria opened her Bible to a Scripture. "Listen, Texas. In the Book of Daniel, chapter 7, verse 23," she thought of her own Daniel, "it says the fourth beast is a fourth kingdom that will appear on earth. It will be different from all the other kingdoms and will devour the whole earth, trampling it down and crushing it." Victoria drew in a breath. "That's pretty scary." She already felt trampled down. Her freedom to worship Christ openly had been blatantly taken away by powerful people who made the rules.

"What?" he detected a question forming on her lips.

"Do you believe we're in the *Last Days*?"

"Yes, I do," he said. "Read some more."

"Daniel 7, verse 24," Victoria continued. "The ten horns are ten kings who will come from this kingdom. After them another king will arise, different from the earlier ones; he will subdue three kings. He will speak against the Most High and oppress the saints and try to change the set times and the laws. The saints will be handed over to him for a time, times and half a time."

"You don't fully understand Daniel's interpretation of his vision?" Texas smiled. "Don't feel bad, honey, nobody does."

The kindness steeped in Texas' gaze comforted Victoria.

"But you get the gist of the Revelation verses," he said. "The oppression this fourth kingdom will wage against the saints will be horrendous. When the mark of the beast is required to buy and sell—well, a lot of folks are going to sit up and take notice."

Texas was grateful he could share his thoughts with Victoria.

"On the forehead or the hand," Victoria recalled. "It's a mystery that will be revealed in the future."

"Maybe sooner." He gazed through glossy green eyes. "Have you heard of the Vera chip invented in Florida in 2002?"

"No," said Victoria. "What does the device do?"

"It is a small microchip implanted under the skin of an individual which allows the GPS to track a person. Originally, it was only to be used with criminals on probation or the mentally challenged. Today, companies are exploring further usage."

"Oh. To buy and sell?" Victoria's eyebrows lifted.

"Possibly. Near the end of the Book of Daniel, God instructed His prophet to go his way, reminding him that the words were closed up and sealed until the time of the end."

"Many would be purified, made spotless and refined, but the wicked would continue to be wicked," Victoria quoted Scripture. "I believe much of this prophecy will occur after the Rapture."

"I agree," said Texas.

"When Jesus snatches His Bride, His holy church, from the world, many people will be confused," declared Victoria.

"Because Jesus Christ won't be seen by most people," he explained. "Not until He returns to Earth seven years later, and plants his feet on the Mount of Olives will every eye behold Scripture fulfilled according to the Bible. What an event!!"

Victoria was full of impending tears by now.

"Most Christians view the events of the *Rapture* and *Christ's Triumphant Reentry* as separate events," Texas continued. "Only Believers will meet Christ in the air at the Rapture, while the Great White Throne Judgment will occur at the end of the Tribulation."

"We see in part, but as events unfold, we will know . . ."

"Exactly."

"Texas! You should have been a preacher instead of a helicopter pilot!" Victoria felt energized with enthusiasm.

"Can't I be both?" Texas smiled. "I love talking about the future and heavenly things to come. Joann—" he choked up. "Sorry." Hurt bloomed in his eyes.

Victoria was certain that he had been about to say Joann would be waiting for him when he got to Heaven.

"It's all right, Texas," Victoria empathized. "I feel the same way about Jeffrey. In Heaven there will be no stronger bond than love among all Christians. I can love both you and Jeffrey."

Texas was stunned. "Do you realize you just told me that you loved me?" Inside, he was flooded with joy.

"Yeah, I did, didn't I?" Victoria laughed. "I suppose I just realized I need a warm body to hold me in the night." She blushed at her presumptuousness of a happy-ever-after ending.

"Not just a warm body, dear. My warm body." He captured the moment with a glint in his eyes. "Don't worry about how life will work out, we'll do it together. All right?"

"Thank you, Texas, for being in my life."

"My pleasure."

37

The J.W. Marriott in Rome

Sunday evening's banquet honoring the presence of two hundred Americans in Rome was spectacular. Red, white and blue dominated the color theme as a Marine Band played *Stars and Stripes Forever*. When the national anthem was announced, the crowd stood and cheered, waving banners. The Fernwood foursome proudly joined in on the patriotic salute to America.

An Italian diplomat introduced the Pope who said the Invocation in Latin. Catholics made the sign of the cross while others simply bowed their heads. Religion was respected in the New World Order. Interfaith conferences had brought millions of people together and fostered respect, promoting peace.

After a heart-healthy salad, the entrée was served: steak with a side of Idaho potatoes, green beans and mushrooms. The sourdough rolls were made from a California recipe and melted in your mouth. Drink choices consisted of ice tea or coffee.

La Madeline Restaurant in New Orleans had sent one of their chefs over to prepare an array of delicious desserts consisting of chocolate torts and almond pastries to serve with Community Coffee. Everything was absolutely delicious.

A few elderly Americans had brought along their children or grandchildren. The old and young blended together like a colorful patchwork quilt, bound together by the English language.

After the meal, the Vice-President of the United States was introduced and came to the podium. A hand of applause followed in honor of America's first female second-in-command chief.

"Welcome to Rome, Italy, patriots of America," said Vice-President Allison Lightfoot. A round of applause followed. "It's my great pleasure to represent our great country at this historic world event." Her rich alto voice echoed over the microphone.

More applause followed her recap of how the good old USA came into existence. With much praise for Alexander Luceres Ramnes, Vice-President Lightfoot named the committee members who had served on the International Religious Economic Committee, thanking them for making the world a safer place.

"God bless Luceres!" someone screamed out. "Praise to Luceres!" another said, foot stomping and hip-hoorays following.

But has the fighting ended? Karen mused. Wasn't Daniel always involved in negotiations between opposing factions? And when negotiations failed didn't the well-armed UN Peacekeeping troops under the strong leadership of the United States Army move in to take control of the situation?

The banquet ended and people stood to leave.

"What?" Mark peered at Karen as they exited the ballroom.

"Oh, I don't know. My mother's Biblical teachings keep playing over in my head—like she's here reminding me of right and wrong." Karen felt agitated over the vice-president's speech.

"You don't agree with the vice-president, that the world is a better place to live? Why?" They entered the promenade.

"It's not that, Mark. I keep thinking how Mother said a world leader would change the way things are done," Karen replied, thinking he wouldn't understand if she could explain.

"How can any one person change everything? Really Karen! Don't you think you're being a little paranoid? I know exactly where this conversation is headed and I don't like it. You think Luceres is the Antichrist. Well, he's not! So drop the subject."

Karen glared at Mark. "But what if the Bible is right? It's no secret that Luceres opposes Christianity. Will persecution result in mass eradication of Christians because they oppose international religious laws? Can you say for sure that won't happen?"

Mark shrugged, having no defense against the Bible.

***

Memphis, Tennessee

Due to swarming storms, Texas had made an emergency landing in Little Rock, Arkansas, to wait for favorable weather. The delay had put them off schedule, but better safe than sorry.

In their approach to Memphis, Victoria spied a large flat barge lazily floating down the Mississippi River, probably headed to New Orleans to deliver merchandise. Old Man River hadn't changed much in thousands of years, unlike her yoyo memory.

The helicopter safely landed at the Shelby County Airport late Sunday as dusk settled over the city like a dark blanket. Points of light across the city flickered on like one person had flipped a master switch, reminding Victoria of the time she had slipped away to Memphis to look for Burn Gordon in Southaven.

Nothing had happened the way she had planned. *Did life ever?*

After pigging out on a fattening McDonald's hamburger special, she had driven downtown in search of an attorney, thinking any professional would know how to find a reliable, low-profile investigator. Having failed to question anyone at the Shelby County Courthouse, she had ventured inside the covered downtown mall and enjoyed a Coke at the Yellow Rose Café.

On her way back to the car, she'd noticed a new Municipal Building across the street from THE ONE HUNDRED NORTH MAIN BUILDING. In the Office of Deeds and Records, Larry Baldwin had kindly directed her to his cousin, Attorney Devin Baldwin, who in turn had given her Georgie's telephone number.

Thank God. Georgie was a Godsend.

"Texas, I need to do one thing while we're in Memphis." Victoria's eyelids shuddered at the prospect of knocking on Devin Baldwin's door again, but she needed to get a message to Georgie.

"What?" He shut down the helicopter engine.

"It's important or I wouldn't ask."

"Uh oh, that gleam in your eye spells trouble. What're you thinking now?" He helped Victoria out of the Bird. "We don't have a lot of time to meander the streets of Memphis."

"I won't be meandering," said Victoria. "I need to see a friend about a friend." Her lips folded inside.

"Names, please. We're not keeping secrets, are we?"

"Not too much." She tried to downplay her next statement. "I want to go over to Attorney Devin Baldwin's house and ask him if he's seen or heard from Georgie Hendricks lately."

"Your PI friend whose apartment got bombed. And what if somebody is watching the attorney's house when you show up?"

"Well . . ." in Victoria's way of thinking Texas had proposed the worst possible scenario. She couldn't afford to be apprehended just when their love story was getting interesting.

"They won't see me," she said, "because *you* are the one who's going to knock on Devin's door." No one knew of her connection with Texas outside of Jon Branson and the CPA.

"All right. Say I agree to do it. You just want me to look Devin in the face and point-blank ask him where Georgie is?"

"Yeah." The solution seemed satisfactory.

"Baby . . ." Texas folded Victoria inside his strong arms. "I can't do that. It's far too risky. Sorry."

"Please." She begged with her eyes, lips pouting.

***

Texas finally convinced Victoria to spend Sunday night at Safehouse #36 and put off their visit to Devin Baldwin until later, when they returned to Memphis. She agreed, graciously reluctant.

Jon Branson received them warmly, showing Victoria to her old room, which he'd kept for her. His sandy hair was longer than usual, oily and tasseled. "So how was the flight over?"

"Fine," said Texas.

"What's wrong, Jon?" Victoria noticed the disturbed look tucked away in his lime-colored eyes.

"I could never fool you, Victoria." He trembled. "It's my mother—" he choked on tears, "—she's dying." The hurt cut though his heart like a sharp knife, wounding to the soul.

"I'm so sorry." Victoria embraced Jon tightly. "I'll pray that Jesus will comfort her." She meant it. Jon was like a son to her. He had been Paul's best friend, and now he was hers.

Almost bitterly Jon said. "Oh, she's already comforted—doesn't believe she will die. She thinks Jesus will rapture us before it happens. She's refusing treatment. I spoke with Hospice and they are going to send someone over to see her on Monday."

"Don't be embittered over death." Victoria shared a bit of wisdom. "The other side is more desirable than our world. Your mother has a beautiful future in Heaven." She should take her own advice and let Jeffrey rest in the grave as Mark suggested.

"Texas?" Jon looked at the NASA satellite expert. "You can bunk with me, if that's all right." He was unprepared to discuss grief, more comfortable with the Good Samaritan role of a host.

"Fine by me," Texas said. "Okay with you, honey?"

"Honey?" Jon reacted, a smile emerging. "Now I really like the sound of that. Two lovebirds taking flight."

Victoria blushed as Texas punched Jon lightly on the arm.

"The CPA has your credentials ready, on their way over as we speak. A professional makeup artist will be here later tonight, to complete your disguise." Jon glanced over at Victoria.

"Don't worry about being recognized, you won't," Jon added, thinking that nothing was full proof. The unexpected happened.

However, in Jon's way of thinking, Victoria and Texas were special in God's plan. They would fare well in Rome, Italy, and accomplish God's divine purposes. Truth would prevail.

***

Sunday night had proven an all-nighter. When the makeup artist finished, Victoria returned to her bedroom feeling right at home. The mirror's image was a reminder that she had been reinvented with a new face, reshaped eyebrows, straight-arrow nose, and frosted-brown hair—compliments of the layers of simulated skin no heavier than ordinary makeup. Mark should take a few lessons from Tootsie before he cut on a new patient.

Victoria was posing as Alisha Carol Hammerstein, an aging but still-beautiful former model. Texas, as Jack, represented the reclusive Texan oil baron whose real name was Jackson Lloyd.

Appearing younger with age lines camouflaged, Texas let Tootsie cut his salt-and-pepper hair short and dye it brown like Jackson's. In his eyes were contact lenses to match, and he didn't need a quick-tanning bed to look like a seasoned Westerner.

Victoria approved of the innovative results. Dressed in expensive preppy clothes, Jack was a knock-off of the real Jackson Lloyd without question. And unmistakably, Victoria bore a strong resemblance to Alisha Carol. However, she had a major concern regarding the spirited personality-plus Texas. Given, he looked like Jack, but he might have trouble impersonating the multimillionaire who in real life was a shy recluse seldom venturing out in public. If Texas looked worried it was okay, he should be.

The real Jackson Lloyd Hammersteins had received a valid invitation from NATO to attend the festivities in Rome honoring the popular Alexander Luceres Ramnes. Positive they wouldn't attend, the Christian Protection Agency had inquired about borrowing their identities. Jackson Lloyd agreed for the CPA to send spies in their place. Obviously, the high-profile couple were devoted Christians or the trip to Rome wouldn't be happening.

Though excited, Victoria was chagrined to learn Jon's mother wasn't expected to live. Texas put Marilyn Branson's name on the CPA Internet prayer chain. God was still in the miracle business.

MONDAY, JUNE 16

38

Rome, Italy

Monday afternoon, Karen and Mark took a rambunctious buggy ride through the streets of Rome to view the remains of archaic buildings left after centuries of wear and tear. According to the guide, most buildings had been constructed to honor Rome's greatest rulers, Caesar Augustus and Trajan.

Simon's historical comments droned on and on. Mark listened with great interest while Karen's mind floated elsewhere. She was tired and felt queasy, and the air blew hot as a furnace.

"Rome is known as the 'eternal city', exemplifying the political efficiency and artistic achievement of the past."

Karen didn't care. Rome could burn; give her America.

"For example," Simon continued, "a replica of the Parthenon was reconstructed in Nashville, Tennessee."

Nashville reminded Karen of her missing mother again.

"Rome is divided into four Sectors: North-West, South-West, South-east, and North-east." Professor Simon was a pro.

Who cares? Karen thought. *Everyone's dead who lived back then.*

Still, she pretended to enjoy the tour, so as not to disappoint Mark. According to the historical pamphlet, the much-acclaimed structures were a pride thing. Men, they hadn't changed.

By three-thirty in the afternoon, Karen's swollen feet were hurting and she was rudely yawning. "I love Rome, but it's getting hot and Daniel is coming over soon to see me at the hotel."

Karen did not need Mark's permission to return to the Marriott, but she wanted his approval. Especially after the way he'd scolded her for distrusting him following the fund-raiser banquet Saturday night. My word, she'd actually accused him of being in cahoots with Dick and participating in her father's death.

But today, Karen realized that proving Mark's guilt or innocence was unimportant. Forgiven of all transgressions, she loved him with all her heart. *Some things are best left unsaid.* She adopted Fernwood's favorite copout phrase and widely yawned.

"What time is Daniel meeting you?" asked Mark, interested in continuing the tour. "I wish you hadn't promised him."

"Around four. Stay with Dick and Marjorie if you like, but I really need to go back to the room and rest. I don't feel so well." The heat was sapping her energy and perpetuating the virus.

"I'm sorry, dear," said Mark. "Professor Simon, thank you for your time, but we're going back to the hotel to rest."

Mark's willingness to accommodate Karen made her feel totally selfish. "You don't have to go with me," she reiterated.

"Really, I don't mind," said Mark. Dick and Marjorie were in the buggy behind them, gung-ho on continuing the tour.

Thank Heavens! Karen wanted Mark to herself for a while.

The Branson duo hustled from the shaky buggy and rushed over to the Theater of Balbus to view a William Shakespeare play about to be performed on the site dedicated in 13 BC by Cornelius Balbus, a Roman banker-friend of King Augustus.

"Sure you don't want to see the play?" Mark asked.

"Absolutely." Karen had all the sightseeing she could take. According to one tract she'd read, on the day the famous theatre opened, the Tiber River had flooded the site. Its remains were later found buried beneath the *Palazzo Mattei-Paggancia*, a portico commercially used by bronze and rope makers. All history.

A breeze drifted off the Mediterranean Sea in the direction of the city, relieving the blast of heat. It wasn't that she hadn't loved spending the afternoon with Mark, she had. And goodness she'd learned a lot about Roman history. But talking to Daniel about their mother's disappearance couldn't wait. *He had to be brought up to snuff,* as Granddaddy Martin used to say.

They were back at the Marriott in plenty of time to intercept her brother at four, but Daniel did not call as promised. Mark was sorry and trotted off to his bedroom for a nap. Karen was mad.

Later that evening they were attending another dinner. The Prime Minister of England was going to be there along with a Presbyterian Bishop to pronounce the invocation.

While Mark slept, Karen sat on the edge of the bed angrily staring at the phone. "Ring, will you?"

At five fifteen the phone rang, waking Karen from her nap.

"What?" She rolled over in the bed and reached for the phone. "Yeah?" She was sleepy-eyed and twisted out of sorts.

"It's me, Daniel. I'm on a plane headed for Africa. Appears there's a problem there. I'm sorry I missed our appointment."

"It's okay." Karen didn't ask what kind of problem. She knew it involved some uprising the Peacekeeping Taskforce needed to fix, to verbally salve a few old wounds and offer international assistance with financial aid if required.

"Thanks for being so understanding," he said.

"Will you be back on Friday?" Karen asked.

"Yes," said Daniel. "I'm losing you, Sis. We'll talk before the banquet, I promise. I—"

"It's urgent," Karen said to a dead line.

***

Safehouse # 36 in the States

Saying goodbye to Jon Branson Monday morning felt more like leaving one of her own children. Victoria's and the lad's bond was strong. How Dick's son could turn out so decent after a terrible childhood was a puzzle for the Holy Spirit to solve. Victoria's distaste for Dick Branson bordered on hate, an emotion a faithful Christian should never harbor under any circumstance.

"I like your hair frosted, Victoria." Texas glanced over as they drove through the open gates of the old state mental institution. "You make a beautiful Alisha Carol."

"Thank you." She pulled down the visor and flipped on a light to study her reshaped face. Every minor blemish had been eradicated by the application of a new layer of skin. It felt weird peering into a pair of green eyes that belonged to another woman, compliments of contact lenses. And the fall added to the crown of her head made her hair appear thicker and longer.

During the drive over to Memphis, all Victoria could think about was seeing her son. Of course, she couldn't let him know who she was. Warned that Daniel had a strong resemblance to his daddy, Jeffrey, Victoria tried to prepare her heart for the shock.

In the past she had done a poor job at preparing her heart for most things—pretty much taking life at face value. But on this dangerous CPA mission, she could not afford vacillating emotions. She was party to a dangerous undercover plan.

And Texas is depending on me.

"Are you sure you're okay with this sting?" Texas detected hesitancy in Victoria's expression.

"I suppose." She turned off the light of the visor shade and flipped it up. "What am I supposed to do? How am I supposed to act? I'm not a model, and this spy thing is new to me."

"It's no different than any other undercover assignment. Just play your part, have a good time, and keep your mind open to news," said Texas, his hand firmly on the steering wheel.

"What kind of news?" she wondered.

"Anything to do with political favors being negotiated under the table—like conversations regarding personal comments about Luceres. The CPA wants to know who his friends are. Just be your sweet self and let me take the lead. You'll do just fine."

That is the problem, thought Victoria. Her impulsive nature had a tendency to erupt at the unexpected moments.

"I'll try hard to be good." She weakly smiled, fearing she would fail. "Be *good?* You make it sound like a mandate."

He said nothing in response, making Victoria nervous.

"Well, you certainly have seen my impulsive nature." She shut her eyes and thought of all the times she'd spoken her mind before thinking. One wrong word and they might get caught.

"Of course, dear, if you have any ideas on how to handle this assignment, I'd sure like to hear about it before you act. We can't afford to get caught, Victoria. The CPA is depending on our report as a launch pad for defending Christians against a hostile world government. There is no room for failure."

Duh. Victoria was in no position to make judgments.

"One. No running ahead of the game. Second. No slipping off to search for Daniel. Last, and most important: no conversations with anyone who might know you. Call it the ABC's of safety." He had a half smile curling his lips

"I'll try," Victoria tentatively said, privately grimacing.

"No. You *will* comply, and we won't have any trouble."

Victoria nodded her head in agreement. And she thought she liked strong-willed men who took control. "Anything else?"

"No. Except we need to take care of your little mission."

39

Memphis, Tennessee

Victoria stayed in the rented 2008 gray Buick while Texas walked a few blocks over to the address she had given him.

There were lights on at Devin Baldwin's house, which meant he was probably home. Texas walked up to the front door and rang the bell. A pretty redhead came to the door in a pair of shorts and a tie-dyed shirt. "Yes?" Eyes were wide with interest.

"Excuse me, but does Devin Baldwin live here?"

"Devin!" Melanie turned her head and called out loudly. "Someone's at the door asking for you."

Texas waited. The attorney's smoky eyes, red around the rims, said that he had experienced a rough day.

"I'm sorry to bother you, Mr. Baldwin, but an acquaintance of mine is lookin' for a detective friend of yours."

Devin's expression tightened. "We shouldn't be having this conversation, mister," he said with his hand firmly on the door.

"Eyes and ears pointed your way?" Texas asked.

"Exactly. So tell your acquaintance her buddy is missing—maybe permanently. I'm doing all I can to help." Devin leaned out the doorway and looked down the street both directions.

"Thank you for the information," Texas said. "I take it I'd better go." Fear was tucked away in Devin's cryptic gaze.

"It would be best." Devin rudely slammed the door.

"Well, that didn't go well." Texas took a few steps into Devin's yard. "I don't think Victoria's going to like this."

Out of the corner of his eye Texas noticed a big guy trotting across the street, heading his way. Sensing danger, he turned in the opposite direction and quickened his pace, immensely grateful that the CPA required regular rigorous physical training.

Fifteen minutes later, after outrunning his shadow, Texas lunged into the passenger seat of the Buick and ordered Victoria to drive while he coughed and chugged to catch his breath.

"I lost him." Texas swiped his sweaty forehead with the back of his hand. "Good thing. He was a big dude."

"Lost *who*? Big dude? What happened back there?" Victoria asked all at once while igniting the engine with the key.

"Go! *Now!*" Texas kept an eye on the street for his stalker.

"You're scaring me." Victoria rammed the pedal with her right foot and lunged away from the curb. "Did you see Devin?"

"Georgie's gone—maybe permanently." Texas was pouring sweat through his shirt. "Somebody got to the attorney. You'll have to decide what that means since you know him better."

"Gone as in *dead*?" Victoria jerked the car to the right as a man in a green truck honked at her for hogging the curve.

"I don't know. Devin was frightened. I don't think he wants anything to do with Georgie anymore. Then there's the matter of the big guy back there who tried to get his hands on me."

"Dick's hired thug, probably," Victoria surmised.

"Maybe." Texas peered through the rear window. "I don't see anybody following us. I think we're safe for now."

"I hate that man!" Victoria fussed.

"Which man?"

"Dick Branson!" Raw anger flew all over Victoria like an erupting volcano. "I wish he was dead."

"No, you don't. You despise the way he thinks and lives."

"Don't tell me how to hate, Texas! I'll hate any way I choose. It's my sin, and mine alone!" She hugged the steering wheel.

"Sorry." Texas grasped the dashboard for support. "Please don't speed. We don't want to get stopped by a cop."

Victoria eased her foot off the accelerator, her heart jumping. "We won't be safe until we're out of Memphis," she said.

Texas kept his mouth shut, unable to cope with Victoria's sudden wrath. She would love as hard as she hated.

Victoria stewed over her profession of hate.

"You're right, Texas, it's wrong to hate," she suddenly confessed. "I'm supposed to love Dick's soul."

"Supposed to?"

"Yeah." She made eye contact, inwardly wishing that God would punish Dick for his lies, strike him down with the plague, give him a swift lightning jolt, or simply boil him in oil.

"Dick Branson needs a Savior. Jesus would change him."

"I suppose." Victoria wasn't convinced, mad as a wet hen in a rainstorm, ready to hit Dick over the head with a big umbrella.

***

On Monday, after a few hours of badly needed sleep at Sarah's, Georgie Hendricks departed Fernwood around noon. On a mission, tucked away in her backpack was the undeveloped Kodak film showing Branson employees packing cocaine inside packages of meat. Add to that a clear plastic zip-lock bag of cocaine, and there was probably enough evidence to bury Dick.

It was time for PI Georgie to drop out of sight.

The motorcycle ride over to Memphis took a little over two hours. Avoiding the interstate, she traveled the back roads until reaching city limits. Locating a United States Post Office, she took care of business then got lost in a crowded discount mall.

After nightfall, Georgie approached Devin Baldwin's house on her motorcycle and noticed a beat-up gray Buick parked against the curb. To avoid passing the vehicle, she circled the block and entered Devin's yard from the opposite direction.

The attorney's residence was dark—like no one was home. Oh yeah, Devin was there. He was in the habit of shutting off the lights in the outer rooms at night in order to avoid solicitations.

Georgie left the motorcycle parked behind Devin's shed out back and moved across the yard on foot. She gave the basement window a tug to see if it was unlocked. No such luck.

A subtle growl grabbed Georgie's attention. It was Devin's unimpressive guard dog sleepily stumbling around. Tied to a post on a short leash, he wasn't going too far. The German shepherd objected to anyone stepping on his green turf after dark.

"Go back to sleep, puppy," Georgie whispered as she passed him on her way to the shed. Firmly grasping the handle of the door, she discovered it was unlocked.

After gathering a few tools to open the basement window, she approached the house again. Devin wouldn't mind her breaking in for the night, seeing they were good friends. About to crawl through the window, her neck snapped back.

"What?" Pain splintered through her skull. "That hurts!"

"Well, look what I caught!" A big man, six-foot four or taller, had Georgie by the neck, flopping her around like she was a rag doll. "You wouldn't happen to be Detective Hendricks?"

Hulk's grip was so intense, Georgie gasped for breath. The toes of her shoes tipped the tall grass as she was pinned to the house like a paper target. "Put me down, you brute!"

"Whatever you say, sweetie." Hulk dropped his prey like a sack of potatoes, brushing his hands together as he chuckled.

"Ouch." Georgie studied her assaulter. "What do you want from me? I don't have any money." She showed empty pockets

"You," Hulk answered, propping his right foot on her back, grinding Georgie into the ground. Out of the corner of her eye, she spied two more big men stepping from the tree shadows.

"Tie and gag her," ordered Hulk. "We'll finish up back at my place." His yellow gaze fell heavily on Georgie like cold gold.

Seeing no opportunity for escape, Georgie quit struggling. When her assailants had masked, tied and gagged her, she felt the weight of a heavy metal object strike her temple. Darkness swooped down. Whatever else happened next didn't matter.

Attorney Anthony Vorices instructed his men to carry the detective back to the motel. After extracting information from her—by force if necessary—he would decide her fate.

Georgie awakened hours later, bound and gagged. The lump on her head hurt like the dickens. She was no longer in Devin

Baldwin's backyard, probably locked inside a closet since the room was musty, small and dark—not even close to the Holiday Inn.

So what was a girl to do?

Struggling to loosen the ropes, Georgie miserably failed. It was obvious her unidentified assailants were professionals, but they would not glean information from her, not a peep. She never betrayed a client, even if it meant being tortured. *Like this.*

Gratefully, the photos showing Jerry Loafer and his motley crew packing cocaine in meat packages were already in the mail. Devin would soon receive her two-day priority package and get an eyeful. The photos proved that Dick Branson was peddling illegal drugs. Hopefully, Devin would contact the FBI on her behalf.

If he didn't, nobody else would.

TUESDAY, JUNE 17

40

Rome, Italy

Karen was beat on Tuesday. Needing to rest, she told Mark to join Dick and Marjorie on yet another sightseeing tour of Rome. Welcoming the solitude, she crawled back in bed and slept until noon. Fully awake now, she felt ravenously hungry.

After dressing she ventured downstairs to the promenade, thoughts of her mother nestling in her brain. Realizing that she'd become somewhat cynical over how life was working out, she found a small restaurant and ordered brunch, eating crazy like a lazy pig in a quagmire of mud. What was going on with her?

Binging and purging—was she becoming bulimic?

The buzz at the Marriott placed Alexander Luceres Ramnes arriving late Wednesday, though he'd likely be kept under wraps until showcased on Friday evening at the final banquet.

Karen wandered over to the buffet and refilled her plate with delicacies. Feeling better after eating, she didn't buy into the idea that she had contracted a bug as Mark suggested. Gratefully, she hadn't wasted a morning visiting a health clinic. This was her long-dreamed-of vacation, too, and she was going to be just fine.

Like her mother, Karen preferred to steer clear of doctors—except for the one she dearly loved.

Anyhow, she needed time alone to plan how to tell her little brother that their mother was missing and wanted by the police. Daniel seemed so happy when they had last spoken she hated to burst his balloon. In love for the first time, he had a bright future with the world government. All was perfect in his world.

Karen grimaced. So what would she say to him? Mother has her old memories back and she's run away? The police think she plotted our father's murder, so she's gone undercover to gather information to clear her name? I have no idea where she is?

Oh boy, Karen envisioned how Daniel would react. He'd argue that the idea of his mother being wanted by the police was preposterous, that she would never even step on a spider much less contemplate murder. And he would be right. Furious, of course, and with good reason, she fully understood.

Karen believed in her mother's innocence, but there was still the large insurance policy taken out on her father two weeks before he died. The fact that Mark's *Little Vicki* had signed on the bottom line made her look guilty in the eyes of the law.

The problem is, Karen grimaced, *Victoria Martin Tempest has no memory of ever collecting the two million dollars.*

"I'd sure like to know if anyone else did." Karen polished off a sticky vanilla pastry. If her mother hadn't collected on the policy, who had? Without a motive, there would be no case.

Since the insurance company had bellied up at the end of 1989, how could she find out? Even if the policy existed, it might not pay off. A ticket was only good as long as the show lasted.

So now that little issue had been settled, what was she going to do with the rest of the day?

Karen recalled that Marjorie and Dick were going to the coast later today to meet with one of Dick's European business associates. Fine by her, she and Mark could use some down time alone. Why not plan a romantic evening to curl his toes?

After downing the remainder of her espresso, Karen left a nice tip on the table and paid the tab at the cash register.

"*Buon giorno,*" said the Italian cashier.

One thing Karen had already learned from the Italians, they adored pasta and cheese dishes prepared with almost any kind of fish, beef, and poultry. And wine. Don't forget the wine.

M. Sue Alexander

***

Somewhere in the States

When the sun came up on Tuesday morning, the family of Big-and-Tall finally let Georgie out of the closet to feed and water her, which made her feel more like a battered animal than human.

The Chinese cuisine served cold was pasty. Chucking down the food like it was prime filet mignon, Georgie guzzled a half-gallon of milk while her assailants stood around and watched.

"What?" She glared at Hulk, thinking it might be her last meal. He appeared amused, his arms crossed, his mouth taut.

"What have you been up to, Detective?" asked the leader of the rat pack, the big golden-eyed man who had dangled Georgie by the hair and dropped her on the ground like trash.

"Me? Nothing." She played innocent. "I've been working for the Shelby County Garbage Management Company." *It was the truth.* "Check it out under the name of Jaycee Moore."

"Are you still employed by Victoria Tempest?" Anthony Vorices inquired in a low, growling voice, the rapid-rising muscles on his arms rippling to signify he was capable of violence.

"No," lied Georgie. "I have to think of myself now. Because of guys like you." Eyes skittered in several directions.

Anthony received the compliment well.

"You're smart, Georgie. That's why you're still alive." Hulk's half grin was more of a curved smirk. "And exactly what did you do after you quit your garbage job?" He was going fishing.

Anthony had already received a call from Jerry Loafer, advising him that a package of cocaine had turned up missing, and that his most recent employee hadn't shown up for work.

"Well, actually, like," Georgie stammered, "I'm in the process of lookin' for a new line of work—something less dangerous."

Anthony chuckled and looked at the others. "Girl, I think you'd fit right in with the criminal element."

Georgie wasn't laughing like the others.

"Except you can't be trusted," Golden-eyed Hulk said.

A wise investigator, Georgie kept her mouth shut.

"Now exactly where did you hide the evidence you stole from Branson?" Anthony proceeded with his inquiry.

"What evidence?" Georgie brushed crumbs from her hands.

"Enough bull!" Anthony grabbed Georgie by the nap of her neck. "The pack of cocaine you stole from Branson Meatpacking Company? Where is it?" His expression mimicked a snarling dog.

Boy, did Dick's grapevine work well!

"I don't know what you're talkin' about!" Georgie tried to hide her smoldering fear, acid churning in her stomach. Maybe she should just give back the evidence and run like Victoria.

A fish on a sharp hook could only flop.

***

Back in Rome

Mark James opened the door of his hotel suite around 4 p.m. Tuesday afternoon and found Karen waiting for him with a chilled bottle of champagne and a tray of appealing appetizers.

"Karen!" His mouth fell open. Never had Victoria's daughter looked more stunning. Impetuous hazel eyes glistened in the candlelight as naughty tongues of frosted hair teased her pretty face. Lips of cherry were fully sensuous. Neiman Marcus must have borrowed the flimsy red negligee from Aphrodite.

"You like it?" Karen had a surprise for Mark that would change their lives forever. "I'm all yours."

"We've had this conversation before," Mark's throat constricted, "and you know exactly how I feel about *us*." He angrily tromped past Karen into his bedroom and tossed his billfold on the dresser. This was not happening a second time.

"Wait!" Karen followed Mark, not about to let her plans end unproductively. "Don't act like this. I have something to show you." *Seize the moment and make him listen.*

"You've already shown me quite enough." Mark struggled with his lusty thoughts. "Get dressed."

"No, this!" Karen handed Mark a pregnancy indicator.

"What's this? So somebody's pregnant. What's that got to do with us?" He glanced into the parlor at the tray of goodies. "Look. How sweet of you to order a snack! I'm famished."

"Mark?" Karen stewed. "This is *not* about food, or flattering your huge ego. I'm pregnant with your child."

He blinked with understanding. "Impossible. It only happened once." He tossed his tie on the back of the chair.

"Biologically, once is all it takes." Karen made dreamy eye contact. "I'm having this child with or without you, Mark." She'd done the abortion route. It had left her with regret and emptiness.

"What will your mother say?" Mark choked back a wave of panic. "My baby?" He had believed it was too late to become a father and grow a family. Yet, euphoria rose up inside of him.

"Yes. *Your* baby." Karen fondly rubbed Mark's arm.

"You're sure it's mine." His blue gaze was direct.

"Mark!" Karen reacted, hurt by his opinion. "The last person I was with before you was my husband Teddy."

Mark's gaze softened like putty. "I don't know what to say, Karen." He felt both remorse and glee. *My own child?*

"What do you want me to do?" he asked. "Pay for an abortion?" Reality set in like a fog. He was sixty years old.

"Heavens, no!" Karen said, closing the gap between them. "Marry me, Mark James, and make an honest woman out of me." She ran her hands inside his unbuttoned shirt. "I will have this baby with or without you. I will *never* abort a child again."

Mark grasped Karen's hands and studied her pretty face. With no forethought, he picked her up in his arms and carried her to his bed. Right or wrong, he would marry her and have a son who would enrich his life and inherit all his earthly possessions.

Though Mark didn't love Karen in the way a man ought to love a woman—like he did Victoria—in time he would learn to cherish their relationship. *Oh, Victoria, if only it was you.*

WEDNESDAY, JUNE 18

41

Texas and Victoria boarded a jet in Atlanta, Georgia, late Tuesday. The plane touched down at *Aeroporto di Fiumicino* Wednesday morning at seven a.m. Rome, Italy time.

While deplaning, Victoria glanced up at Jack and batted her lacquered eyelashes. She might just keep her nose job and the exquisite tooled-linen beige suit with a matching Ann Klein straw hat—which Texas claimed had cost over a thousand dollars.

Actually, the outfit felt more like a million when Texas looked at her, no slouch himself in Calvin Klein designer sportswear.

The man even wore his good looks with humility. What was there not to love about him? From his fun-loving spirit to his remarkable intellect, he was near perfect.

For the first time since awakening to old memories, Victoria felt truly content. Here she was in the most romantic city in the world, on a vacation site most people only dreamed about.

So blessed, Victoria thought she might burst.

Hand in hand, the Jack Hammersteins walked through the jetway connecting the aircraft to the terminal.

"Well, darlin', we're here," Texas fondly remarked.

Victoria decided a kiss was in order. Neither did he object when she grabbed him by the neck and firmly planted a syrupy wet one on his lips. "Thank you, dear, for bringing me here."

As expected, Jackson Lloyd and Alisha Carol Hammerstein made it just fine through customs.

"I need to check with the airline to make sure our tickets home are confirmed," Jack informed Victoria.

"Sure," she replied. "You go ahead and I'll wait right here." The concourse bustled with a mix of nationalities.

Sensing a pair of eyes on her back, Victoria slowly turned around and spied a man in a black suit rudely staring. In response, she frantically looked for Texas, some twenty feet away and talking to a Delta employee. At a second glance, he was still there.

And still staring . . . does he know who I am?

Victoria's breathing was ragged, heart thumping in her chest. Incredibly threatening, his staring bore a hole through her soul.

His eyes are almost reptilian . . . like the steamy breath of a predator.

Embarrassed, Victoria quickly looked away and hurried over to the Delta desk to find Texas.

Don't look. Stay calm. It's probably nothing.

"Are we ready to go?" She tapped Texas on the arm.

"You look troubled, dear. Are you all right?"

"I don't know," Victoria replied. "That man—" she turned around and he wasn't there anymore. "Never mind."

The stranger—he probably recognized Alisha Carol Hammerstein.

Still, the incident had left Victoria trembling inside.

"We'll pick up our suitcases at BAGGAGE CLAIM and settle into the hotel before doing anything else," Texas said. "The CPA has booked us at the Marriott. You'll love it."

"I'd love staying in a hut if you were there," Victoria rashly said before thinking. Should she tell Texas about the man?

No, I should expect stares. Alisha Carol had been a famous model, and the wife of Jackson Lloyd, a worldwide-acclaimed oil icon from Texas. *It's probably nothing to be worried about.*

"Just remember that we've been married for over twenty years so we can't act like newlyweds," Texas teased as they walked down the concord. "Honey? Are you listening to me?"

Huh? "What I said, I only meant, uh, about living in a hut," Victoria stuttered, unwilling to compromise Christian principles.

"I know what you meant, Victoria," he said with a smile. "And I agree that material possessions won't seal a relationship."

She walked faster following the signs to BAGGAGE.

"Have you ever been to Rome?" Texas had visited twice.

"No, and I'm excited. I've seen *Three Coins in a Fountain*."

"I saw that movie, too," Texas remarked. "Maybe we'll toss in a few coins—not that I believe in luck."

"But it's kind of fun, you know, to follow tradition, don't you think?" Side by side, they stepped on the descending escalator to the lower level of the terminal and caught a tram.

When Victoria's two red suitcases rolled out on the baggage conveyor belt, she breathed a sigh of relief. Texas had an airport attendant grab their bags and put them on a pushcart.

The young Italian followed them through double electronic doors leading to the covered parking lot beyond the four lanes used by cars and buses to pick up passengers.

"What upset you so much back there?" he asked.

"What?" Her mind was in a thousand places.

"While I was talking to the Delta gal, you looked as if you'd seen a ghost," he reminded her of the incident.

"Oh, that." Victoria could still see the man's reptilian eyes bearing down on her. They stood on the curb while their Italian escort screamed and motioned at cabbies to pull over to the curb.

"Explain *that*, please," Texas said, thinking it was important.

"I noticed a man staring, and it unnerved me."

"You think he recognized you?" Texas' pulse leaped.

"Maybe Alisha Carol. But isn't that going to happen?"

"Possibly," he replied. "However, no one who knows Alisha Carol intimately is supposed to be attending the conference."

"What do you mean?"

"A precautionary measure, to protect our cover."

"My imagination is probably working overtime," Victoria nervously admitted. She wasn't about to let fear ruin their trip.

The new bolder Victoria implicitly trusted God.

Outside the terminal, taxi drivers in white limousines frantically honked at pedestrians. Texas had his eye on a cab pushing its way through the horrific traffic like a maniac. In response to his crooked finger, the feisty driver swerved his vehicle across two lanes of traffic and hit the curb with a screeching halt. Seconds later, he hopped out of the limousine, white teeth gleaming at Texas, and opened the trunk.

"Let's go!" Texas grasped Victoria's arm and rushed toward the cab. The driver rattled off Italian phrases as he loaded their suitcases in the back. "Get in Alisha." Texas opened the door for her. "The J.W. Marriott," he said to the cabby.

"*Sì.*" The driver ignited the engine.

"There's more than one way to skin a cat." Texas winked.

"Thank you, Jack." She felt safe again, warming up to the idea of being married to Texas if only for a week.

Driving through the eternal city was a step back into medieval history with its archaic buildings and old world charm. A party spirit permeated the seasonably warm air as couples congregated on restaurant terraces to enjoy a cup of café espresso or a glass of vintage wine. Inhaling the odors of fresh-baked pastries and dark European blends of coffee enticed Victoria to satisfy her appetite.

"Do you smell that wonderful aroma?" she asked Texas.

He nodded and squeezed her hand as the driver stopped for a man selling bouquets of roses to cross the street.

"Aren't you getting hungry?" Victoria dropped another hint.

"We'll eat as soon as we check in the hotel." Texas said and yawned. "It's been a long trip and we need to rest for a while."

Victoria's pupils grew large as the limousine pulled up to the hotel. The building was a replica of the old Roman Coliseum, a popular convention center and tourist attraction with guests coming and going in mass and money exchanging hands.

"This is magnificent!" Victoria exclaimed. Like a true debutante, she stepped lightly from the vehicle as the door opened. Texas was right behind her as they approached the entrance and entered the hotel through revolving doors.

"*Buon giorno,*" the young Italian manning the doors greeted Victoria, his appreciative gaze intimately disarming.

"*Ciao,*" she returned.

"You speak Italian, too?" Texas reacted. "Master of two languages, I'm impressed." She also spoke fluent Spanish.

"So it appears." Victoria understood what the doorman privately said to his friend, that she was a beautiful woman. Whether she had *mastered* the Italian language remained to be seen.

The interior décor of the hotel was magnificent, furnished with expensive European antiquities and original artwork. Where the cherry wood railing stopped, regal red-and-gold wallpaper climbed the walls to the ceilings. Sparking chandeliers of tinkling glass beads lit up the place like a beautiful banquet hall.

Victoria caught her breath, not recalling ever having been in so opulent a setting or around so many influential people. She stepped outside the flow of traffic and waited for Texas while he made his way over to the check-in counter. Within a stone's throw was a gigantic fountain spewing water into the air and the entrance to the hotel's promenade of retail stores. She couldn't recall shopping for anything since . . . since Wal-Mart.

A giggle rippled off Victoria's full pink lips. "You've come a long way down baby." She recalled Beverly James' astute assessment of her life when they last spoke at the CROSS-COUNTRY MOTEL in Denver. "Well, Bev, that's all changed."

"We're checked in," Texas came over to Victoria with the electronic keys to their suite in his hand. "Ready to go up?"

"I suppose." She was sensitive to the their situation—blushing like a new bride about to be carried over the threshold. The CPA had reserved a one-bedroom suite with a king-sized bed.

"What about our suitcases?" she suddenly asked.

"Got it covered." Texas didn't miss a beat, grinning from ear to ear. "This isn't a honeymoon, Victoria," he whispered in her ear. "I'm saving that for later when we *really* get married."

Red is the color of roses, not faces.

Room 515 was only a few steps away from where the elevator let them off. Texas opened the door and waited for her to enter.

Giddily, Victoria stepped inside the quaint parlor painted in muted mauve tones and furbished with a loosely woven Persian rug, a ruby-red sofa, and a black-velvet covered Queen Anne.

A silver box of candy and a bottle of vintage red wine had been placed on the marble table for arriving guests. In the corner fireplace leaped a jet of yellow gas flames. It was a gracious room.

"Please don't let me pig out on chocolate," she said to Texas as she spied a small veranda beyond the French doors.

In a flowing motion Victoria stepped outside and breathed in the fresh morning air, appreciative eyes taking a giant swath of the city's old-world buildings and the countryside beyond. Five stories below raged a colorful garden of flowers, shades of red and gold brilliantly gleaming in the sunlight. *So this is Rome* . . .

A few moments later, Victoria returned to the parlor. Testing the agility of the sofa, she questioned the sanity of sharing with Texas a dream she was convinced stemmed from a lost memory.

She was in a large room with a stone fireplace, seated in a wheelchair with bare feet nestled into a soft shaggy rug. She recalled glancing into the kitchen and viewing a set of patio doors. Somehow she had known beyond the sliders stretched a lazy, flowing river. It was uncanny—the vivid dream impression.

Feeling that she had eaten many meals at the oak table in the breakfast nook, she knew which kitchen cabinet contained the crystal glasses. And the plates inside the china closet were white, rimmed in pink roses with squiggly green vines.

The door to Victoria's left opened into a hallway leading to a half bath flanked by two guest bedrooms. Hers was on the right. She could visualize the bedroom even now, how it looked, its wallpaper and the large wall closet that housed her clothes.

Beyond the double French doors beside her queen-sized bed was a garden with fragrant Gardenia bushes, Bachelor's Button and Nasturtium. Its sweet aroma was still playing at her nostrils.

However, there was no way to prove that the realistic dream impressions had been spawned by an actual memory. Would Texas think she was crazy to embrace such a theory? Indeed, like Karen had said, did she need to see a psychiatrist?

A knock had come at the door. *Don't open it!* Fear had stabbed at her senses. Something hideous was on the other side.

Victoria had heeded the warning and awakened.

Now, here in Rome, real danger threatened. She could be apprehended by the police and sent home.

And there was the Antichrist to deal with . . .

A knock jolted Victoria to the present. Her wide eyes fastened on Texas, who was opening the door to their suite.

It was only the bellhop with their suitcases. Pulling out some Euro coins, he handsomely tipped the Italian and thanked him.

"*Grazie*," the suntanned lad replied with a bow and left.

"I'll put our suitcases in the bedroom," Texas said as he secured the door. "Don't look so worried, we'll be fine."

Which door do I fear opening? Victoria shivered. *The one leading to lost memories, or the door the Antichrist is standing behind?*

"I don't know about you, sweetheart, but I need a shower and a nap." Texas scrubbed his oily scalp. "I have to clear my head from jetlag if I'm ever gonna think straight again." He lent her his world-weary eyes. "Do you want to shower first?"

"No, I'll curl up on the sofa and read. You go and do whatever." Her gaze skidded to the bedroom, a slight thrill coursing her veins as she considered sleeping beside Texas.

She peered at him, weak from love knocking at her heart.

"Don't look at me like that, or I can't promise to act like a gentleman." He was so in love with this woman, it hurt.

"I can't talk about our future now, Texas."

"I know," he said, "but when this week is over, we're talking about our future. We can't go on denying our feelings."

I know, Victoria said in her mind. Texas would ask her to marry him again and this time she was thinking of saying yes.

42

The Penthouse Suite

"Did you notice that unusual woman at the airport?" Alexander Luceres Ramnes asked his personal assistant.

"Which woman?" Donald Wetherfield inquired, using a brush to remove lint from the leader's light-gray woolen jacket.

"The beautiful American who was accompanied by the tall Texan. They came out of Delta Gate B-7 as we passed by."

Luceres noted something in the woman's eyes that had deeply disturbed him. *Something about her he couldn't quite . . .*

"I'm sorry, Sir," Donald paused from his task, "but I don't know which woman you mean. Is she someone of importance?"

"Perhaps." He studied the idea.

"Shall I obtain a list of passengers who arrived at Delta Gate B-7 around the same time we did?" Donald asked.

"No, don't bother." Luceres waved a hand. "If the mystery woman is in Rome to attend the festivities, I'm bound to run into her." He now knew what it was that caught his attention. She had an aura of *holiness*, an uncommon trait found in most people.

Luceres removed his billfold from the back pocket of his slacks, counted his cash, and reached for his jacket on the sofa.

Donald's watchful eye didn't miss a move. He would not always be a servant, one day moving into the leader's orbit.

"If you're thinking of a stroll down the promenade," Donald warned, "hotel security advises against it. You might be the target of a religious dissentient. Don't place yourself in harm's way."

Luceres tossed his jacket aside, loosened his tie, and tore it from his neck. "I'm not afraid of my adoring public—though I would likely be mauled for my autograph." He chuckled.

"It would be tragic if—"

"Nothing will happen to me!" Luceres snapped. "But, of course, you are right. A casual stroll is out of the question."

Luceres admired his image in the mirror, craning his neck to the left and right to view his handsome profile at different angles. The forces of nature had been kind. Having inherited superior genes, royal red blood ran through him from his mother's side.

"What, my man, speak up!" Donald was staring at him.

"I'm curious, Sir. What will you say at the banquet when you are honored? It would frighten me to stand before so great an audience—kings, queens, presidents, and dignitaries."

"Say? Do?" Luceres chuckled to himself. "I have no clue. I'm spontaneous, as you well know. The words will come."

"From inspiration?" Donald delved deeper. "And where does one get that sort of spontaneous guidance?"

"It's not just inspiration, it's clairvoyance. Aware of what people are thinking about in the audience helps me understand what I need to say to command their interest."

"You read minds, as in witchcraft?" Donald's eyebrows arched. "Interesting. I recently viewed an old Harry Potter flick."

"I'm hardly into witchcraft," Luceres denied the accusation. "That's an archaic term for the willful force of mind over matter."

"Isn't it the idea of man's control over his destiny that's got Christians in such a stitch?" Donald asked out of curiosity.

"Christians are hateful, narrow-minded, and view clairvoyant people as a threat to true spirituality. Stupid."

"And you prefer to believe that man evolved from an accidental combination of atoms, with a higher intelligence than other animals, and capable of making wise choices."

Donald loved these little fireside chats.

"I like the way you think, Donald. Remind me to give you a raise when my . . ." Luceres had almost said, "When my kingdom comes." He didn't think Donald was ready to hear about his dream of ruling the world. Would he embrace a new savior?

"Manipulation is not necessarily an unhealthy ploy." Luceres decided to pursue the conversation in more depth. "Think of the process as a form of time management by inducing people to act in ways that accomplish your personal goals."

"And your heart is in the right place," said Donald. "You've done the world a great service in ending religious bickering. I'm proud to serve you, Sir. Keep up the good work."

"Thank you, Donald. Flattery will get you everywhere."

43

Gaeta, Italy

The *Grand Hotel Le Rocce* was only a ninety-minute drive from Rome. Dick and Marjorie climbed out of their rented Lamborghini Jeep and viewed the hotel from roadside. The Mediterranean-styled structure, resembling a Moorish villa, occupied an entire hillside outside of Gaeta, Italy and overlooked its own secluded inlet of the pristine blue-green Tyrrhenian Sea.

Dick's veins pumped adrenaline as he parked the jeep in the hotel lot. Old-timers rode the tram down the hillside to the hotel while healthy joggers walked along the flagstone trail lush with vegetation. At sixty-five, Dick was certainly long past the athletic stage, not that he'd ever been physically fit.

Peter Coates had phoned on his cell over an hour ago to inform Dick that he had already checked in the hotel with his sweetie-pie, Lindsey Rhymes—a thirty-something French model. They were scheduled to meet for dinner at eight o'clock tonight, a purely social occasion with companions present. Later, they would do their *real* business without witnesses.

"You ready to go up to the room?" Dick asked Marjorie.

"Let's walk out on the terrace first. I want to take a picture of the sea. Such a lovely shade of lime." She'd brought along her miniature 3-D digital camera, the most advanced of its kind.

"Let's not linger, though. I need a nap before supper." Dick said with a yawn. "Mercy, I can't get used to the time change."

"I know this trip is not purely social," said Marjorie, peering into her husband's cagey eyes. "I only hope you know what you're doing in Europe. I've looked the other way a lot of the time, but doing something illegal on a grander scale, the authorities might not ignore." He'd get the gist of her warning.

Dick chuckled. "What a little woman! No wonder I love you so much." She didn't understand how the world worked.

***

J. W. Marriott in Rome

"Are we having dinner in the room?" Victoria asked Texas.

"If it's all right with you, I'd like to walk the promenade and get a look at the people." He straightened the knot in his tie. "You look lovely. I like your outfit. Yours or Alisha Carol's?"

"Oh, this ol' rag!" Victoria laughed. She was wearing a Rosh Vincent original worth a mint. The silk pantsuit had cost in the neighborhood of twenty-five hundred American dollars.

"Don't underestimate the power of wealth, dear. It buys a lot of friends." Texas smiled. "Anyhow, you could wear nothing and look great!" His face turned beet-red. "Sorry, Victoria."

"Don't apologize. As of late, my thoughts have been no purer. I don't want to act on feelings alone."

"Oh, honey . . ." Texas embraced Victoria and inhaled the clean odor of her freshly shampooed hair. "The time is not quite right for us to formally make plans, but we're getting there."

Victoria knew what Texas meant, and was forced to agree. He had his agenda; she had hers. One day theirs might blend.

"Texas?" Victoria peered up into his eyes, a deep aqua-blue in the dim lighting of the room. "What if this gig doesn't work out and we get caught? What will happen to *us*?"

"My love for you won't change," he said. "Besides, nothing bad will happen to either of us. God is on our side."

Texas was keenly aware that bad things did happen to good people. The enemy had an agenda, too: taking down the cross of Jesus in people's hearts and eradicating their faith in God.

***

Feeling pleasantly full after dining on Mexican cuisine prepared by a popular chef from Monterrey, Mark and Karen took a leisurely stroll down the hotel promenade.

"The Mexican food was great!" she said.

"The company, too," he added.

"I've waited a long time to hear you say that, Mark."

"I like that you're smiling. Are you feeling better? Any queasiness?" He had to look after his baby growing inside of her.

"I feel wonderful now that we have settled our future." Karen wondered how her mother would take the news of their sudden engagement. *You didn't want him, Mommy.*

"Are you positive you want to be married on the same date your mother and I set aside at the country club?" It was doable because Mark hadn't yet cancelled the wedding chapel.

"Do you think Mother will be hurt when she finds out?"

"Does it matter? Vicki's gone," he pointed out. "Sorry if I sound cold, but your mother made it crystal clear that she wants nothing to do with me." Overtones of bitterness laced his words.

"So we're going on with our lives with or without her?"

"Yes, unless you have a better idea."

"I don't. I suppose I should heartily agree, but . . ." Karen worried the news of their betrothal would upset her mother and precipitate another memory episode.

"But what?" Mark's poignant gaze targeted his fiancée.

"I'm angry, but still I worry how she's handling life."

"I understand. The two of you have always been close."

"Like you *were*. Mark, I hope you won't let any personal grudges influence your good judgment regarding the trumped-up murder charges against Mother." He was a spurned lover.

"What are you talking about?" *Was he so transparent?*

"Mother was cruel to you, but she's not a criminal."

Mark nervously chuckled, the conversation beyond weird.

"What?" She took exception.

"You. Sometimes I'm amazed." He shook his head, pausing at the fountain to toss in a few coins for good luck.

"Why?"

"You do *everything* in your power to pull me into your world, and now that I'm committed to you, you assault my character on the pretense of protecting your mother. Isn't that being a little two-faced? Let's call a spade a spade." *Get real, sweetheart.*

"That hurts, Mark." Tears poised to flow in Karen's iridescent hazel eyes. "I didn't mean to chastise you."

"All right. Let's not talk about this any more."

He gazed at the shiny coins at the bottom of the fountain. What did Karen want from him? Victoria had meant—did mean the world to him, but circumstances had drastically changed.

"One more untouchable subject, then I'm through," Karen said. "It's true I didn't want you to marry my mother!" she confessed. "But when your *Little Vicki* tossed you aside, you became fair game—not that you would ever turn down a little free gratis sex when it was offered." *Let's air a little truth here.*

"Wow!" Mark smacked his lips. "That temper of yours has gotten you into trouble before." He was talking about her deceased husband, Teddy, whom Karen removed permanently.

"You know it's not like that with us." Karen touched Mark's arm. "I'm sorry I'm so out of control. Chalk it up to hormones."

"So how is it with us?" Mark plowed deeper.

"I never loved Teddy like I love you. He was abusive and cheated on me. You are the kindest man I've ever known."

Mark's blue gaze softened. "And you know I would never do anything to hurt you or your mother." He embraced Karen and kissed her lightly on the lips. "You're my life now."

"I know." Karen had unresolved questions about Mark's participation in her daddy's murder. *Could she move past the doubt?*

***

Victoria stepped into the promenade traffic in front of the fountain. "Did you see *that?*" She hid behind Texas.

"What?" He turned around and faced her.

She pointed over his shoulder. "Dr. Mark James just kissed my daughter. What do you suppose *that* means?"

"I don't know, and it isn't any of our business." He escorted Victoria into a candy store. "If you're thinking of having a little motherly chat with your daughter, this isn't the time or place."

Victoria took in a strangling breath. Mark was going to take advantage of Karen now that she was out of the picture. She should have returned home weeks ago and explained everything to Karen. She would have understood and offered her help instead of camping out with the enemy. *Were they sleeping together?*

***

Donald Wetherfield stood outside Caesar's Cigar Shop watching the pedestrians stroll the mall. A tall Texan pulled a pretty American woman away from the fountain and into a candy store. What was going on? Why was the lady so upset?

Donald decided to follow the couple and observe them. Call it a hunch, but this had to be the American Luceres had seen at the airport, not many women so beautiful. If she or her partner used a credit card for purchases, he would learn their identities. The Internet highway was chockfull of information regarding world citizens. Find the right route and it was a walk in the park.

***

Victoria purchased a box of *Crema Cioccolato* with nuts and exited the shop with Texas. By now, her head was exploding.

"I think we should pick up some take-out deli sandwiches and return to the room. You are in no mood to socialize."

"Right." They walked down the promenade and found a deli. Texas ordered for them and paid the tab in cash. "Ready?"

"I'm sorry I ruined our evening," Victoria apologized to Texas going up on the elevator. "I see flashes of red every time I think of my daughter in the arms of that womanizer."

"Isn't that being a little hard on Mark, your so-called best friend?" Texas lifted an eyebrow. "What about compassion?"

"I have none. Compassion was before Beverly suggested that that Mark received a monetary payoff from Dick Branson. I know he was involved with my husband's death, and that makes me hopping mad." She had been the object of his manipulation.

The elevator doors crunched open. "Let's talk in the room," Texas suggested, slicing his card through the security lock.

They entered the suite and stood motionless. Victoria was crushed by what she had seen: Karen kissing Mark. She had to do something to stop this ill-fated romance, doomed from the start.

"I can't just sit by and watch Karen ruin her life again." Her first marriage had been disastrous. "Can I break my promise and talk to her?" Eyes begged for mercy, resolve inching in.

"I don't think it's a good idea, Victoria. How are you going to explain posing as Alisha Carol Hammerstein?"

"I know I'm not reacting rational, but I don't care! I love my daughter, and I don't want that snake influencing her."

"Look," said Texas, hoping to reason with Victoria. "Karen is a grown woman, seasoned in relationships. Is it possible she knows what's she's doing and wants a relationship with Mark?"

Tears clouded Victoria's vision. "I've known for a while that Karen loves him," she admitted. "I thought he knew better than to take advantage of her feelings. I was wrong."

Texas had never seen Victoria so distraught. He walked over and put his hands squarely on her shoulders. "You need to calm down and get perspective, or you'll ruin our sting."

"I know." But saving Karen took priority. "Coming here with you may have been a mistake."

"What?" Texas took a step back, disappointed.

Rain slithered down the glass panels of the French patio doors, reminding Victoria of the time she stood outside the Sagewood Movie Theater in Memphis, Tennessee, waiting for Georgie Hendricks to call her back on the payphone. She felt just as helpless now as she did then—like she had no control over life.

"To harbor hate is a mistake, Victoria," Texas reasoned. "You can't control other peoples' lives. Let Karen work out her problems without your interference. She deserves your trust."

Victoria glared at her escort. *He's preaching to me.*

"I know you want to jump in and make things right, but you can't. By any chance, are you jealous of their relationship?"

"What?" Victoria couldn't believe her ears. "You think I still care for Mark? I thought you knew me better than that!"

"Doesn't it make you furious that after only a few weeks of missing you Mark has turned to another woman?"

Texas knew he bordered cruelty, but he had to make Victoria see the futility of her anger. Blowing her cover for a mother-daughter chat in the midst of thousands of law enforcement officers was dangerous. He needed Victoria's undivided attention to pull off the CPA sting, a far more important agenda.

"I know what you're trying to do." Victoria collapsed on the sofa and threw her face into her hands.

Texas gathered Victoria into his arms. "I'm sorry, but I can't afford a sympathetic ear. If I came down too hard on you, forgive me. But we must look at the bigger picture, our mission. We can't let our vision become clouded with personal agendas."

"You're right." Victoria broke his hold on her and walked over to the coffee table. From the brown paper sack, she removed a ham sandwich and took a bite, recalling her picnic with Mark on the banks of Chickasaw Lake. "Aren't you eating?"

44

Somewhere in South America

Georgie Hendricks was left in the dark hole of an aircraft for what seemed like days. When the plane landed hours later, she had no idea where she had been taken. Blindfolded, she was at the mercy of golden-eyed Hulk, the man who had kidnapped her from Devin's house and treated her unkindly. Shame on him!

"Take it easy!" Georgie fussed as rough hands pulled her out of the plane and ground her face into the dirt for speaking. She spit out the stinking sand and cursed her captors. The men who had detained her spoke Spanish, and from their nasty tone of voice, they weren't too happy about the situation either.

It appeared she was somewhere south of the border in a dessert since the air was blazing hot and arid. Still blindfolded, feeling thirsty and hungry, Georgie was further abused when someone picked her up and tossed her into the bed of a truck.

The hot, bumpy ride through the desert gave her ample time to consider if death might actually win out. Over the past few weeks, she had lost a lot of weight. Flesh hung on her usually taut body like excess baggage. Her stomach felt glued to her ribs. She would not die without a fight. She couldn't. Not like this.

Not now!

Someone opened the back of the canvas-covered truck and said, "Get out." Georgie didn't argue. Any place would be better than the dusty, rat-infested flat bed of the truck. Rattlesnakes were treated better. "I'm thirsty," she said, hoping for mercy.

A hand shoved a canteen to Georgie's lips and she drank like a camel at the end of a hot journey. "Where are you taking me?"

"You've been assigned to work in the fields," the man said with an English accent that made Georgie think he was a Latino.

Sunlight slapped Georgie in the face like a bolt of lightning as someone tore the cloth mask from her face. She shaded her squinted eyes with her hands and glanced at her assaulters.

"Where am I?" she asked.

A flat sheet of white sand stretched for hundreds of miles in every direction. Jagged mountaintops on the distant horizon cut into the blue sky like black cutouts. Peru or Paraguay? Argentina? *Or on the backside of the moon?*

"No questions, *Donna*! You pick beans and live," said the skinny Colombian. "You do as we say, you live."

"Coffee beans?" Georgie queried.

The Colombian pair bent over with laughter and conversed rapidly in Spanish. Georgie suddenly wished she'd taken school more seriously and learned a couple of languages in the process.

Still, she got the picture in living color. The likelihood of her ever seeing the US of A again was dubious. Victoria would have to carry on by herself. PI Georgie had her own drama to play out.

***

J.W. Marriott in Rome

Donald Wetherfield checked with the deli owner to see if any of his customers had used a credit card to charge their meal and learned that the American couple had paid in cash. Afterwards, he trailed them to the fifth floor and noted their room number.

At the front desk Donald used his security clearance to obtain the couple's identities from the clerk. The Jackson Hammersteins had also paid cash in advance for their suite, highly unusual for world travelers. *Did they have something to hide?* He wondered.

***

On Wednesday evening, Dick went to bed at the *Grand Hotel Le Rocce* in Gaeta, Italy, happy as a Tennessee lark. The financial drug deal was sealed. Peter Coates, representing a group known as Taurus, had agreed to all Dick's terms. The Arab world would soon be receiving illegal drugs packed in Branson meats, just as soon as the International Business League approved the plan.

Supplying illegal drugs to residents of nervous, confused countries had become big business in the new millennia. The spread of democracy, coupled with the decline of moral values, had created a playground for experimentation. Folks were unhappy, needed an aphrodisiac to get them through the day. It might be sex, more likely, sex with drugs. He could help.

Fast asleep and snoring, Marjorie lay beside Dick. She was the best woman ever, never complaining about his late nights out, and always trusting that he would come home to her. And he had.

Tomorrow morning, she could thank him.

***

Back at the Marriott

Donald Wetherfield was up nearly all night Wednesday making inquiries on the Internet. He was not disappointed.

Married for ten years, Jackson Lloyd and Alisha Carol Hammerstein were U.S. citizens, residents of Dallas, Texas. Jack owned a chain of oil wells from Houston to El Paso, a recluse by nature. And Alisha Carol, former super model, had appeared on the front pages of numerous magazines around the world.

Having kept a low profile for years, what were they doing in Rome, involved in all the hoopla? *Why* were they here?

Donald critiqued the information again. No question the couple had received an invitation to the festivities or they would not be here. Those who had organized the NATO event required that participants make a financial contribution. They qualified.

However, something about the wealthy couple bothered Donald, though he couldn't quite put his finger on what. While exiting the Internet, he heard a knock at the door. Removing the latch, he peered into the dimly lighted hallway. The hour was late.

"Luceres? What can I do for you?" Donald asked.

"I couldn't sleep. I see you're up, too. What have you been doing?" The world leader pushed open the door and walked into Donald's suite, glancing around the parlor. "Am I intruding?"

"No." Donald threaded his fingers through his nappy blond hair. "Just playing around on the Internet. You?" He wasn't ready to share inconclusive information regarding the woman who had fascinated Luceres. "Would you like some coffee?"

"Decaf would be great," he replied. "I was looking over the schedule of activities offered tomorrow and I've decided to attend the High Tea given in honor of the young peacekeepers. What do you think? Should I go, or would it cause a ruckus?"

Donald smiled. "It might. Are you sure you want to draw attention to yourself before Friday evening?"

"I don't want to separate myself from the people," Luceres said. "I'm a politician, and I depend on the support of friends."

"I see," said Donald. "Well, if you do attend, I should accompany you." He was a jujitsu expert, Luceres' bodyguard. Having learned martial arts while training to become a CIA operative, Donald's career had abruptly ended when a cohort discovered that he had betrayed his country by accepting money from a South American drug lord in exchange for information.

Donald placed a glass container of water in the microwave to heat, pre-measuring instant coffee into two cups as he peered at his boss. "Anything else I should know about your agenda?"

"No," answered Luceres. "This appearance is purely social. I'm interested in meeting my supporters."

"Oh," said Donald, "the loyal, rich ones."

"Exactly." Luceres privately aspired to see the American woman again. This time, he had questions for her. "Of course, I have no problem with you attending, but I need my space."

"No problem, Sir. That's why you pay me the big bucks."

Luceres heartily laughed. "I do like you, Donald—always the congenial one, honest and up front. We make a great team."

Was he? If his boss could read minds, didn't he know a great deal more about Donald Jay Wetherfield than he was letting on?

"I like you, too, Sir." Mutual respect was important.

"I should go and let you get some rest." Luceres' eyes fell on the computer. "Were you doing research?"

"Yes," said Donald. "It's personal."

"Oh," said Luceres. "Is the coffee ready?"

Donald took the hot liquid from the microwave, filled two mugs, and handed Luceres one. "To a good week!" he toasted.

"To success!" Luceres took a sip of coffee. "Thanks for entertaining me so I could unwind." He was a light sleeper and usually read himself to sleep at night. "Well, I should be going." He set down his cup. "Continue on with what you were doing."

Donald saw Luceres out the door. "Goodnight, Sir."

"Goodnight, Donald. Thanks for the coffee."

He knows what I'm doing, thought Donald.

THURSDAY, JUNE 19

45

Dick and Marjorie took a sailboat ride Thursday morning before checking out of the Grand Hotel Le Rocce in Gaeta, Italy. He wanted to be back in Rome before High Tea was served.

Daniel Tempest would be in the reception line. And if his sister Karen had anything to say about her mother, he wanted to hear it with his own ears. "You ready to roll, Marjorie?"

"Just about." She finished up in the bathroom and came out smiling. "Oh, Dick. I had such a nice time today. Thank you for the sail. The sea is beautiful, calm as a sheet of glass."

"And you weren't all that bad yourself this morning." He was referring to their little tryst in bed. "I might just want to sail a little more, if you . . ."

"No, I think it's time to leave."

"You're right." Dick smiled. "We don't wanna miss High Tea." He was planning on cornering Alexander Luceres Ramnes if he got the chance. *Friends in high places*, he knew the routine.

"I hear the Queen of England will be there with her court," Marjorie said. "I'd sure like to shake her hand."

"Hell's bells! The Man of the Hour could show up."

"I doubt it." Marjorie plugged a diamond earring into one ear. "Luceres would be mobbed if he came. Too dangerous."

"Unlikely," Dick said, "considering the elite class of folks who will be attending." He latched their suitcases.

"You're right. The Queen of England wouldn't mob the man who brought religious peace to the world." She picked up her sweater. "Did you already check out of the hotel?"

"Done. We're through here. Let's get back to Rome."

***

Back at the Marriott

Karen awakened Thursday morning with Mark in the bed beside her. She didn't care that she was about to throw up. Her dream of owning Mark's affections had come true. He was going to marry her; it was only a matter of time. She would be patient.

Mark rolled over in the bed and opened his eyes. "Good morning, Sunshine. What time is it?"

"You haven't called me that since I was a little girl."

"Don't remind me." Mark was all too aware of their age difference. "People are bound to say I robbed the cradle."

"So what? Shall I order breakfast sent up?"

"That would be nice. But keep it light." The clock said 9:30. "Every time I turn around, somebody's feeding us."

"Isn't High Tea scheduled for this afternoon?" Karen asked.

"Yes. Our invitation is over there on the dresser."

"I think I'll have an order of black coffee and a cream-cheese bagel." Karen studied the hotel menu.

"I'll have the same," Mark said, heading off to the bathroom to shave and shower.

Karen flipped on the TV. "Look, Mark! There's a news clip on the television about the Rome festivities," she called out to him in the bathroom. A camera shot of Luceres appeared as he deplaned at the airport in Rome. "Who's that man?"

"What?" Mark called back, unable to hear Karen.

"Never mind." The cameras rolled to the left and focused on a famous American model, Alisha Carol somebody—not anyone that Karen recognized from a magazine cover.

"I wish Mother would call," Karen said, aware that her words fell on deaf ears with the radio turned up and Mark in the shower.

***

"Are you ready to meet your adoring public?" Texas asked.

Victoria looked beautiful in Alisha Carol's velvet green after-five dress and matching shoes. A diamond crescent graced her slender neck like it belonged there. He wanted to lean over and kiss the nap of her neck and drink in her sweetness, but dared not.

"What time are we supposed to be there?" Victoria eyed her escort, wearing a shiny black tuxedo and screaming-red bowtie.

"Ready as I'll ever be," Texas said. "Remember, as soon as we are in the ballroom, we separate and mingle with the crowd. The micro-recorder installed in your necklace is voice activated so you don't have to do anything. Any questions?"

"None." She wanted to see her son. Daniel was the most important reason she was here. "I'll behave, I promise."

"Then, let's go downstairs and have a spot of tea."

***

Dick and Marjorie Branson returned to the J. W. Marriott in Rome around noon. After bathing and resting, they dressed for the afternoon tea. Marjorie donned a shimmering pink chiffon dress with matching shoes. Dick wore a tuxedo. Fit to be tied, he was supercharged over socializing with the rich and famous.

The ballroom doors opened at 2:30 p.m. and Dick wanted to be among the first to congratulate the peacekeeping do-gooders for their contribution to world peace. He was not disappointed when he saw the decorated banquet hall, a testimony to finery.

On the long serving tables covered in white linen cloths were European delicacies fit for royalty. And the silver was polished to perfection, the finest china waiting to be used by the guests.

Jeffrey Daniel Tempest was second in the reception line. Lance Jacobs, a young Canadian with a doctorate in Human Resources, would offer the first handshake. Daria Langstead stood to Daniel's right, dressed elegantly in a blue sateen dress covered in French lace. Altogether, the twenty peacekeepers waited to greet the guests, well rehearsed in social etiquette. The International Peacekeeping Taskforce had an image to protect.

"Are you nervous about meeting my sister?" Daniel leaned over and privately asked Daria.

"Should I be?" She adoringly peered at Daniel. "Is Karen the overprotective type? Will she be upset that you're engaged?"

"Look! They've officially opened the doors." He pointed.

In response, the orchestra leader waved his baton for the music to begin. First to be formally announced were Richard and Marjorie Branson from Fernwood, Tennessee. Dr. Mark James and Miss Karen Tempest were second through the doorway.

"Hi, Sis." Daniel grasped his sibling's hand, giving her a tight hug. "You look great! Where's Mother?"

"Uh," Karen stumbled, thinking it was bad timing to discuss her mother's situation. "Congratulations on your good work, Bro. Do you think you could spare me a little time when the formalities are over?" She eyed Mark. "We'll save you a seat at our table."

"Great! I have some good news to share."

"Oh?" Karen glanced over at the pretty girl from Holland.

"Later, Sis. You're holding up the line." Daniel chuckled.

When Mark and Karen had greeted all twenty of the young peacekeepers, they found Table Number 30 and took their seats.

"Thank you," Karen said as Mark pulled out a chair for her.

An artistic arrangement of chrysanthemums, primroses, green ivy and baby breaths in a pastel pink-glazed vase graced the middle of the large, round table. Before Karen was a magnificent setting of fine white china set on a tablecloth of French lace, complete with silver and linen napkins, no expense spared.

One of eight couples, Dick and Marjorie Branson located their nameplates and sat down. Mr. and Mrs. George T. Bernard were seated on their right, Karen and Mark on their left.

The other spaces at the table filled quickly as scores of people filed into the ballroom, cordially greeted by the peacekeepers. After formal introductions, private conversations were in order.

"The music is divine," Marjorie leaned over and whispered to Dick. "After we're served, could we dance?"

"Anything to make you happy, dumplin'." He consumed the wine like it was cola, feeling light as a feather, as giddy as a boy.

Midway through the first course, Karen noticed a tall, lean Italian standing in the doorway. His eyes were—

"Look Mark! Alexander Luceres Ramnes is here!"

"What? Who's that muscleman with him?"

"His bodyguard, I suppose."

The fanfare music announced the arrival of Queen Ann Marie. She made a triumphant entry and took her royal seat on the podium. The orchestra played England's national anthem as her royal court joined the procession. Luceres was the first to kneel at the queen's feet, kissing her hand.

"Now, isn't that just the sweetest thing you ever saw?" Dick said to Marjorie. "Luceres is such a great person."

Karen scribbled a note on a white napkin and passed it over to Daniel as he passed by. It said, "I need to speak to you about Mother when you get a chance." He smiled and nodded.

Following the meal and a generous portion of gourmet tea, the tables were cleared for the dancing to begin.

During the second song, Karen tapped Daria on the shoulder. "Excuse me, but may I have this dance with my brother?" She flew into his arms, finally alone.

"I'm so glad to see you, Karen. How is life treating you?" Daniel smiled, whirling her around on the dance floor.

"Great! Mother's missing," she said.

"What do you mean missing??" Daniel led Karen to the side so they could speak privately. "I thought Mother and Doc James were getting hitched the end of this month—June 28th, isn't it?"

"The wedding's off. Mother broke their engagement weeks ago and ran away with our grandmother."

"Kimberly Ann?" Daniel blinked at the whirlwind news. "No wonder you wanted to see me. Are they all right?"

"I have no idea," said Karen. "The police have issued a warrant for Mother's arrest." This news was the worst part.

"For taking Grammy out of the Nashville healthcare facility? Isn't that a little harsh punishment for the deed?"

"No, for plotting our father's murder."

"I'm afraid you've lost me. Mother can't be responsible for actions she can't recall. Besides, the case is closed."

"Not anymore!" Karen exclaimed. "Mother got back her memories." The saga sounded like a fantasy.

Daniel's face turned white as a sheet. "How?"

"I'm sorry I had to break the news like this, but you've been out of touch." She paused. "I'm afraid there's more."

Daniel profoundly sighed. "Go on."

"Mother's memories have flip-flopped. Although she recalls many events prior to her accident, nothing afterwards registers," Karen explained the weird amnesia the best she could.

"She doesn't recall being engaged to Mark James?"

"No," said Karen. "She doesn't love him anymore."

"Does she recall giving birth to me? " Daniel asked.

"No, Daniel. I'm so sorry. Mother didn't recognize me or Mark when her memories switched on April 14."

Daniel stared down at the polished wood floor beneath his feet. "Wow! No wonder you were in stitches to see me. That makes my news a whole lot less eventful."

"What news?"

"I'm engaged to Daria. We are to be married in September."

"I have some other news," Karen said. "I'm going to marry Mark in Mother's place." Saying the words sounded bizarre.

"Why?" Daniel cornered his sister's hazel gaze.

"Because I love him, and because I'm pregnant with his child. Please don't scold me and be happy for us."

"Dance with me, honey?" Daria showed up in the nick of time to keep Daniel from saying the wrong thing.

46

Karen found Mark at the open bar. "I'm ready to leave."
"Don't you want to meet Luceres?" he asked.
"No, I've had all the excitement I can take for one afternoon. I told Daniel about Mother. *Every* alarming detail." She grabbed Mark's hand and pushed though the crowd toward the exit.
Victoria and Texas observed their departure.
"Did you notice how upset Karen is?" she whispered to Texas, who was standing a few feet away from the Queen of England and recording every interesting conversation on his micro-recorder. "Should we go after her?" she asked.
"Excuse me," Texas said, effectively ignoring Victoria's question. "I see someone I know. Wait here, I won't be long."
"Who?" Victoria glanced around the room.
Leaving her side, he ventured across the ballroom. Feeling abandoned, Victoria guessed she'd have to fend for herself.
"Could I assist you in locating someone?" a mellow male voice addressed Victoria from behind. Startled, she spun around and faced Alexander Luceres Ramnes, the suspect Antichrist.
Duh. More handsome than his photos, Luceres' sharp gaze disarmed Victoria's desire to insult him.
"You dropped this," the leader said, smiling as he handed Victoria her white linen handkerchief. "Are you alone today?"
"No. My husband, Jack is with me." *Go ahead and tell all, foolish girl.* Victoria slipped the hanky inside her jeweled handbag, staring at her shoes to avoid eye contact. "Thank you."
"My pleasure. And you are?"
Victoria lifted her eyes. "Alisha Carol Hammerstein."

Luceres sensed the beautiful American was hesitant to befriend him, unlike most people who vied for his attention. Did Alisha Carol have something to hide? "And your husband is?"

"Jackson Lloyd. We're from Dallas." She glanced around for Texas. *Help!* "Texas. In America." *And live on a ranch with horses. Eat bacon for breakfast . . .* Victoria was foolishly jabbering like she hadn't a brain cell behind her false eyelashes.

"Interesting." Luceres laced his hands behind his back and rocked on his feet. "So how do you like Rome?"

Victoria stared at the politician, speechless and confused over what she should do next. "Fine." *Cat hair was fine, not Rome.*

"Would you like to waltz while you're waiting for Jackson?" Luceres offered his hand, stumped that she didn't immediately take it. What was it with this woman? Didn't she like him?

"I know who you are!" Victoria said a little too quickly as she was swept into Luceres' arms, feeling more like she'd been jailed than held by the most popular personality in the world.

Antagonism? Was that what he detected? Luceres was unable to read the American woman's thoughts. Something was blocking her thoughts. *It was—*

"Excuse me, but I think you have my wife." Texas tapped Luceres on the shoulder. "Mind?"

"Of course not." The world leader spun around to see who addressed him. "I assume you are Jackson Lloyd."

"Jack. And it's wonderful to meet you, Mr. Ramnes."

"Please call me Luceres. Let's not be formal." He clicked his heels together and bowed slightly before Victoria. "You have a charming wife and she dances delightfully. I understand you are from the state of Texas. It's been a while since I was in Dallas."

"Jack!" Victoria declared, immensely relieved. "May I have a word with you in private?" She pulled him to the side.

"What? The conversation was just getting off to a good start. Are you recording? Why did you break away?"

"Because I can't stand that man and I don't want to socialize with him. You talk to him. I'm going back to the room."

Luceres had an opportunity to walk away, but he wasn't yet ready. He was curious about Alisha Carol, what it was about her that disturbed him so. At first, he thought it was her spirituality, but now he was uncertain. His chameleon eyes the color of wheat and seaweed skittered to the couple, indulged in an argument of some sort, so typical of long-term married couples.

Luceres couldn't dismiss a feeling of—what? He shook his head, stumped. Was she a Christian dissident, a rebel in Paradise?

Texas took Victoria by the hand and led her into the presence of the diplomat. "I'm sorry, but Alisha Carol isn't feeling well. Maybe we can arrange a meeting later—"

Hearing Texas making an appointment with the Antichrist, Victoria pretended to have an attack of gout, doubling over like poison was invading her body. "You'd better attend to your sick wife," Luceres advised. "If she needs medical attention—"

"No, I'll be fine," Victoria lifted her head. "I just need to lie down. Will you excuse us?" She reached out for Texas' hand.

"I'm so sorry we didn't get to visit with—"

"Jack! Please, I need to leave."

"Perhaps you could join me for lunch one day?" Luceres gazed at Victoria with interest. "I'm staying in the penthouse. Maybe you could ring me when you're feeling better?"

Victoria's eyes skittered to Texas. "Actually, our schedule is pretty full." She winced from pain when Texas pinched the underside of her arm. "I don't think it will be possible." Victoria had no desire to chitchat with a man who had a devilish agenda.

"Surely, you can find time to socialize—oh say for thirty minutes?" Luceres was irritated at being put off.

Victoria bent over and gagged. "Oh . . ." she pretended to be in pain. "I think you'd better take me to the clinic, Jack."

Luceres snapped his finger at Donald Wetherfied and he came running. "See that Mr. and Mrs. Hammerstein get back to their suite. I'll send my personal physician over to check her out."

"Really, that won't be necessary. Like my wife said, it's the gout. I think a few antacid tablets will do the trick. Rich foods, you know." Texas tried to maneuver out of the mess Victoria had spontaneously created. "Thank you for caring so much."

"Sure, phone me if I can be of any assistance."

Donald observed the dialog, certain that the American woman was only pretending. But it wasn't his call.

Texas made one more attempt to rectify Victoria's rude response to the Antichrist. "I'll call you about setting up a time to meet. I would love to hear more about your future plans."

Victoria bent over and gagged again.

"Well . . ." Luceres crossed the ballroom to engage in another conversation, thinking it took all kinds to make up a world.

"Are you crazy, woman?" Texas let Victoria have it once they had exited the ballroom. "You just insulted the most influential man in the world! What were you thinking?"

"What I'm thinking is X-rated, so don't ask."

***

"Who was that woman talking to Luceres?" Mark wondered.

"I have no idea," returned Karen. "Wait! She was the woman at the airport—on the news. Is she a friend of Luceres'?"

In some strange way, the confident manner in which the American woman carried herself reminded Karen of her mother.

Could it be? Karen rudely stared. *No way!*

"What's wrong?" asked Mark. "You look like you've seen an apparition. Are you sick again? Maybe we should return to the room before you embarrass yourself and upchuck on someone."

"No. I want to meet Luceres in person." She walked back into the ballroom with attitude, her mind chasing rabbits.

The Queen had just finished dancing with Luceres when Karen seized her opportunity to speak with him. With no forethought of how the politician would view her straightforwardness, she approached him and said: "Excuse me, Mr. Ramnes. May I have a word with you in private?"

"It's Dr. Ramnes," he replied, thinking American women had a corner on beauty. "I just completed my doctorate in psychology last month. And you are?" He managed a smile.

"Karen Tempest." She hooked her arm in his, ignoring Mark, and walked the politician into a corner. "I have a grave problem, and I was hoping that you might lend some assistance."

Luceres' lips pursed with amusement. "What kind of problem?" He crossed his arms in a deadlock. American women were not only lovely and charming, they were outspoken.

"My mother is in trouble. Without going into great detail, let me just say I believe she has been falsely accused of a crime."

Standing within hearing distance, Mark turned a pig pink over Karen's presumption that the world leader cared a whit what happened to Victoria. *What is she thinking?*

"And where is your mother?" Luceres glanced around the room. "Perhaps we could settle this matter now."

"She isn't here," Karen said. "Mother has been missing for several weeks. She has amnesia. Confused, she's afraid to come home because of the trumped-up charges against her."

"Oh?" Luceres lifted one eyebrow. "Explain, please."

"It's bad." Karen removed a tissue from her purse and dried a pretend tear. "They believe she plotted my father's murder."

"They? Who are *they*, Miss Tempest?" The drama unfolding was far too serious for the gala occasion. "Wouldn't you prefer to dance, and let's discuss this matter later in my suite?"

"Here is fine. I don't want to take up your precious time," Karen said. "Just say you'll help her when she returns home."

Luceres meditated a moment. "And you are convinced that your mother is innocent because you know her well?"

"As sure as I stand here, she wouldn't step on a fly. If she is apprehended by the police, will you promise to have *your* people look into the matter?" Eyes burnished in green pleaded.

"It's a simple request." He reached in his coat pocket and pulled out a business card. "Call this number and tell the operator the password." He leaned over and whispered in Karen's ear.

"Don't tell anyone or the phones will ring off my wall." He smiled, straightening his lean, perfectly sculptured body.

"Excuse me." Mark interrupted the serious conversation. "I apologize for my fiancée's cornering you like this," he said to Luceres. "Forget about helping. It's not your problem."

"Mark!" Karen exclaimed.

"Thank you for your time, Dr. Ramnes."

"And you are?" Luceres gazed at Mark.

"Dr. Mark James from Fernwood, Tennessee. Karen's mother is the infamous fugitive from Tennessee, Victoria Martin Tempest. You may have seen her picture on the news."

"Oh yes, the woman with the unusual amnesia. I'm so sorry, Karen. This must be terribly hard on you."

"It is! And if we don't find my mother soon I'll go crazy. Just knowing you will help her is such a great comfort."

"Enough, Karen!" Mark grabbed her by the elbow. "I'm afraid we have to leave now," he said to Luceres.

"Wait." Luceres thought a moment. "Thank you for putting your trust in me, Karen."

"You're welcome, Sir." She jerked away from Mark, sending him a chilling message to butt out!

"I'll look into the matter and lend my assistance, should you need it." He smiled. "Perhaps the problem will work itself out."

"I doubt it," Karen replied. "Here's my business card."

Luceres studied it. "I see your are in real estate. I might be able to use your services one day." *When my kingdom comes.*

"I apologize for being a nuisance. You are more of a gentleman than the media reports. You have my vote."

Luceres grinned. "On the contrary, Karen, I value your friendship and admire your spunk. It took a great deal of courage for you to approach me on your mother's behalf. I am honored that you place such high esteem upon my capabilities.

"Thank you, Sir." Karen swelled with elation.

47

"What was *that* all about in there?" Texas asked Victoria as soon as they exited the ballroom. "You had the *perfect* chance to get information from the horse's mouth. You blew it!"

"I'm in no mood to be scolded, Texas! Why don't you go up to the room and relax?" *Get over it!* "I need to purchase film from the camera shop." A cold fire burned in her eyes.

"Shouldn't we talk about this?"

"No," said Victoria. "And don't follow me."

The fugitive-in-flight was complicated like Jon Branson had said, as unpredictable as a lightning strike. Texas wasn't about to chase Victoria down and apologize. She'd been rude to him and the Antichrist, an action not so easy to forgive or forget!

As Victoria walked away, Texas disappeared into the steel jaws of the elevator. He knew she'd seen the fury boiling in his angry eyes and heard his fist slam against the elevator button.

Let him get the anger out of his system, Victoria thought.

No way was she meeting privately with the Antichrist. In a room alone with the vain leader she was certain to go for his jugular vein. *Bad idea.* No, distancing herself from him was best.

Surely, Texas would see the wisdom of her thinking when he had time to think about it. Then they could kiss and make up.

Victoria walked the equivalent of a block and located the camera shop. There she purchased colored film for her camera, failing to notice that a man was following her.

***

Donald Wetherfield had cautiously trailed the American couple when they left the ballroom. He had witnessed the brief argument that had taken place between Jackson Lloyd and Alisha Carol, applauding them for their wise decision to separate until tempers cooled. Unfortunately, he didn't hear what was said.

Alisha Carol entered the promenade, walking fast.

Good, thought Donald, it would give him the opportunity to observe her actions from a distance without the protection of her spouse. Women acted in different ways when alone.

Donald entered the camera shop behind Victoria and played with some video equipment while she paid cash for film.

After the fugitive had gone, he approached the sales girl at the counter. "The woman that was just here. Do you know her?"

"What about her?" the sales lady asked.

"Your security camera . . ." Donald pointed overhead. "Did it take her picture?"

"Yeah, I suppose," she replied.

"I need a copy." Donald pulled out his CIA credentials and showed them to the woman. "As soon as possible."

"No problem, Sir. Come back in thirty minutes and I'll have the photo ready," she replied, happy to assist in a security risk.

***

When Donald returned to his suite around five, he fed Alisha Carol Hammerstein's photo into the INTERPOL Internet identification program designed to track missing persons. Notices were color-coded. Red for immediate arrest, blue for unclear identity and persons likely to commit crimes. Yellow was used for missing persons and black notices indicated the deceased.

Donald had read all of Patricia Cornwell's crime novels.

It would be interesting to see if the woman's photo turned up a match. There were valid reasons for people to hide their true identities. Of all people, Donald understood, christened William Lynn Baker at birth. Need always outweighed the risks.

Well into Donald's late twenties, poor decisions led to chastisement by his CIA peers. After having extensive facial reconstruction, he'd decided to embark on a better life and officially changed his name to Donald Jay Wetherfield. With no living siblings and dead parents, his new identity had never once come into question. In fact, he liked himself even better.

Investigating Alisha Carol Hammerstein had been Donald's idea alone. He wanted to please his boss; it was as simple as that. The woman had upset Luceres because she lacked proper respect when encountered at High Tea on Thursday. She had refused his personal invitation to visit him in his suite, wounding his ego.

Despite the American's rude behavior, Luceres wanted to see her again. Why he was obsessing with this particular woman was a mystery. Was she so different from any other woman?

***

Victoria rushed to catch the elevator before the doors crunched shut. "Great!" She stepped aboard, leaking unwanted tears around her eyes, already sorry for her immature behavior toward Texas and the Antichrist. *Some undercover agent, huh?*

The day had been ratty with her making many wrong choices.

"Excuse me, Miss, but you dropped this." Someone tugged at the hem of Victoria's dress. *Huh?* She glanced down.

"On my," was all Victoria could think to say.

"Ms. Victoria? Why are you here?" the carrot-topped boy asked. "Here." In his hand he held a small, glassy disc. "You dropped your contact on the floor."

Victoria blinked, fear catapulting through her body like a bullet. "Cory Lindsey? How did you know it was me?"

"Ms. Victoria, why is one eye brown and other one green?" he innocently asked. "Are you going to a Halloween party?"

"No, Cory. What are you doing in Rome?"

"Oh, it's okay, I'm here with my grandfather. You know, your friend, Bud Lindsey from Fernwood, Tennessee."

Luckily, they were alone in the elevator. The ten-year-old lad was head and shoulders beyond his years in intelligence.

"Cory, you can't—"

"Tell anyone. I know," said Cory. "It's a secret because the police are looking for you. I saw you on TV. They think you're in Denver, Colorado. But you didn't murder nobody, did you?"

"No, Cory, I didn't." The lad's copper eyes glistened in the florescent elevator light. "I came to Rome to help out a friend."

"Dr. Mark and Miss Karen? They're here, too."

"Yes," said Victoria. "Don't tell them we talked, okay?"

"The police just made up that story on TV 'cause they're mad at you. Ain't that true, Ms. Victoria?" Cory favored justice.

"Oh, I'm so glad to see you." Victoria knelt on the elevator and hugged him. "You are such a blessing."

"My granddaddy doesn't think you kilt nobody either." The lad clung to Victoria. "Why don't you jest tell everybody so."

"I wish it were as simple as that, sweetheart."

"I believe you, Ms. Victoria. Everything will turn out just fine in the end." Cory's lower lip trembled.

The wisdom of a little child! No wonder Jesus loves them so.

"Now dry those eyes, Ms. Victoria." Cory used his hands to swipe her cheeks. "Somebody might see you crying and wonder."

"Oh, Cory!" Victoria wrung his little hands between hers. "I think God sent you into my life today to encourage me."

"I won't tell nobody I saw you, and friends don't take money for favors." His ruddy face erupted in a big smile.

"Thank you, Cory." Officer Sarah Boswell had once said the same thing. "You'd better start up the elevator before somebody reports a malfunction." Victoria put in her contact.

"Sure." Cory hit the RESUME button. "I get off at the fourth floor." The elevator doors opened. "Bye, Ms. Victoria." He waved a hand while backing off the elevator.

FRIDAY, JUNE 20

48

At exactly 4 a.m. Friday morning, the nearest match to Alisha Carol Hammerstein's photo locked on the computer screen. An alarm sounded and awakened Donald Wetherfield. He hurried over to the desk to view the results. Elation flooded his face.

"Victoria Martin Tempest, a.k.a. Alisha Carol. Gotcha!"

***

The *Finale Banchetto* was at 8 p.m. Friday evening in the Grand Ballroom of the J.W. Marriott Hotel in Rome, Italy. Five thousand people had crowded inside to watch Alexander Luceres Ramnes receive the *International Man of the Year* award and hear his personal remarks. Dick Branson and his party were there, too.

Before Luceres took a seat at the head table, he whispered in Donald Wetherfield's ear: "Pick up Victoria Tempest following the banquet. I want to speak to her. If I am satisfied she's innocent, I will honor her daughter's request and seek a pardon."

"But she's a fugitive from the law—an American citizen!" Donald protested. "Is it wise to get involved with her problems?"

Luceres didn't bother to answer his personal assistant.

Seated beside Texas at the table, Victoria was a quiet as a clam with no pearl to share. In fact, they were barely speaking.

After returning from her trip to the camera shop, the expert "spy" had left the suite and hadn't returned until around six. If

Texas was waiting for her to apologize, he could forget it. She was not in the least bit sorry for shunning the Antichrist.

Bud Lindsey's *Tennessee Blackberry Cobbler* was on the dessert menu along with *Bread Pudding Soufflé*, a specialty prepared by a New Orleans Commander's Palace chef. Victoria selected the cold peach tea as a waiter passed by with a tray of drinks.

No longer able to take the cold shoulder from Texas, Victoria excused herself and left the ballroom in search of a public restroom. The romantic trip to Rome had not turned out as she envisioned. If this was what it was like being married to Texas, she could forget about wedded bliss. It was evident he was not going to forgive her for failing the Christian Protection Agency.

No one was in the hallway outside the Grand Ballroom. The chefs were in the main kitchen completing the food preparations and the servers were cloistered in a room upstairs receiving last-minute instructions. Victoria was alone, and that was just fine.

Another scare—like running into Cory Lindsay—would do her in. *Dear Lord, just get me out of here.*

"Mother?"

"What?" Victoria turned around and peered into the eyes of her husband. "Jeffrey?" she squeaked. "Is that you? Have I died and gone to heaven and don't know it yet?"

"Of course, not. This way, Mother. And don't dare give me any problem." Jeffrey's knockoff firmly grasped Victoria's arm and led her down the hall away from the ballroom.

"Let go of me," Victoria protested, struggling to be free.

"Why in the world did you come here, Mother?"

"Daniel?" Victoria peered into a pair of seaweed colored eyes, feet solidly planted on the carpet. "Are you really my son?"

"Yes, Mother, I'm *really* your son, the one you forgot about having. Karen explained what happened to you. We'll talk about all *that* later. Meanwhile, the authorities know you're here."

"The authorities—how? Who ratted on me?" Her mind shot to Texas. Surely he wouldn't. *But who else knew she was here?*

"Listen to me, Mother! It doesn't matter. Luceres ordered Donald Wetherfield to pick you up following the banquet. You are two hours from being arrested and sent back home."

Questions circled Victoria's mind. *Fear.* "What about my friend? I can't just leave him." Texas would be tried in a court of law and convicted of crimes against PEACE FIRST.

"Forget about your handsome escort, we're going *now*."

"No, I can't." Victoria struggled to get free.

"Where are you taking me?" She resisted, peering down the long empty hallway. "My friend will think I skipped out on him."

"That's exactly what you are doing, Mother. So forget about your handsome partner in crime. Let's roll."

"No!" Victoria stood her ground. "I won't leave."

"Look." Daniel sensed her apprehension. "Would you feel better if I told you that Karen is warning your friend?"

"Some." Victoria winced. "I just don't feel right running off like this." Daniel's face and eyes were so like Jeffrey's it melted her heart. "Is there any other option available to me?"

"No." Daniel dragged Victoria down the hall. "I don't know why you ran away from home. Karen and Mark have been worried sick about you. Why did you break your engagement?"

Victoria glared at her pertinent son.

"How could you forget I exist? I hate all this."

"Well, you certainly are like your father!" Victoria swelled with indignity. "He *never* hesitated to put me in my place."

This was not the family reunion she had expected.

"Sorry." Daniel moved rapidly toward the exit door, dragging Victoria by the hand along with him.

"You never said where you are taking me? Is it far? Do I have time to get my suitcase from my room?"

"No." Daniel moved quickly.

"Where are we going? Tell me, please!"

"Away from here. Far, far away," he said.

THE END

DON'T MISS BOOK 4
IN THE *RESURRECTION DAWN* SERIES
In the continuing saga of Victoria Martin Tempest

VEIL OF LIES

Shocked when her son Daniel cornered her in the hallway of the J.W. Marriott Hotel, Victoria Tempest was forced to leave Rome without Texas Holmes. After talking to Daniel on the plane going to Switzerland, she realizes he doesn't share her faith in Jesus Christ. As a young UN peacekeeper, he mistakenly believes PEACE FIRST will free the global community of hate and war.

The true nature of Alexander Luceres Ramnes has not been fully realized by admirers who have no inkling of the political leader's lust for international power and to what ends he is willing to go. Peace on earth is but a tentative veil of lies clouding the truth.

Prompted by the antics of a sick dog in Attorney Devin Baldwin's backyard, *Memphis Commercial Appeal* reporter Cannon Fieldstone unearths Georgie Hendricks' incriminating photos of Branson employees packing cocaine in meat packages and alerts the press. Forewarned, Dick Branson loads his verbal shotgun, ready to fire at any accuser who blames him for drug trafficking, or the toxic sludge found on his property. He won't be convicted of a crime.

Meanwhile, Victoria returns to America without Daniel's approval and joins new Christian friends in Nashville, Tennessee. Having returned from Rome, Texas and his son Lucas visit Jon Branson at Safehouse #36 in preparation to attend a cave revival. The conclusion to this exciting sequel is both surprising and satisfying.

ABOUT THE AUTHOR

In the midst of writing this futuristic series, *Resurrection Dawn 2014*, M. Sue Alexander learned she had ovarian cancer in July of 2001. After the removal of two cancerous growths by an oncologist-surgeon, she underwent chemotherapy. During her four months of illness, Sue worked to complete book three, *Rebels in Paradise*.

God spoke to Sue's heart early on and warned her she would be very ill. But as the weeks went by, she was not as sick as anticipated. But two days following her fifth chemo treatment in early December, Sue developed a fever. Three days later, her temperature had spiraled to 104 degrees and she was taken to the hospital emergency room for treatment and sent home.

The hospital ER phoned Sue two days later and told her she had contracted a serious blood infection. For the next ten days, she was hospitalized and given powerful antibiotics to fight a staphylococcus infection that had entered through her *portocath*.

During Sue's hospital stay, her white blood count bottomed out leaving little resistance to fight the dangerous infection. Sue lay in the bed and prayed for God's deliverance, trusting that the doctors would provide the medical care she needed. Sue testifies that she was not afraid to die because of her faith in Jesus Christ.

God is in control.

Currently, Sue is working on the seventh book in the series and is cancer-free. And that is . . . the rest of the story.

CHARACTERISTICS OF THE ANTICHRIST

1. He will be an intelligent man who is powerful, persuasive, and deceptive, ruling the world with international consent. (Daniel 8:19-23 and 24-25; Revelations 17:12-13).

2. He will establish laws to control the global economy, unify religious thought, and establish peace. (Rev.13: 16-17)

3. He will be supported by a religious figure the Bible calls the False Prophet. (Rev. 13:11-18; 2 Thessalonians: 2:4)

Many antichrists over the centuries have opposed Christianity and the principles of righteous living taught by Jesus Christ, the Messiah who fulfilled Old Testament Bible prophecy. *The* Antichrist will be a man, a puppet of Satan, who will achieve international status and respect from the global community, establishing laws that require people to receive a mark on the hand or forehead to conduct business by forging a one-world monetary system. He will rule the world with unprecedented lawlessness.

CHARACTERISTICS OF JESUS CHRIST

"For I have come down from heaven not to do my will but to do the will of him who sent me . . . for my Father's will is that everyone who looks to the Son and believes in him shall have eternal life, and I will raise him up at the last day." (A portion of Scripture quoted from John 6: 38-40, The NIV Study Bible)

Printed in the United States
PP993700002B/5